ACCLAIM FOR JORGE AMADO'S

GABRIELA,

Clove and Cinnamon

"*Gabriela* is on its way to conquer the world. . . . Conquer it will, for it is a tale full of zest for life and love . . . a full-bodied, hot-blooded novel. *Gabriela* is unique. When the book is finished, the reader feels as though he had been, temporarily, sitting in Illheus's plaza and watching its world go by."　　　　　　　　　　　—*Chicago Tribune*

"If its other translations are as expertly smooth as the English translation . . . Mr. Amado's 'cinnamon-colored' heroine has a chance of becoming as internationally famous as those other Latin charmers, Gina Lollobrigida and Sophia Loren. . . . Gay . . . diverting. . . . *Gabriela* is a novel that grows on one."　　　　　—*The New York Times*

"Witty, warm, charming. . . . The translation is faultless."
　　　　　　　　　　　　　　　　　　　—Roald Dahl

"But it is Gabriela, a woman for all senses, who makes the book and makes it memorable."　　　　　　　　—*Show*

"One of the greatest writers alive . . . also one of the most entertaining."
　　　　　—Mario Vargas Llosa, author of *Death in the Andes*

JORGE AMADO

GABRIELA,

Clove and Cinnamon

Jorge Amado was born in 1912, in the Brazilian state of Bahia, which he would portray in more than twenty-five novels. His first novels, published when he was still a teenager, made a case for social justice for the workers on Bahian cacao plantations. Amado was later exiled for his leftist politics, but his novels would always have a strong political perspective. Not until he returned to Brazil in the 1950s did Amado write his great comic novels— *Gabriela, Clove and Cinnamon* and *Dona Flor and Her Two Husbands*—which take aim at every level of society, even as they pay exuberant tribute to the region of his birth. One of the most renowned and admired writers of the Latin American boom of the '60s, Amado's work has been translated into more than forty-five languages. He died in 2001.

INTERNATIONAL

ALSO BY JORGE AMADO

GABRIELA,

Clove and Cinnamon

GABRIELA,

Translated from the Portuguese by

JAMES L. TAYLOR *and* WILLIAM L. GROSSMAN

JORGE AMADO

Clove and Cinnamon

VINTAGE INTERNATIONAL

Vintage Books

A Division of Random House, Inc.

New York

FIRST VINTAGE INTERNATIONAL EDITION, SEPTEMBER 2006

The Library of Congress has cataloged the Knopf edition
as follows:
Amado, Jorge, 1912–2001.
[Gabriela, cravo e canela. English]
Gabriela, clove and cinnamon. Translated from the Portuguese
by James L. Taylor and William L. Grossman.—1st American ed.
p. cm.
1. Brazil—Fiction. I Title.
PZ3.A478 Gab2
62-8689

VINTAGE ISBN-10: 0-307-27665-1
VINTAGE ISBN-13: 978-0-307-27665-0

Book design by Warren Chappell

www.vintagebooks.com

Printed in the United States of America
10 9 8 7 6 5 4 3

Color of cinnamon,

Clove's sweet smell,

I've come a long way

To see Gabrielle.

SONG OF THE CACAO REGION

CONTENTS

GABRIELA,

Clove and Cinnamon

FOREWORD

ON A BRIGHT spring day, old Filomena finally carried out her long-standing threat. That is, she abandoned the kitchen of Nacib the Arab and took the eight o'clock train for Água Preta to live with her son. This was, however improbably, the beginning of Nacib's great love story. On the same day, by the strangest coincidence (as Dona Arminda would say), Colonel Jesuíno Mendonça shot and killed his dark-haired, slightly overweight wife, Dona Sinhà-zinha Guedes Mendonça, and the elegant young Dr. Osmundo Pimentel. News of this tragedy, involving three prominent members of the community, shocked the entire town of Ilhéus. The colonel owned a large cacao plantation, his wife was a leader of local society and a conspicuous figure at church functions, and the doctor, although he had lived in Ilhéus only a few months, had already attained a fine reputation as a dentist and, within a relatively narrow circle, as a poet.

According to João Fulgêncio—a man of considerable learning and the proprietor of the Model Stationery Store, the center of the town's intellectual life—the day had been badly chosen. The first clear sky after an unusually long rainy season, with the sun fairly caressing one's skin, this was no day for bloodshed. But such aesthetic considerations never passed through the cuckold-horny, aching head of Colonel Jesuíno Mendonça. He was a man of little learning but of great honor and determination. At precisely two in the afternoon he surprised the lovely Sinhàzinha and her seducer and dispatched them with two well-aimed bullets each. The town forgot all the other matters of current interest: the stranding of a ship of the Costeira Line that morning on the sandbar at the harbor entrance, the establishment of the first bus line between Ilhéus and Itabuna, the grand ball recently held at the Progress Club, and even the burning issue raised by Mundinho Falcão about dredging the bay.

By way of contrast, Nacib's little domestic problem—the loss of a cook—was known only to his most intimate friends, and even they considered it of minor importance. Everyone thought only about the crime of passion, the story of the plantation owner's wife and the dentist, enhanced as it was by the social prominence of the persons involved and by the richness and piquancy of the details. For, despite the town's much vaunted progress ("In Ilhéus civilization marches on in leaps and bounds," wrote Dr. Ezequiel Prado, famous lawyer, in the *Ilhéus Daily*), nothing pleased the townspeople so much as a good juicy story of love, jealousy, and violence. The echo of the last shots in the struggle for the cacao lands was fading away, but those heroic years left the people of Ilhéus with a taste for bloodshed. And with certain customs: gambling, drinking, flaunting one's courage, carrying a revolver. And with certain laws of conduct, one of the most binding of which was observed on this fateful day: the law that required a deceived husband to avenge his honor by killing the deceivers. It came down from the old days, from the strong men who razed the forests and planted the first cacao. It was engraved in the collective conscience of the people—even now, in 1925, when plantations were flourishing on the land fertilized with corpses and blood, when fortunes were being multiplied, and when progress was changing the face of the town.

The taste for bloodshed was so pervasive that Nacib the Arab, despite the emergency resulting from Filomena's departure, forgot his troubles and joined heart and soul in the talk about the double murder. New streets had been opened, automobiles brought in, mansions built, roads constructed, newspapers published, clubs organized—Ilhéus was transformed. But the ways men think and feel evolve more slowly. Thus it has always been, in every society.

PART ONE § ADVENTURES AND MISADVENTURES OF A GOOD BRAZILIAN (BORN IN SYRIA), ALL IN THE TOWN OF ILHÉUS IN 1925, WHEN CACAO FLOURISHED AND PROGRESS REIGNED, WITH LOVE AFFAIRS, MURDERS, BANQUETS, CRÈCHES, DIVERS STORIES FOR ALL TASTES, A REMOTE AND GLORIOUS PAST OF PROUD SEIGNEURS AND ROGUES, A MORE RECENT PAST OF RICH PLANTATION OWNERS AND NOTORIOUS ASSASSINS, WITH LONELINESS AND SIGHS, DESIRE, HATRED, VENGEANCE, WITH RAIN AND SUN AND MOONLIGHT, INFLEXIBLE LAWS, POLITICAL MANEUVERS, CONTROVERSY ABOUT A SANDBAR, WITH MIRACLE, DANCERESS, PRESTIDIGITATOR, AND OTHER WONDERS

OR

A BRAZILIAN FROM THE ARABIES

The Rondeau of
OFENÍSIA

Listen, oh my brother,
Luís Antônio, my brother:

Ofenísia on the veranda
Swinging in her hammock.
The heat and the fan,
The soft sea breeze,
A maid massaging her head.
With half-closed eyes she sees
The glorious Monarch appear,
His beard as black as night,
Oh splendor!

Teodoro's verses,
The rhymes for Ofenísia,
The gown from Rio,
The bodice, the necklace,
The black silk mantilla,
The monkey you gave me,
Of what good all this,
Luís Antônio, my brother?

His eyes are as coals
   (The Emperor's eyes!),
They burn into mine.

His beard a sheet of dreams
   (The Imperial beard!)
To wrap around my body.
With him I wish to marry
   (You cannot marry the King!).
With him I wish to lie
And in his beard to dream
   (Oh sister, you dishonor us!).
Luís Antônio, my brother,
Why not kill me now?

I want no count or baron,
I want no sugar planter,
No verses of Teodoro.
I want no pinks or roses
Or diamond earrings.
I want only the beard,
So black, of the Emperor!

My brother Luís Antônio
Of the illustrious house of the
   Ávilas,
Listen, oh my brother:
If I do not become
The Emperor's concubine,
I shall die in this hammock
Of languor.

FIRST CHAPTER

The Languor of OFENÍSIA

*(whose importance must not be judged by the brevity
of her appearance)*

"In this year of headlong progress . . ." (FROM AN ILHÉUS NEWS-
PAPER OF 1925)

OF THE SUN AND THE RAIN AND A SMALL MIRACLE

IN THAT YEAR of 1925, when the idyll of the mulatto girl
Gabriela and Nacib the Arab began, the rains continued long
beyond the proper and necessary season. Whenever two planters met in the street, they would ask each other, with fear in
their eyes and voices:

"How long can this keep up?"

Never had they seen so much rain. It fell day and night, almost without pause.

"One more week and we may lose everything."

"The entire crop . . ."

"God help us!"

The crop gave promise of being the biggest in history. With
cacao prices constantly rising, this would mean greater wealth,
prosperity, abundance. It would mean the most expensive
schools in the big cities for the colonels' sons, homes in the
town's new residential sections, luxurious furniture from Rio,
grand pianos for the parlors, more and better-stocked stores, a
business boom, liquor flowing in the cabarets, more women
arriving in the ships, lots of gambling in the bars and hotels—in
short, progress, more of the civilization everyone was talking
about.

But this unending downpour might ruin everything. And to

think that only a few months earlier the colonels were anxiously scanning the sky for clouds, hoping and praying for rain. All through southern Bahia the cacao trees had been shedding their flower, replacing it with the newly born fruit. Without rain this fruit would have soon perished.

The procession on St. George's Day had taken on the aspect of a desperate mass appeal to the town's patron saint. The gold-embroidered litter bearing the image of the saint was carried on the shoulders of the town's most important citizens, the owners of the largest plantations, dressed in the red gowns of the lay brotherhood. This was significant, for the cacao colonels ordinarily avoided religious functions. Attendance at Mass or confession they considered a sign of moral weakness. Church-going, they maintained, was for women.

Not that the colonels played no part in the religious life of the community. Their role, as they saw it, was to provide funds, upon request of the Bishop or the local priests, for church buildings and activities. They financed the parochial school for girls, the episcopal residence, catechism classes, novenas, the month of Mary, charity bazaars, and the feasts of St. Anthony and St. John.

That year, instead of spending St. George's Day swilling in bars, there they all were, walking contritely in the procession, each with a candle in his hand, promising the saint everything in the world in exchange for the precious rains. The crowd followed the litters through the streets, praying along with the priests.

Adorned in his vestments, hands joined, face touched with compunction, Father Basílio led the prayers in his sonorous voice. He had been chosen for this important function not only because of his professional capacity but also because he was himself a plantation owner and therefore had a special interest, not shared by his colleagues, in divine intervention. He could be relied upon to pray with all the strength at his command.

Father Basílio's exaltation inspired transports of ecstasy in the old maids clustered around the image of Mary Magdalene. They could hardly recognize in him the indifferent priest whose Masses were breathtakingly short and who listened so inattentively to their long confessions—unlike Father Cecílio, for example.

The priest's vigorous and self-interested voice rose high in ardent prayer. So did the nasal soprano of the old maids and the mixed chorus of colonels and their families, tradesmen and their employees, exporters, workers from the country come to town for the occasion, longshoremen, sailors, prostitutes, professional gamblers and assorted good-for-nothings, the boys of the catechism classes, and the girls of the Daughters of Mary. The prayer rose to the diaphanous, cloudless sky, with its pitiless sun—a murderous ball of fire set on destroying the newborn sprouts of cacao pods.

At the latest ball of the Progress Club, some ladies prominent in local society had agreed to walk barefoot in the procession, and they were now fulfilling this promise, offering the saint their elegance as a rain sacrifice. Further delay on his part was wholly inadmissible. He could see the affliction of his people, he could hear their appeals—all sorts of desperate promises in exchange for a quick miracle.

Nor did St. George remain unaffected by their prayers, the sudden and inspiring piety of the colonels, and the ladies' bruised feet. Doubtless he was touched especially by the anguish of Father Basílio. The priest was so fearful of the fate of his cacao that, between prayers, he swore to give up the sweet favors of his housekeeper Otália for the entire month. She had borne five children—three girls and two boys, all as sturdy and promising as Father Basílio's cacao trees. She had wrapped them in cambric and lace and carried them to the baptismal font, where the priest became their godfather. He could not adopt them but, in Christian charity, he let them have his family name—Cerqueira, a fine and honorable name.

Indeed, how could St. George remain indifferent to such affliction here in his own land, the land whose destiny he had been directing, for good or ill, since early colonial days? As a token of friendship, the king of Portugal had given the region, with its savages and brazilwood trees, to one Jorge de Figueiredo Correia. This gentleman, however, preferred the pleasures of the court at Lisbon to the hardships of the wilderness. In his stead he sent his

Spanish brother-in-law, who, at his suggestion, placed the region under the protection of the donee's namesake, St. George. Thus it was that the holy killer of dragons, astride his horse on the moon, had been following the history of this land for more than four hundred years. He saw the Indians massacre the first colonists and in turn be slaughtered and enslaved. He saw the building of sugar mills and a little planting of coffee. And for many years he saw his land unprosperous and stagnant. Then came the first cacao seedlings, and the saint, seeing them, ordered the kinkajous to undertake the large-scale propagation of cacao trees. Perhaps he was tired of looking at the same landscape for so long and had no purpose in mind other than to change it a little. Quite possibly it never occurred to him that cacao would bring wealth and a new era in the history of his land.

Then the saint saw frightful things happen: men killed one another for possession of hills, rivers, and valleys; they burned the forests and feverishly planted acre on acre of cacao. He saw the region suddenly develop, with towns and villages. He saw progress come to Ilhéus and, along with it, a bishop. He saw ships arriving with passengers. He saw so many things that he thought he could no longer be much impressed by anything. But he was wrong: the unexpected and profound devotion of the colonels moved him deeply. After all, they were uncultivated men, little given to law or to prayer. And he was impressed by that mad promise of Father Basílio Cerqueira, a man impulsive and incontinent by nature, so impulsive and incontinent, indeed, that the saint doubted whether he could really keep such a promise for a whole month.

When the procession arrived at St. Sebastian Square and stopped before the little white church; when Nacib the Arab came out of his deserted bar to enjoy the spectacle; when Gloria, smiling from her notorious window, crossed herself—it was then that the miracle happened. No, black clouds did not suddenly fill the sky, rain did not immediately begin to fall; for this, as the saint knew, would have spoiled the procession. But a pale moon appeared, clearly visible despite the blinding brightness of the sun. The first to notice it was Tuísca, a little Negro boy. He called it to the attention of his employers, the Dos Reis sisters.

They shouted "miracle." From them the cry spread to the other black-clad old maids, then to the rest of the crowd, then to the entire city. For two days no one spoke of anything else. St. George had heard their prayers; the rains would soon come.

And they did come, early one evening a few days after the procession. But apparently St. George was excessively affected by the prayers, the ladies' bare feet, and the promises, including Father Basílio's incredible vow of chastity. For he provided a super-abundance of rain. It had already continued two weeks beyond the rainy season. If it lasted a week or ten days longer, the entire record-breaking crop would be ruined. The situation was desperate. Candles were lit on the altars of St. George, St. Sebastian, and Mary Magdalene, and even on the altar of Our Lady of Victory in the cemetery chapel.

And then, at four o'clock one morning, a planter—known as Colonel Manuel of the Jaguars because his plantations were out in the wilds where the roars of jaguars could still be heard—stepped out of his house in Ilhéus and saw a clear sky, with a glow over the ocean joyfully announcing the sun. He raised his arms to heaven and cried out in immense relief:

"At last! At last!"

Early every morning a group of old acquaintances met down at the fish market near the waterfront. Colonel Manuel was always the first to arrive, yet this morning he fairly ran to the meeting-place as if all the others were already there eagerly awaiting his wonderful news. He smiled in anticipation.

The record crop was saved and cacao prices were rising. But this was only one of the circumstances that made the 1925–1926 harvest year, in the opinion of many, the most significant in the history of the region. To some, it was primarily the year of the controversy about the sandbar in the harbor. To others, it was the year of the political struggle between Mundinho Falcão, cacao exporter, and Colonel Ramiro Bastos, the old political boss. Still others remember it chiefly for the sensational trial of Colonel Jesuíno Mendonça, or for the arrival of a Swedish ship to carry cacao, for the first time, directly from Ilhéus to foreign countries. But no one speaks of it as the year of the love of Nacib and Gabriela. Yet, in an important sense, the story of their passion was central to the entire life of the town at this time when progress and the innovations of civilization were transforming the face of Ilhéus.

OF THE MIXTURE OF PAST AND FUTURE IN THE STREETS OF ILHÉUS

The prolonged rains had turned the roads and streets into quagmires, churned daily by the hooves of pack animals and saddle horses.

For a time, even the recently opened highway from Ilhéus to Itabuna was impassable: small bridges were washed away and some stretches of road were so muddy that drivers turned back. Before the coming of the rains, Jacob the Russian and his young partner, Moacir Estrêla, had organized a transportation company and had ordered four small buses from the south to operate over the new road between the two principal cacao markets. The trip by train took three hours when there was no delay; by bus it could be made in an hour and a half.

Jacob owned some trucks that hauled cacao from Itabuna to Ilhéus. Moacir Estrêla had opened a garage in town; he, too, worked with trucks. They joined forces, borrowed some money from a bank, and ordered the buses. They tacked notices on poles throughout the town announcing the early establishment of the bus line with quicker and cheaper service than by train. Then they rubbed their hands in anticipation of profitable business. That is, the Russian rubbed his hands. Moacir just whistled.

But the buses were late in coming, and when they were finally unloaded from a small Lloyd Brasileiro freighter before the admiring eyes of the townspeople, the rains were at their peak and the road was in miserable condition. Even the wooden bridge over the Cachoeira River, the very heart of the highway, was threatened by the rising water. The partners decided to postpone the inauguration of the line. The new buses remained in the garage for nearly two months while the Russian cursed in an unknown language and Moacir whistled angrily. The notes fell due at the bank and, if Mundinho Falcão had not come to the rescue, the business would have failed before it had started. It was Mundinho himself who asked the Russian to come to his office and volunteered to let him have the needed funds, without interest. For Mundinho Falcão not only believed in the progress of Ilhéus: he sought to promote it.

With the lessening of the rains the river had gone down, and although the weather continued bad, Jacob and Moacir repaired some of the small bridges at their own expense, dumped crushed rock on the worst spots in the road, and started running the buses. The inaugural trip, with Moacir himself driving, provided an occasion for speeches and jocularity. All the passengers were guests: the Mayor, Mundinho Falcão and other exporters, Colonel Ramiro Bastos and other planters, lawyers, physicians, and the gentlemen known respectively as the Captain and the Doctor. Some, fearful of the road conditions, offered various excuses. Their places were eagerly taken by others. In some cases, indeed, two took the place of one, so that in the end several of the passengers had to stand. The trip took two hours—the road was still very bad—but all went well. Upon the arrival of the bus in Itabuna there were fireworks and a luncheon. The Russian then announced that, after a couple of weeks of regular bus service, he would invite the leading citizens of both towns to a banquet at Nacib's place in Ilhéus to celebrate this milestone on the road of local progress.

Progress was the word heard most often in Ilhéus and Itabuna at that time. It was on everyone's lips. It appeared constantly in the daily and weekly newspapers. It came up again and again in the discussions at the Model Stationery Store and in the bars and cabarets. The townspeople repeated it in connection with the new streets, the new parks, the new buildings in the business center (including the four-story branch building of the Bank of Brazil), the modern homes at the beach, the printing plant of the *Ilhéus Daily,* the buses leaving every morning and afternoon for Itabuna, the trucks hauling cacao, the brightly illuminated night spots, the new Ilhéus Cine-Theatre, the soccer field, Dr. Enoch's school, the hungry lecturers from Bahia and even from Rio, and the Progress Club with its tea dances. "It's progress!" They said it proudly, for they felt they all were contributing to the town's modern appearance and way of life.

In short, the town was losing the armed-camp atmosphere that had characterized it during the violent days of the struggle for the land. Planters on horseback with pistols in their belts, hired assassins clutching their revolvers as they roamed the muddy (or dusty) streets, gunshots filling the turbulent nights with fear, peddlers spreading their wares on the sidewalks—all this was disappearing. The town glittered with bright and colorful shop windows; many new stores were being opened; the peddlers traveled about the country and appeared in Ilhéus only at the weekly open-air markets. Bars, cabarets, movies, schools. A land of little religion, its people were nevertheless proud of its promotion to a diocese and welcomed their first bishop with memorable festivities. Planters, exporters, bankers, businessmen—all gave money for the building of the parochial school for girls and for the episcopal residence, both on Conquista Hill. They gave money also for the establishment of the Progress Club, an organization of business and professional men led by Mundinho Falcão, where Sunday tea dances and now and then a ball were held. Soccer clubs and the Rui Barbosa Literary Society were organized. Ilhéus began to be known as the Queen of Southern Bahia, an area of the state dominated by cacao. The cultivation of this crop was immensely profitable; fortunes grew and so did Ilhéus, the cacao capital.

But the streets still revealed, along with the progress and future greatness, some remnants of the recent past, of the time of bandits and bloodshed. Trains of pack donkeys, bringing cacao to the exporters' warehouses, still invaded the business center, mingling with the trucks that were beginning to replace them. Men wearing boots and carrying guns still were seen; fights broke out in alleys; known assassins pushed people around in cheap bars and occasionally murdered someone right out in the street. These characters mingled on the clean pavements with prosperous exporters, elegantly clothed by tailors who came down to Ilhéus from the city of Bahia; with innumerable loud-spoken traveling salesmen, who knew all the latest jokes; with physicians, lawyers, dentists, agronomists, engineers, who arrived by every boat. Many planters no longer wore boots or carried weapons but went about peacefully, building good homes, living in town part of the time, and enrolling their sons in Enoch's school or sending them to boarding school in Bahia. Their wives visited the plantation only during holidays, wore silks and high-heeled shoes, and went to parties at the Progress Club.

Many things still reminded one of the Ilhéus of former days. Not the days of the sugar mills, of the poor coffee plantations, of the Negro slaves, of the illustrious house of the Ávilas—almost nothing of that remote past remained—but the more recent past, the period of struggle for possession of the land after the Jesuit priests had brought the first cacao seedlings, the period when men in search of fortune invaded the forests and with rifle and pistol disputed every foot of soil, when the Badaróses, the Oliveiras, the Brás Damásios, the Teodoros das Baraúnas, and many others, spread over the region, hacking out new trails and leading their bands of armed ruffians in mortal combat, when the forests were felled and the cacao was planted over corpses and blood, when crooked land deals were common and justice was perverted to serve the interests of the strong, when behind every big tree a gunman lay in wait for his victim. This was the era of which vestiges remained in the life of the town and in the habits of the people. But little by little these vestiges were disappearing, yielding to new ways—not without resistance, however, especially from customs that time had virtually transformed into laws of conduct.

Some men still clung to the past, viewed the innovations with suspicion, and spent nearly all their time on the plantations; they came to town only for business with the exporters. Such a man was Colonel Manuel of the Jaguars. As he walked along the deserted street in the rainless dawn, the first in so long a time, he was thinking of his departure later that day for the plantation. Harvest time was approaching, the sun would now turn the cacao pods golden yellow, the groves of fruit-laden trees would look beautiful. That was what he really liked. The city failed to capture him despite its many seductions—motion pictures, bars, cabarets with beautiful women, well-stocked stores. He preferred the expansive life of the plantation, the hunting trips, the sight of the cacao groves, the chats with his workmen, the swapping of stories about the good old days, the humble country girls in the village whore houses, and even the snake bites. He had come to Ilhéus to talk business with Mundinho Falcão, to sell cacao for later delivery, and to draw money for improvements on the plantation. But finding that the exporter had gone to Rio and not wishing to deal with the manager, he had decided to await Mundinho's expected return on the next ship of the Ita Line.

And, while he waited, in a town gay despite the rains, he was dragged by his friends to the movies (he usually fell asleep in the middle of the picture, it tired his eyes) and to the bars and cabarets. Women with so much perfume, my God, it was ridiculous. And they charged such high prices and wanted you to give them jewelry. This new Ilhéus was a snare and a delusion. Nevertheless, the sight of the limpid sky, the assurance of a fine crop, the vision of the cacao spread out on trays to dry, dripping its juice into the troughs beneath, and of the pack animals carrying it to town—it all made him so happy and benevolent that he decided to be kinder to his family. It was unfair to keep them on the plantation, where there was no school for the children and where his wife had nothing to do but spend her life in the kitchen like a colored woman. The other colonels lived in town; they built fine homes, they dressed like decent people. . . .

Of all the things the colonel did in Ilhéus during his brief stays there, nothing pleased him more than the early morning talks with his friends at the fish market. Today he would tell them about his decision to have a house in Ilhéus and to bring his family there. He was thinking of this as he walked the empty street when, on reaching the waterfront, he ran into Jacob the Russian, red beard unshaven, hair uncombed, and excitedly happy. As soon as he spied the colonel, he opened his arms and shouted something, but in his excitement he spoke in a foreign tongue. The planter knew what he meant and replied:

"That's right, my friend. The sun at last."

The Russian rubbed his hands.

"Now we'll run the buses three times daily—at seven in the morning, at noon, and at four p.m. And we're going to order two more buses."

They walked together to the garage, where the colonel declared:

"This time I'm going to travel in your machine. I've made up my mind."

The Russian laughed.

"The road is dry, so the trip will only take a little over an hour."

"Imagine that! Who would have thought it! Thirty-five kilometers in an hour! It used to take us two days on horseback. . . . Well, if Mundinho gets here today on the Ita boat, you can reserve a ticket for me for tomorrow morning."

"Sorry, Colonel, but not for tomorrow."

"Why not?"

"Because tomorrow we're giving our celebration dinner, and you are invited to come as my guest. A first-class banquet, with Colonel Ramiro Bastos, our Mayor and the Mayor of Itabuna, the judges from both towns, Mundinho Falcão, all high-class people . . . the manager of the Bank of Brazil. . . . It'll be a wonderful party."

"Who am I, Jacob, for such an important affair? I live in my little corner."

"I insist on your coming. It will be held at the Vesuvius Bar—Nacib's place."

"In that case, I'll stay until day after tomorrow."

"I'm going to reserve a place for you on the front seat of the bus."

The planter started to leave.

"Is there really no danger of that thing turning over?" he asked. "At such speed. . . . It seems impossible."

OF THE NOTABLES AT THE FISH MARKET

On hearing the ship's whistle, they all fell silent for a moment. "He's calling for a pilot," said João Fulgêncio.

"It's the Ita boat from Rio. Mundinho Falcão is returning on it," said the Captain, always abreast of the news.

The Doctor resumed where he had left off, underscoring his words with a categorical finger:

"As I say, in five years or so Ilhéus will be a real city. Bigger than Aracaju, Natal, Maceió. . . . No other town in the north is making such progress. Only a few days ago, I read in one of the Rio papers. . . ." He let his words fall slowly; even in conversation, his voice maintained a certain oratorical tone and his opinions were listened to with respect. A retired public servant highly esteemed as a man of culture and talent, who published long historical articles in the Bahia newspapers, Pelópidas de Assunção d'Ávila was an ornament of the town.

Those around him—planters, municipal functionaries, businessmen, exporters—nodded in agreement. The undeniable progress of the cacao region was a source of pride to all of them. Except for Pelópidas, the Captain, and João Fulgêncio, none of the men engaged in conversation that morning at the fish market had been born in Ilhéus. They had been drawn there by cacao, but they all considered themselves real Ilhéans.

Gray-haired Colonel Ribeirinho reminisced:

"When I landed here in 1902, twenty-three years ago next month, this place was a hell of a hole, run-down, falling to pieces. The real town then was Olivença. . . ." He laughed. "There was no pier for ships, no pavement on the streets, practically no business. A good place to wait to die in. Nowadays, see what you have: a new street every day, the harbor clogged with shipping . . ."

He pointed to the wharves: a Lloyd freighter at the railroad pier, a ship of the Bahiana Line docked in front of the warehouses, a launch casting off from a nearby pier to make room for the Ita boat. Small craft were coming and going between Ilhéus and Pontal, others were coming down the river from upcountry.

They were conversing near the fish stands erected on vacant land at the foot of Unhão Street, where the traveling circuses set up their tents. Negro women were selling porridge, corn on the cob, tapioca cakes, and steamed rice with coconut milk. Planters who were in the habit of getting up at dawn at their plantations, and certain notables of the town—the Doctor, João Fulgêncio, the Captain, Nhô-Galo, and sometimes the Judge and Dr. Ezequiel Prado (who came, as a rule, directly from his paramour's house nearby) —would gather there every morning before the town awoke. Under pretext of coming early to buy the best fish, which were alive and flopping on the tables, they would discuss the latest events and make predictions about the weather, the crop, and the price of cacao. Some, including Colonel Manuel of the Jaguars, would show up so early that they could see the last customers leaving the Bataclan cabaret and the fishermen arriving, their baskets filled with snooks and dorados gleaming like silver blades in the morning light. Colonel Ribeirinho, owner of the Mountain Princess plantation, whose wealth had not affected his good-natured simplicity, was nearly always there by five o'clock. That was the hour when Maria de São Jorge, a handsome Negro woman and a specialist in manioc meal with coconut milk, would come down the hill, her tray on her head, in brightly colored skirt and low-cut, starched white waist. The colonel had developed a special skill: he would help Maria arrange her tray without taking his eyes from the plunging neckline that revealed a good part of her firm breasts.

Some came in their slippers, wearing a pajama coat and a pair of old pants. Not the Doctor, of course. He gave the impression that he never took off his black suit, his high laced shoes, and his turned-around collar and solemn tie, even to go to bed. The group went through the same routine every day: first the glass of porridge, the animated conversation, the exchange of news, the loud laughter. Then they would leave the fish market and walk to the main pier, where they would stop a moment before continuing on to the front of Moacir Estrêla's garage. There they watched the passengers getting on the seven o'clock bus for Itabuna—this spectacle of recent origin—before going their separate ways.

The ship let out another blast, a long, cheerful whistle, as if it wanted to wake up the whole town.

"The pilot's on board. They're going to start in."

"Yes, Ilhéus is terrific. You won't find any place with a greater future."

"If cacao goes up no more than five hundred reis this year, with the crop we're going to have, we'll be using money for kitty litter," declared Colonel Ribeirinho with greed in his eyes.

"I'm going to buy a house in town for my family. Or maybe build one," announced Colonel Manuel of the Jaguars.

"Well, that's great! At last!" exclaimed the Captain, patting the planter on the back.

"You should have done it long ago," Ribeirinho observed.

"The younger children are reaching school age and I don't want them to be ignoramuses like the older ones and their father. I want at least one to be a 'doctor' with a ring and a diploma."

"Not only that," said the Doctor, "but the rich men of the region, like yourself, have an obligation to contribute to the progress of the town by building fine homes. Look at the mansion Mundinho Falcão built at the beach, and he arrived here only a couple of years ago—and he's a bachelor, besides. After all, what's the use of accumulating money and burying yourself in the country, without modern conveniences?"

"You know what I'm going to do?" asked Colonel Amâncio Leal, who was blind in one eye and had something wrong with his left arm—souvenirs of the bloody era of struggle. "I'm going to buy a house for my family in Bahia."

"That is what I call lack of civic loyalty," said the Doctor indignantly. "Was it in Bahia or here that you made your money?"

"Keep your shirt on, Doctor. Ilhéus is fine, but after all Bahia is the state capital. It has everything, including a good school for the kids."

The Doctor would not be appeased.

"Bahia has everything," he replied, "because you fellows land here empty-handed, you glut yourselves with money, then you go and spend it there."

"But—"

"I think, Amâncio," said João Fulgêncio, "that our Doctor here is right. If we don't look out for Ilhéus, who will?"

"I don't say you're wrong," the colonel conceded. He was an easy-going man and did not like to quarrel. It was hard to believe that he had been a famous bandit chief, the man who, in the fight for the forests of Sequeiro Grande, had caused more blood to flow than any other man in the history of Ilhéus. "For me, personally, there's no place like Ilhéus. The only thing is, in Bahia there are greater comforts and better schools. Who can deny that? I've got my youngest sons enrolled in the Jesuit school there, and the missis doesn't want to be so far away from them. She's already pining for the one who's in São Paulo. What can I do? So far as I'm concerned, I'd stay right here."

The Captain intervened:

"You're wrong about schools, Amâncio. Now that Enoch's school is open, it's ridiculous for anyone to think he has to send his children to Bahia." The institution to which the Captain referred employed modern teaching methods, with no corporal punishment. It had been founded by Dr. Enoch Lira, an unsuccessful lawyer. The Captain himself taught Universal History there, not because he needed the money but just to help out.

"But it's not government-accredited."

"By now it probably is. Enoch received a telegram from Mundinho Falcão saying that the Minister of Justice had promised accreditation within a few days."

"Even so. . . ."

"That Mundinho Falcão, when he sets out to do something. . . ."

"What the devil do you suppose he's really after?" asked Colonel Manuel of the Jaguars, but the question was left unanswered because a discussion broke out among Ribeirinho, the Doctor, and João Fulgêncio regarding teaching methods.

"It may be all you say it is. But when it comes to teaching the

ABC's there's nobody like Dona Guilhermina. Any kid of mine goes to her to learn to read and figure. This idea of teaching without the switch. . . ."

"That's out-of-date, Colonel," said João Fulgêncio, smiling. "Those days are gone forever. Modern pedagogy. . . ."

"What?"

"You can't teach kids without the switch."

"You fellows are a century behind the times. In the United States—"

"Sure, I send my girls to the parochial school. But for the boys it's Dona Guilhermina."

"Modern pedagogy has abolished the switch and all other forms of corporal punishment," João Fulgêncio managed to get in.

Arguing thus over the teaching methods of Dr. Enoch and of the famous Dona Guilhermina, of legendary severity, they continued to stroll toward the pier to await the arrival of the ship. Other people, coming out of nearby streets, were headed in the same direction. In spite of the early hour, there was a certain amount of activity. Longshoremen were carrying cacao bags from the warehouses to a ship of the Bahiana Line. A sail barge was preparing to leave; it looked like an enormous white bird. A blast on a conch trumpet, announcing its departure, vibrated in the air. Colonel Manuel repeated his question:

"What's Mundinho Falcão trying to accomplish? The man is a demon. He's not content with his own affairs; he gets involved in everything."

"Hell, that's easy. He wants to become mayor in the next election."

"I don't think so. It's too small a job for him," said João Fulgêncio.

"He has plenty of ambition."

"He'd make a good mayor. Very enterprising."

"He's practically a stranger; he only came here recently."

The Doctor, an admirer of Mundinho, cut in:

"Men like Mundinho Falcão are what we need. Men of vision, courageous, willing. . . ."

"Hell, Doctor, men around here have never lacked courage."

"I don't mean shooting and killing people. I mean something a lot harder than that."

"Something harder?"

"Mundinho Falcão arrived here just recently, as Amâncio says. And see how much he has already accomplished: he built the avenue along the beach, when nobody thought he could do it. It turned out to be a fine deal for him and a beauty spot for the city. He brought in the first trucks. If it weren't for him, we wouldn't have the *Ilhéus Daily* or the Progress Club."

"They say he loaned money to the Russian and Moacir for their bus line."

"I agree with the Doctor," said the Captain, who until then had remained silent. "It's men like that we need—men with vision, who can promote progress."

At the pier they met Nhô-Galo, a functionary of the Tax Board. He was an inveterate bohemian, sociable, nasal-voiced, and uncompromisingly anticlerical.

"Hail to this illustrious company!" he greeted them, shaking hands. "I'm dying for want of sleep, hardly slept at all. I went to the Bataclan with Nacib, and we ended up in Machadão's house —had something to eat and then women. But I had to be here to welcome Mundinho home."

The passengers for the first bus were gathering in front of Moacir Estrêla's garage. The sun had risen; it was a glorious day.

"The crop is going to be tremendous."

"Tomorrow there's a dinner, the bus-line banquet."

"I know. Jacob invited me."

The conversation was interrupted by a series of short, distressful blasts from the ship's whistle. There was an expectant stirring on the pier. Even the longshoremen stopped to listen.

"She's run aground!"

"That damned sandbar!"

"If it keeps on this way, even the Bahiana ships won't be able to get into the harbor."

"The Costeira Line people have already threatened to suspend service."

The dangerous bar extended across the channel from Unhão Hill on the mainland to an island off Pontal. The sands of the narrow, shallow channel shifted with every tide. Ships ran aground frequently and sometimes it took them a whole day to get free. Large steamers would not risk crossing the fearful bar, in spite of the splendid anchorage inside the harbor.

The anguished blasts continued. Some persons started for Unhão to see what was happening out on the bar.

"Let's go."

"This is revolting," said the Doctor as the group walked along the unpaved street skirting the hill. "Ilhéus produces a large part of the world's supply of cacao, we have a first-class harbor, and yet the revenue from export taxes stays in Bahia. All because of that damned sandbar."

Now that the rains had stopped, this was the most absorbing subject to the Ilhéans. Every day, everywhere in town, people talked about the bar and the need to make the channel safe for large vessels. Measures were suggested, the state government was criticized, and the Mayor was accused of neglect. But no solution was forthcoming; the authorities made promises and the docks in Bahia continued to collect the export taxes.

While the discussion was going on, the Captain hung back and took the arm of Nhô-Galo, whom he had left at the entrance to Machadão's establishment at about one o'clock that morning.

"How was she?"

"First class," murmured Nhô-Galo in his nasal voice. "You don't know what you missed. You should have seen Nacib the Arab making love to that new cross-eyed girl. You would have pissed yourself laughing."

The ship's whistles grew more distressful. The men hastened their steps. People were coming from all directions.

OF THE DOCTOR'S CLAIM TO NOBLE BUT NOT IMPERIAL BLOOD

The Doctor was not a doctor and the Captain was not a captain. Just as most of the colonels were not colonels: the title was merely a traditional symbol of ownership of a large plantation, generally one producing more than a thousand arrobas annually; it had no military significance whatever. João Fulgêncio, who liked to ridicule local customs, used to say they were "colonels of the most irregulars," for many of them had led bands of outlaws in the bloody struggle for control of the land.

Some of the younger generation had never even heard the noble and sonorous name of Pelópidas de Assunção d'Ávila, so accustomed were they to addressing him respectfully as Doctor. Miguel Batista de Oliveira, the Captain, was the son of Cazuzinha, who had been mayor at the beginning of the era of struggle, who had been rich but had died poor, and whose reputation for kindness was still talked about by old women. Even as a boy, Miguel was called Captain, for he always commanded the other children.

They were two of the town's illustrious personalities and, though old friends, they were rivals for acceptance as the town's most eloquent and thrilling orator. Each had his fanatical supporters. On every conceivable occasion—national holidays, Christmas and New Year festivities, visits of literary figures from the state capital—the Doctor and the Captain delivered speeches, and the controversy started anew.

Some preferred the Captain's high-flown phrases in which grandiose adjectives followed one another in passionate procession, the tremolos in his husky voice provoking delirious applause. Others preferred the Doctor's ingeniously long sentences, abundant in quotations and bejeweled with words of such classicism that only a few of his listeners knew what they meant.

Even the Dos Reis sisters, so united in everything else, were divided in their opinions on this subject. The slight and nervous Florzinha felt exalted by the Captain's outbursts, by his "shining dawns of freedom"; she thrilled to the quavers in his voice vibrating in the air at the close of a period. The fat and jolly Quinquina, on the other hand, preferred the Doctor's vast knowledge, his time-honored phrases, the pathetic tone in which, with finger upraised, he cried: "My people, oh my people!" Returning from civic meetings at the town hall or in public squares, the two sisters argued, as the whole city argued.

"I don't understand a thing he says, but it's so beautiful," said Quinquina, referring to the Doctor.

"I feel a shiver running up and down my spine when the Captain speaks," said Florzinha.

They were memorable days, those on which the Captain and the Doctor followed each other as speakers on the flower-ornamented stand erected in the plaza before the Cathedral of Saint George. One of them was the official orator of the Thirteenth of May Euterpean Society, the other spoke in behalf of the Rui Barbosa Literary Society. All the other speakers would be forgotten—even Professor Josué, whose lyrical utterances found favor among the young ladies at the parochial school—and a solemn silence would reign when there advanced upon the stage either the dark and captivating figure of the Captain, impeccably clothed in a white suit, a flower in his buttonhole, a ruby pin in his tie, his large, hooked nose giving him the air of a bird of prey, or the Doctor's thin silhouette, small and lively, like a garrulous, hopping bird, wearing those eternal black clothes, with high collar and stiff shirt, his pince-nez attached to his coat by a ribbon, his hair almost totally white.

"Eloquence just flowed from the Captain's lips today. What beautiful language!"

"But empty. The Doctor, on the other hand, everything he says has marrow in it. The man is a dictionary!"

Only Dr. Ezequiel Prado himself could compete with them, on those rare occasions when, nearly always blind drunk, the lawyer ascended the rostrum. He, too, had his supporters and, in courtroom oratory, public opinion unanimously conceded his invincibility.

Pelópidas de Assunção d'Ávila (the Doctor) maintained that he was descended from the Portuguese noblemen named Ávila who had settled near what was now Ilhéus during the period of royal land grants. The line of descent could be clearly traced, he found, in family documents. The solid opinion of a historian. He was descended also from certain plebeian, shopkeeping Assunções, and, to his great credit, he cherished the memory of these ancestors and of the Ávilas with the same exalted fervor.

Obviously there was not much to be told about the Assunções, whereas the chronicle of the Ávilas was rich in noble deeds.

The Doctor was a minor federal official, now retired, but he lived in a world of fantasy and greatness: the past glory of the Ávilas and the present glory of Ilhéus. For many years he had been writing a voluminous and definitive history of the Ávila family. At the same time, he was an ardent propagandist and voluntary worker for progress in Ilhéus.

The Ávilas had long since lost their wealth. Pelópidas's father, a collateral descendant, inherited only the name and the aristocratic habit of not working. But it was for love of the girl herself and not, as whispered at the time, for love of her father's money that he married a plebeian Assunção, the daughter of a prosperous dry-goods storekeeper. The old merchant never forgave her the asininity of that noble marriage. Nevertheless, he sent his grandson, the present Pelópidas, to study law in Rio de Janeiro. During the young man's holidays in Ilhéus, his grandfather anticipated his future diploma by addressing him as Doctor, and the servants and neighbors soon did likewise. But old Assunção died, and the nobleman, having stooped to such vulgar diversions as backgammon and cockfighting, gradually consumed the store—the bolts of cloth meter by meter, the hairpins dozen by dozen, the colored ribbons spool by spool. Thus ended the Assunção wealth, leaving the young man stranded in Rio in his third year at law school with no means for continuing his studies.

Some friends of his grandfather arranged a meager job for him in a government office. He rose in position, but not very far, for he lacked both influential support and the useful art of sycophancy. Thirty years later he retired and returned to Ilhéus for good, to dedicate himself to his "life's work," the monumental book about the Ávilas and their role in the history of Ilhéus.

The book was now almost a tradition. It had been talked about ever since the time when the Doctor, still a student, had written his famous article on the love affair between Pedro II and the virginal Ofenísia, a lymphatic and romantic Ávila, during the Emperor's trip to the northern part of the country.

The article, which appeared in the first and only issue of a little Rio review, would have remained in complete obscurity had it not been for a stroke of luck: the magazine happened to be read by a certain member of the Brazilian Academy of Letters who was also a papal count and a great admirer of the Emperor. The count felt his own honor offended by the "depraved and anarchic insinuation" which painted that "honorable gentleman" as a disloyal guest and placed him in the ridiculous posture of a lovesick suitor sighing for the glances of the virtuous daughter of the house of Ávila, which he was distinguishing with his visit. The count flayed the audacious student in vigorous sixteenth-century Portuguese, ascribing to him intentions and purposes he had never thought of. The student was transported with joy over the harsh criticism: it meant recognition. For the second issue he prepared an article in no less classical language in which, by irrefutable arguments based on facts and above all on verses by the poet Teodoro de Castro, he completely demolished the count's denials. But there was no second issue. The newspaper in which the count had attacked Pelópidas refused to publish the latter's rebuttal in full; it grudgingly condensed his eighteen sheets to twenty lines of print at the bottom of a page. But even now the Doctor gloried in his "fierce polemic" with a member of the Brazilian Academy of Letters, a man of national reputation.

"My second article crushed him and reduced him to silence."

In the annals of the intellectual life of Ilhéus that polemic is assiduously and pridefully cited as proof of Ilhéan culture, along with the verses of Teodoro de Castro and the honorable mention received in a Rio magazine story contest by Ari Santos, an employee of an exporting firm and current president of the Rui Barbosa Literary Society.

As to the clandestine romance between the Emperor and Ofenísia, it apparently consisted of no more than glances, sighs, and vows murmured in solitude. It seems that they met at a party in Bahia and that she bewitched the imperial traveler with her dreamy eyes. A noted Latinist, one Father Romualdo, was living in the Ávila mansion, and the Emperor came there several times on pretext of visiting the learned priest. On the mansion's ornate balconies the monarch would sigh in Latin his unconfessed and impossible desire for that flower of the Ávilas. Ofenísia, to the excited delight of her maid servants, hung around the parlor where the Emperor, through his black and scholarly beard, was discussing ancient literature with the priest, under the respectful and uncomprehending eyes of Luís Antônio d'Ávila, her brother and head of the family. In any case, after the departure of the imperial inamorato, Ofenísia launched an offensive to have the household moved to Rio, but failed before the stubborn resistance of Luís Antônio, guardian of the family's honor and of hers.

Colonel Luís Antônio d'Ávila died in the war with Paraguay, during the retreat from Laguna, at the head of troops recruited on his own sugar plantations. The romantic Ofenísia, still a virgin and still pining for the imperial beard, died of consumption at the country estate of the Ávilas. And the poet Teodoro de Castro, the sweet and passionate singer of the graces of Ofenísia, whose verses were popular for a time but whose name is unjustly omitted from national anthologies, died a drunkard.

To Ofenísia he had written his finest verses, exalting in rich rhyme her fragile, languorous beauty, imploring her unattainable love—verses that are still recited at parties by students of the parochial school. According to the Doctor (and who would dispute this with him?), Teodoro, with his tragic bohemian temperament, died of a broken heart ten years after Ofenísia's wasted body was laid in its white coffin. He had drowned himself to death in alcohol produced on one of the Ávila sugar plantations.

There was an abundance of interesting material for the Doctor's unpublished but already famous book: Ávilas of vast lands, with sugar mills, alcohol stills, and hundreds of slaves; Ávilas on the country estate at Olivença and in the mansion in Bahia; Ávilas of Pantagruelian appetites; Ávilas keeping concubines in Rio; beautiful Ávila women, fearless Ávila men, and, at last, an Ávila man of learning. Luís Antônio and Ofenísia were by no means the only Ávilas of distinction. There was, for example, the Ávila who fought for Brazilian independence in 1823 at the side of Castro Alves's grandfather. Another, Jerônimo d'Ávila, after being defeated in an election (rigged by him in Ilhéus but rigged by his adversaries in the rest of the province), organized his men as a little army with which he sacked villages, marched on the capital, and threatened to overthrow the government. Mediators obtained peace through concessions to the enraged Ávila. The decadence of the family was accelerated by wild, red-goateed Pedro d'Ávila. He abandoned his family, together with the country estate (the mansion in Bahia had already been sold) and the mortgaged plantations, and chased after a gypsy of strange beauty and, according to his inconsolable wife, of sinister powers. Pedro is said to have been murdered in a street brawl by another of the gypsy's lovers.

All this belonged to a past forgotten by the citizens of Ilhéus. A new life had begun with the coming of cacao; what had happened earlier did not matter. Sugar mills and distilleries, plantations of sugar cane and coffee, old tales and legends, had disappeared forever. Now the groves of cacao were developing, and so were new stories of how men fought with one another for possession of the land. The blind folk singers were carrying to the remotest country fairs the names and deeds of the men of cacao.

The Doctor alone concerned himself with the Ávilas—a concern which, however, did not deprive him of the townspeople's ever-increasing esteem. These rude land-grabbers, these unlettered planters, had an almost humble respect for knowledge, for learned men who wrote for newspapers and made speeches. One can imagine, then, their reverence for a man of such knowledge and ability that he was writing or had written a book. For, indeed, so much had been said about the Doctor's book, so much praise had been bestowed upon it, that many assumed it had been published and was now an established part of the nation's literary heritage.

OF FILOMENA'S DEPARTURE AND NACIB'S PREDICAMENT

Nacib was awakened by repeated knocks on the door of his room. He had come in at daybreak. After closing his bar for the

night, he had gone off with Tonico Bastos and Nhô-Galo on a
round of the cabarets and had wound up at Maria Machadão's
house in bed with Risoleta, a recent addition from Aracaju.

"Who is it?"

"It's me, Mr. Nacib. To say goodbye. I'm leaving."

A ship nearby whistled for a pilot.

"You're leaving, Filomena? Where are you going?"

Nacib got up, listening absent-mindedly to the ship's whistle.
It sounds like an Ita boat, he thought to himself. He squinted at
the big watch that he kept next to his bed: six o'clock in the
morning, and he had come in around four. What a woman, that
Risoleta! Not that she was a beauty—in fact, one of her eyes was
crossed—but she knew things: she would bite the tip of his ear
and throw her head back, laughing. . . . What kind of craziness
had got into old Filomena?

"To Água Preta, to live with my son."

"What the devil are you talking about, Filomena?"

Half asleep, he tried to find his slippers with his bare feet, his
mind on Risoleta. The woman's cheap perfume clung to his
hairy chest. He went out into the hall barefoot, in his long nightshirt. Filomena was waiting in the front room in her new dress,
with a colored scarf about her head and an umbrella in her hand.
Next to her on the floor, a small trunk and a bundle of saints'
pictures. She had worked for Nacib from the day he bought
the bar, more than four years ago. She was grumpy but clean and
hard-working, upright, honest, careful. "A pearl, a precious
stone," Dona Arminda used to say of her. She had her off days,
when she woke up scowling and would say nothing all day except that she was going away to live in Água Preta, where her
only son owned a small fruit-and-vegetable store. She had talked
so often about leaving, about taking that legendary trip, that
Nacib no longer paid any attention to her. He thought it was just
a silly notion that diverted the old woman. After all, she was so
close to him, more like a poor relative than a servant.

The ship whistled again. Nacib opened the window. It was, as
he had thought, the Ita boat from Rio de Janeiro.

"But Filomena, what madness is this? All of a sudden, without
warning—"

"Why, Mr. Nacib! Ever since I first came through that door I have been telling you that one day I would go away and live with my Vicente."

"But you could have told me yesterday that you were leaving today."

"I did send you a message, by Chico. You paid no attention to it."

Lazy Chico, his employee and neighbor, son of Dona Arminda, had in fact brought him, along with his lunch, a message from the old woman announcing her departure. But this happened nearly every week. Nacib had scarcely listened to him and had made no answer.

"And I stayed up all night waiting for you to come home—till daybreak—while you were out there chasing around. A grown man like you should have a wife and keep his backside at home instead of gadding about every night. In spite of that big body of yours, you're going to get weaker and weaker, until one fine day they'll be carrying you out of here feet first."

She pointed a thin, accusing finger at the Arab's chest showing through the unbuttoned neck of his nightshirt, which was embroidered with little red flowers. Nacib lowered his eyes and saw the smears of lipstick. Risoleta! Old Filomena and Dona Arminda were always making nasty remarks about his bachelor habits and planning marriages for him.

"But Filomena—"

"There are no more ifs and buts, Mr. Nacib. This time I'm really leaving. Vicente wrote me, he's going to get married, he needs me. I've packed my things."

Of all times, why did this have to happen the day before the big dinner—thirty guests—of the Southern Bahia Bus Line! It almost seemed as if old Filomena was doing it on purpose.

"Goodbye, Mr. Nacib. God protect you and help you find a good wife to take care of your house."

"But, woman, it's only six o'clock in the morning. The train doesn't leave till eight."

"I have no faith in trains. I'd rather play safe and be there ahead of time."

"At least wait till I pay you."

It all seemed like an idiotic nightmare. He moved through the room, stepping on the cold cement floor; it made him sneeze and he swore softly. Suppose he caught a cold on top of everything else. Damned crazy old woman.

Filomena extended her bony hand and gave him the tips of her fingers.

"Goodbye, Mr. Nacib. Come and see us if you ever get to Água Preta."

Nacib counted out her salary and added a bonus; she deserved it, despite this untimely abandonment. He helped her lift the trunk and the heavy bundle of framed pictures of saints, which had hung in Filomena's little room in the back yard. The bright morning light was coming in through the window—sun after so many days of rain—and with it an ocean breeze and the song of a bird. Nacib looked at the ship and at the pilot's boat approaching it. He stretched his arms and decided not to go back to bed. He would take a nap at siesta time to get in shape for the night ahead; he had promised Risoleta to return. Damned old woman, she had upset his day.

He went to the window and watched her till she disappeared. The sea breeze made him shiver. His house on steep St. Sebastian Street was almost directly in front of the sandbar. Well, anyway, the rains had stopped. In the house next door, Dona Arminda appeared at the window, waving her handkerchief at old Filomena; they had been close friends.

"Good morning, Mr. Nacib."

"That crazy Filomena—she's left me."

"I know. And it's the strangest coincidence! Yesterday I said to Chico, when he came home from the bar: 'Tomorrow Filomena is going to leave, her son sent her a letter asking her to come.' "

"Chico mentioned it to me, but I didn't believe it."

"She stayed up late waiting for you. We sat talking on your doorstep. But you didn't show up." She gave a little laugh, somewhere between reproof and understanding.

"I was busy, Dona Arminda, lots of work."

She seemed to be staring at the lipstick smears. Nacib started: were there some on his face, too? Very likely.

"Well, as I always say, you won't find many people in Ilhéus who work as hard as Mr. Nacib . . . working right through the night like that."

"And today of all days," grumbled Nacib, "with a dinner for thirty people to be served in the bar tomorrow night."

"I didn't even hear you come in, and it was late when I went to bed, past two in the morning."

Nacib snorted something. This Dona Arminda was curiosity personified.

"I came in about then. . . . Now who's going to prepare the dinner?"

"I wish I could help, but Dona Elisabeth is expecting any minute; in fact, she's overdue. That's why I stayed up last night. I can't tell when Mr. Paulo will come for me. Anyway, I don't know much about fancy cooking."

Dona Arminda—widow, spiritualist, viperous backbiter, and mother of Lazy Chico, a boy who worked in Nacib's bar—was a famed midwife. In the last twenty years, innumerable Ilhéans had been born into her hands, and their first sensations in the world were the strong garlic smell of her breath and the blurred sight of her reddish, freckled, mulatto face.

"And Dona Clorinda, has she had her baby? Dr. Raul wasn't in the bar yesterday."

"She had it yesterday afternoon. But they sent for a doctor, that Dr. Demosthenes. These newfangled ideas. Don't you think it's indecent for doctors to see other men's wives naked? Shameful!"

This was a vital matter to Dona Arminda, for the doctors were beginning to give her serious competition. But Nacib was worried about the dinner for the following day and about the appetizers and snacks for the bar—serious problems created by Filomena's departure.

"It's progress, Dona Arminda. . . . That old woman has really put me in a spot."

"Progress? Shamelessness, that's what it is."

"Where am I going to find a cook?"

"The best thing is to get the Dos Reis sisters."

"They charge too much, they skin you alive. . . . And I already arranged for a couple of kitchen girls to help Filomena."

"That's how the world is, Mr. Nacib. Everything happens when you least expect it. I, fortunately, have my departed husband to advise me. Only the other day, in a séance at Deodoro's house—"

But Nacib was in no mood to listen to the midwife's repetitious stories about spiritualism.

"Is Chico awake?"

"Of course not, Mr. Nacib. It was after midnight when the poor boy got home."

"Please, go wake him up. I have to get busy. A dinner for thirty—all important people—to celebrate the start of the bus line."

"I heard that one of them turned over on the Cachoeira bridge."

"Just talk. The buses are always full. It's a big success."

"You see all kinds of things in Ilhéus nowadays, eh, Mr. Nacib? They were telling me that the new hotel is going to have one of those elevators, a big box that goes up and down by itself."

"Will you please go wake up Chico?"

"I'm going. . . . They say the hotel won't have any stairs at all, can you imagine!"

Nacib remained at the window a few moments longer, looking at the Ita ship, toward which the pilot was heading. Mundinho Falcão was supposed to be on her, someone at the bar had said. Full of news, no doubt. Some new women were supposed to be coming, too, for the cabarets and for the houses on Unhão, Sapo, and Flores streets. Every ship from Bahia or Aracaju or Rio brought a contingent of strumpets. Perhaps Dr. Demosthenes's new automobile was also on board. The physician was making a pile of money; he had the largest practice in town. It would be worthwhile dressing and going to the pier to watch the debarkation. He would be sure to find the usual bunch there, the early risers. And, who knows, maybe he would learn of a good cook who could handle the work for his bar. Cooks in Ilhéus were scarce, much sought after by housewives, hotels, boarding houses, and bars. Damned old woman! And just when he had discovered

that wonderful Risoleta. Just when he most needed to be free of
worries. There was no alternative: he would have to place himself, for a few days at least, in the talons of the Dos Reis sisters.
Life is puzzling: only yesterday everything was going so well, he
had no worries, he had won two sets of backgammon in a row
from no less powerful an adversary than the Captain himself, he
had eaten a glorious crab stew at Maria Machadão's place, and
he had discovered Risoleta. And now, first thing in the morning,
he was loaded down with problems. A hell of a mess! Crazy old
woman! The truth was that he missed her already—her break-
fasts of coffee, manioc meal, potato, fried banana, and tapioca
pudding; her neatness, her maternal solicitude, even her grum-
blings. Once when he had been sick with the fever—typhoid at
that time was as endemic in the area as malaria and smallpox—
she had not left his side; she had slept on the floor next to his
bed. Where would he find another like her?

Dona Arminda returned to the window.

"He's awake, Mr. Nacib. He's taking a bath."

"I'm going to do the same. Thanks."

"When you've finished, come and have coffee with us. I want
to tell you the dream I had about my husband. He said to me:
'Arminda, old lady, the devil has taken possession of everybody
in Ilhéus. All they think about is money and bigness. They're on
the road to hell. Things are going to start happening—' "

"Well, for me they've already started, Dona Arminda, for me
they've already started."

He spoke in a bantering tone, not knowing that his troubles
had really just begun. The ship had taken on the pilot and was
maneuvering toward the entrance to the harbor.

OF LAW, JUSTICE, BIRTH, AND NATIONALITY

He was commonly called Arab or Turk, and it therefore becomes necessary to clarify Nacib's status as a Brazilian. He was

born neither in Arabia nor in Turkey but in Syria. He arrived in Bahia on a French ship and came to Ilhéus at the age of four. His parents were among the hundreds and hundreds arriving daily in this suddenly famous town, attracted by cacao and the wealth it promised. They came by ocean, river, and land. They came in ships, launches, and canoes; on muleback and on foot, trampling out new trails. Brazilians from Sergipe, Ceará, Alagoas, Bahia, Recife, and Rio. Foreigners from Syria, Italy, Lebanon, Portugal, Spain, and various ghettos. Experienced workers, young men looking for jobs, traders, bandits, adventurers, women of every description. And all of them, even the blond Germans of the newly established chocolate factory and the tall Englishmen of the railroad, became men of the cacao land, adjusted to the customs of the still semibarbarous region. They arrived, and soon they were true Ilhéans, breaking through the forest, planting cacao trees, setting up stores, opening roads, killing people, gambling in the cabarets, drinking in the bars, founding villages, making and losing money, feeling as close to the land as the oldest natives, sons of the families of pre-cacao days.

As these people of varied nature and origin continued to pour in, Ilhéus began to lose the appearance of a bandit camp and became more and more an urban community. And all of them, even the vagrants who came to live off the newly rich colonels, contributed to the astounding growth of the region.

Certain of Nacib's kinsmen, the Aschars, were naturalized Brazilians and thorough-going Ilhéans. Their deeds were among the most heroic and renowned of the region, comparable only with those of the Badaróses, of Braz Damásio, of the celebrated Negro, José Nique, and of Colonel Amâncio Leal. One of them, Abdula, the third oldest, died in the back room of a cabaret in Pirangi, where he had been engaged in a quiet poker game, but not until he had killed three of the five hired assassins sent to get him. His brothers avenged his death in an unforgettable manner. To learn about these rich kinsmen of Nacib's you need only consult the court records.

His many friends called him Arab or Turk, and they did so as an expression of intimacy, of affection. He did not much mind Arab, but he hated to be called Turk.

"Maybe your mother's a Turk. I'm not."

"But Nacib—"

"Call me anything you want except Turk. I'm a Brazilian—" he pounded his hairy chest with an enormous hand—"of Syrian parentage, thank God."

"Arab, Turk, Syrian—it's all the same."

"All the same, my ass. You're showing your ignorance. You don't know history and geography. The Turks are bandits, the rottenest people in the world. The worst insult for a Syrian is to be called a Turk."

"Hell, Nacib, don't get mad. I didn't mean to offend you. It's just that these foreign differences are all the same to us."

Perhaps his nicknames were due less to his Levantine ancestry than to his enormous black mustache, which made him look like a dethroned sultan. It came down around the corners of his mouth, and he stroked its ends while talking. His face was fat and good-natured, with enormous eyes that turned covetous at the sight of a woman, and a large, greedy mouth that broke easily into laughter. A tremendous Brazilian, tall and fat, with a flat head and a luxurious growth of hair. His belly was far too big—a "nine-month belly," as the Captain would say after losing a game of checkers.

"In my father's country. . . ." Thus he would begin his stories on evenings when only a few customers, all friends of his, remained at the tables in the bar.

For his own country was Ilhéus and the cacao groves, that fertile region where he had grown into manhood. His father and his uncles, following the example of the Aschars, had come ahead of their families. He had come afterwards with his mother and six-year-old sister. Nacib himself was not yet four. He vaguely remembered the voyage in the steerage and the landing at Bahia, where his father, the peddler Aziz, had gone to meet them. And the subsequent arrival at Ilhéus, where they went ashore in a rowboat, for at that time there was no pier for debarkation. He remembered nothing at all about Syria, so thoroughly had he blended into his new environment and so completely had he become both a Brazilian and an Ilhéan. It was as if he had been born at the moment of the arrival of the ship in Bahia when he was being kissed by his weeping father.

The first thing Aziz did after reaching Ilhéus was to take his children to the registry office of old Segismundo in Itabuna, then known as Taboca, to have them registered as Brazilians. The notary charged only a modest fee for this rapid naturalization procedure and thus made the privilege of immediate and authentic Brazilian citizenship available without discrimination to the children of all immigrants.

In the fight for land, some men burned down the registry office in order to destroy certain deeds and records. All the registry books of births and deaths were consumed in the flames. Accordingly, hundreds of Ilhéans had to be re-registered. Fortunately, there were qualified witnesses ready to swear that little Nacib and the timid Salma, the children of Aziz and Zoraia, had been born in the village of Ferradas and had been previously registered in the office, before the fire. How could Segismundo, without being gravely discourteous, doubt the word of José Antunes, a rich planter, or of Fadel, the prosperous owner of a dry-goods store? Or even the more modest word of the sacristan, Bonifácio, always ready to supplement his meager salary by serving in such cases as a trustworthy witness? Or of the one-legged Fabiano, who had been chased out of Sequeiro do Espinho and who had no other means of livelihood than to serve as witness?

About thirty years had gone by since these events. Old Segismundo had lived on for a few years, enjoying the esteem of the entire community. The orators at his funeral—attended by everyone in town and still remembered—proclaimed him an admirable public servant and an example for future generations.

Segismundo's services had, indeed, been admirably suited to the time and place. Had he been highly critical or sceptical, he would have been swept aside in the rapid development of the region. Crooked land deals, the falsification of deeds and land measurements, fraudulent mortgages, were all part of the process; the registry offices and notaries public were therefore important persons in the battle for the clearing and planting of the land. Besides, how could one tell true documents from false?

Old Segismundo applied the same attitude to questions of birth. He cheerfully registered all the children that appeared before him as having been born in the County of Ilhéus, State of Bahia, Brazil. He asked no questions, even when it was obvious that the birth had occurred after the fire. How could one be bothered with such miserable legal details as the exact place and date of a child's birth when one was living dangerously in the midst of gun fights, armed bandits, and deadly ambushes? Life was beautiful and exciting: how could Segismundo be finicky about the names of places? What did it matter, really, where the little Brazilian about to be registered was born—whether in Syria or Ferradas, the south of Italy or Pirangi, Portugal or Rio do Braço? He had already too many complications with documents relating to ownership of the land; why should he complicate the lives of honorable citizens when all they wanted was to obey the law by registering their children? He simply took the word of these friendly immigrants and of their witnesses—respectable men whose word was worth more than any legal document—and accepted their modest gifts.

And if, perchance, an occasional doubt assailed him, it was not the payments for the registries and birth certificates nor the things they enabled him to buy—the dress goods for his wife, the hen or turkey for his back yard—that eased his conscience. He believed, with the majority of the people, that what made a man a native was not his place of birth but his courage in entering the jungle and braving death, the cacao seedlings he planted, the shops and warehouses he opened—in short, his contribution to the development of the region. This was the mentality of Ilhéus and of old Segismundo, a man of wide experience in life, of broad human understanding, and of few scruples. Experience and understanding placed at the service of the land of cacao. As to scruples, they played no part in the development of the towns of southern Bahia, in the building of roads, in the creation of plantations, in the promotion of commerce, in the construction of buildings and port facilities, in the founding of newspapers, in the exportation of cacao to the entire world. These things were accomplished rather by bullets and ambushes, by false documents and fraudulent land surveys, by adventurers and hired outlaws, by prostitutes and gamblers, by blood and bravery.

On one occasion Segismundo remembered his scruples. It was in connection with a survey. When the bribe they offered him was small in relation to the size of the deal, his scruples suddenly came to the fore. This is why his registry office was burned down and he got a bullet in one of his legs. The bullet in the leg was a mistake: it was intended for Segismundo's heart. From that time on, he became even less scrupulous, less expensive, more truly native, and more beloved. When he died in his eighties, his funeral was transformed into a veritable tribute to one who had been, in those parts, an example of civic pride and devotion to justice.

By that venerable hand, on a certain afternoon many years ago, little Nacib, dressed in green French velvet pants, was turned into a native-born Brazilian.

IN WHICH MUNDINHO FALCÃO, AN IMPORTANT CHARACTER, MAKES HIS APPEARANCE LOOKING AT ILHÉUS THROUGH BINOCULARS

From the captain's bridge on the ship, which had lain to while awaiting the pilot, a well-dressed, clean-shaven, youngish man was looking at the town with a slightly bemused air. Something about him—perhaps his black hair, perhaps his large eyes—gave him a romantic look that caused women to notice him at once. But the firm mouth and strong chin suggested a resolute, practical man of action. The captain, tanned by the wind and gripping a pipe in his teeth, handed him the binoculars. As he took them Mundinho Falcão said:

"I hardly need them. I know the place house by house, man

by man." He pointed his finger. "That's my house there, on the avenue along the beach, to the left of the two-story one. I might add that I built that avenue myself."

"The place has a lot of money and a great future," said the captain, speaking as one who knew. "The trouble is, the sand-bar—"

"We're going to take care of that, too," declared Mundinho, "and very soon."

"I hope to God you do. Every time I put in here I'm afraid for my ship. There's not a worse sandbar in the whole of the north."

Mundinho raised the glasses to his eyes. He saw his modern house, built by an architect he had brought from Rio. The gardens of Colonel Misael's mansion, the cathedral towers, the public school. The dentist Osmundo, wrapped in a bathrobe, just stepping out of his house for his morning dip in the ocean, which he always took very early in order not to scandalize the neighbors. No one on St. Sebastian Square. The Vesuvius Bar still closed. During the night the wind had blown down a bill-board in front of the motion picture theatre. Mundinho observed every detail attentively, almost emotionally. The fact was, he liked the place more and more. He did not regret the mad impulse that had brought him there a few years before. He had been like a man adrift in the open sea who finally sights land. But this was not just any land. Cacao grew here. Where could he better invest his money? All one needed here was boldness, good sense, a head for business, and a willingness to work. He possessed all these and something more: a memory to be erased, an impossible passion to be rooted out of his heart and thoughts.

This time, when he visited Rio, his mother and brothers all found him greatly changed.

Lourival, the oldest brother, conceded disdainfully:

"No doubt about it, the kid's grown up." His voice, now as always, suggested an unremitting state of boredom.

"And he's making money," said Emílio, smiling and sucking on his cigar. Then, addressing Mundinho: "We shouldn't have let you go away. But we never guessed that our young ladies' man had a knack for business. The only talent you ever showed here was for girls and liquor. So when you left and took your money with you, we assumed you were off on a super-binge of some sort. We've been waiting for you to come back so we could straighten you out."

"He's not a boy any more," said the mother, almost crossly.

With whom was she annoyed? With Emílio for saying such things, or with Mundinho because he no longer came to her every month for money after squandering his allowance?

Mundinho let them talk. When they had nothing more to say, he announced:

"I'm thinking of going into politics and getting myself elected . . . congressman, maybe. You know, I'm gradually becoming the important man in that region. Emílio, how would you like to see me take the floor and answer one of your speeches defending the government? I plan to join the opposition."

The three brothers were talking in the large, austere parlor of the family residence—a scene which their mother, with her proud eyes and white hair, dominated like a queen. Lourival, whose clothes came from London, had always refused to run for Congress. He had even declined an appointment to a ministry. The Governorship of São Paulo? He might accept it if all the political factions combined to offer it to him. Emílio was a congressman, elected time after time without any effort on his part. Much older than Mundinho, the two brothers were astonished to see him a man, managing his own affairs, exporting cacao, earning enviable profits, talking about the barbarous region to which he had run off (no one ever understood why), and now announcing himself as a soon-to-be-elected congressman.

"We can help you," said Lourival paternally.

"We can have your name placed near the top of the government's slate," added Emílio. "Your election would be certain."

"I didn't come here to ask for anything. I came to tell you what I'm going to do."

"The kid's become conceited," muttered Lourival.

"By yourself, you can't get elected," predicted Emílio.

"Don't worry, I'll get myself elected all right. And in Ilhéus. I didn't come here for your help, thanks just the same."

The mother raised her voice:

"You can do whatever you wish, no one will try to stop you. But why do you rise up against your brothers? Why do you separate yourself from us? They only want to help you, they are your brothers."

"I'm no longer a boy, as you just said."

Then he told them about Ilhéus—the past struggles, the progress, the problems.

"I want them to respect me, to send me to Congress to speak for them. What would be the use of your including my name in the government's slate? You don't need me to represent the family business in Congress; Emílio is taking care of that. I'll represent Ilhéus."

"Small-town politics. With shooting and band music," smiled Emílio, ironic and condescending.

"Why expose yourself to danger when it isn't necessary?" asked the mother, concealing her real fears.

"To keep from being just a brother of my brothers. To be somebody."

He turned Rio upside down. He marched into the ministries, addressed the ministers familiarly, barged into their private offices. Hadn't he often met each of them at his mother's home, seated at the table over which she presided, or at Lourival's home in São Paulo, smiling at Madeleine? When the Minister of Justice, his rival in a contest for the favors of a Dutch woman years before, told him that he had already replied to the Governor of Bahia that Enoch's school could not be accredited until the beginning of the following year, Mundinho laughed.

"Listen, friend, you owe a lot to Ilhéus. If I hadn't moved there, you would never have slept with Berta, that hot little Dutch number. I want the certificate right now. You can quote the law to the Governor but not to me. I want the illegal, the difficult, the impossible."

In the Ministry of Transportation and Public Works, he demanded an engineer. The Minister went over the whole story with him—the sandbar at Ilhéus, the docks at Bahia, the interests allied with the son-in-law of the Governor of Bahia. It was impossible. It was right, no doubt, but impossible, my dear fellow, utterly impossible; the Governor would howl with rage.

"Did he appoint you to office?" asked Mundinho.

"No, of course not."

"Can he fire you?"

"I don't believe so."

"Well then?"

"But don't you see—"

"No. The Governor's an old man, his son-in-law is a thief, they're not worth a damn. It's the end of their clan and the end of their regime. Are you going to stand against me, against the most prosperous and powerful region in the state? That would be stupid. I'm the future, the Governor is the past. Besides, if I come to you, it's just out of friendship. I can go a lot higher, as you well know. If I speak to Lourival and Emílio, you'll get orders from the President of the Republic to send an engineer. Isn't that so?"

He enjoyed this bit of blackmail, especially in view of the fact that under no circumstances would he have asked his brothers for this or any other favor. He dined with the Minister that evening; there were women and music, champagne and flowers. The engineer would be in Ilhéus the following month.

He spent three weeks in Rio, during which he reverted to his former life: the parties, the sprees, the debutantes, the musical comedy actresses. He was astonished to find that all this, which had filled his life for years and years, now held little charm and soon bored him. He missed Ilhéus, his busy office, the intrigues, the rumors, certain local personalities. He had never thought he could adapt himself so easily, become so attached to the place. His mother introduced him to girls of important families, rich girls. She hoped he would marry one of them and that his wife would then drag him away from Ilhéus. Lourival wanted to take him to São Paulo, for Mundinho was still a partner in the coffee plantations and ought to visit them. He did not go; the wound in his heart had only recently healed, Madeleine's image had finally disappeared from his dreams, and he did not want to see her again, to suffer her haunting eyes. Their passion, although never confessed, had been recognized by both; they had always been on the verge of throwing themselves into each other's arms. He owed his cure to Ilhéus, and for Ilhéus he would now live.

Lourival, so supercilious, so superior, so British in his self-sufficiency, the childless widower of a wealthy woman, had unexpectedly remarried on one of his frequent trips to Europe. Madeleine had been a French fashion model. She was much younger than he, and her reasons for marrying him were obvious. Mundinho knew that if he remained near her nothing—no moral consideration, no scandal, no prospect of remorse—could keep them from becoming lovers. They followed each other with their eyes, their hands trembled when they touched, their voices froze. The cold, disdainful Lourival never imagined that it was out of consideration and love for him that his wild brother Mundinho had gone away.

Mundinho scanned the town of Ilhéus through the binoculars. He saw Nacib the Arab at his window and smiled because the owner of the bar brought to mind the Captain, his constant adversary at checkers and backgammon. The Captain was going to be of great service. He had become Mundinho's best friend and for some time had been throwing out vague hints that Mundinho should enter politics. The Captain's enmity for the Bastos family was no secret; twenty years previously they had driven his father out of politics. Mundinho had not taken the Captain's bait. But now the time had come. He must prompt the Captain into speaking out frankly and offering him the leadership of the opposition. He would show his brothers what he could do. The colonels had no real conception of the specific problems of the region, but they knew that, to accelerate or even maintain its progress, Ilhéus needed a new type of leader, someone like himself.

Mundinho handed back the binoculars, the pilot came aboard, and the ship moved toward the bar.

OF THE SHIP'S ARRIVAL

Despite the early hour, a crowd had gathered at the foot of Unhão Hill. The ship was stuck deep in the mud and it looked as if they would never get her free. Officers and seamen rushed about while the captain and pilot shouted orders. Small boats, coming from Pontal, circled the ship. Passengers, nearly all in pajamas and slippers, were leaning over the rail. They were shouting to the people on land who had come to meet them, exchanging news, commenting on the trip, making jokes about the grounding. Someone on board reported to a family on shore:

"She suffered horribly at the end, poor little thing."

This news tore sobs from the breast of a middle-aged woman, dressed in black and standing next to a thin, somber man with crape on his sleeve and lapel. Two children were watching the activity, unaware of their mother's tears.

Groups were forming among the spectators, exchanging greetings, commenting on the event.

"That sandbar is a disgrace."

"It's dangerous. Some day one of those ships is going to get stuck for good and that'll be the end of the port of Ilhéus."

"The state government doesn't care."

"Doesn't care? They leave it that way on purpose so that big ships can't come in. So that we'll have to go on sending all our exports through Bahia."

"It's about time Ilhéus stood up for its rights and began to throw its weight around a little."

The group coming from the fish market joined the conversations. The Doctor, with his usual excitability, cried out against the politicians in Bahia for scorning the county of Ilhéus, as if it were not the richest, the most prosperous in the state, the one that paid the highest taxes. Not to mention Itabuna, which was growing like a mushroom and was also being sacrificed to the incapacity of the rulers, to their negligence, to their ill will toward the port of Ilhéus.

"The fault is ours and we should admit it," said the Captain.

"How so?"

"Ours and ours alone. And it's easy to prove: who controls politics in Ilhéus? The same men as twenty years ago. Whom do we elect as mayor and whom do we elect to the state legislature and to Congress? People we know have no real interest in Ilhéus. They're picked on the basis of antediluvian commitments that have nothing to do with our present needs."

João Fulgêncio chimed in:

"That's it exactly. The colonels go on backing the men who stood by them in the old days."

"And what's the result? The interests of Ilhéus are completely neglected."

"But a commitment is a commitment," said Colonel Amâncio Leal. "In our hour of need they were the ones we could depend on."

"The needs are different now."

"This state of affairs must end," said the Doctor, wagging his finger. "We have to elect men who represent the true interests of the region."

Colonel Manuel laughed.

"But the votes, Doctor, where will you get the votes?"

Colonel Amâncio Leal spoke in his soft voice:

"Listen, Doctor. There's a lot of talk about progress, about civilization, about the need to change everything in Ilhéus. That's all I hear all day long. But tell me one thing: who brought about this progress? Wasn't it us, the planters? We made promises in exchange for help when we needed it. We're not the kind of men who go back on their word. As long as I live, my votes belong to my friend Ramiro Bastos and whoever he names. I don't care who they are. When I was fighting for my life in the forests back there and I needed help, I could always depend on him. Now he can depend on me."

Nacib the Arab joined the group. He was still sleepy, worried, and depressed.

"What's it all about?"

The Captain explained:

"It's the everlasting backwardness of our politics. The colonels can't understand that times have changed, that today things are different, that the problems are no longer the same as they were twenty or thirty years ago."

But the Arab took no interest in the discussion, though at another time it would have engrossed him. His thoughts were absorbed in his immediate problem: no cook for his bar—a catastrophe! He nodded his head automatically at his friend's words.

"You look down in the dumps. What's the matter?"

"My cook has left me."

"So what?" The Captain turned back to the discussion, which was growing more heated. Several persons had gathered around the group.

So what! Nacib took a few steps as if to put distance between himself and the unsympathetic Captain, as the Doctor's oratory clashed with the soft but firm voice of Colonel Amâncio. What did Nacib care about the Mayor or about congressmen and senators! The thing that concerned him was the dinner next day—thirty people! The Dos Reis sisters, if they took the job, would hold out for a lot of money. And just when everything was going so well.

His purchase of the Vesuvius Bar five years ago had been derided by his uncle and some of his friends as an act of insanity. The bar was located in a residential district some distance (not very far, for all distances in Ilhéus were ridiculously short) from the business center, where its principal competitors were located. These bars—the Café-Ideal, the Bar Chic, and Plínio Araçá's Golden Nectar—were close to the waterfront and very prosperous. The Vesuvius, on the contrary, was run-down, fly-infested, empty. But after his father's death Nacib did not want to go on measuring out cloth in the dry-goods store. He had little liking for that kind of work and less still for the business association with his uncle and brother-in-law. (His sister had married an agronomist at the Cacao Experimental Station.) While his father was alive the store did all right; the old man had initiative and was well liked. But now his uncle, a timid man with a large family, was running the store in a routine, unimaginative way, content with small profits. Nacib sold his share. For a while he speculated in the cacao market; then he gave this up and bought the bar. He bought it from an Italian, who went off into the interior to make a fortune in cacao.

Bars in Ilhéus were well patronized, almost as well as the cabarets. The streets were filled with traveling salesmen, new-comers attracted by stories of quick wealth, and businessmen of all sorts. Many deals were closed right at the tables in the bars, which were especially crowded in the late morning and again in the late afternoon. This was partly because of a custom intro-duced by the Englishmen who built the railroad: the shaking of poker dice to see who would pay for drinks before lunch or dinner.

The Vesuvius was the oldest bar in town. It occupied the ground floor of a two-story house on a corner of the small but beautiful square where the church of St. Sebastian was located. On the corner across the street, the Ilhéus Cine-Theatre had recently been opened. The decadence of the Vesuvius Bar re-sulted less from its location outside the business district than from neglect by its Italian owner. His head was so completely turned toward the cacao groves that he even neglected to renew his stock of liquor. The name of the bar, painted in fire-red letters over the picture of a volcano in eruption, had faded. An old gramophone, on which the Italian used to play opera arias, was out of order and covered with spider webs. Rickety chairs, tables with broken legs, rips in the green baize of the billiard table. Nacib bought the whole mess plus the name and location for a small sum; the Italian kept only the gramophone and the records.

Nacib had the place painted, ordered new tables and chairs, brought in backgammon and checkerboards, sold the billiard table to a bar in Macuco, and built a private room in the back for poker games. He offered a large variety of drinks. He pro-vided ice cream for the family trade, which was lively just after the movies and at the time for afternoon walks on the new avenue along the beach. As an apparently unimportant addi-tion, he served appetizers and tidbits at the apéritif hours. They included such delicacies as crabmeat paste, shrimp paste, manioc balls, cornsticks, and bean-paste balls flavored with onion and palm oil. This added attraction grew out of a casual remark by João Fulgêncio. One day, in Nacib's house, he was munching a bean-paste ball made by Filomena. "Why don't you sell some of this stuff in the bar?" he said.

At first, only Nacib's friends frequented the bar: the bunch from the Model Stationery Store, the backgammon and checker players, and certain highly respectable men, such as the Judge and Dr. Maurício, who did not like to be seen with the motley crowd in the waterfront bars. Soon the ice cream and fruit drinks began to attract the family trade. But it was when Nacib started to serve appetizers that business really prospered. The poker games in the back room also were a great success. The players frequently included Colonel Amâncio Leal, the rich Maluf, Colonel Melk Tavares, Ribeirinho, Dr. Ezequiel Prado, Fuad the Syrian, who owned the shoe store, and Osnar Faria, whose only occupations were poker and the Negro girls on Conquista Hill. Nacib saved a few plates of tidbits as a midnight snack for these customers. Drinks and money flowed freely.

In a short time, the Vesuvius Bar had more business than the Café-Ideal or the Bar Chic and was topped only by the Golden Nectar. Nacib worked like a slave. For help he had only Lazy Chico, Eaglebeak, and sometimes the Negro boy Tuísca, who had his shoeshine box on the broad sidewalk in front of the bar near the outside tables. Everything was going fine, he liked the work, and in the bar he heard all the latest news and comments on national and world events and, of course, on everything that happened in town. All the customers liked Nacib—"an honest, hardworking fellow," the Judge would say as he sat down after dinner at a sidewalk table to look at the ocean and the people in the square.

Everything was going fine until the day when that crazy Filomena carried out her long-standing threat. Now who would cook for the bar—and for him, Nacib, whose weakness was good food, well seasoned? To think of the Dos Reis sisters as a permanent replacement was absurd. They would not accept the job and, anyway, he could not afford to pay them: their wages would absorb all the profits. On that very day he must somehow find an accomplished cook; otherwise—

"They may have to throw all the cargo overboard to get loose," remarked a man in shirtsleeves. "She's really stuck."

The ship's engines were straining without success. Nacib forgot his troubles for a moment. Meanwhile the discussion continued.

"This has got to end," asserted the Doctor.

"No one really knows much about this Mundinho Falcão," said Amâncio Leal, quietly as always.

"We know he's on board that ship and we know he's the kind of man Ilhéus needs. What else do we have to know?"

The ship shuddered, dragging on the bottom, the engines roared, the pilot shouted orders. On the captain's bridge a well-dressed young man, shading his eyes with his hand, was trying to identify friends on shore.

"There he is!" exclaimed the Captain. "Mundinho!"

"Where?"

"Up there."

Other cries followed:

"Mundinho! Mundinho!"

The young man spotted them and waved his hand. Then he went down the companionway, disappeared for a few minutes, and reappeared, smiling, among the passengers at the rail. He cupped his hands to his mouth and shouted:

"The engineer is coming!"

"What engineer?"

"From the Ministry of Transportation, to study the entrance to the harbor."

"See? What did I tell you?"

Behind Mundinho Falcão one could see a blond woman, wearing a large, green hat. She smiled and placed her hand on his arm.

"Wow! What a woman! Mundinho loses no time."

"A knockout!" Nhô-Galo nodded agreement.

The ship jerked violently, the passengers looked frightened, the blond uttered a little cry, and the ship broke free of the mud. A joyful clamor arose on shore and on board. A dark, extremely thin man with a cigarette in his mouth stood next to Mundinho, looking without interest at the prospect of the town. The exporter said something to him and he smiled.

"That Mundinho is a smooth article, all right," remarked Colonel Ribeirinho approvingly.

The ship whistled, loud and clear, and headed for the pier.

"He's high Carioca society; he's different from us," replied Colonel Amâncio Leal disapprovingly.

"Let's go get the details from him," proposed the Captain.

"Me, I'm going to the boarding-house to change my clothes and have breakfast," said Manuel of the Jaguars.

"Me too," said Amâncio Leal. They left together.

The crowd started towards the wharf. The group of friends discussed what Mundinho had said.

"Sounds as if he managed to get the Ministry moving. It was certainly high time."

"The man really has influence."

"What a woman! A morsel for a king," sighed Colonel Ribeirinho.

When the crowd reached the pier, the ship was already maneuvering to come alongside. Passengers continuing on to Bahia, Aracaju, Maceió, and Recife were gazing curiously over the side. Mundinho Falcão, among the first to come down the gangplank, soon found himself embraced on all sides. The Arab virtually kowtowed to him.

"You put on weight."

"You look younger."

"Rio makes one young again."

At close range the blond woman looked a little older than at a distance but even more beautiful, better dressed, and more expertly made-up. She was, in Colonel Ribeirinho's words, "a foreign doll." She and the very thin man stood near the group, waiting. Mundinho introduced them playfully in the voice of a circus barker:

"Prince Sandra, the world-famous magician, and his wife, the amazing ballerina Anabela! They're going to give some performances here."

The man on board who had announced someone's piteous

death, embraced now by his family on shore, was relating the sad details:

"She suffered terribly for a whole month before she died. Moaning day and night, poor little thing. It cut your heart to pieces."

The woman sobbed louder. Mundinho, the artists, the Captain, the Doctor, Nacib, and the planters started walking along the pier. Porters went by, carrying baggage. Anabela opened a little sunshade. Mundinho Falcão suggested to Nacib:

"Wouldn't you like to engage the young lady to perform in your bar? She does a dance of the veils. I'm sure it would be a tremendous success."

Nacib raised his hands and replied:

"In the bar! That's for the theatre or the cabarets. What I'm looking for is a cook."

Everyone laughed. The Captain took Mundinho by the arm. "What about the engineer?"

"He'll be here by the end of the month. The Minister gave me his word."

OF THE DOS REIS SISTERS AND THEIR NATIVITY

SCENE

The Dos Reis sisters—chubby, roly-poly Quinquina and skinny Florzinha—were returning from seven o'clock Mass at the cathedral when they saw Nacib waiting at their gate; they quickened their short steps. The sisters were twins, and between them they had lived one hundred and twenty-eight years of undoubted, indisputable virginity. These two spry little ladies were all that remained of an old Ilhéan family of pre-cacao days. Many a rich plantation owner coveted the fine house on Adami Street in which they lived. They had inherited it along with three houses on Cathedral Place, which they rented. Tuísca peddled their cakes and candies in the afternoon, thus augmenting their income. Renowned as kitchen magicians, they would on occasion agree to cater for an important luncheon or dinner. What made them a municipal institution, however, was the large Nativity tableau they set up every Christmas in one of the two front rooms. They worked at it the whole year, cutting pictures out of magazines and pasting them on cardboard to supplement the figures used the Christmas before; this was their amusement and their devotion.

"You got up early this morning, Mr. Nacib."

"Just one of those things."

"What about the magazines you promised?"

"I'm going to bring them, Dona Florzinha, I'm going to bring them. I'm getting them together."

Nervous Florzinha collected magazines from all their acquaintances while placid Quinquina smiled. Sprightly and bright, with scarfs on their heads and dresses long out of style, they looked like caricatures from an old book.

"What brings you here at this time of day?"

"I wanted to talk with you about something."

"Well, come in."

The gate led to a side veranda where carefully tended potted plants and flowers were growing. A servant, bent by the weight of years, older still than the two old maids, was moving among the plants, watering them with a sprinkler.

"Come into the Nativity room," said Quinquina.

"Anastácia, bring a liqueur for Mr. Nacib," ordered Florzinha. "What do you prefer? Genipap or pineapple? We also have orange and passionflower."

Nacib knew from prior experience that if he wanted to do business with the sisters, he would have to drink the liqueur—at that time of morning, my God!—and praise it. He would also have to ask questions about the progress of the work on the tableau. They must be induced to prepare not only the dinner for the bus line the following night but also tidbits and appetizers for the bar until he could get a good new cook.

It was one of those old-fashioned houses with two parlors facing the street. One of them, however, had long ceased to function as a parlor; it was reserved for the Nativity scene. Not that the tableau remained standing the whole year. It was set up in December and exhibited to the public from then until around carnival time in February or March, when Quinquina and Florzinha would take it down and promptly start working on the next year's tableau.

It was not the only Nativity scene in Ilhéus. There were others, some rich and beautiful, but when people spoke of "the crèche" they meant the one of the Dos Reis sisters, for none of the others could compare with it. They had been enlarging and improving it for more than fifty years. When they set up their first, small tableau, Ilhéus was still a backward little town, and Quinquina and Florzinha were restless and fun-loving young girls, much sought after by the boys. Even now it is a small mystery why they never married—perhaps they were too choosy. In that almost forgotten Ilhéus of the days before cacao, a rivalry had arisen among the families as to which would exhibit the most beautiful, complete, and richest Nativity scene. Christmas in Ilhéus was very different from Christmas in the United States and certain European countries. There was no Santa Claus bringing presents for the children in a sleigh driven by reindeer. Instead, there were Nativity tableaus, visits to homes where a continual buffet was offered, suppers after midnight Mass, and traditional street dances and pageants.

Year after year the Dos Reis girls went on increasing the size of their tableau. And, as the number of dances diminished with the changing times, they devoted more and more of their attention to it. They added new figures, enlarged the platform on which it was mounted, and eventually extended it around three sides of the room. From March till a few weeks before Christmas, they devoted all their spare time to it—that is, all the time when they were neither attending church, nor gossiping with neighbors, nor visiting friends, nor making the delicious confections peddled for them by Tuísca. Among those who faithfully supplied magazines to the sisters were João Fulgêncio, the Captain, Diogenes (a Protestant and owner of the Ilhéus Cine-Theatre), pupils of the parochial school, Professor Josué, and, despite his fervent anticlericalism, Nhô-Galo. In December when the work became pressing, neighbors and friends, and girl students after their final examinations, came in to help the old ladies. In the final setting up of the tableau and its multicolored lights, they were assisted by Joaquim, a clerk in the Model Stationery Store. He considered himself a man of artistic temperament and played the bass drum in the Thirteenth of May Euterpean Society. The people of Ilhéus took pride in the great tableau, which had become almost a community property. On the day of its annual inauguration the Dos Reis house was always full of people; many others admired the tableau through the open window, and Joaquim got a little drunk on the old maids' sweet liqueurs.

The tableau represented, of course, the birth of Christ in a rude manger in distant Palestine. But this basic element had become little more than a detail in the center of a kaleidoscopic, growing world in which the most diverse scenes and figures, from the most divergent periods of history, mingled democratically with one another. Statesmen, scientists, military men, artists, famous writers, domesticated wild animals, and saints with drawn faces—all side by side with the radiant fleshiness of semi-nude movie stars.

On the platform there rose a series of hills with a small valley in the center where one could see the stable with Jesus' cradle, Mary seated beside it, and St. Joseph holding a docile ass by its halter. These figures seemed small and poor beside the others, but they had come down from the very first tableau and so Quinquina and Florzinha insisted on keeping them.

A great and mysterious comet announced the Savior's birth. It hung, suspended by wires, between the stable and a blue, star-studded cloth sky. It was Joaquim's masterpiece and an object of encomiums that left him misty-eyed: an enormous cellophane star with a red tail, so well conceived and executed that all the light illuminating the vast scene seemed to radiate from it.

Near the stable, cows—awakened from their stolid sleep—horses, cats, dogs, roosters, ducks, chickens, a lion, a tiger, and a giraffe stood about, worshipping the newborn babe. And, guided by the light from Joaquim's Star of Bethlehem, there were the Three Wise Men of the East: Caspar, Melchior, and Balthazar, bringing gold, frankincense, and myrrh. Two of the Biblical figures, the white kings, had been cut out of a calendar long ago. The Negro king, however, had been ruined by dampness and had been replaced recently by the Sultan of Morocco, whose picture appeared frequently in the newspapers and magazines of the period because of his struggle to preserve his nation's independence.

A river—a thread of water running over a bed of rubber tubing cut in half—flowed through the hills into the valley, and even a waterfall had been provided by the ingenious Joaquim. Roads ran over the hills toward the stable, and tiny villages dotted the landscape. And on the roads, in front of houses with illuminated windows, one could see, intermingled with the animals, men and women who had in some way distinguished themselves in Brazil and in the world and whose pictures had therefore been published in magazines. There was Santos Dumont, wearing his sporty, turned-down hat and a somewhat dejected look; he was standing beside one of his primitive airplanes. Near him, on the right-hand slope, stood Herod conversing with Pilate. Farther off, heroes of the war: King George V of England, the Kaiser, Marshal Joffre, Lloyd George, Poincaré, Czar Nicholas. On the slope to the left, the splendid Eleanora Duse, a crown on her head, her arms bare. Near her were Ruy Barbosa, J. J. Seabra, Lucien Guitry, Victor Hugo, Dom Pedro II, Emílio de Menezes, the Baron of Rio Branco, Zola, Dreyfus, the poet Castro Alves, and the bandit Antônio Silvino. Interspersed among these great men were some ingenuous colored pictures from magazines, included for no better reason than that the sisters had found them "just lovely for the tableau."

In the last few years the number of movie stars—the principal contribution of the pupils at the parochial school—had greatly increased. William Farnum, Eddie Polo, Lia de Putti, Rudolph Valentino, Charlie Chaplin, Lillian Gish, Ramon Novarro, William S. Hart, and the others were threatening to dominate the tableau. Even Vladimir Ilyich Lenin was there; João Fulgêncio had cut the picture out of a magazine and given it to Florzinha, saying: "An important man. You mustn't leave him out."

There were also some local figures, such as ex-Mayor Cazuza

Oliveira and the deceased Colonel Horácio Macedo, tamer of the wilderness. A drawing, made by Joaquim at the Doctor's suggestion, represented the unforgettable Ofenísia. Clay bandits with rifles were placed as if in ambush.

Magazines, scissors, glue, and cardboard lay scattered on a table beside one of the windows. Nacib was eager to get to the point of his visit. He sipped the genipap liqueur and praised the work on the tableau:

"I can see that it's going to be wonderful this year!"

"God willing."

"Lots of new things, eh?"

"My heavens! We can't keep track of them."

The two sisters were seated on a sofa, very upright, smiling at the Arab, waiting for him to speak again.

"You know, old Filomena left me. She went to live with her son in Água Preta."

"You don't say so! She really left? She has been saying all along that she was going to." Both sisters spoke at the same time. And both were thinking what a tasty bit of news this was for them to spread around.

"I didn't expect her to do it, though. And today especially, market day, when we're always so busy at the bar. And to make it worse, I have to provide a dinner for thirty people."

"A dinner for thirty people?"

"Yes, it's being given by Jacob the Russian and Moacir to celebrate the inauguration of their bus line."

"Ah!" said Quinquina. "I heard about it. They say the Mayor of Itabuna is coming."

"Our Mayor, the Mayor from Itabuna, Colonel Misael, the manager of the Bank of Brazil, Mr. Hugo Kaufmann—all high-class guests."

"Do you think the bus line is going to work out all right?" Quinquina wanted to know.

"It is already. Pretty soon nobody will go by train. There's a difference of an hour."

"What about the danger?" inquired Florzinha.

"What danger?"

"The danger of turning over. One turned over the other day

in Bahia. I read about it in the paper. Three persons were killed."

"They'll never get me in one of those contraptions, I can tell you that," said Quinquina. "I have trouble enough not getting run over by them."

"The other day," added Florzinha, "Mr. Eusébio tried to make us go for a ride in his motor car. His wife says we're behind the times."

Nacib laughed.

"In another two or three years I'll bet you ladies will own an automobile."

"Us? Even if we had the money. . . ."

"Well, let's get down to business."

He asked if they would help him out; they resisted, made him plead, and finally gave in. They would not undertake such a job, they said, for anyone else, but Mr. Nacib was such a fine, decent young man. Who ever heard of ordering a dinner just the day before, and for thirty important people! Not to mention the two days that would be lost from work on the tableau. Besides, they would have to find someone to help them.

"I already hired two colored girls to help Filomena."

"No, we prefer Dona Jucundina and her daughters. We're used to her. And she's a good cook."

"Do you suppose I could get her as my regular cook?"

"Who? Jucundina? Don't even think of it, Mr. Nacib. Her house, her three grown sons, her husband—who would take care of them? She just helps us out now and then, as a favor."

Their price was high, so high that he could not possibly make a profit on the dinner. If he had not committed himself to Moacir and the Russian. . . . He was a man of his word: he would not leave his friends without food for their guests. And he could not leave the bar without snacks and appetizers; his customers would turn elsewhere and his loss would be all the greater. But he could afford the Dos Reis sisters for no more than a few days.

"Good cooks are hard to find," lamented Florzinha.

"And when there is one, everybody fights for her," added Quinquina.

It was true. A good cook in Ilhéus was worth her weight in gold. The rich families used to send for them in Aracaju, in Feira-de-Sant'Ana, and in Estância.

"All right, then, we're agreed. I'll send Lazy Chico with the groceries."

"The sooner the better, Mr. Nacib."

As he stood up and extended his hand to the old maids, he saw again the piles of magazines on the table and the paper boxes stuffed with pictures.

"Those magazines I promised, I'll bring them in a day or two. Well, much obliged for getting me out of a tight spot."

"Don't mention it, we're glad to do it for you. What you need, Mr. Nacib, is to get married. If you had a wife, you wouldn't get caught like this."

"With so many unmarried girls in town. . . ."

"I know a splendid wife for you, Mr. Nacib. A fine girl, not one of these flibbertigibbets who think of nothing but movies and dances. She's poor but she's talented. She can even play the piano."

The old ladies were inveterate matchmakers.

"If I ever decide to get married, I'll certainly let you ladies pick my bride for me."

OF A DESPERATE SEARCH

On that first sunny morning after the long rains, Nacib set out in search of a cook. His coat under his arm, his large body sweating profusely, he started on Unhão Hill and covered virtually the entire town. The streets were gay with animation, as planters, exporters, and businessmen exchanged greetings and congratulations. People thronged the open-air markets, the stores, and even the doctors' offices.

Nacib swore. On arriving home late the night before, tired after the day's work and Risoleta, he had made plans for the following day. He would sleep until ten, the hour when Lazy

Chico and Eaglebeak, having cleaned the bar, would be serving the first customers. After lunch he would take a nap, then play a round of backgammon or checkers with Nhô-Galo and the Captain, chat with João Fulgêncio, and hear the latest local and world news. Then, after closing hours, he would drop in at the cabaret and maybe spend the rest of the night with Risoleta. Instead of all that, here he was. . . .

On Unhão he canceled his arrangement with the two colored girls he had engaged to help Filomena. One of them, showing her toothless gums in a grin, said she could cook a few plain dishes. The other could not even do that. Nacib made inquiries here and there and descended the hill on the other side.

He inquired along the waterfront and called at his uncle's house. Did anyone happen to know of a good cook? His aunt complained that she had had one, so-so, not really very good; the girl had quit without notice, for no reason, and now she, the aunt, was doing the cooking until she could get another. Why didn't Nacib come there for lunch every day?

He heard about a wonderful cook who lived on Conquista Hill. Felipe the Spaniard, his informant, was an expert mender of shoes, boots, harnesses, and saddles. A formidable adversary at checkers and a great talker, foul-mouthed but not bitter, Felipe represented the extreme left in Ilhéus. He called himself an anarchist and threatened to rid the world of capitalists and priests, though he was a friend and table guest of several rich planters, including Father Basílio. He sang anarchist songs as he pounded shoe leather, and he joined Nhô-Galo in cursing the priests whenever the two played checkers together.

"She's in a class by herself," said Felipe. "Her name is Mariazinha."

Eduardo, who kept some milk cows, confirmed Mariazinha's talents. She had worked in his house awhile and her seasonings were exquisite. Her only fault was a fondness for liquor. Once or twice, when drunk, she had been disrespectful to his wife, and Eduardo had fired her.

"But for a bachelor like yourself. . . ."

A lush or not, if she was a good cook he would hire her. At least until he could find another.

Nacib hurried to Conquista, whose steep street was still slippery from the rains. A bunch of little Negro girls laughed when he fell and got mud on the seat of his pants. By persistent questioning he found the cook's house. It was a miserable little hut of wood and tin. Mariazinha, in bare feet, sat at the door combing lice out of her long hair. She was a woman of thirty or thirty-five, ravaged by drink, but with traces of good looks still left in her peasant's face. She listened to him, with the comb in her hand. Then she laughed as if the proposal amused her.

"No, suh," she said. "Now I cook just for my man and me. He don't even want to hear about me goin' to work."

A man's voice came from inside the hut:

"Who is it, Mariazinha?"

"A gentleman lookin' for a cook. He's offerin' to hire me—says he'll pay good."

"Tell him to go to hell. There's no cook for him here."

"You see? That's how he is. Won't even listen about me takin' a job. He gets jealous about the least little thing. He's a police sergeant." Mariazinha seemed pleased with herself.

"Why are you still jabbering with that stranger, woman? Tell the man to beat it before I get mad."

"You better get goin'."

"Don't you know of some other cook?"

She did not answer, just shook her head. Nacib went down Vitória Street and passed the cemetery. Down below, the busy town sparkled in the sunshine. The Ita boat, arrived that morning, was unloading. A hell of a place: all that talk about progress and you couldn't even find a cook.

"That's a sign of progress," João Fulgêncio explained to him, when the Arab stopped at the Model Stationery Store to rest. "Labor becomes scarce and wages go up as the demand increases. Have you tried the market place?"

The weekly open-air market was as noisy and colorful as a festival. It took place in a vast open space facing the bay and extending almost to the railroad tracks. Slabs of beef—jerked, sun-dried and salted, or smoke-cured; slaughtered pigs, sheep, deer, agouties, and pacas. Golden bananas, yellow pumpkins, green eggplant, okra, and oranges. In the stalls, served in tin plates: tripe, fish stew, and black beans with pork and sausage. People from the country were eating these dishes and washing them down with white rum. Nacib made inquiries. A fat Negro woman, wearing a turban and several necklaces and bracelets, turned up her nose.

"Me work for somebody? God forbid!"

Birds of incredible plumage, talking parrots.

"How much do you want for the parrot, lady?"

"Only eight milreis, because it's for you."

"I can't pay that much."

"But he's a real talker. He knows a lot of dirty words."

The parrot demonstrated his ability by screeching the popular song, "Oh, Mr. President." Nacib moved between the mountains of cheeses. The sun shone on the yellow surfaces of ripe jack fruit. The parrot screeched: "Hey, rube! Hey, rube!" Nobody knew of a cook.

A blind man, his gourd cup on the ground in front of him, played a guitar and sang ballads of the early days of cacao.

> *"The best gun in the land*
> *For vengeance or for pelf*
> *Was young Amâncio.*
> *Only Juca Ferreira himself*
> *Could match his bravery.*
> *They met one dark, dark night*
> *In a clearing of the woods,*
> *Both spoiling for a fight.*
> *His finger on the trigger,*
> *'Who goes there?' Juca cried.*
> *'The last man you'll ever see,'*
> *Amâncio replied.*
> *And the monkeys quaked with fright*
> *In the darkness of the night."*

The blind men generally kept well informed, but they did not know where Nacib could find a cook. One of them, a Pernambucan, added that nobody knew how to cook here; for real food you had to go to Pernambuco; the people here didn't know the difference between good food and bad or they wouldn't eat this garbage.

Poor Arab road peddlers exhibited their opened packs of gewgaws and trinkets, cheap dress goods, costume jewelry, and perfumes with foreign names but made in São Paulo. Brown and black women, servants in the homes of the rich, crowded before the open boxes.

"Buy, miss, buy. It's very cheap." Funny accent, seductive voice.

Long drawn-out negotiations. Strings of beads on black bosoms, bracelets on brown arms—what temptation! The rhinestones in the rings sparkled in the sun like diamonds.

"Everything genuine, best quality."

Nacib interrupted the haggling: did anybody know of a good cook? Yes, there was a very good one, she could do both plain and fancy cooking, but she worked for Commander Domingos Ferreira. And the way they treated her, why, you'd never know she was a servant.

The peddler held out some earrings to Nacib.

"Buy them, fellow-countryman, a present for your wife, your fiancée, your woman."

Nacib continued on his way, indifferent to all temptations. The colored girls bought things at half the stated price but at double their value.

A medicine man, exhibiting a tame snake and a small alligator, proclaimed to a group around him a cure for all the ills of mankind. He held up a bottle containing the miraculous remedy, discovered by the Indians in the jungle far beyond the cacao plantations.

"It cures coughs, colds, consumption, the itch, chicken pox, smallpox, measles, malaria, headaches, bubos, venereal diseases of every kind; it cures fallen breastbones, rheumatism. . . ."

For a trifle, one and a half milreis, he would let you have that bottle of health. The snake slithered up the man's arm; the alligator remained absolutely motionless. Nacib continued to make inquiries.

"A cook? Don't know none, sir. But a bricklayer, now. . . ."

Household articles and statuettes sold for a tostão each, two for a crusado. Made by hands at once rough and skilful, they included water pitchers, clay jugs, pots, pans, horses, cows, dogs, roosters, outlaws with rifles, men on horseback, soldiers, policemen, and groups of figures representing ambushes, burials, and weddings. A Negro almost as tall as Nacib downed a glass of white rum in one gulp and spit big on the ground.

"Wonderful stuff, our Lord Jesus Christ be praised."

To Nacib's tired question he replied:

"No, I don't, sir. Hey, Pedro Paca, do you know a cook? For the colonel here."

Pedro Paca did not know a cook. Maybe at the slave market, only there was no one there now, no newly arrived group from the backlands.

The so-called slave market behind the railroad station was the place where migrants from the drought area waited for employment. The colonels would go there to hire workers and trigger men, and housewives went there to look for servants. But just now the slave market was deserted.

Nacib was advised to extend his search to Pontal. At least he would not have to climb hills there. He took a skiff and crossed the bay. He walked the few sandy streets, under the hot sun. Some kids were playing soccer; instead of a ball they used rags rolled up in a stocking. Euclides, owner of a bakery, dashed his hopes.

"A good cook? You can't even get a bad one. They earn more money working at the chocolate factory. Forget it, don't waste your time."

Nacib returned to Ilhéus, exhausted and sleepy. By now his bar should be open and very busy, too, for it was market day. It needed his presence, his attentions to the customers, his remarks, his congeniality. His two employees—a couple of dopes they were —couldn't handle things alone. But at Pontal they had told him about an old woman who was a fine cook; she had worked in several homes and now lived with her married daughter near Seabra Plaza. Nacib decided to go there first and then to the bar.

The old woman had died six months before. The daughter wanted to tell him all about her mother's last illness, but Nacib did not have time to listen. He felt despondent; he wished he could go home and sleep. He entered Seabra Plaza, where the town hall and the Progress Club were located. He was walking along, mulling over his troubles, when he came upon Colonel Ramiro Bastos sunning himself on a bench in front of the town hall. He stopped to speak to him, and the colonel made him sit down.

"I haven't seen you in a long time, Nacib. How is the bar? Still prospering, I hope."

"The damnedest thing happened to me this morning, Colonel. My cook left me. I've tramped all over Ilhéus, I even went to Pontal, and there's not a cook to be found."

"The only thing you can do nowadays is send for a cook from outside. Or go around in the country and look for one."

"And me with a dinner on my hands tomorrow for Jacob the Russian."

"I know. I've been invited."

The colonel smiled. The sun warmed his tired body and comforted him.

OF A POLITICAL BOSS IN THE SUN

Nacib tried to get away but Colonel Ramiro Bastos would not let him. Who could disobey an order of the colonel's, even when he gave it with a smile as if asking a favor?

"It's early. Let's talk awhile."

On sunny days, invariably at ten o'clock, Colonel Ramiro Bastos would leave his house. Leaning on his gold-headed cane, his step slow but firm, he would walk to Seabra Plaza and sit down on a bench.

"The snake has come to sun itself," the Captain would say, standing in the doorway of the tax-collection office across the plaza from the Model Stationery Store.

When he saw the Captain, the Colonel always raised his panama hat and nodded his white head. The Captain returned the greeting, but he would have preferred not to.

It was the most beautiful plaza in Ilhéus. The Mayor, according to some local cynics, saw that it got special care because of its proximity to Colonel Ramiro's house. But there was reason enough on the plaza itself, for the town hall, the Progress Club, the Vitória movie theatre, and some of the finest homes in town were located there. Above the theatre were some bachelors' rooms and the headquarters of the Rui Barbosa Society. It was natural, therefore, that the public authorities should accord the area special treatment. It had been landscaped during one of Colonel Ramiro's own terms of office as mayor.

Today the old man—he was eighty-two—felt expansive. The sun had finally reappeared and he could feel it on his back, on his bony hands, and in his heart. This daily exposure to the morning sun was his diversion and his luxury. During rainy spells he felt unhappy; he remained in the armchair in his living room, receiving visitors, listening to requests, promising solutions. Scores of persons sought him daily. But on sunny days at ten o'clock, no matter who was there, he stood up, excused himself, took his cane, and walked to the plaza. He sat on one of the benches; before long someone came along to keep him company. His eyes wandered over the plaza and rested on the town hall. Colonel Ramiro Bastos contemplated the scene as if it all belonged to him, which in a way it did, for he and his henchmen had ruled Ilhéus for many years.

He was a rugged old man, defiant of age. His small eyes retained the commanding brightness of a man accustomed to give orders. As one of the great planters of the region, he had made himself a respected and feared political chieftain. After overthrowing Cazuza Oliveira, he had served two terms as mayor. Now he was a state senator. Rigged elections for the mayoralty were held every two years, but nothing really changed, for the power behind the throne continued to be Colonel Ramiro. His full-length portrait hung in the town hall's grand salon, where lectures and receptions were held. Relatives and reliable friends of the colonel took turns as mayor and would not lift a finger without his approval. One of them was his son Alfredo, a pediatrician and now a state assemblyman. Alfredo made a name for himself as a good administrator. During his term of office the outward appearance of the town began to change. He opened streets and parks; he planted gardens. It was said that the colonel ordered these changes to facilitate the young man's election to the state legislature. The truth, however, was that the colonel loved Ilhéus, in his way, as he loved the orchard on his plantation or the garden of his town house, where he had planted, among other things, apple-tree and pear-tree seedlings imported from Europe. He liked to see the town clean (he had made the municipal government buy garbage wagons); he liked it to have well-paved streets, landscaped parks, and a good sewerage system. He stimulated the building of good homes, and it made him happy when out-of-towners spoke of the beauty of Ilhéus, with its parks and gardens. On the other hand, he remained obstinately deaf to certain problems and needs: the building of hospitals, the establishment of a municipal high school, the opening of roads to the interior, the construction of athletic fields. He turned up his nose at the Progress Club and would not even listen to talk about dredging the harbor. He attended to such matters only when there was no way of avoiding them and when his prestige was at stake. This is how it had been with the road connecting Ilhéus and Itabuna, finally built through the joint efforts of the two towns. He looked with suspicion upon certain undertakings and, above all, upon certain new customs. Because the opposition consisted of a small group of ineffectual malcontents, the colonel nearly always did just as he wanted. Nevertheless, in spite of his stubbornness, he had recently begun to feel that his prestige and dictatorial power were being somewhat undermined. Not by the opposition—those nobodies—but by the very growth of the town and the surrounding area, which seemed at times to want to escape from his now shaky hands. Had not his own granddaughters criticized him for causing the Mayor to deny a subsidy to the Progress Club? And had not Clóvis Costa's newspaper dared to discuss the problem of an accredited high school? He had overheard one of his granddaughters saying: "Grandpa's a reactionary."

He understood and accepted the cabarets, the brothels, the unrestrained orgy of night life in Ilhéus. Men needed these things: he had been young once himself. What he could not understand

was a club where young men and women talked until late at
night, where they danced these new dances (if you could call
them that), where married women whirled about in the arms of
men other than their husbands—it was indecent! A woman's
place was in the house, taking care of her children and home. A
young woman's occupation was to wait for a husband and, meanwhile, to learn to sew, play the piano, and run the kitchen. He
had tried unsuccessfully to prevent the founding of the club.
This Mundinho Falcão, recently come from Rio, avoided his
control, never came to call on him or consult him, decided matters for himself, did what he damned well pleased. The colonel
felt vaguely that the exporter was an enemy who in time would
give him trouble. To outward appearances they maintained excellent relations. Whenever they met, which happened rarely,
they exchanged polite greetings, protested their friendship, and
placed themselves at each other's disposal. But this Mundinho
was beginning to stick his nose into everything. The number of
his adherents was growing steadily. He talked about Ilhéus, its
life, its progress, as if they concerned him, as if they were his
business, as if he had authority. He belonged to a family accustomed to political power in the southern part of the country;
his brothers had prestige and money. To him, it was as if Colonel
Ramiro did not exist. Had he not completely ignored the colonel
in deciding to build the avenue along the beach? He had presented himself unexpectedly at the Mayor's office with the draw-
ings, deeds to the property, and complete plans.

Nacib related the latest news. The colonel had already heard
about the grounding of the Ita boat.

"Mundinho Falcão came back on her. He says that the sandbar—"

"An outsider," the colonel cut in. "What the devil is he looking for in Ilhéus? He never lost anything here." It was the harsh
voice of a man who had mercilessly set fire to plantations, invaded villages, and killed people. Nacib trembled.

"An outsider." As if Ilhéus were not a land of outsiders, of
people who had come from everywhere. But this was different.
The others arrived modestly and soon bowed to the authority of

the Bastoses; they wanted only to make money, establish them-selves, invade the forests. They did not take it upon themselves to promote the progress of the town or to make decisions about its needs. A few months before, Clóvis Costa, owner of a weekly newspaper, had approached the colonel. He wanted to organize a company to publish a daily. He had the presses already lined up in Bahia but needed capital. He went into the matter at length. He hoped to raise the money by selling stock to the plan-tation owners. It would be the first daily paper in the state out-side of Bahia itself; it would represent a great step forward in the progress of Ilhéus; it would defend the interests of the cacao re-gion. The idea did not please Ramiro Bastos. Defend against whom, against what? By whom was Ilhéus being threatened? Cer-tainly not by the state government, and the opposition in Ilhéus was negligible. No, a daily newspaper seemed to him a needless luxury. If he could be of service in some other way, just call on him. But a daily newspaper, no.

Clóvis left disheartened. He told his troubles to Tonico Bastos. Tonico was the colonel's other son and a notary public. Clóvis said he could raise a little money from a planter here and there, but the majority of them would be influenced by Ramiro's re-fusal. They would inevitably ask: "How much did Colonel Ra-miro pledge?"

The colonel gave the project no further consideration. A daily newspaper would be a menace. If he just once denied some re-quest of Clóvis's, the paper would stir up opposition, interfere in municipal affairs, make investigations, drag reputations in the mud. When Tonico came to him that evening to discuss the mat-ter, the colonel told him this and added:

"Do *you* need a daily paper? Well, I don't either. And so neither does Ilhéus." After which, he changed the subject.

How great, therefore, was his surprise a few days later to see announcements, tacked on poles and walls around the plaza, that the newspaper would soon be published. He sent for Tonico.

"What's this story about a daily newspaper?"

"You mean Clóvis's?"

"Yes. I saw the announcements."

"The machinery has already arrived and is being installed."

"How can that be? I refused him my support. Where did he find the money? In Bahia?"

"Right here, Father. Mundinho Falcão."

And who had promoted the Progress Club? Who had provided funds for the young commercial employees to organize soccer clubs? Mundinho Falcão's shadow was spreading everywhere. His name was falling on the colonel's ears more and more often. Even now, Nacib the Arab was speaking of him and about his announcement of the coming of engineers from the Ministry of Transportation to study the sandbar problem. Who had asked him to arrange for engineers, who had turned the town's problems over to him for solution? Since when was he elected to office?

"Who authorized him to do this?" the old man demanded of Nacib in a harsh voice, as if Nacib was in some way responsible.

"Ah, that I don't know. I'm just selling the fish for what it cost me."

The flowers in the park flaunted their colors in the brilliant sunlight; birds trilled in the trees. The colonel frowned darkly. Nacib lacked the nerve to get up and leave. The old man was angry and suddenly started to speak. If they thought he was finished, they were mistaken. He hadn't died yet and wasn't senile. Did they want to fight? All right, let's fight—what else had he done all his life? How had he planted his lands, defended their boundaries, built up his power? It wasn't by inheriting from relatives and growing up under the protection of his brothers in a big city, like this Mundinho Falcão. How did he wipe out his political enemies? By crashing through the forests, pistol in hand, with his men at his heels. Any of the older Ilhéans can tell you about it. This Mundinho Falcão is very much mistaken. He comes from outside, he doesn't know Ilhéus's history, he'd better learn about it before he takes on more than he can handle. The colonel tapped his cane on the cement sidewalk. Nacib listened in silence.

The monologue was interrupted by the cordial voice of Professor Josué, a teacher and assistant director at Enoch's school:

"Good morning, Colonel. Sunning yourself?"

The colonel smiled and extended a hand to the young man.

"Having a chat with my friend Nacib here. Sit down." He made room on the bench. "At my age the only thing left is to sit in the sun."

"Come now, Colonel, not many young fellows are the man you are."

"Well, I was just saying to Nacib that I'm not buried yet. There are some around here who think I'm no good any more."

"Nobody thinks that, Colonel!" said Nacib.

Ramiro Bastos changed the subject and asked Josué:

"How's the school doing?"

"Well, very well. It's been accredited. Ilhéus now has a high school. It was great news."

"It's been accredited? I hadn't heard. The Governor sent me word that the accreditation couldn't be granted until the beginning of next year, that the Ministry couldn't do it any sooner, that it was forbidden by law. I took a lot of interest in the matter."

"The Governor was right, Colonel: accreditations are always made at the beginning of a new year, before classes start. But Enoch asked Mundinho Falcão, when he went to Rio, to—"

"Ah!"

"And he persuaded the Minister to make an exception. It means that we'll have a federal inspector at our final examinations this year. It's great news for Ilhéus."

"No doubt, no doubt."

The young teacher went on talking and Nacib took the opportunity to say goodbye, but the colonel did not hear them. His thoughts were far away. What the devil was his son Alfredo doing? A state assemblyman in Bahia, who could walk into the executive mansion and talk to the Governor whenever he wished—what the devil was he doing? Hadn't he instructed Alfredo to ask for the immediate accreditation of the school? To him, the colonel, and to no one else, would Enoch and the town have been indebted for the accreditation if the Governor, pressured by Alfredo, had really taken an interest. He, Ramiro, had not gone to Bahia lately (although he was a member of the Senate) ; the trip was such a hardship. And here was the result: his requests to the government were stalled in the ministries, dragged themselves through normal bureaucratic channels, while. . . . The Governor had sent him word, as if promptly complying with his request, that the school would be accredited without fail at the beginning of the year. He had conveyed the news to Enoch, stressing the speed with which the government had acted at his solicitation:

"Next year the school will have federal inspection."

Enoch had thanked him but had expressed regret:

"It's a pity we can't get it right now, Colonel. We're going to lose a whole year. Many of the boys will go to Bahia."

"It can't be done any sooner, my dear fellow. In the middle of the year accreditation is impossible. But you have only a few months to wait."

And now, suddenly, this bombshell. The school was being accredited out of season, thanks to Mundinho Falcão. The colonel would go to Bahia and tell the Governor plenty. He was not a man to be trifled with. And what the devil was his son doing in the State Assembly? The boy really had no aptitude for politics. A good doctor, a good administrator, but too soft for politics, didn't know how to impose his will on others. He certainly didn't take after his father. The other son, Tonico, thought about nothing but women.

Josué was taking his leave.

"Goodbye, my boy. Give Enoch my congratulations. Tell him I was expecting the good news at any moment."

He was alone again on the bench. He no longer felt the comfort of the sun. He thought of the old days when such things were easily settled. If someone stood in his way, all he had to do was send for a trigger man, promise him money, and mention the person's name. Now it was different. But this Mundinho Falcão was fooling himself. True, Ilhéus had changed a lot over the years. Colonel Ramiro had striven to understand this new life, this new community being born out of his old Ilhéus. He had thought he understood it, sensed its problems, its needs. Had he not beautified the town, had he not built parks and gardens and paved the streets? Had he not even run a road to Itabuna, contrary to his commitments with the Englishmen of the railroad? Why was everybody now beginning to do whatever he pleased, without consulting him, without waiting for orders from him? What was happening in Ilhéus?

He was not a man to let himself be beaten without a fight. This was his territory, no one had done more for it than Ramiro Bastos, no one was going to take it away from him. He sensed a new period of struggle approaching, different from the old and perhaps more difficult. He rose and stood erect, as if the years weighed lightly on him. He might be old but he was not yet buried, and as long as he lived he would be the one to rule here. He crossed over to the town hall. The soldier on duty at the entrance snapped to attention. Colonel Ramiro Bastos smiled.

OF A POLITICAL CONSPIRACY

Colonel Ramiro Bastos entered the town hall. At about the same time Nacib entered the Vesuvius Bar, and Mundinho, in his house at the beach, was saying to the Captain:

"It was a battle, my dear fellow. It wasn't easy, by any means."

He set down his cup, stretched his legs, and sprawled in the armchair. He had stopped for a moment at his office, then had brought his friend home with him for the ostensible purpose of telling him about his trip. The Captain took a sip of coffee and asked:

"But where does all the resistance come from? After all, Ilhéus is not just some little village. It produces more than a thousand contos in annual tax revenue."

"Well, my dear man, a minister is not all-powerful. He has to consider the wishes of the Governor of Bahia. Now, the last thing in the world the Governor would like to see is the removal of the sandbar here. Every bag of cacao that passes through Bahia means more money for the docks there, and the Governor's son-in-law is tied in with the dock interests. The Minister said to me: 'Mundinho, you're going to get me in bad with the Governor.'"

"That son-in-law is a low character. The colonels don't want to understand the situation. Only this morning we had an argument about it while the boat was being freed. They support a state government that plunders us and then practically ignores us."

"While our local government does absolutely nothing."

"That's right. In fact it actually places obstacles in the way of improvements. Incredible stupidity. Ramiro Bastos just crosses his arms and sits there. He has no vision. And the colonels go along with him."

Perceiving the Captain's impatience, Mundinho took pains to conceal the eagerness that had caused him to leave an office full of customers, postpone important business opportunities, and come home with the Captain for a talk. It would be better if he made no suggestion but let the Captain take the initiative and offer him the leadership of the opposition. The offer must come as a surprise. He must hesitate, be coaxed, and finally accept. He got up, walked to the window, and looked out at the breakers.

"Captain, sometimes I wonder what the devil I'm doing here. After all, I could be enjoying life in Rio or São Paulo. Only the other day my brother Emílio, the congressman, said: 'Aren't you sick and tired of Ilhéus by now? What mad attraction does it have for you? Why do you bury yourself in a hole like that?' You know that my family's in coffee, don't you? Has been for many years." He drummed on the window with his fingers and looked at the Captain. "Don't think I'm complaining. Cacao is a fine business. The best. But you can't compare life here with life in Rio. Still, I don't want to go back there. And do you know why?"

The Captain was enjoying this intimacy with the exporter. He felt proud to have so important a man for a friend.

"I confess my curiosity, which is not mine alone but everybody's. Why you ever came here, that's one of our local mysteries."

"Why I came doesn't matter. But why I stayed, that's the question. When I arrived here and put up at the Hotel Coelho, that first day, I wanted to sit on the curb and cry."

"You mean, because of our backwardness?"

"Yes. But it was that very backwardness that held me here. A new land, rich, where everything remains to be done, where everything is just beginning. What has been done so far is generally bad. It needs to be changed. There is, so to speak, a civilization to be built."

" 'A civilization to be built'—well put. In the old days we used to say that when a man came to Ilhéus his feet got stuck in the cacao pulp and he could never get away. Haven't you ever heard that?"

"Yes. And my feet got stuck all right, but not in the cacao pulp. I'm no planter; I'm an exporter. My feet got stuck right here in the mud of the streets of Ilhéus. I felt I had to stay and build something, do something constructive. I don't know if I make myself clear."

"Perfectly."

"Naturally, if I didn't make money, if cacao exporting were not profitable, I wouldn't stay. But that's not enough to hold me; it's more than that. I guess I just have a pioneer spirit." He laughed.

"So that's why you get involved in so many things. Now I understand. You buy land, open up streets, build houses, invest in all kinds of businesses. . . ."

The Captain's enumeration of Mundinho's activities brought forcefully to his attention the scope of the exporter's interests and the leading part he played in almost every progressive innovation in Ilhéus: additional branch banks, the bus line, the avenue along the beach, the daily newspaper, the pruning of cacao trees under expert supervision, and modern architecture. The architect who designed and built Mundinho's house was called crazy at first; now he had more work in Ilhéus than he could handle.

". . . and now you even bring show people," he concluded laughingly.

"She's pretty, eh? Poor people! I met them in Rio. They wanted to go on the road but didn't even have enough money for their fares. So I became an impresario."

"Under the circumstances, my friend, I'm not at all surprised. I think I would have done the same. Her husband looks as if he belonged to the Fraternity of St. Cornelius." *

---

* A play on the word *corno* (cuckold).

Mundinho made a gesture with his hands.

"They're not even married; their kind don't marry. They live together but each goes his own way. How do you suppose she gets along when she has no dancing engagements? For me, it was just a diversion to break the monotony of the trip. And that's the end of it. She's at the disposal of any of you. All you have to do, my dear fellow, is pay her price."

"The colonels will go crazy over her. But don't tell anybody that they're not married. Every colonel's fondest dream is to sleep with a married woman. Only, if anybody tries to sleep with *his* wife—oh boy! But getting back to the sandbar: are you really going to see the thing through?"

"To me it has become a personal challenge. I made contact in Rio with a Swedish steamship company. They're willing to establish a direct line to Ilhéus as soon as the harbor can be entered by ships of a certain draft."

The Captain listened attentively. Certain political plans that he had long nurtured were running through his mind. The time had arrived to put them into action. Mundinho's coming to Ilhéus was a blessing from heaven. But how would he react to the proposals? The Captain told himself that he must proceed carefully.

Mundinho felt moved by the Captain's admiration. He was in a mood for confidences; he let himself be carried away:

"Look, Captain, when I came here . . ." He fell silent for a moment, as if in doubt whether to continue. ". . . when I came here I was more or less running away." Silence again. "Not from the police. From a woman. Some day I'll tell you the whole story, but not today. Do you know what passion is? More than passion: madness? That's why I left everything and came here. I had heard about Ilhéus and the cacao. I came to look things over, and I never went back. You know the rest: my exporting firm, my life here, the good friends I've made, the enthusiasm I have for the place. It's not only on account of the business or the money, you understand. I could make as much or more exporting coffee. But here I'm accomplishing something, I am somebody, you know? I'm doing it with my own hands." And he looked at his delicate hands, with nails manicured like those of a woman.

"That's what I want to talk to you about."

"Wait, let me finish. I came here for intimate personal reasons; I was running away. But I've stayed so long partly because of my two brothers. They're much older. I figure I was born too late. By the time I grew up, everything was arranged, everything was taken care of. I was the baby: no effort on my part was required or expected. And my brothers always came first. It didn't suit me, it didn't suit me at all."

The Captain was swimming in delight; these confidences came at just the right moment. He had become friendly with Mundinho Falcão soon after the latter's arrival in Ilhéus. He was the federal tax collector and had to orient the exporter in fiscal matters. They began to spend a good deal of time together, and the Captain acted as a guide to the newcomer. He took him to Ribeirinho's plantation, to Itabuna, to Pirangi, to Água Preta; he explained the local customs; he even recommended women to him. Mundinho, in turn, was unpretentious, friendly, easy to get along with. At first the Captain merely felt proud of his intimacy with the rich young southerner, this brother of a federal congressman and relative of several diplomats. The oldest brother had even been mentioned for appointment as Minister of Finance. It was only later, after observing Mundinho's manifold activities, that the Captain began to cogitate and to plan: here was the man to lead a movement against the Bastoses.

"I was a spoiled boy. In the firm, I had nothing to do: my brothers decided everything. Although I was a grown man, to them I was still a boy. They just let me have a good time. My turn would come later, my 'hour of responsibility,' as Lourival used to say." He frowned as he spoke about his oldest brother. "You understand? I got tired of doing nothing, of being just the kid brother. I might never have rebelled, I might have gone on and on in that soft, easy life. But then came the woman. It was a problem with no possible solution." His eyes were turned toward the ocean through the open window, but he was looking into the past.

"Was she pretty?"

Mundinho Falcão gave a short laugh.

"It's an insult to speak of her as pretty. Do you know what

beauty is, Captain? Perfection in every feature? You can't call a woman like that pretty."

He passed his hand over his face to wipe out the vision.

"Deep down, I'm happy. Here I'm not the little brother of Lourival and Emílio Mendes Falcão. I'm myself. This is my land, I have my own firm, and, Captain, I'm going to turn Ilhéus inside out, I'm going to make this place a—"

"—a metropolis, as the Doctor was saying this morning," interrupted the Captain.

"This trip, my brothers saw me in a different light. They've given up hope of seeing me return beaten, with head bowed. The truth is, I'm not doing so badly, eh?"

"Badly? Man, you just got here and you're already the leading exporter of cacao."

"Not yet. The Kaufmanns export more than I. Stevenson, too. But I'll get ahead of them. What holds me here, though, is the newness of the place. Everything is still to be done, and I feel I can do it all. At least," he corrected himself, "I feel I can help. This is stimulating to a man like me."

"You know what they're saying around town?" The Captain stood up and walked across the room. The moment had arrived.

"What?" Mundinho waited. He could guess what the Captain was going to say.

"That you have political ambitions. Only this morning—"

"Political ambitions? I never thought of politics, at least not seriously. I've thought only of making money and of trying to stimulate progress here."

"That's all very nice. But you'll earn twice as much if you get into politics and change the existing situation."

"How?" The cards were on the table, the game had begun.

"You said yourself: the Minister can't do much because he has to consider the Governor's wishes. The state government takes no interest in Ilhéus. The local politicians here are a bunch of zebras. The colonels can't see beyond the end of their noses. All they think about is planting and harvesting cacao; nothing else interests them. They do whatever Ramiro Bastos tells them to. The mayoralty passes from one of Ramiro's sons to one of his cronies."

"But the colonel does some good, doesn't he?"

"He paves streets, builds parks, plants flowers—and that's about it. Roads? Not a chance. It was a big struggle just to get the highway to Itabuna built. Said he had commitments with the Englishmen of the railroad and this and that. The sandbar? He has commitments to the Governor. He has commitments to everybody except the people of Ilhéus."

The Captain spoke passionately; he had to convince Mundinho. The exporter listened in silence. He knew that the Captain was right, that the colonels had no conception of the needs of this rapidly growing region.

"There's a lot in what you say."

"You bet there is." He tapped Mundinho on the shoulder. "My dear friend, even if you want to, there is no way in good conscience that you can keep out of politics."

"And why not?"

"Because the people here need you. Because Ilhéus has a right to demand this of you."

The Captain spoke gravely, extending his arm as if he were making a speech. Mundinho lit a cigarette.

"It's something to think about." And he envisioned himself in Congress, sent there by the land of cacao, just as he had told Emílio.

"You can't imagine." The Captain went back and sat down, pleased with himself. "That's all they talk about, people who are really interested in the progress of Ilhéus and Itabuna and the whole region. They would all support you."

"It's an interesting thought, but I won't say yes or no right now. I don't want to get involved in a quixotic adventure and look ridiculous."

"You won't. If I told you that it's going to be easy, that there won't be a fight, I'd be lying to you; it'll be tough, you can be sure of that. But one thing is certain: we can win and win big."

"It's something to think about," Mundinho repeated.

The Captain smiled to himself. Mundinho was interested, all right; it was just a step from this point to a commitment. In the whole of Ilhéus no one but Mundinho Falcão could challenge Colonel Ramiro Bastos's power; he alone could avenge the Captain. Had not the Bastoses unseated his father, old Cazuzinha, ruining him in an inglorious political struggle and leaving the Captain without a penny of inheritance?

Mundinho, too, smiled to himself. Here was the Captain offering him the power he wanted, or at least a means of attaining it.

"Something to think about! The elections are coming up soon. We have to get busy immediately."

"Do you really think there are large numbers of people ready to support me?"

"You have only to make yourself available. Look, this business of the sandbar can be decisive. It's something that concerns everybody. And not just here but in Itabuna, too, and Itapira— all through the interior. You'll see, the arrival of the engineer will create a sensation."

"After the engineer the dredges will come, and the tugboats."

"And to whom will Ilhéus owe it all? Don't you see how many trumps you hold?" He paused. "You know the first thing to be done?"

"What?"

"A series of articles in the *Ilhéus Daily* exposing the government and the Mayor and showing the importance of the sandbar issue. Look, we even have a newspaper at our disposal."

"Yes, but it's not mine. I just invested some money in it to help Clóvis Costa. He's not committed to me. As a matter of fact, I think he's a friend of the Bastoses'—at least of Tonico's; they go around together."

"He's a friend of whoever pays the most. Leave him to me."

The exporter affected one last vacillation:

"I wonder if it's really worth it. Politics are always so dirty. But, if it's for the good of the region. . . ." He felt slightly ridiculous. "It might be fun," he added.

"There's no other way, old man, if you really want to help Ilhéus. Idealism alone is not enough."

"You're right, there."

There was a knock at the door, and the maid went to open it. It was the Doctor.

"I went to your office to welcome you back. I didn't find you there, so I came here." He was sweating under his turned-around collar and stiff shirt front.

The Captain hastened to speak:

"What would you say, Doctor, if I were to tell you that we are to have Mundinho Falcão as a candidate in the next elections?"

The Doctor raised his arms.

"Great! Sensational!" He turned to the exporter. "If in my modest way I can serve you. . . ."

The Captain looked at Mundinho as if to say: "You see, I wasn't lying. The best men in Ilhéus. . . ."

"But it's still a secret, Doctor."

The three men sat down, and the Captain began explaining the inner workings of local politics in the region, the connections among those who controlled votes, the interests at stake. Dr. Ezequiel Prado, for example, a man with many friends among the planters, was annoyed with the Bastoses; they had not made him president of the Municipal Council. . . .

ON THE ART OF GOSSIPING

Nacib rolled up his sleeves and looked over his customers. Nearly all were strangers to him, mostly persons who had come to town for market day. There were also a few passengers off the Ita boat, in transit to northern ports. It was still too early for his regular trade. He caught hold of Eaglebeak and took the bottle out of his hand.

"What are you doing?" It was a bottle of Portuguese cognac. "Don't you know better than to serve this to these yokels?" He walked the waiter back to the bar, where he took down another bottle. It looked just like the first one and had the same label, but it contained a mixture of Portuguese and Brazilian cognac— one of the Arab's prescriptions for increasing profits.

"It wasn't for them, Mr. Nacib. It was for the men from the boat."

"So what? Are they something special?"

Pure Portuguese cognac, unmixed vermouth, undiluted port

and madeira were reserved for his regular customers, those who came every day, his friends. He had to be there all the time; otherwise his employees would ball things up and he would lose money. He opened the cash register. This was going to be a busy day. And there would be lots of interesting talk. Filomena's departure not only caused him fatigue and material loss but also robbed him of the peace of mind necessary for complete enjoyment of his friends at the bar. In Nacib's opinion, there was nothing more enjoyable—except food and women—than to discuss the news and speculate on the latest rumors.

Gossip was the art supreme, the superlative delight, of the town. The old maids raised it to a level of incredible refinement. "The Congress of Viperine Tongues has convened," João Fulgêncio would say on seeing them in front of the church at the hour of benediction. But was it not in Fulgêncio's own Model Stationery Store that the local male gossips gathered?—and their tongues were quite as sharp as those of the old maids. There and in the bars, on the wharves, at poker games, everywhere. Someone once told Nhô-Galo that his adventures in bordellos were being talked about. In his twangy voice he replied:

"My boy, I don't give a damn. I know they talk about me, as they do about everybody else. I merely try, as a patriotic citizen, to give them something interesting to talk about."

Not everyone accepted gossip about himself with Nhô-Galo's good humor. The spreading of rumors frequently led to fights in the bars. Sometimes the offended party would draw a gun and demand an apology. Gossip, however enjoyable, was not always free from peril.

On that day there was much to be discussed. At the head of the list was the question of the sandbar, a complex subject involving many factors, such as the grounding of the Ita boat, the coming of the engineer, Mundinho Falcão's activities ("What the devil is he after?" asked Colonel Manuel of the Jaguars), and Colonel Ramiro Bastos's violent reaction. Here alone was material for several days' lively talk. And how could one overlook the two show people: the beautiful woman and the phony prince, who looked like a starved rat? This delicate and delicious subject would give rise to wisecracks by the Captain and João Fulgêncio, to sarcastic remarks by Nhô-Galo, and to much laughter by others. Tonico Bastos would soon be prowling after the ballerina, but this time he would find Mundinho Falcão blocking the way. It was certainly not because he admired her dancing that the exporter had brought her here, with her husband in tow; he had probably paid both their fares. Then there was the dinner for the bus line, the following evening, to be discussed, with conjectures as to why so-and-so had not been invited. And the new women at the cabaret. And Risoleta. . . .

Nhô-Galo sat down for a moment at one of the sidewalk tables but would not go inside. It was not his regular hour, and besides, he should have been at his desk in the Revenue Department.

"I made the mistake of going back home after the arrival of the boat, and slept until now. Give me a quick drink, I've got to go to work."

Nacib served him his usual mixture of vermouth and white rum.

"How about that cross-eyed girl, eh?" Nhô-Galo laughed. "Yesterday you were magnificent, Arab, just magnificent. The women here are improving, no doubt about that."

"I never had a woman who knew so much." Nacib whispered some details.

"You don't say so!"

The colored boy Tuísca arrived with his shoeshine box and with a message from the Dos Reis sisters: everything was under control, Nacib was not to worry. In the afternoon, they would send over the two trays of appetizers.

"Speaking of appetizers, let me have something. Anything to kill the taste in my mouth."

"Don't you see there aren't any? Not until this afternoon. My cook left me."

Nhô-Galo, trying to be funny, said:

"Why don't you hire Machadinho or Miss Pirangi?"

He was referring to the town's two official homosexuals. One was the mulatto Machadinho, always clean and neat, a launderer by trade, into whose delicate hands the families entrusted their white linen suits, fine shirts, and stiff collars. The other was an ugly Negro, a servant at the Caetano boarding-house, who could be seen on the beach at night in quest of a partner. The street urchins used to throw stones at him and yell his nickname: "Miss Pirangi! Miss Pirangi!"

Nacib became annoyed.

"Oh, go to hell!"

"That's just where I'm going: to my job. I'll make believe I'm working. But I'll be back soon, and I want you to tell me about last night—every detail."

The activity in the bar increased. Nacib saw the Captain and the Doctor coming from the direction of the beach, one on each side of Mundinho Falcão. They were talking animatedly and the Captain was making gestures. Now and then the Doctor interrupted him. Mundinho listened, nodding his head in agreement. There's something going on there, thought Nacib. What in the world had the exporter been doing at home (for he was certainly coming from there) at that time of day, in the company of the other two? Having returned only that morning after a month's absence, Mundinho should have been in his office receiving colonels, discussing business, buying cacao. This Mundinho Falcão was unpredictable; he didn't behave like other people. There he was, as if he had no business, no customers to take care of, engaged in lively conversation with two friends. Nacib turned the cashier's post over to Eaglebeak and went out to the sidewalk.

"Have you found a cook yet?" asked the Captain, taking a seat.

"I tramped all over Ilhéus. Not a trace of one."

"Cognac, Nacib—and the real stuff, eh?"

"And some codfish balls."

"I haven't any just now."

"Say, Arab, you're falling down on the job."

"You'll lose your trade. We'll all go to another bar."

"I'll have some in, this afternoon. I've ordered them from the Dos Reis."

"It's all right, then."

"All right! They charged me a fortune. I'm losing money."

"What you need, Arab, is to modernize your place. Put in a refrigerator, make your own ice, install modern equipment."

"What I need is a cook, that's what I need."

"Send for one in Sergipe."

"And until she gets here?"

Nacib noted their air of conspiracy, the Captain's satisfied smile, and the sudden termination of the conversation upon his approach. He sat down at the table with them.

"Mr. Mundinho, what the devil have you done to Colonel Ramiro Bastos?"

"To the colonel? I haven't done anything. Why do you ask?"

It was Nacib's turn to be secretive.

"Oh, nothing."

"Out with it, Arab. What was it?"

"I met him today, in front of the town hall. He was sunning himself on a bench. We started to talk, and I told him that Mr. Mundinho got back today and that the engineer was coming soon. The old man went wild. He wanted to know what business that was of Mr. Mundinho's, why he was sticking his nose where it didn't belong."

"You see?" the Captain interrupted. "The sandbar—"

"But that's not the only thing. When Professor Josué came along and told him that the school was accredited, the colonel almost jumped out of his skin. It seems he made a request of his own to the government and it didn't go through. He started tapping his cane on the sidewalk, mad as hell."

Nacib enjoyed his friends' silence, the effect his story had on them; he felt avenged for their conspiratorial air. Before long now he would discover what they were up to. The Captain spoke:

"The old sachem was furious, eh? He thinks he owns the whole town. Well, he's going to get a lot more furious than that."

"To him, Ilhéus is like a part of his plantation," declared the Doctor, "and we Ilhéans are merely his sharecroppers and hired hands."

Mundinho Falcão smiled but said nothing. At the door of the theatre on the opposite corner. Diogenes, Prince Sandra, and Anabela appeared. They saw the group at the table and came toward them. Nacib added:

"That's exactly it. To him, Mr. Mundinho is an outsider."

"Did he say 'outsider'?" asked the exporter.

"Outsider, yes, that's the word he used."

"That does it." Mundinho Falcão touched the Captain on the shoulder. "You can go ahead with your plans, Captain. We'll call the tune and the old man will have to dance to it." He addressed these last words to Nacib.

The Captain stood up. drained his glass, greeted the newcomers, and said:

"Excuse me, I was just leaving—something urgent."

The other men rose and drew more chairs to the table. Anabela, holding her open sunshade, smiled coquettishly. The prince extended a long, thin, nervous hand that held a long cigarette holder.

"When is the opening?" inquired the Doctor.

"Tomorrow. We still have some details to settle with Mr. Diogenes."

The owner of the theatre, his face unshaven, explained, in the eternally depressed and mournful voice of a singer of sacred hymns:

"His act may go over all right. The kids like magic tricks; even some of the grown-ups do. But her act. . . ."

"What's wrong with her act?" inquired Mundinho, while Nacib served more drinks.

Diogenes scratched his chin.

"You know how it is. This is still a backward place. Those dances of hers—almost naked. The families won't come."

"But you'll fill the theatre with men," said Nacib.

Diogenes tried to explain his position—very clumsily, for he did not want to admit that it was he himself, a chaste Protestant, who felt doubt about the propriety of Anabela's daring exhibition.

"It's all right for a cabaret, but not for a motion picture theatre."

The Doctor, in his very polite and refined manner, made excuses for the town to the smiling artiste:

"You must forgive us, Madam. This is an old-fashioned place where the freedom of art is not understood. They look upon everything as immoral."

"Artistic dances," said the magician in his cavernous voice.

"Of course, of course, but—"

Mundinho Falcão found it amusing.

"After all, Mr. Diogenes—"

"She can earn more at the cabaret. She can help her husband with his tricks in the theatre, then she can go and dance at the cabaret."

The thought of greater earnings brought a gleam to the prince's eye. Anabela asked Mundinho's opinion.

"It sounds like a good idea," he said. "Magic in the theatre, dances in the cabaret—perfect."

"And what about the owner of the cabaret? Do you think he'll be interested?"

"We'll soon find out." He turned to the owner of the bar. "Nacib, do me a favor: send a boy to get Zeca Lima. I want to talk with him. Tell him to come right away."

Nacib shouted an order to Tuísca, who started off at a run, for Mundinho was a good tipper. The Arab was struck by the note of command in the exporter's voice; it sounded like the voice of Ramiro Bastos when he was younger, always giving orders, laying down the law. Something was certainly about to happen.

The activity in the bar increased, new customers kept arriving, the conversation at the tables became louder. Lazy Chico ran from one side to the other. Nhô-Galo returned and joined the group at the table. Colonel Ribeirinho did likewise, while his eyes devoured the dancer. Anabela shone brightly among all those men. Prince Sandra, maintaining his dignified air, made mental calculations of the money he and his partner would make. It looked as if they would remain in Ilhéus for some time —and eat well.

"That idea of the cabaret is not bad."

"What idea?" Ribeirinho wanted to know.

"She's going to dance in the cabaret."

"Not in the movie theatre?"

"In the theatre, just the magic act, for the families. In the cabaret, the Dance of the Seven Veils."

"In the cabaret? Wonderful. The place will be jammed. But why not in the theatre? I thought—"

"Modern dances, Colonel. The veils start dropping off, one by one."

"One by one? All seven?"

"The families might not like it."

"Ah! You're right about that. One by one. All of them? I guess it would go better in the cabaret. Livelier crowd."

Anabela laughed and looked at the colonel with a promise in her eyes. The Doctor repeated:

"A backward place, where art must hide in the cabarets."

"You can't even find a cook here," lamented Nacib.

Professor Josué came down the street in the company of João Fulgêncio. It was now the before-lunch apéritif hour. The bar was crowded. Nacib himself had to wait on customers at the tables. Many of them called for snacks and appetizers, and the Arab was kept busy explaining why there were none—damn that old Filomena! Jacob the Russian, sweat pouring off him, his red hair in disarray, wanted to know about the dinner for the next day.

Don't worry: I'm not the kind of louse to go back on my word."

Josué, full of savoir faire, kissed Anabela's hand. João Fulgêncio, who did not frequent the cabaret, protested against Diogenes's Puritanism:

"Scandalous? Nonsense. It's just this sanctimonious Protestant."

Mundinho Falcão looked down the street to see if the Captain was returning. Now and then, he and the Doctor exchanged glances. Nacib observed those glances and the exporter's impatience. You couldn't fool him: something was up. The breeze from the ocean carried away Anabela's sunshade, which she had left open on the sidewalk beside her chair. Nhô-Galo, Josué, the Doctor, and Colonel Ribeirinho all jumped up; only Mundinho Falcão and Prince Sandra remained seated. But it was Dr. Ezequiel Prado, on his way to the bar, who caught the parasol and brought it back to her. He had the baggy eyes of a confirmed drunkard.

"With my compliments, Madam."

Anabela's eyes, with their long black lashes, traveled from man to man and came to rest on Ribeirinho.

"We are in the company of real gentlemen!" said Prince Sandra.

Tonico Bastos, coming from his office, fell into Mundinho Falcão's arms, both men making a great show of friendship.

"And Rio, how was it when you left? That's where a man can really live."

He took in Anabela with his seductive eyes, the eyes of the town's irresistible lady-killer.

"Who will introduce me?" he asked.

Nhô-Galo and the Doctor sat down before a checkerboard. At another table, someone was telling Nacib about a marvelous cook. Seasoning like hers you never tasted. Only, she was working in Recife for the Coutinhos, an important Pernambucan family.

"What the hell good does that do me?"

GABRIELA ON THE WAY

As the migrants moved southward, the landscape changed. The inhospitable dry scrubland gave way to fertile valleys, green meadows, dense woods, brooks, and rivers. They spent a night near a small distillery, with fields of sugar cane waving in the wind. A workman explained to them the route they must follow. In less than one day of walking they would reach Ilhéus, the end of their frightful journey.

"Migrants always camp at the end of the market grounds over by the railroad."

"Don't they go aroun' lookin' for work?" asked the Negro Fagundes.

"It's better to stay there and wait. People come there and offer you a job, sometimes out on the cacao plantations, sometimes in town."

"Sometimes in town?" said Clemente, frowning. A concertina hung from his shoulder.

"Yes, for anybody who's got a trade: bricklayer, carpenter, house painter. They're building houses in Ilhéus faster than you can count them."

"Suppose you don't have a trade?"

"There's jobs also in the cacao warehouses and on the docks."

"Me, I'm goin' out into the woods," said a strong, middle-aged man. "They say you can make good money there."

"There was a time you could. Today it isn't so easy."

"I hear a good trigger man can always get work," said the Negro Fagundes, passing his hand almost caressingly over his revolver.

"Used to be that way."

"No more?"

"Not so much."

Clemente had no trade. He had always worked in the country; all he knew was how to plant, hoe, and harvest. Moreover, he had come with the specific intention of working on the cacao plantations. He had heard many accounts of people like himself—beaten by the drought, refugees, half dead with hunger—who made a fortune there in a short time. That was what people said in the backlands. The fame of Ilhéus had spread everywhere; the blind beggars sang ballads about it to the accompaniment of their guitars; traveling salesmen talked about its abundance and daring: a man could make his pile there in no time, there was no other crop in the world as profitable as cacao. Bands of migrants were streaming out of the backlands, the drought at their heels; they abandoned the arid land, where their cattle were dying and their crops withering, and trudged southward. The trails were rough; in places they had to be hacked out with machetes through virgin woods. Many fell by the wayside, unable to withstand the rigors of the journey; others died when they reached the rain belt, where typhus, malaria, and smallpox awaited them. They neared their destination with their numbers decimated, just remnants of families now, almost dead with fatigue; but their hearts pulsated with hope. One final effort would bring them to the "city" of wealth and easy living—to the land of cacao, where money was like garbage in the streets.

Clemente was loaded down. In addition to his own belongings —the concertina and a half-filled sack—he was carrying Gabriela's bundle. Their pace was slow; there were old people

among them, and even the young were approaching the limit of
their endurance. Some were virtually dragging themselves along,
sustained only by their hopes.

Gabriela alone seemed unmindful of the hardships. She
moved as if her feet were gliding over the rugged trail, as if
there were no stones, no jagged tree stumps, no tangled vines.
The dust of the roads in the dry scrubland had so completely
covered her that it was impossible to distinguish her features.
Her piece of comb could no longer penetrate her hair. She
looked like a wild woman wandering through the country. But
Clemente knew what she was really like and he knew it with
every particle of his being, with the tips of his fingers and the
hair on his chest. When the two groups had come together at the
beginning of their journey, the color of Gabriela's face and legs
was still visible, and her hair, falling over the back of her neck,
diffused a lovely scent. Even now, through the dirt that covered
her, Clemente could envision her as she appeared on that first
day, leaning against a tree, her body tall and slender, a smile on
her face, eating a guava.

"You don't look like you came such a long way."

She laughed.

"We're gettin' close now," she said. "It'll be good to get there."

His frown deepened.

"Not for me."

"Why not for you?" She raised her eyes to the man's somber
face, eyes that were sometimes shy and ingenuous, sometimes
bold and provocative. "Didn't you leave home to come and work
in cacao, to earn money? That's all you used to talk about."

"You know why," he muttered angrily. "For me this road could
go on forever."

In her laugh there was a faint suggestion of resignation—one
could not call it sadness—as if she had come to terms with the
inevitable.

"Everything good comes to an end. So does everything bad."

A sudden impotent fury rose up in him. Once again, con-
trolling his voice, he repeated the question he had been asking
her along the way and during the sleepless nights:

"Don't you want to go with me? Clear some land and plant cacao together, just the two of us? Soon we'd have our own little plantation and really begin to live."

Gabriela's voice was gentle but definite:

"I told you what I want to do. I'm goin' to stay in Ilhéus. I'm goin' to hire me out as a cook or a washwoman or a housemaid." Then she added, as a happy memory: "I used to work for rich folks. I learned how to cook."

"You won't get anywhere that way. Out in the country, you and me, we'd be building up a little nest egg and gettin' ahead. . . ."

Gabriela did not answer him. She moved along the road almost trippingly. She looked like a demented woman with her dirty face, unkempt hair, bruised feet, and ragged clothing. But Clemente saw her slender and beautiful, her hair loose, her face delicate, her legs long, her breasts high. He scowled even more darkly; he wanted her with him forever. How could he live without the warmth of Gabriela?

When, at the beginning of the journey, the two groups had come together, she had caught his eye at once. She was with her uncle, whose persistent cough racked his sick, wasted body. Clemente watched her as she moved among the other migrants, talking, helping, consoling; but for the first few days he lacked the courage to go near her.

At night the scrubland was thick with snakes and fear. Clemente filled the solitude with the sound of his concertina. The Negro Fagundes told stories of his adventures with a band of outlaws, stories of violence, courage, and death. He watched Gabriela with humble eyes and hurried to obey whenever she asked him to go fill a can of water.

Clemente played his harmonica for Gabriela but did not dare speak to her. It was she who came close one night, with light feet and innocent eyes. Her uncle was asleep, every breath a struggle for air. She leaned against a tree. The Negro Fagundes was telling a story:

"There was five soldiers, and we spitted them on our knives like monkeys to keep from wastin' ammunition. . . ."

The night was dark and scary. Clemente could feel Gabriela's nearness. As the sounds from the concertina died down, Fagundes's voice resounded in the silence. Gabriela spoke in a whisper:

"Don't stop playin' or they'll notice us."

He struck up a melody of the backlands. His throat was tight, his heart pounding. Gabriela began to sing softly. It was late and the fire was dying when she lay down beside him, as if it were nothing. The night was so dark they could hardly see each other.

Ever since that miraculous night, Clemente lived in dread of losing her. He thought at first that after what had happened she would be eternally his and would go with him into the country to plant cacao. But he soon learned otherwise. During the daytime she acted as if there was nothing between them; she treated him as she treated all the others. She was naturally cheerful and playful, she bantered even with the Negro Fagundes, she spread her smiles about and got from everyone whatever she wanted. But when night fell and she had attended to her uncle, she would go to the distant spot where Clemente awaited her and lie down with him as eagerly as if she lived for nothing else. She would give herself to him with complete abandon—sighing, moaning, and laughing.

The next morning Clemente, attached to her now as if she were his very life, would try to make plans with her for the future. But she would laugh at him, almost mockingly, and go off to care for her uncle, who was daily becoming thinner and more exhausted.

One afternoon they had to make a halt on the road: Gabriela's uncle was dying. He was gasping and spitting blood. The Negro Fagundes picked him up and carried him on his back for a while. Gabriela walked beside them. The old man died in the early afternoon, with the blood oozing out of his mouth. Buzzards were already circling overhead.

Then Clemente saw Gabriela as a lone orphan, destitute and sad. For the first time, he thought he understood her: she was just a poor young woman, little more than a girl, whom he could protect. He approached her and talked at length about his plans. He had heard a great deal about the land of cacao. He knew of persons who had left Ceará without a penny and had returned a few years later on a pleasure trip, flaunting their money. That was what he was going to do. He wanted to clear virgin forests—there were still some left—plant cacao, have his own land, earn plenty. Gabriela could go with him; when a priest came around, they would get married. She shook her head in disagreement, but without her mocking laugh, and said only:

"I'm not goin', Clemente."

Other persons died along the way and their bodies were left to the vultures. They reached the end of the scrub, fertile lands appeared, and the rains fell. She continued to lie with him, to moan and to laugh, to sleep with her head on his bare chest. Clemente continued talking, growing ever more somber; she only laughed and shook her head. One night he shoved her away from him.

"You don't really want me."

Suddenly, out of nowhere, the Negro Fagundes appeared with gun in hand, his eyes blazing.

"It was nothin', Fagundes."

Her body had struck against the trunk of the tree under which they had been lying. Fagundes lowered his head and went away. Gabriela laughed, while Clemente's anger mounted. He approached her and seized her by the wrists. She had fallen back on the undergrowth, and her face was scratched.

"I feel like killin' us both."

"What for?"

"You don't love me."

"You're silly."

"God, what am I goin' to do?"

"It don't matter so much," she said, and drew him toward her.

Now, on this last day of the journey, confused and disoriented, he reached a decision at last. He would stay in Ilhéus, abandon his ambitions; the only thing that mattered was to be near Gabriela.

"If you don't want to go with me, I'll find some way of stayin' in the city. The only thing is, I got no trade. Farmin' is all I know."

She took his hand in an unexpected gesture, and for a moment he felt victorious and happy.

"No, Clemente, don't stay. What for?"

"What for!"

"You came to make money, to clear some ground and be a planter. That's what you want. Why stay in the city and be poor and miserable?"

"Just to see you. So we can be together."

"And is it so bad if we can't see each other? We want different things: we should go different ways. Some day, maybe, we'll meet again. When you're rich, you won't even want to recognize me."

She spoke calmly, almost as if they were mere acquaintances, as if the nights they had slept together did not mean anything.

"But, Gabriela. . . ."

He did not know what to say; he momentarily forgot his arguments, the appropriate insults, and his urge to beat her and teach her not to toy with a man. He managed only to blurt out:

"You don't love me."

"I'm glad we met: it made the trip shorter."

"You really don't want me to stay?"

"What for? To go hungry? You know what you want; go and see if maybe God will give it to you."

"And what'll you do?"

"I don't know for sure. I just know I don't want to go out in the country and plant cacao."

He felt a pain in his breast and a desire to kill her and himself before the end of the journey. She smiled.

"It don't matter so much, Clemente."

Gloria's LAMENT

I have a fire in my breast,
Oh! in my breast a fire.
(Who would burn himself in me?)

From the colonel I have riches,
Riches without end:
Louis XV chairs
To set my rump upon,
Pure silk lingerie,
And pure white cambric blouse.
Bodice of silk or satin,
Bodice of finest cambric
Cannot contain the fire,
The loneliness in my breast.

I have a parasol,
Money to squander at will;
I buy at fancy stores
And charge it on my bill.
I have every luxury
And in my breast a fire.
What good is all I have
If I lack what I desire?

The women turn their faces,
The men look from afar:
I am the colonel's Gloria,
The old planter's concubine.
Snow-white linen sheets
And in my breast a fire;
On this bed of loneliness
How hot my breasts, my thighs
Aflame, athirst my lips!
I am the colonel's Gloria,

Within my breast a fire;
On snow-white linen sheet
I lie in loneliness.

My eyes bewitch. My breasts,
Scented with lavender,
Press warm. I will not tell
The secret of my womb,
But all the fire within me
Comes from a small live coal
Aglow within a nook
In Gloria's moon-round belly.
I will not tell the secret
Of womb or glowing ember.

I shall find a timid student,
Growing his first mustache;
I shall find a boastful soldier,
All confidence and flash;
I must find a love to quench
The fire in my breast,
A love to end
This loneliness.

Push open my heavy door,
I have removed the bar,
There is no lock and key.
Come, quench this glowing ember,
Come share this bed with me;
And bring what love you can
For I have much to give.

I have a fire in my breast,
Oh! in my breast a fire.
(Who would burn himself in me?)

SECOND CHAPTER

The Loneliness of GLORIA

(asighing at her window)

> "Backward and ignorant, hostile to the new world in which they live, incapable of understanding the very meaning of civilization or of progress, these men must no longer be allowed to rule." (FROM AN ARTICLE BY THE DOCTOR IN THE ILHÉUS DAILY)

OF TEMPTATION AT THE WINDOW

GLORIA'S HOUSE was on a corner of the square, and she spent the afternoons at the front window, her elbows on the sill, her robust breasts uplifted as in an offering to the passers-by. The old maids went by every day on their way to the church and always made the same remarks:

"Shameless hussy!"

"The men sin even without meaning to, when they just look at her."

"She even makes the young boys sin. They lose the chastity of their eyes."

Sharp-tongued Dorotéia dared to express the indignation they all felt:

"Really, the colonel could have set up his woman on a side street. But no, he plants her down where the best families have to look at her. And right in front of the men's noses."

"And so close to the church. Why, it's an offense against God!"

At five o'clock every afternoon, the men at the crowded bar would begin to stretch their eyes toward Gloria's window on the other side of the square. Professor Josué, tall and skinny—"like a sad, solitary eucalyptus," he had once written in a poem—

wearing a blue bow tie with white polka dots, his cheeks sunken like those of a consumptive, brilliantine on his hair and a book of verses in his hand, would cross to the sidewalk that ran in front of Gloria's window. It also ran in front of Colonel Melk Tavares's new house, which stood on a corner at the far end of the square. This house had aroused profound and bitter arguments among the intelligentsia at the Model Stationery Store, for it was a house in the modern style, the first to be built by the architect brought from Rio by Mundinho Falcão. In its clean, simple lines it contrasted sharply with the high, heavy houses of the other colonels.

The house was surrounded by a small, well-kept garden of tea roses and madonna lilies, with jasmine at the front gate. Malvina knelt among the flowers (which she excelled in beauty), tending them and dreaming. She was Melk's only daughter, a pupil at the parochial school and the object of Josué's sighs. Every afternoon after classes and after the indispensable confabulation at the Model Stationery Store, the teacher came for a walk in the square; twenty times he passed in front of Malvina's garden, and twenty times his suppliant eyes fell in mute declaration upon the young woman. At Nacib's place, the regular customers observed and commented on the daily peregrination:

"The Professor never gives up."

"He wants to marry a cacao plantation and become financially independent."

"There he goes, doing his daily penance," the old maids would say. They understood his ardent, unrequited passion and sympathized with him.

"I know her for what she is, a stuck-up little minx. Does she think she can catch somebody better than an intelligent young man like that?"

"Intelligent but poor."

"She doesn't need a rich husband. Such a good young man, so well educated; he even writes poetry."

When he neared the church, Josué would slow his steps, remove his hat, and bow nearly double in salutation to the spinsters.

"So mannerly. A fine young man."

"Fine but with weak lungs."

"Dr. Plínio said there was nothing the matter with his lungs. He's just frail."

"A conceited minx, that's what she is. Just because she has a pretty face and a rich father. And the poor young man is so much in love." A sigh rose from the wrinkled chest.

Followed by the sympathetic remarks of the spinsters and by the unjust opinions expressed in the bar, Josué neared Gloria's window. It was to see Malvina, beautiful and cold, that he slowly paced that stretch of sidewalk twenty times every afternoon, with a book of verses in his hand. But, in passing, his romantic gaze would pause upon Gloria's erect breasts, resting on the window sill as on a blue tray. And from her breasts his gaze rose to her dark-complexioned face, with the heavy, avid lips and the eyes that poured forth a continual invitation. Josué's romantic eyes would light up in sinful, physical desire, and a warm flush would suffuse his usually pallid cheeks. For only an instant, however; once he had passed the temptation at the notorious window, his eyes took on again their look of entreaty and despair, and his face became even paler than before—the eyes and face he wore for Malvina.

Privately Professor Josué censured Colonel Coriolano Ribeiro. a wealthy plantation owner, for installing his seductive mistress on St. Sebastian Square, right on a street where the best families lived and just two steps from Colonel Melk Tavares's house. Were she on any other street, farther away from Malvina's garden, he could perhaps have risked it: on some moonless night he might have accepted the invitation that he read in Gloria's sultry eyes and in her parted lips.

"Look at that piece of scum giving him the eye."

In long, black dresses buttoned at the neck, with black shawls over their shoulders, the spinsters looked like nocturnal birds. Standing in the forecourt of the little church, they could see the movement of Gloria's head as she turned to watch Josué pacing the sidewalk in front of Colonel Melk's house.

"He's an upright young man. He has eyes only for Malvina."

"I'm going to make a vow to St. Sebastian," said plump Quinquina, "so Malvina will fall in love with him. I'm going to light a candle, one of the big ones."

"I'll light one, too," added skinny Florzinha, who stood resolutely with her sister on all issues.

At her window Gloria emitted a deep sigh, almost a groan. It expressed a mixture of desire, sadness, and resentment. Her bosom was filled with indignation against men in general. They were cowards and hypocrites. During the heat of the day, in the middle of the afternoon, when the square was deserted and the shutters of the family residences were closed, men passing alone in front of Gloria's open window would smile at her and wish her good afternoon with visible emotion. But if they were walking with someone, or if any other person was in the square—even just one old maid—the men deliberately looked the other way, as if they were repelled by the sight of her at the window with her high breasts almost leaping out of her embroidered cambric blouse. The very same men who had previously murmured gallantries as they passed alone now wore a look of offended propriety. Gloria would have liked to slam the window in their faces, but alas! she could not bring herself to do it, for those gleams of desire in the men's eyes, those smiles, those fearful, fleeting phrases, were all she had in her loneliness. Much too little for her thirst and hunger, but if she closed the window she would lose even that little. No married woman in all of Ilhéus, where married women lived indoors and took care of their homes, was so well guarded and so inaccessible as Gloria. Colonel Coriolano was not one to stand for any foolishness.

Men were so afraid of him that they dared not even speak to poor Gloria if anyone was near. Josué constituted the lone exception. Twenty times each afternoon the fire in his eyes would blaze as he passed under her window, only to die down again as he neared Malvina's gate. Gloria was aware of the teacher's passion for the girl and disliked her for her indifference; she considered the girl an insufferable fool. But her knowledge of his love did not cause her to withhold from him her smile of invitation and of promise, and she was grateful to him, for even when Malvina stood at the jasmine-covered gate of the new house, he did not turn away his face. Ah, if only he were a little bolder, if only, late some night, he would push open the street door, which Gloria purposely left unlocked, she would soon make him forget that haughty child.

Josué did not dare push open the heavy door. Nobody dared, for fear of scandal, of the old maids' tongues, and still more for fear of Colonel Coriolano Ribeiro. Everyone had heard about Juca and Chiquinha.

On this day, Josué had come to the bar a little earlier than usual; it was still the siesta hour and the square was deserted. Apart from the Doctor and the Captain, engaged in a game of checkers, the only customers in the bar were a few traveling salesmen. To celebrate the accreditation of his school, Enoch had given the pupils the afternoon off. Professor Josué had gone for a walk; he had witnessed the arrival of a large band of migrants at the slave market, he had stopped awhile at the Model Stationery Store, and now he was having a drink at the bar and talking with Nacib.

"A big crowd of migrants. The drought must be burning up the backlands."

Nacib displayed interest:

"Any women?"

"Why? Are you that hard up?"

"No joking. My cook left me and I've got to get another. Sometimes you can find one among the migrants."

"Yes, there are a few women. Horrible-looking people, covered with rags, filthy, look as if they had the plague."

"I'll go there later."

Malvina had not appeared at the gate, and Josué was getting impatient. Nacib informed him:

"Your girl is on the avenue down by the beach. I saw her pass by a little while ago with some of her friends."

Josué paid for his drink and got up to leave. Nacib stood at the entrance to the bar, watching him go and thinking that it must be good to be in love that way. The girl gave him no encouragement, but he wanted her all the more; sooner or later the thing would end in marriage. Gloria appeared at her window, and Nacib's eyes turned covetous. If some day the colonel let her go, there would be a stampede. He would never have a chance, in competition with all the rich colonels. The trays of tidbits and appetizers had been delivered, much to the pleasure of the customers at the apéritif hour. But Nacib could not continue to pay the Dos Reis sisters a fortune. When business slacked off at the dinner hour, he would visit the migrants' camp. Who knew, maybe he would be lucky enough to find a cook there.

Suddenly the afternoon quiet was shattered by shouts and the hubbub of many voices. The Captain held up his move, the checker in his hand. Nacib stepped outside; the clamor increased.

The colored boy Tuísca, who had been peddling the Dos Reis sisters' confections, came running from the avenue, his tray balanced on his head. He was yelling something but could not make himself heard. The Captain and the Doctor turned around, curious, and other customers stood up. Nacib saw Josué and several others hastening along the avenue. Finally they heard Tuísca shout:

"Colonel Jesuíno killed Dona Sinhàzinha and Dr. Osmundo. There's blood all around. . . ."

The Captain pushed away the table and left almost at a run. The Doctor went with him. After a moment's hesitation, Nacib hurried after them.

OF THE CRUEL LAW

The news of the crime spread like wildfire. From Unhão Hill to Conquista Hill, in the elegant homes along the beach and in the huts on Cobras Island, in Pontal and in Malhado, in private homes and in houses of prostitution, everyone was talking about the tragedy. Because it was market day the town was crowded with people who had come from the interior, from villages and farms, to buy and sell. In the shops, in the food stores, in the pharmacies and doctors' offices, in the lawyers' offices, in the cacao exporting firms, in the Cathedral of St. George and in the Church of St. Sebastian, it was the only topic of conversation.

The bars were crowded with people discussing the news—especially the Vesuvius Bar, situated so close to where the shocking event had taken place. A crowd of the curious gathered in front of the dentist's house, a small bungalow on the beach. A policeman posted at the door explained what he could. The stunned housemaid was surrounded by questioners demanding details. Girls from the parochial school walked up and down the beach avenue in joyous excitement, whispering to one another. Professor Josué seized the opportunity to get close to Malvina and told the girls about other famous love affairs: Romeo and Juliet, Héloise and Abelard, Dirceu and Marília.

At every table in Nacib's bar, men were discussing the crime. They all approved the planter's action. Not one voice was raised, even among the women in the church vestibule, in defense of poor, beautiful Sinhàzinha. Colonel Jesuíno had proved himself a real man, resolute, brave, honorable, as he had done so often during the period of struggle. People remembered that the colonel and his hired assassins had been responsible for many crosses in the cemeteries and at roadsides. He had not only engaged the assassins but had led them himself on certain famous occasions, such as the encounter with the men of the now deceased Major Fortunato Pereira at the crossroads of Boa Morte in the dangerous area of Ferradas. He was a fearless and stubborn man.

This Colonel Jesuíno Mendonça, of the famous Mendonças of Alagoas, had come to Ilhéus as a young man. He had cleared jungles and laid out plantations. He had defended his claim to the soil by shooting those who challenged it. His properties had increased and he had made his name a respected one. He had married Sinhàzinha Guedes, a local beauty twenty years his junior. She was a member of an old Ilhéan family (to which the Doctor was distantly related) and had inherited from her father a coconut plantation in the vicinity of Olivença. She was the principal organizer of festivities at the Church of St. Sebastian and an indefatigable customer of the shoe stores and dry-goods shops. She spent long periods at her husband's plantation. Never, in all her married years, had Sinhàzinha given the town busybodies anything to talk about. Suddenly, on that beautiful sunny day, during the quiet of the siesta hour, Colonel Jesuíno Mendonça shot her and her lover to death.

The impact on the town was tremendous, for the shooting stimulated emotions associated with the old days. For the moment, Nacib forgot his terrible problem, the Captain and the Doctor forgot their political concerns, and Colonal Ramiro Bastos even forgot his hatred for Mundinho Falcão. The news, spreading like wildfire, increased the respect and admiration that already surrounded the planter's thin and somewhat somber figure. For this was how it was in Ilhéus: the honor of a deceived husband could be cleansed only by blood.

This is how it was. For the customs of the region were still strongly affected by the era of constant fighting and disorder, when a human life was considered of little value and when trails hacked out by trigger men and bordered by the graves of ambush victims were broadening into roads for donkey trains. The only treatment for a faithless wife was violent death. Whenever a man was tried for his observance of this unwritten law (and consequent violation of the written law against homicide), the jury brought in a unanimous verdict of not guilty.

The court sessions, held twice a year, were still the liveliest and most heavily attended diversions in Ilhéus, despite the new competition of three movie houses, dances at the Progress Club, soccer games on Sunday afternoons, and lectures by literati from Bahia and Rio. Famous lawyers, such as Dr. Ezequiel Prado and Dr. Maurício Caires, not to mention the shyster João Peixoto with his thunderous voice—renowned orators and eminent rhetoricians all—made the audience tremble and weep. Dr. Maurício Caires, president of the Brotherhood of St. George, was a specialist in quoting the Bible; he had been a seminarian before entering law. He was fond of Latin phrases, and some considered him as erudite as the Doctor. When a case was being tried before a jury, the oratorical duels went on for hours and hours, with replications and rejoinders that lasted till daybreak. These occasions were the most important cultural events in Ilhéus.

There was heavy betting on the outcome of almost every trial. The people of Ilhéus loved gambling, and anything served as a pretext for it. On some occasions, now rarer than in earlier days, the jury's verdict gave rise to gun fights and additional deaths. Colonel Pedro Brandão, for example, was killed on a staircase of the town hall after being acquitted by a jury. The son of Chico Martim, whom the colonel and his henchmen had barbarously murdered, dealt out this justice with his own hands.

No bets were laid, however, when the crime was the murder of an unfaithful wife by her husband. Everyone knew that a unanimous acquittal would be the inevitable and just result. They only went to listen to the lawyers' speeches and to pick up whatever scabrous or picaresque details might be brought out at the trial.

The tragedy of Sinhàzinha and the dentist was passionately discussed. Opinions varied as to exactly what had happened, there were conflicting details, but on one thing all were agreed: the colonel had done the right thing and deserved praise for performance of his duty as a husband and as a man.

OF BLACK STOCKINGS

On the afternoon of the crime, the number of customers in Nacib's bar was far above normal, even for a market day. Many persons went to the beach, stared at the dentist's house, and then hurried to the bar to learn the latest rumors and to discuss the tragedy with their friends.

"Who would have thought it! Such a good churchwoman!"

Moving busily from table to table, speeding up his helpers, Nacib made a mental calculation of his profits. A juicy crime like that every day and he could soon buy his cacao plantation.

Mundinho Falcão, who had an appointment to meet Clóvis Costa at the bar, found himself surrounded by the talk. He smiled indifferently, preoccupied with the political plans to which he was devoting himself body and soul. That is how he was: when he decided to do something he never rested until it was accomplished. But both the Doctor and the Captain seemed interested in nothing but the crime, as if their conversation with him that morning had not taken place. Mundinho merely lamented the death of the dentist, his neighbor at the beach and one of his few swimming companions, for ocean bathing was considered almost scandalous in Ilhéus at the time. The Doctor, whose rapturous temperament gave him a sense of well-being in that climate of tragedy, used Sinhàzinha to bring up the subject of Ofenísia:

"Don't forget, Dona Sinhàzinha was related to the Ávilas. A family full of romantic women. She must have inherited her cousin Ofenísia's propensity for misfortune."

"Ofenísia? Who was she?" asked a merchant from Rio do Braço. He had come to market in Ilhéus and wanted to take back a larger collection of details about the crime than any of his fellow townsmen.

"A forebear of mine, a fatal beauty who inspired the poet Teodoro de Castro and infatuated Dom Pedro II. She died of frustration and regret for not having gone with him."

"Gone where with him?"

"Gone where! To bed of course, where else?" said João Fulgêncio.

The Doctor explained:

"To Rio. It did not matter to her that she would have had to be his concubine. Her brother had to lock her up with seven keys. The brother was Colonel Luís Antônio d'Ávila, of the war with Paraguay. She died of a broken heart. In Dona Sinhàzinha's veins there flowed some of Ofenísia's blood, the blood of the Ávilas, marked by tragedy!"

Nhô-Galo burst in, out-of-breath, and dropped his news in the middle of the group:

"It was an anonymous letter. Jesuíno found it at the plantation."

"Who could have written it?"

They fell into silent thought, and Mundinho took the opportunity to ask the Captain, in a low voice:

"What about Clóvis Costa? Did you speak to him?"

"He was busy writing up the crime. I arranged for us to meet tonight, at your house."

"In that case I'll get going."

"You're leaving? At a time like this?"

"I'm not from Ilhéus, my dear man," said the exporter, laughing.

Everyone was astonished at his indifference to so rare and exciting an event. Mundinho left and started across the square. Coming toward him was a group of girls from the parochial school, escorted by Professor Josué. At the approach of the exporter, Malvina's eyes brightened; she smiled and straightened her dress. Happy to be in Malvina's company, Josué congratulated Mundinho again on the accreditation of the school:

"Ilhéus is once more in debt to you."

"Oh, it was nothing." He seemed like a magnanimous prince handing out favors, money, titles of nobility. . . .

"And what do you think of the crime, sir?" asked Iracema, an ardent brunette, whose conduct with young men at the gate to her house was a subject of gossip.

Malvina moved closer to hear the answer. Mundinho spread his arms and replied:

"It's always sad to learn of the death of a beautiful woman. Especially such a horrible death. A beautiful woman is sacred."

"But she was deceiving her husband," protested Celestina, so young and already so like an old maid.

"Between death and love, I choose love."

"Do you write poetry?" asked Malvina, smiling.

"Me? No, miss, I'm not gifted that way. The poet here is our Professor."

"I only wondered. What you said just now sounded poetic."

"It was a fine phrase," said Josué.

For the first time, Mundinho took a good look at Malvina. A beautiful girl. Her deep, mysterious eyes held him.

"You take that attitude," said Celestina to Mundinho, "because you're not married."

"But you take the opposite attitude, and you're not married either."

Everyone laughed. Mundinho took his leave. Malvina's eyes followed him pensively. Iracema laughed, an almost shameless laugh.

"That Mr. Mundinho . . ." And as she watched the exporter heading toward his house, she added: "What an attractive man!"

In the bar, Ari Santos—who worked in an exporting firm, was president of the Rui Barbosa Literary Society, and wrote a column for the *Ilhéus Daily* under the name of Ariosto—leaned over the table and whispered:

"She was stark naked."

"Entirely?"

"All over?" It was the Captain's greedy voice.

"Stark naked. The only thing she had on was a pair of black stockings."

"Black stockings! Oh, my!" The Captain clicked his tongue.

"A lewd woman," said Dr. Maurício Caires.

"She must have been beautiful." Nacib suddenly saw Dona Sinhàzinha nude, in a pair of black stockings. He sighed.

The details would come out in the testimony. The black stockings were a refinement doubtless introduced by the dentist, for he came from Bahia. After getting his degree there, he had been attracted by the wealth and prosperity of Ilhéus. He had rented a bungalow on the beach, had set up his office in the front room, and had done well. From ten to twelve in the morning and from three to six in the afternoon, persons passing by could look in at the large window and see the shiny new chair, made in Japan, and the elegant young dentist in his white gown working on his clients' teeth. His father—a well-to-do merchant in Bahia with a store on Chile Street—had given him the money for his equipment and, during the first few months, had sent him an allowance to help with his expenses. But it was not in the well-equipped dental office, it was in the bedroom at the back that the planter found his wife, dressed only, as the prosecuting attorney subsequently expressed it, in "depraved black stockings." As to Dr. Osmundo Pimental, he was completely undressed, without socks of any color or any other garment covering his arrogant, seductive youth. The planter fired two fatal bullets into each. He was a man of famed marksmanship, practiced in the use of firearms from the old nights of roadside ambushes and bloodshed.

Nacib had more business that day than he could handle. As

they served the customers at the tables, Lazy Chico and Eaglebeak listened eagerly to the conversations. Tuísca also helped,
but the boy's mind was elsewhere: he was worried about payment of the previous week's bill for the confections of corn,
cassava, and manioc that he delivered to the dentist's house
every afternoon. As Nacib looked at his overcrowded bar, in
which the snacks and appetizers provided by the Dos Reis sisters
had long since been consumed, he occasionally swore at old
Filomena. On a day like this, of all times, to go off and leave him
without a cook! He moved from table to table, joined in the talk,
took a drink with friends, but he could not give himself over
completely to enjoyment of the tragedy, as he would have done
if his mind had been free. Episodes of illicit love and mortal
revenge with such savory details—black stockings, my God!—did
not happen every day. But he would have to go out soon to look
for a cook among the new migrants at the slave market.

Lazy Chico, his hands filled with glasses and bottles, stopped
at a table to listen.

"Come on, loafer, move."

But when Nacib was not looking, Chico, an incurable dawdler
at best, repeated his offense. After all, he was one of God's children, too, and he wanted to hear all about the black stockings.

"The finest quality, my dear fellow, imported," said Ari Santos.
"You can't get merchandise like that in Ilhéus."

"He must have ordered them from Bahia. Probably from his
father's store."

"They were in each other's arms when Jesuíno entered the
room. They didn't even hear him."

"But the maid screamed when she saw Jesuíno."

"At a time like that you don't hear a thing," said the Captain.

"The colonel gave them what they deserved."

Dr. Maurício seemed to think he was already in the courtroom:

"He did what any one of us would have done in such a case.
He acted like a man: he was not born to be a cuckold, and there
is only one way a man can tear off his horns."

Everyone was talking, to people at the same table and to people at other tables. But in all that noisy assembly, which in-

cluded some of the town's notables, not one voice was raised in defense of Sinhàzinha. No one forgave the sudden awakening of her long dormant desires. They had been transformed into blazing passion by the dentist's smooth talk, black curls, and mournful eyes, like those of St. Sebastian in the picture above the altar of the little church on the square. Indeed, Sinhàzinha's infatuation began when she noticed this resemblance, for St. Sebastian had been her favorite saint; so, at least, said Ari Santos, who had often shared the platform with the dentist at the Sunday morning meetings of the Rui Barbosa Literary Society.

"That's what happens when people go to church too often," observed Nhô-Galo.

"Right," said Colonel Ribeirinho. "It's bad business for a married woman to tie herself to a priest's cassock."

Three cavities to be filled; the dentist's mellifluous tones to the accompaniment of the Japanese motor; the poetic compliments. . . .

"He had a gift for poetry," affirmed the Doctor. "He once recited some sonnets to me—exquisite. Superb rhymes. Worthy of Olavo Bilac."

So different from her harsh and taciturn husband, twenty years older than she (the dentist was twelve years younger). And those suppliant eyes of St. Sebastian—my God, what woman could resist them! Especially one at the peak of womanhood, with a husband who lived more on the plantation than at home, who was tired of his wife, and who was crazy about young colored country girls just coming into bloom—a woman, moreover, without children to think about and to keep her busy.

"My dear Mr. Ari Santos, don't come defending her to me, the shameless creature," Dr. Maurício Caires cut in. "An honorable woman is an impregnable fortress."

"The blood," said the Doctor, "the terrible blood of the Ávilas, the blood of Ofenísia."

"You and your blood. Trying to compare this filthy orgy with a platonic romance that never went beyond a few harmless glances. Comparing an innocent noblewoman with an adulteress, and our wise Emperor, a paragon of virtue, with a depraved dentist."

"Who's comparing? I'm talking about heredity, the blood of my people."

"I'm not defending anybody," declared Ari. "I'm just reporting."

Sinhàzinha had begun to stay away from church affairs and to attend tea dances at the Progress Club.

"The dissolution of old customs is an important factor in these cases," said Dr. Maurício.

The treatment at the dentist's had been prolonged, but the motor was no longer needed and the chair in the office, with its shiny metal, had been exchanged for the dark bed in the back room. Lazy Chico stood stock still, with a bottle and a glass in his hands, listening avidly to the details, his adolescent eyes opened wide and an idiotic grin on his gaping mouth. Ari Santos concluded with a phrase that struck him as exquisite:

"And thus fate transforms an honest, religious, and modest woman into the heroine of a tragedy."

"Heroine? Don't come to me with literary phrases. Don't try to absolve the sinner. Where would we end?" Dr. Maurício raised his hand in a gesture of warning. "All this is the result of the degeneration of old customs that is taking place in our land: balls and afternoon dances, intimate little parties everywhere, love-making in the dark at the theatres. Motion pictures are teaching women how to deceive their husbands. It's a disgrace."

"Now, Dr. Maurício, you shouldn't blame the movies and the dances," said João Fulgêncio. "Women were betraying their husbands long before these things existed. It's a custom that goes back to Eve and the serpent." He laughed.

The Captain came to João's support. The lawyer was tilting with windmills. He, the Captain, did not condone a married woman's infidelity. But why blame the Progress Club or the movies? Why not blame the husbands who ignored their wives, treated them like servants, while giving everything—jewels, perfumes, expensive dresses—to wantons, to prostitutes, or to the mulatto girls whom they set up in private houses? You had to look no farther than right there on the square: Gloria, in the lap of luxury, dressed more expensively than any lady in town—did you suppose Colonel Coriolano spent that much on his own wife?

"After all, his wife is a decrepit old woman."

"I'm not talking about her; I'm talking about what goes on. Isn't it the way I said?"

"A married woman's function is to stay at home, raise the children, take care of her husband—"

"And what's the function of the other woman—to squander the husband's money?"

"The one I don't consider at fault is the dentist. After all . . ." João Fulgêncio interrupted the discussion, for the Captain's indignant words might be taken amiss by the planters present.

The dentist had been a bachelor, young, fancy-free. Was it his fault if the woman thought he looked like St. Sebastian? He had not even been a Catholic; he and Diogenes had been the only two Protestants in Ilhéus.

"He wasn't even a Catholic, Dr. Maurício."

"Why didn't he think of the husband's honor before taking a married woman to bed?" inquired the lawyer.

"Women are a temptation, they turn a man's head."

"And you think she threw herself into his arms—just like that? That he did nothing, that he was innocent?"

The argument between the two admired intellectuals—the lawyer and João Fulgêncio, the one solemn and aggressive, a defender of established morality, the other good-natured and smiling, fond of raillery and irony, so that one could never tell when he was speaking seriously—held those around them spellbound. Nacib loved to listen to discussions like that, all the more when people like the Doctor, the Captain, Nhô-Galo, and Ari Santos were present and taking part.

No, João Fulgêncio did not think Sinhàzinha had thrown herself into the dentist's arms just like that. The dentist had, very likely, said sweet things to her. But, he asked, wasn't that the minimum obligation of a good dentist—to pay a few compliments to his clients, frightened as they were by the chair, the motor, and the dreadful instruments? Osmundo had been a good dentist, one of the best in Ilhéus—who could deny it? And who could deny also the fear that dentists inspire? Phrases to create the proper atmosphere, allay fears, inspire confidence—

"A dentist's obligation is to treat teeth and not to recite verses to pretty clients, my friend. It is as I say and repeat: we are threatened by these depraved customs of decadent lands. The society of Ilhéus is being dissolved by the solvent slime of imported modernism."

"It's progress, sir."

"Such progress I call immorality," said the lawyer, casting a fierce look around the bar. It made Lazy Chico tremble.

Nhô-Galo raised his nasal voice:

"Of which customs do you speak, sir? Of the dances, the movies? But I have lived here more than twenty years and have always known Ilhéus as a land of cabarets, heavy drinking, gambling, prostitutes. These are nothing recent, they have always existed."

"Those are things for men. Not that I approve of them. But they do not affect families, like these clubs where girls and grown women go to dance, neglecting their household duties. The motion pictures are a school of depravity."

Now the Captain posed another question: how could a man —and this, too, was a question of honor—refuse a beautiful woman, when she, charmed by his words, seeing in him a resemblance to a picture in the church and intoxicated by the perfume of his curly black hair, falls into his arms, with her teeth fixed but her heart forever wounded? A man has his pride as a male. In the Captain's view, the dentist was more to be pitied than blamed.

"What would you do, Dr. Maurício, if Dona Sinhàzinha, with that body which God gave her, should throw herself upon you, naked, with nothing on but a pair of black stockings? Would you start running and yelling for help?"

Some of the listeners—Nacib, Colonel Ribeirinho, even Colonel Manuel of the Jaguars with his white hair—weighed the argument and thought it irrefutable. They had all known Dona Sinhàzinha. They had often seen her, serious and withdrawn, crossing the square on her way to church, with her body imprisoned in a tight dress. Lazy Chico, his work forgotten, sighed before the vision of Sinhàzinha, naked, throwing herself into his arms—a dream from which he was rudely awakened by Nacib.

"Get to work, you loafer! Where do you think you are?"

"*Vade retro!*" said Dr. Maurício in his courtroom voice. The dentist, he contended, was not the innocent that (he started to say "my noble colleague" but checked himself) the Captain had made him out to be. He would turn to the Bible, the Book of Books, and confront the Captain with the example of Joseph.

"Which Joseph?"

"The one that was tempted by Pharaoh's wife."

"That guy must have been impotent," said Nhô-Galo, and he laughed.

Dr. Maurício squelched the Revenue Board clerk with a look.

"Such jokes are not in keeping with the seriousness of the subject. This Osmundo was not innocent. A good dentist he may have been, but he was also a danger to the Ilhéan family."

And the lawyer went on to describe Osmundo as if he were standing before judge and jury: yes, the dentist was well-spoken, careful in his dress—but why all that elegance in a land where the planters wore riding britches and high boots? Was this in itself not proof of the decadence of customs, responsible in turn for the moral decadence of our beloved community? Soon after his arrival in Ilhéus, the dentist had exhibited his expertness in the Argentine tango. Ah, that den where modesty and propriety disappeared, where, on Saturdays and Sundays, young people of both sexes and even married women would meet and whirl about together, that so-called Progress Club; a better name for it would have been the Hug-and-Squeeze Club. Like a butterfly, Osmundo had courted, during his eight months in Ilhéus, a half-dozen of the town's most beautiful girls, flitting from one to another, fickle-hearted. But he married none of them; marriageable girls did not really interest him; what he wanted was a married woman, so that he might feast gratuitously at someone else's table. Just another of the many sneak thieves that were beginning to appear in Ilhéus. Dr. Maurício cleared his throat and bowed his head, as if to acknowledge the applause which would have broken out in the courtroom in spite of the judge's repeated warnings.

Nor was applause lacking in the bar.

"Well said," exclaimed Manuel of the Jaguars.

"That's it exactly," said Ribeirinho. "Jesuíno undoubtedly did the right thing."

"I don't dispute that," said the Captain. "But the fact remains, Dr. Maurício, that the change in Ilhéus that you and many others are opposing is really progress."

"Since when is depravity progress?"

"How can the movies and social clubs bring depravity to a town already full of cabarets and loose women, where every rich man has a mistress? You and others like you want your women locked up at home, in the kitchen—"

"The home is the fortress of the virtuous woman."

"For my part, I'm not against any of those things," explained Colonel Manuel of the Jaguars. "I like to go to the movies when there's a good comedy showing. Dancing's all right, too, although I'm a little old for it now. Those things are all right, but it's a different thing entirely to say that a married woman has the right to deceive her husband."

"Who said she has?"

Not even the Captain, a man of experience in life, who had lived in Rio and disapproved of many of the customs in Ilhéus, not even he had the courage to stand up in opposition to the cruel law. So fierce and rigid was this law that poor Dr. Felismino, who had come to Ilhéus a few years before to open an office, had been virtually forced to leave because after he had discovered his wife Rita's affair with the agronomist Raul Lima, he had abandoned her to her lover. He had been delighted with this unexpected opportunity to rid himself of the insufferable woman. He had rarely been so pleased as when he found them together and saw the agronomist, mistaking his intentions, run half-naked through the streets. To Felismino no revenge seemed greater, more appropriate, more exquisite, than to burden Rita's lover with her extravagances, her love of luxury, and her unbearable domineering. But Ilhéus lacked the sense of humor necessary to understand him: everyone looked upon him as a cowardly and immoral cynic. He was nicknamed Tame Ox. His incipient clientele vanished completely. Some even refused to shake hands with him. There was nothing else for him to do: he left Ilhéus and never came back.

OF THE LAW OF CONCUBINES

On that day, in the excited, almost festive air of the bar, many stories were repeated besides the melancholy adventure of Dr. Felismino, terrible stories of love, betrayal, and gruesome acts of vengeance. Someone recalled the famous case of Juca Viana and Chiquinha. It was not, of course, exactly the same as what happened that afternoon, for the colonels reserved the death penalty for faithless wives; their concubines did not merit such radical treatment.

When a colonel learned of the faithlessness of the woman he supported, whether kept by him in a boarding-house for prostitutes or in a house by herself on a side street, he simply threw her out and got himself another mistress. There had been cases, however—more than one—of violence over some trollop. Recently, for example, Colonel Ananias and Ivo, a clerk known as The Tiger because of his skill as center-forward of the Vera-Cruz Soccer Club, had exchanged shots in the Golden Nectar over Joana, a pock-marked girl from Pernambuco.

Colonel Coriolano Ribeiro had been one of the first to fell the forests and plant cacao. Few plantations could compare with his magnificent lands, where the cacao trees began to produce in their third year. A man of great influence, very close to Colonel Ramiro Bastos, he controlled one of the richest districts in the county of Ilhéus. He was an old-fashioned man of simple habits and simple needs; his only extravagance was to keep a girl in a house in town. He spent most of his time on the plantation, which he loved. He came to town from time to time, always on horseback, for he disdained the greater comfort of the trains and buses. He wore a pair of cheap store-bought pants, a weather-beaten coat, a hat of respectable age, and mud-soiled boots. The gossips said he was so parsimonious that at the plantation he ate rice only on Sundays and holidays, contenting himself the rest of the time with beans and a piece of jerked beef, like the workmen.

His wife and children, however, lived in great comfort in Bahia, where he rarely visited them. His son was in law school, and his daughter frequented the dancing parties at the Athletic Association. His wife had grown old prematurely during the anxious nights when the colonel went off at the head of his henchmen to battle for the land.

"An angel of kindness but homely as the devil," João Fulgêncio would say whenever someone criticized the colonel for neglecting his wife.

Even when his family lived in Ilhéus—in the same house in which Gloria was now installed—the colonel always kept some young mulatto girl in room and board. Sometimes, on coming to town from the plantation, he would go straight to his "branch office" even before going to see his family. These girls were his luxury, his main happiness in life, and they treated him as if he were a king.

As soon as his children reached school age, he transferred the family to Bahia and moved in with his mistress. There, stretched out in a hammock and smoking corn-husk cigarettes, he received his friends, handled his business affairs, and discussed politics. His own son, when he visited Ilhéus and the plantation during school holidays, had to go there to see him. Though frugal where he himself was concerned, he was open-handed with his mistresses; he opened charge accounts for them at the stores and liked to watch them enjoy their luxuries. But he required them to stay indoors almost all the time, alone, with no right to friends or visitors. He was, a people said, "a monster of jealousy."

"I don't keep women for others to enjoy," the colonel would explain when someone touched on the subject.

Nearly always it was the woman who left him, tired of the captive life of a well-fed and well-dressed slave. Some wound up in bordellos, others returned to their homes in the country, one went to Bahia with a traveling salesman. Occasionally, however, it was the colonel who became surfeited and felt the need for new flesh. He would discover, usually on his own plantation or in one of the villages, some pleasing little country girl and would pack the old mistress off. In such cases he would pay the fallen favorite a large severance bonus. For one of them, with whom he had lived more than three years, he opened a fruit and vegetable store on Sapo Street. He went there now and then to visit her; he would sit down and ask how she was getting on.

Many stories were told about Colonel Coriolano and his girls. There was Chiquinha, for example, a frail, shy girl of sixteen. She seemed afraid of everything, and her gentle eyes sometimes almost leaped out of her face. The colonel discovered her and brought her from his plantation to a house on a side street. She was so timid that the colonel himself, then about fifty, went out and did her shopping for her. Even at the moments of greatest intimacy, she addressed him respectfully as "Senhor" and "Colonel." Coriolano drooled with happiness.

Juca Viana, a second-year law student on holiday, discovered Chiquinha one day as she sat at her window watching a street procession. His friends warned him of the danger: nobody fooled around with Colonel Coriolano's women. Juca Viana, almost twenty and bold by nature, shrugged his shoulders. Chiquinha's timidity melted away before the daring student's mustache, his elegant clothes, his promises of love. First she opened her window, which was nearly always closed when the colonel was not there. Then, one night, she opened the door, and Juca made himself a partner of the colonel in the girl's bed. A partner without capital and without obligations, who took the greater share of the profits with an intensity of passion that soon became known and discussed all over town.

The story in all its details is still told over games of backgammon, among the old maids, and at the Model Stationery Store. Juca Viana lost all sense of caution and in broad daylight began going in and out of the house on which the colonel paid the rent. The timid Chiquinha was transformed into a brazen sweetheart; she even went out with him arm in arm and lay on the deserted beach in the moonlight. They looked like two children out of a pastoral poem.

The colonel's ruffians arrived early one evening, downed some drinks at Toínho Cara de Bode's poorly patronized bar, muttered some threats, and left for Chiquinha's house. The two young people, passionate and unsuspecting, were smiling at each other and playing love games on the bed paid for by the colonel. The next-door neighbors could hear laughs and gasping sighs and now and then Chiquinha moaning: "Oh, my love!" The colonel's men entered through the back, and then there were new, louder sounds. Indeed, the whole street was awakened by the screams, and a crowd quickly gathered in front of the house. They say the boy and girl both took a terrible beating; their hair was shaved off—Chiquinha's long black braids and Juca's blond curls—and they were ordered, in the name of the outraged colonel, to disappear that very night and forever from Ilhéus.

Juca Viana was now the prosecuting attorney in Jequié: even after his graduation in Bahia he had not returned to Ilhéus. Chiquinha was never heard of again.

Knowing this story, who would dare to cross, except at the colonel's express invitation, the doorsill of his mistress? Especially the doorsill of Gloria's house, for she was the most enticing, the most luscious of all the women Coriolano had ever kept and he was deeply attached to her.

OF A CHARMING RASCAL

Tonico Bastos was by far the most elegant man in Ilhéus. He had dark circles under his eyes and a romantically abundant head of hair streaked with silver. Dressed in a blue jacket, white trousers, and brightly shined shoes, he was entering the bar with his customary nonchalance when he heard his name mentioned. An embarrassed silence fell on the group, and he asked suspiciously:

"What were you talking about? I heard my name."

"About women," said João Fulgêncio, "and so of course your name came up."

Tonico's face broke into a smile and he pulled up a chair; he delighted in his reputation as an irresistible lady-killer. While his brother Alfredo, a pediatrician and state assemblyman, examined children in his office in Ilhéus and made speeches in the legislature at Bahia, Tonico gadded about town, associating with trollops and cuckolding the colonels in their mistresses' beds. At once polite and bold, he made gallant advances to every pretty woman newly arrived in Ilhéus. His efforts met with considerable success, which he nevertheless exaggerated in the telling. He usually came to the bar at the siesta hour, when it was empty, and astonished his friend Nacib with stories about his conquests and about women's jealousy over him. Nacib admired him more than anyone else in Ilhéus.

Opinions about Tonico Bastos varied. Some looked upon him as a genial young man, somewhat self-seeking and a bit of a braggart but an agreeable talker and, at bottom, inoffensive. Others thought him a conceited ass, incompetent and cowardly, lazy and altogether mediocre. But his charm was undeniable, what with his delightful conversation and his smile of a man satisfied with life. The Captain himself would say of him:

"He's a charming rascal, a bad character but irresistible."

His father, Colonel Ramiro, fed up with Tonico's escapades in Bahia, had sent him to an engineering college in Rio. Tonico spent seven years there but never managed to get beyond the third year in his courses. The colonel considered it unlikely that he would ever become an engineer; so he brought Tonico back to Ilhéus and got him the best notary's office in town and the richest bride.

The only daughter of her planter father, who had died at the end of the land struggles, Dona Olga was fat and preeminently hard to live with. Tonico had not inherited his father's courage —more than once he had been seen to pale and stammer when involved in some row in the red-light district—but this did not wholly explain his fear of his wife. It was fear, no doubt, of a scandal that might hurt his highly respected father, for Dona Olga was forever threatening scandal. She thought every woman in town was after her Tonico. The neighborhood could hear her daily threats:

"If I ever find out that you're mixed up with a woman. . . ."

Maids did not last long in her house: Dona Olga suspected them all of coveting her handsome spouse and dismissed them on the slightest pretext. She also regarded with suspicion the girls at the parochial school and the ladies at the Progress Club dances.

Her jealousy had become a legend in Ilhéus. So had her rudeness and bad manners.

Not that she knew about Tonico's adventures or suspected that he frequented bordellos when he went out evenings "on political matters." Tonico was a smooth talker; he always found some way of deceiving her and of allaying her jealousy. No man could have been more circumspect than he when, after dinner, he took his wife to the movies or for a stroll on the avenue along the beach and they stopped at the Vesuvius Bar for ice cream.

"Look how sedately he walks with his elephant," people would say.

After returning his wife to their home on Paralelepípedos Street, where he also had his office, he would go out again "to talk with some friends about political matters." He would then go dancing in the cabarets and to supper in the bordellos, where, in their rivalry for him, the girls would exchange insults and tear one another's hair.

"Some day the roof will fall in on him," people said. "When Dona Olga finds out, it'll be the end of the world."

On several occasions it almost happened. But Tonico would surround his wife with a net of lies and dispel her suspicions. It was a high price to pay, but his position as the town's number one Don Juan was worth it.

"What do you think of the crime?" asked Nhô-Galo.

"Horrible!"

They told him about the black stockings, and Tonico winked knowingly. They recalled similar crimes, such as that of Colonel Fabrício: he stabbed his wife to death and ordered his henchmen to shoot her lover as he was returning from a Masonic meeting.

Despite his worries (the supply of snacks and appetizers from the Dos Reis sisters had run out), Nacib joined in the conversation—and, as always, to make extravagant claims for the land of his fathers. Standing next to the table, he dominated the scene with his huge size. The silence spread to the other tables so that everyone could hear him.

"In my father's country it's much worse. There, a man's honor is sacred, no one trifles with it, because—"

"Because what, Arab?"

He moved his eyes slowly over his listeners—his customers and friends—and assumed a dramatic pose, pushing forward his big head.

"There, a faithless woman is put to death by the knife—slowly. They cut her into small pieces."

"Small pieces?" queried Nhô-Galo, in his nasal twang.

Nacib brought his big face, with the bulging white cheeks, close to Nhô-Galo's. He assumed a murderous look and twisted the end of his mustache.

"Yes, my friend, there they are not content to kill the woman with two or three little bullets. That's a country of he-men, and the treatment for a shameless woman is different: they cut her up into bits, beginning with the nipples of her breasts."

"The nipples of her breasts! What barbarity!" Even Colonel Ribeirinho felt himself shiver.

"Barbarity, nothing! A woman who deceives her husband deserves it. If I was married and my wife put horns on me, ah! with me it would be the Syrian law: I would make hash of her body."

"And what about the lover?" asked Dr. Maurício Caires, obviously disturbed.

"The besmircher of another's honor?" The Arab paused, almost terrifying to look at. He raised his hand and gave a little hollow laugh. "The miserable dog! He's held fast by a bunch of those tough Syrians from the hills; they take off his pants, spread his legs—and the husband, with a sharp razor . . ." With a quick downward movement of his hand, Nacib described the rest.

"What! You don't mean . . ."

"That's right, Doctor. Cut off at the root."

João Fulgêncio rubbed his chin.

"Strange customs, Nacib. I guess each country has its own ways."

"Seeing how passionate those Turkish women are," said the Captain, "there must be a lot of eunuchs around there."

"Well, who told them to go into someone else's house and take what wasn't theirs?" said Dr. Maurício approvingly. "Especially the honor of the home."

Nacib the Arab felt triumphant; he smiled and looked lovingly at his customers. He liked this business of running a bar, these conversations, the games of backgammon and checkers, the little poker games. . . .

"Let's get to our game," said the Captain.

"Not today. Too busy. And pretty soon I have to go out and look for a cook."

The Doctor accepted in Nacib's place and seated himself opposite the Captain, the checkerboard between them. Nhô-Galo kibitzed; he would play the winner. While they played, the Doctor said:

"There was a case like that with one of the Ávilas. He seduced the wife of an overseer; there was scandal; the husband found out—"

"And did he castrate your relative?"

"Who said anything about castration? The husband showed up with a gun; only, my great-grandfather shot him first."

The group began to break up slowly; the dinner hour was approaching. Diogenes and the two artists were seen walking from the hotel toward the motion picture theatre.

"Mundinho's exclusive property?" asked Tonico Bastos.

The Captain, feeling himself somewhat privy to Mundinho's personal affairs, stated:

"No. He's not attached to her in any way. She's completely at liberty, free as a bird."

Tonico whistled between his teeth. The couple said good afternoon. Anabela was smiling.

"I'm going over and greet her in the name of the town of Ilhéus."

"Don't get the town involved in this, you rascal."

"Watch out for her husband's razor," warned Nhô-Galo, laughing.

"I'll go with you," said Colonel Ribeirinho.

But at that moment Colonel Amâncio Leal appeared, and their curiosity proved stronger than their interest in Anabela. Everyone knew that Jesuíno had taken refuge in the colonel's house after the killing. His vengeance accomplished, Jesuíno had calmly left the scene to avoid being taken *in flagrante delicto*. He had crossed the city, without hastening his steps, had gone to the house of his friend and companion of the early days, and had sent word to the Judge that he would appear in court the next day. He knew that, in accordance with the custom in such cases, he would be permitted to remain at liberty while awaiting trial. Colonel Amâncio was looking for someone and spotted Dr. Maurício.

"May I have a word with you, Doctor?"

The lawyer stood up and together they went to the far end of the bar. The planter said something. Maurício nodded and then came back for his hat.

"Excuse me. I must leave."

"Good afternoon, gentlemen," said Colonel Amâncio.

They set out along Adami Street toward Amâncio's house. Some, more curious than others, stood up to watch them. They walked up the street as silent and grave as if they were accompanying a religious procession or a funeral.

"He's going to hire Dr. Maurício for the defense."

"Jesuíno is in good hands. We'll have plenty of Scripture at the trial."

"He doesn't really need a lawyer. He's bound to be acquitted."

The Captain turned around, a checker in his hand, and said:

"That Maurício is a big hypocrite."

"They say that none of the colored girls will put up with him for very long."

"So I've heard."

"There is one, from up on Unhão Hill. She goes to his house almost every night."

The prince and Anabela reappeared at the door of the theatre, escorted by Diogenes. The woman had a book in her hand.

"They're coming this way," murmured Colonel Ribeirinho.

They stood up at Anabela's approach and offered chairs. The book, a leather-bound album, was passed from hand to hand. It contained clippings and handwritten opinions about the dancer.

"After my debut, I want all you gentlemen to write something," she said, still standing. She had not accepted the invitation to sit down. "We are on our way to the hotel." She was leaning against Colonel Ribeirinho's chair.

She would open at the cabaret that same evening, and on the following day she and the prince would give an exhibition of magic at the theatre. He was a hypnotist and a marvelous telepathist. They had just put on their act for Diogenes, the owner of the theatre, who confessed he had never seen anything like it. Gathered in front of the church, the old maids, already in a state of excitement because of the double killing, surveyed the scene at the bar and noticed the woman.

"Another one to turn the men's heads."

Anabela was saying in a gentle voice:

"Did I hear there was a crime committed here today?"

"Yes. A planter killed his wife and her lover."

"Poor thing," said Anabela with emotion, and these were the only words uttered by anyone that afternoon in lamentation of Sinhàzinha's sad fate.

"Feudal customs," pronounced Tonico Bastos, addressing the dancer. "Here we're still living in the last century."

The prince smiled superciliously, nodded his head in approval, and swallowed a slug of white rum; he did not like mixed drinks. Anabela wanted to rest before her opening performance. João Fulgêncio handed back the album.

"I'll expect you all tonight at the Bataclan."

"We'll certainly be there."

The old maids in front of the church crossed themselves. A land of perdition, this Ilhéus. At the gate to Colonel Melk Tavares's garden, Professor Josué was talking with Malvina. Gloria sighed at her lonely window. It was late afternoon. The bar began to empty. Colonel Ribeirinho left and followed the artists.

Tonico Bastos leaned against the counter near the cash register. Nacib was putting on his coat and giving orders to Lazy Chico and Eaglebeak. Tonico was absorbed in contemplating the bottom of his almost empty glass.

"Thinking about the dancer? That's a pretty fancy dish; it'll cost you plenty. The competition's going to be stiff. Ribeirinho has his eye on her."

"I was thinking about Sinhàzinha. A terrible thing, Nacib."

"Someone told me about her and the dentist. I swear I didn't believe it. She always seemed like such a respectable woman."

"You're very naïve." He poured himself another drink. He was an old and trusted customer, who filled his own glass and charged it to his account, which he paid at the end of the month. "But it could have been worse."

Nacib, dumbfounded, lowered his voice:

"Did you sail in those waters, too?"

Tonico did not reply: he was satisfied to instill doubt, suspicion. He made a gesture with his hand.

"She seemed so respectable." Nacib's voice now had a leer in it. "Who would have thought it. You, too, eh!"

"Never speak evil of the dead, Arab."

Nacib opened his mouth to say something but only sighed. So the dentist had not been the first. This rascal Tonico with his streak of white hair, this peerless woman-chaser, had also held her in his arms, had also possessed her body. How often he, Nacib, had followed her with lustful eyes as she passed in front of his place on her way to church.

"That's why I don't get married or get involved with a married woman."

"Me too," said Tonico.

"Cynic."

Nacib started toward the street.

"I'm going to see if I can find a cook. Some migrants just arrived. Who knows, maybe one of them can cook."

Tuísca was standing under Gloria's window and giving her all the details about the crime, things he had heard in the bar. Gloria patted his head in gratitude and pinched his cheek. The Captain, having won his game, observed the scene.

"Lucky little devil!" he said.

OF TWILIGHT

Walking toward the railroad in the melancholy twilight, wearing his big, wide-brimmed hat, his revolver in his belt, Nacib thought about Sinhàzinha. From inside the houses came the laughter and talk of people at dinner. The subject of conversation undoubtedly was Sinhàzinha and Osmundo. Nacib remembered her with tenderness and wished secretly in his heart that her despicable husband, Jesuíno Mendonça, an arrogant and repulsive fellow, would be convicted—an impossibility, of course.

For Nacib's callousness to cruelty was as fictitious as his fierce stories. How could anyone think that a young and beautiful woman deserved death for having deceived an old and brutal man, incapable of a caress, of a tender word? This Ilhéus, this land of his, was far from being really civilized. There was a lot of talk about progress; money flowed freely; the cacao built roads, established settlements, changed the face of the city. But the backward old customs remained unchanged. Nacib did not have the courage to say such things out loud—only Mundinho Falcão would dare do that—but at this melancholy hour of falling shadows he was thinking, and a sadness came over him. He felt tired.

Nacib had never married because, among other reasons, he did not want to be deceived, he did not want to have to kill, to spill blood, to pump bullets into a woman's breast. And yet he would have liked to marry. He felt the need of tenderness, of caresses, of a home, of a house filled with the presence of a woman waiting for him in the middle of the night when he returned after closing his bar. It was a thought that pursued him from time to time, as it did now on his way to the slave market. He was not the sort of man to go hunting for a bride; besides, he had no time, busy as he was all day in his bar. His romantic activity consisted only of temporary liaisons with girls he met in the cabarets, girls who belonged to others at the same time—light adventures in which there was no room for love. When he was much younger, he had had two or three sweethearts. But, as he could not then think of marriage, these little affairs had never progressed beyond timid kisses in the movie theatres.

Nowadays he had no time for courtship, for the bar took up his whole day. He wanted to make money so that he could buy land and plant cacao. Like all Ilhéans, Nacib dreamed of cacao groves, of trees bearing golden yellow fruit, golden also in value. Perhaps then he would think of marriage. For the present, he would remain content to ogle the pretty women in the square, including the inaccessible Gloria at her window, and to discover newcomers like Risoleta and sleep with them.

He smiled as he thought of Risoleta, with her slightly crossed eye and her know-how in bed. Would he or would he not go see her again that night? She would surely be expecting him at the cabaret, but he was tired and depressed. His mind turned again to Sinhàzinha: how often he had, in fantasy, sullied her husband's honor. He did not know pretty words and verses, he did not have curly locks, he did not dance the Argentine tango at the Progress Club—fortunately, perhaps, for otherwise it might have been he lying in a pool of blood, his chest riddled by bullets, alongside the woman in black stockings.

Nacib walked in the twilight, responding mechanically now and then to a "good afternoon." His chest and his paramour's white breasts, ripped by bullets. He could see the picture: the two corpses lying in blood, side by side, naked, she with black stockings. With or without garters? he wondered. Without garters struck him as more chic, finely knit stockings clinging unaided to the flesh. Beautiful! Beautiful and sad. Nacib sighed. He no longer saw Osmundo, the dentist, beside Sinhàzinha; it was Nacib himself, somewhat thinner and less paunchy, stretched out dead, murdered, beside the woman. Beautiful! His breast riddled by bullets. He sighed again. He was a romantic at heart. The horrifying stories he told were really alien to his personality. So was the revolver he carried in his belt, as did all the men in Ilhéus at that time. It was just an old custom. He had no taste for violence. What he really liked was to eat well—good, highly seasoned dishes and a bottle of cold beer; to play backgammon or join an all-night poker game, with fervent pleas to Lady Luck lest he lose the profits he was accumulating to buy land; to maximize these profits by adulterating drinks and padding the bills of customers who had charge accounts; to go to a cabaret; and to end the night in the arms of some Risoleta. Also, to talk with his friends and to laugh.

OF THE INTRICATE WAYS OF LOVE, OR HOW NACIB

HIRED A COOK

Nacib walked through the market place, where the stalls were being dismantled and the goods packed up. He crossed between the railroad buildings to the place at the foot of Conquista Hill where the migrants camped while waiting for work. Someone had once referred to the place as the "slave market" and the name had stuck; now no one ever called it anything else.

Plantation owners slapped their riding crops against the side of their boots and looked over the new arrivals. The backlanders were said to be good workers.

Exhausted and famished, the migrants waited. They could see the market place with its promise of abundance, and hope filled their hearts. They had won out against the dry scrub, the endless roads, hunger, snakes, disease, and fatigue. They had reached the land of plenty; their days of misery seemed ended. They had heard frightening tales of death and violence, but they had heard also about the rising price of cacao. They knew of men who, like themselves, had arrived there destitute and who were now walking about in shiny boots, flipping silver-handled riding whips. Owners of cacao plantations.

A fight broke out at the market place; people started running; a knife flashed in the sun's last rays; shouts rose in the air. There were always drunks and fights at the close of a market day. A woman of the backlanders began to sing a slow, sad song, accompanied by a concertina.

Colonel Melk Tavares motioned to the concertina player, and the music stopped.

"Married?"

"No, sir."

"Do you want to work for me?" He pointed to some other men he had already selected. "We need a good concertina player to put a little life into the dances." According to his reputation,

Melk knew better than any of the other planters how to pick good workers. His plantations were situated up-river at Cachoeira do Sul, and his big rowboats were waiting alongside the railroad wharf.

"As a hired hand or on shares?"

"Whichever you prefer. I have some land to be cleared and I could use some sharecroppers." The backlanders preferred to work that way; the planting of new cacao lands on a share basis gave them an opportunity to earn money on their own.

"All right, sir."

Melk caught sight of Nacib.

"What are you doing here, Arab? Hiring workers for your plantation?"

"I'm just looking for a cook. My old one left me this morning."

"What do you think of the news?"

"Well . . . a thing like that . . . all of a sudden . . ."

"I've been to Amâncio's house to give Jesuíno my embrace. Now I'm going to take these men up to the plantation." He pointed to the men he had selected, now gathered in a group near him. "These backlanders are good workers. They're not like the people around here. Ilhéans don't like heavy work; they'd rather stay in town and loaf."

Another planter was looking over the migrants. Melk continued:

"Backlanders don't measure out their work. At five o'clock in the morning they're out in the field and they don't drop their hoes until sundown. Give them enough beans and jerked beef, coffee and liquor, and they're happy. For my money, there are no workers who can compare to them." He spoke as an authority on the subject.

Nacib looked at the men contracted by the colonel. He envied the big landowner. He himself, as he told the colonel, was only trying to find a woman to take care of his small house on St. Sebastian Street, wash his clothes, cook his meals, and make appetizers for the bar.

"A good cook is hard to find around here," said Melk.

Instinctively, Nacib was looking among the migrants for someone like Filomena, some woman of her age, more or less, and with her grumpy manner.

The boats were loaded and waiting. Colonel Melk shook Nacib's hand and said:

"Jesuíno did right. He's a man of honor."

Nacib felt he had to say something:

"They tell me an engineer is coming to study the sandbar."

"So I heard. It's a waste of time. Nobody can do anything about that bar."

Nacib started walking among the migrants. Old men and young looked at him hopefully. There were a few women, nearly all with children clinging to their skirts. Finally he observed one, about fifty, large, robust, without a husband.

"He died on the way, suh."

"Can you cook?"

"Not fancy, suh. No real family cookin', nothin' like that."

My God, where to find a cook? He was paying the Dos Reis sisters a fortune. Such a busy time, too—murders today, funerals tomorrow. And to make matters worse, he had to take his meals at the Hotel Coelho—rotten, tasteless food. His best solution would be to send to Aracaju for a cook and pay her fare. He stopped in front of an old woman, so old she might die before she could reach his house. She was stooped over a cane. How in the world had she survived the journey to Ilhéus! It made him sad to look at her, so old and dried out, just a remnant of a person. So much sorrow in the world . . .

Another woman came up, dressed in rags and so covered with dirt that he could not make out her features or guess her age. Her unkempt hair was filthy with dust, her feet bare. She brought a gourd of water and placed it in the tremulous hands of the old woman, who drank from it greedily.

"God bless you."

"Don't mention it, grandma." It was the voice of a young woman, perhaps the one who had been singing when Nacib arrived.

Colonel Melk and his men were disappearing behind the railroad cars. The concertina player paused a moment and waved goodbye. The woman lifted her arm and fluttered her hand;

then she turned to the old woman and took the empty gourd. She was about to go when Nacib, still astonished at the old woman's endurance, said to her:

"Is she your grandmother?"

"No, sir." She stopped and smiled, and Nacib saw that she really was young, for her eyes shone when she laughed. "We found her on the road about four days ago."

"Who do you mean, 'we'?"

"Over there." She pointed to a group with her finger, and again she laughed—clearly, brightly, unexpectedly. "We all left together, from the same place. The drought killed every livin' thing, dried up all the water, turned the trees into tinder. On the road we met others. All runnin' away."

"Are you related to them?"

"No, sir, I'm alone in the world. My uncle came with me, but he gave up the ghost before we got to Jeremoabo. He had what they call consumption." And she laughed as if it were naturally a laughing matter.

"Wasn't that you singing a little while ago?"

"Yes, sir, it was. There was a young fellow who played. He was hired for a plantation; says he's goin' to get rich here. When you sing you forget the bad things."

"What can you do?"

"A little bit of everything, sir."

"Wash clothes?"

"Everybody can wash clothes," she said, surprised. "All you need is water and soap."

"And cook?"

"I was once a cook for a rich family." And again she laughed, as if she remembered something amusing.

Perhaps because she laughed, Nacib concluded she would not do. These people coming from the backlands, half-starved, would tell any kind of lie to get work. What dishes could such a girl know how to make? Probably nothing but jerked beef and beans. Besides, he needed an older woman, someone serious and hardworking, like Filomena. The young woman waited, looking him in the face. Nacib did not know what to say. He waved his hand.

"Well, so long. Good luck."

He had turned his back and was leaving when he heard her say to someone, in a low, warm drawl:

"What a beautiful man!"

He stopped. Beautiful! Beautiful? Maybe they used the word a little differently in the backlands. No one had even called him good-looking before, except old Zoraia, his mother, when he was a child. He felt bewildered and confusedly pleased.

"Wait."

He inspected her again. She was strong—why not try her?

"Can you really cook?"

"You take me, sir, and you'll see."

Even if she could not cook, she could take care of the house and do the washing.

"How much do you want?"

"Whatever you decide, sir. Whatever the gentleman wants to pay."

"Let's see first what you can do. Then we'll agree on your wages. All right?"

"Whatever you say, sir, is all right with me."

"Well, then, get your bundle."

She laughed again, showing her bright, white teeth. He was tired. He felt that he had made a mistake, that he was taking home another problem. But it was too late for him to change his mind. If she could at least wash clothes . . .

She returned with a small cloth bundle; it was her only possession. Nacib started walking slowly. With the bundle in her hand, she followed a few steps behind. After they had crossed the railroad tracks, Nacib turned his head and asked:

"What's your name, anyway?"

"Gabriela, sir."

They walked on. He thought again about Sinhàzinha. He reviewed the exciting events of the day: the grounding of the ship Colonel Jesuíno's crime, and the whisperings among the Captain, the Doctor, and Mundinho Falcão. There was something going on there; they couldn't fool him, not Nacib. It would come out before long. News about the crime had almost made him forget the three men, their conspiratorial air, and Colonel Ramiro Bastos's anger. The poor dentist, a charming young man, had paid dearly for his affair with a married woman. It was dangerous to mess around with another man's wife; you generally wound up with a bullet in your chest. Tonico Bastos had better watch out or the same thing would happen to him. Had he really slept with Sinhàzinha or was he just trying to sound big? In any case, Tonico was running risks and some day something would happen to him. But who knows, perhaps a glance, a sigh, a woman's kiss was worth all those risks.

Gabriela followed a few paces behind, carrying her bundle. Her feet barely touched the ground. She had already forgotten Clemente and was glad to leave the filthy, crowded camp. She felt like singing a song of the backlands but did not do so, for the sad, beautiful young man might not have liked it.

OF THE BOAT IN THE FOREST

"They say Colonel Jesuíno killed his wife and a doctor that was sleeping with her," said one of the oarsmen. "Is it true, Colonel?"

"I heard that, too," said another.

"Yes, it's true. He caught his wife in bed with the dentist. He killed them both."

"Women are dangerous, they get you in trouble."

The boat—almost a barge, it was so big—had gone downstream loaded with sacks of dry cacao seeds and was returning with supplies and the new workers. As it moved slowly upstream and the forest on the banks grew thicker, the backlanders stared at the strange landscape, a vague terror in their hearts. The darkening shadows of the trees fell across the water. The oarsmen had to pull hard to keep the boat moving against the current. One of them lit a small lamp on the stern, and its red light threw fantastic shadows on the river.

"Back in Ceará we had a case like that," said one of the backlanders.

"Women'll fool you every time," said the Negro Fagundes. "You never know what they're dreamin' up. I knew one, seemed like a saint. Nobody would've believed . . ."

Clemente remained silent. Melk Tavares talked with his new men; he wanted to know them individually, to learn their good and bad qualities, their history. The backlanders told their stories, which were much alike: the same arid land scorched by the drought, the corn and manioc fields destroyed, the endless journey on foot. They talked soberly. They had heard about Ilhéus: the rich soil, the easy money, the fights and killings. When the drought became unbearable, they abandoned everything and headed south. The Negro Fagundes was the most voluble and told some tall tales.

The workers were inquisitive, too:

"They say there's still a lot of forest land left to be cleared."

"Yes, there's plenty," replied one of the oarsmen, "but you can't get any of it. Somebody already owns it all." He laughed.

"A hard worker can still earn good money, though," said Melk Tavares, consolingly.

"It's just that the time is over when a man could come here with nothing but guts and a gun and take some land and plant cacao," said the oarsman. "Those were the good days. All you had to do was get rid of four or five others who wanted the same land, and you were rich."

"I heard tell of those days," said Fagundes. "That's why I come."

"Don't you like the hoe, my black friend?" asked Melk.

"I don't mind it, no, suh. But I can handle a fire stick better." He patted his rifle and laughed.

"There are still large tracts of forest land left. Over there on the Baforé Sierra, for example. Good cacao land, none better."

"But you have to pay for every foot of it. It's all been surveyed and recorded. You own some land over that way yourself, sir."

"A small piece," confessed Melk. "Doesn't amount to much. I'll begin to clear it next year, God willing."

"Ilhéus nowadays isn't worth a damn," lamented an oarsman. "It's not like it used to be. It's becoming civilized."

"And is that why it's no good?"

"In the old days a man's courage is what counted. Nowadays the only ones who get rich are the Arab peddlers and the Spanish storekeepers. Not like it was."

"Those days are gone," explained Melk. "Now we have progress and things are different. But a good worker can always get ahead; there's room for everybody."

"You can't even fire a few shots in the street. They want to arrest you right away."

The boat moved slowly ahead, enveloped in the night. Animal cries rose out of the jungle and parrots suddenly began screeching in the trees. The men in the boat talked, told stories, discussed Ilhéus. Clemente alone remained silent.

"The day they begin exporting direct is when this region will really start growing."

"That's right."

The backlanders did not understand, and Melk explained that all the cacao destined for England, Germany, France, the United States, Scandinavia, Argentina, and elsewhere had to be shipped via Bahia. The export tax revenue was huge and it all stayed there in the state capital. Ilhéus did not get a cent of it. The channel at the entrance to the harbor was narrow and shallow. It would take a lot of work—some even said it couldn't be done—to dredge the bar so that big ships could enter the harbor. When freighters began to carry cacao directly from Ilhéus to foreign countries, then you could really talk about progress.

"All you hear now, Colonel, is talk about Mundinho Falcão. They say he's going to solve the problem, that he's one hell of a man."

"Thinkin' about the girl?" Fagundes asked Clemente.

"She didn't even tell me goodbye. Didn't even look at me when I left."

"She was drivin' you crazy. You wasn't the same any more."

"Just like we never met. Not even goodbye."

"That's how women are. Best don't fool aroun' with 'em."

"He's a very ambitious man." Melk was referring to Mundinho Falcão. "But how is he going to solve the problem of the bar when even Ramiro wasn't able to?"

Clemente's hand caressed the concertina resting on the bottom of the boat. He could hear Gabriela's voice and looked about as if hoping to see her. He saw only jungle hemming in the river, the tangled trees and lianas, the exuberant verdure turning black, so different from the bare, gray scrub of the backlands. He heard the fearsome cries of animals and the ominous hooting of owls. An oarsman pointed his finger to a place in the woods.

"It was about there, the gunfight between Onofre and Colonel Amâncio Leal's gang. At least ten men were killed."

There was money to be made in this land; you just had to work for it. Earn money and go back to town in search of Gabriela. He would find her, no matter what.

"Best don't think about her," said Fagundes. "Get her out of your head." The Negro's eyes searched the jungle. "Get her out of your head. She's not a woman for me or you."

"I can't stop thinkin' about her."

"You're crazy. She's not the kind of woman for a man to live with."

"What do you mean?"

"You can sleep with her and do things. But to really have her so she's yours—you can't and nobody else can."

"Why?"

"I don't know. The devil knows, maybe."

Yes, the Negro was right. They slept together at night, and the next day she didn't even seem to remember: she looked at him and treated him just as she did the others, as if what had happened didn't matter.

The shadows covered and encircled the boat; the jungle seemed to come closer and closer, hedging them in. The cries of owls cut through the darkness. A night without Gabriela, her cinnamon-brown body, her spontaneous laughter, her cherry-red mouth. She hadn't even said goodbye. A pain gripped his heart; he suddenly knew that he would never see her again, hold her in his arms, crush her against his chest, hear her gasps of ecstasy.

In the silence of the night, Colonel Melk Tavares raised his voice and called out to Clemente:

"Play something for us, young fellow."

Clemente picked up his concertina. The moon shone between

the trees. A light or two glimmered in the far distance. The music swelled into the sobbing of a lost soul, doomed to solitude forever.

GABRIELA ASLEEP

Nacib, with Gabriela, arrived at his house on St. Sebastian Street. Just as he inserted the key in the lock, Dona Arminda appeared at her window next door, all aflutter.

"What an awful thing, eh, Mr. Nacib? She seemed so proper, so decent. In church every afternoon. And that's why I always say—" She suddenly laid eyes on Gabriela and left her remark unfinished.

"I've just hired her. To wash and cook."

Dona Arminda looked the migrant over from head to toe.

"If you need anything, girl, just call me. That's what neighbors are for, to help, isn't it? Except tonight I won't be here, because there's a séance at Deodoro's house. My departed husband is going to talk to me. Maybe even Dona Sinhàzinha will appear." Her eyes moved from Gabriela to Nacib. "A young girl, eh? You don't want any more old women like Filomena." She laughed knowingly.

"She was all I could find."

"Well, as I was saying, it was no surprise to me. Only the other day I saw the dentist on the street. By coincidence, it was séance day, exactly a week ago. I looked at him and I heard the voice of the departed whispering in my ear: 'There he goes, all stuck up, and he's practically dead.' I thought my husband was joking. It wasn't till today, when I heard about it, that I realized he was prophesying."

Nacib had already entered the house. She spoke to Gabriela:

"Anything you need, just call me. Tomorrow we can talk. I'm here to help. Mr. Nacib is just like a relative. He's my son Chico's employer."

Nacib showed Gabriela the little room in the back yard, formerly occupied by Filomena, and explained her duties: to keep the house clean, to do the wash, and to prepare his meals. He did not mention the snacks for the bar because he first wanted to see what kind of cook she was. He showed her the pantry, where Lazy Chico had left the things he had bought for Nacib at the market.

"Anything else you need, ask Dona Arminda."

He was in a hurry: night had fallen, the bar would soon fill again, and he had not yet had his dinner. In the front room, Gabriela looked out wide-eyed at the dark ocean; it was the first time she had seen it.

"And take a bath," said Nacib as he left.

At the Hotel Coelho he found Mundinho Falcão, the Captain, and the Doctor having dinner together. He sat down casually at the table with them and started to talk about his new cook. The others listened in silence; Nacib saw that he had interrupted an important conference. They talked a little about the crime, and Nacib had barely got started on his dinner when his friends, having already finished theirs, got up and left. Those three were certainly planning something, he thought. What the devil could it be?

The bar that night gave him no rest. The place was in a turmoil, all the tables filled, everybody discussing the day's big events. About ten o'clock, the Captain and the Doctor appeared, accompanied by Clóvis Costa, the publisher of the *Ilhéus Daily*. They had come from Mundinho Falcão's house and let it be known that later in the evening the exporter was going to Anabela's debut at the Bataclan. Clóvis and the Doctor talked in low tones. Nacib strained his ears.

At another table, Tonico Bastos was describing the dinner at Amâncio Leal's, which he had attended with several friends of Colonel Jesuíno Mendonça—including Dr. Maurício Caires, whom the colonel had chosen to defend him. It was a regular banquet, Portuguese wine, a monumental affair. Nhô-Galo found it in bad taste, with the woman's body still warm. Ari Santos described the wake for Sinhàzinha at the home of some relatives: a poor, sad little wake, with half a dozen people. As for

Osmundo's wake, it was hardly worth mentioning. There had been hours when the dentist's body was alone except for the housemaid. He, Ari, had dropped by: after all, he was a friend of the deceased and had shared the platform with him at meetings of the Rui Barbosa Literary Society.

"In a little while I'm going there," said the Captain. "He was a good chap, with lots of talent. Excellent poetry."

"I'm going, too," said Nhô-Galo.

Nacib went with them and some others, out of curiosity, around eleven o'clock when business at the bar had slacked off. Osmundo's white face was smiling in death, and his hands were crossed. Nacib felt moved.

"The bullets struck him in the chest—in his heart."

Nacib went to the cabaret to see Anabela's act and to dispel the vision of death. He sat at a table with Tonico Bastos. People were dancing. In a room across the hall, others were gambling. Dr. Ezequiel Prado, already a little high, came and sat with them. He laid his forefinger on Nacib's chest.

"They tell me you've fallen for that cross-eyed gal," he said, pointing to Risoleta, who was dancing with a traveling salesman.

"Fallen for her? No. I slept with her yesterday, that's all."

"Good. I wouldn't want to cut in on a friend's romance. But if that's how it is . . . She's a hot little dish, isn't she!"

"What about Marta, Dr. Ezequiel?"

"She made a fool of herself and I gave her the back of my hand. I'm not going there tonight."

He took a swallow from Tonico's glass. The lawyer's quarrels with his mistress, a blonde whom he had kept for a number of years, occurred every three days and were a constant source of amusement to the town. The more he beat her when he was drunk, the more passionately she clung to him. She went looking for him at the cabarets and brothels, and sometimes dragged him out of another woman's bed. The lawyer was separated from his wife; she and the children lived in Bahia.

He stood up, staggering, weaved his way through the dancing couples, and separated Risoleta from her partner.

"There's going to be trouble," said Tonico Bastos.

But the traveling salesman knew Dr. Ezequiel's reputation; he handed the woman to him and looked around for another. Risoleta resisted, but Ezequiel seized her by the wrist and took her in his arms.

"You've lost your hot little dish," observed Tonico Bastos, laughing.

"He's doing me a favor. I don't want anything to do with her tonight. I'm dead tired. As soon as that woman finishes her dance act, I'm going home. I've had a helluva day."

"What about a cook?"

"I finally found one, a migrant."

"Young?"

"I think so. There was so much dirt on her, I couldn't tell for sure. Those people are all the same age, Mr. Tonico; even the little girls look like old women."

"Pretty?"

"How do I know? Covered with rags, filthy, her hair stiff with dust. She's probably a witch. My house isn't like yours, where the maids look like society girls."

"Not with Olga on guard they don't. If a maid looks like a human being, Olga insults her and throws her out."

"Dona Olga's right. She wants no foolishness. You have to be held in with a tight rein."

Tonico Bastos made a gesture of false modesty:

"Don't exaggerate, old man. Anyone hearing you talk . . ."

Mundinho Falcão arrived with Colonel Ribeirinho, and they sat down with the Captain.

"Where's the Doctor?"

"He never goes to a cabaret. You couldn't drag him here."

Nhô-Galo approached Nacib and said:

"Have you turned Risoleta over to Ezequiel?"

"All I want tonight is to get some sleep."

"Well, I'm going to Zilda's house. I was told she has a girl there from Pernambuco who's terrific." He clicked his tongue. "She might show up here."

"A girl with braids?"

"That's right—with a big fanny."

"She's at the Trianon. She goes there every night," revealed Tonico. "She's Colonel Melk's protégée. He brought her from Bahia. Poor thing, she's homesick."

"The colonel left today for his plantation," said Nacib. "I saw him hiring workers at the slave market."

"I'm heading for the Trianon."

"Before the dance act?"

"Right after."

The Bataclan and the Trianon, the leading cabarets in Ilhéus, were frequented by shippers, planters, merchants, and traveling salesmen from the big companies. Other cabarets, on the side streets, catered to the stevedores, men from the country, and the cheaper women. There was open gambling at all of them—a reliable source of profit.

A small orchestra provided music for dancing. Tonico went looking for a dance partner. Nhô-Galo glanced at his watch. It was time for the dancer to appear, and he was getting impatient. He wanted to chase over to the Trianon after the girl with the braids and the big fanny—Colonel Melk's girl.

It was almost one o'clock in the morning when the orchestra stopped playing and the lights were turned off. Only a few small blue bulbs remained lit. Many people came from the gambling room and sat at the tables, while others remained standing near the doors. Anabela appeared at the far end with enormous fans in her hands. The waving fans alternately covered and revealed segments of her body.

The prince, in a tuxedo, hammered away at the piano. Anabela danced in the center of the room, smiling toward the crowded tables. It was a big success. Colonel Ribeirinho cried "bis" and stood up to applaud. The lights were turned on. Anabela bowed. She was dressed in flesh-colored tights.

"What crap! You think you're seeing skin and it's nothing but pink cloth," commented Nhô-Galo.

With the applause ringing in her ears, Anabela retired, to return a few minutes later for a second and even more sensational number. She was covered with multicolored veils which she slowly discarded one by one, as Mundinho had said. And for a

brief second, when the last veil had fallen and the lights went
on, her slender, well-shaped body was revealed, entirely nude except for a tiny G string and a red something over her small
breasts. The crowd shouted its approval, crying "bis" while Anabela ran out, threading her way among the tables. Colonel Ribeirinho called for champagne.

"Now that was more like it," said Nhô-Galo.

Anabela and the prince came to Mundinho's table. "Everything is on me," said Ribeirinho. The orchestra struck up again,
and Dr. Ezequiel dragged Risoleta around the floor, knocking
over chairs. Nacib decided to leave. Tonico Bastos, with his eye
on Anabela, moved to Mundinho's table. Nhô-Galo had disappeared. The dancer smiled and raised her glass of champagne.

"To everybody's health! To the progress of Ilhéus!"

Her toast was applauded with handclapping. Persons at nearby
tables looked on enviously. Many were returning to the gambling
room. Nacib went down the stairs.

He walked through the silent streets. Light filtered through the
window shutters at Dr. Maurício Caires's house. He must be working on Jesuíno's case, preparing evidence for the defense,
thought Nacib. But a woman's laugh escaped through the window and died in the street. People said that the widowed lawyer
would get young colored girls from the hills to come to his house
at night. But even so, Nacib could not have guessed that at that
moment the counselor—for purely professional reasons, no doubt
—was asking an astonished, snaggle-toothed little mulatto girl
from Unhão Hill to lie down with nothing on but a pair of
black cotton stockings.

"What next!" she said, laughing between her jagged, decayed
teeth.

Nacib felt tired after his hard day. He had finally discovered the
reason for all those goings and comings of Mundinho, for his
secrets with the Captain and the Doctor, and for his confidential
talk with Clóvis. They had to do with the sandbar. He had overheard snatches of conversation. Engineers, dredges, and tugs
would be coming. No matter whom it offended, big foreign ships
would be entering the port and direct exportation of cacao would

begin. Who could be offended by it? Did it mean an open fight with the Bastoses, with Colonel Ramiro? The Captain had always wanted to rule in local politics. But he was not a planter, he had no money to spend; this explained his friendship with Mundinho Falcão. Important things were about to take place. Despite his age, Colonel Ramiro was not a man to give in without a struggle. Nacib did not want to get mixed up in the affair. He was a friend of both sides, of Mundinho and the colonel, of the Captain and Tonico Bastos. A bar owner must never get involved in politics. More dangerous even than getting involved with a married woman.

Sinhàzinha and Osmundo would not see the dredges and tugs. They would not see the days of great progress that Mundinho talked about. A sad thought; but that is the way of the world—joy and sorrow intermingled.

He went around the church corner and continued slowly up the steep street. Could it really be that Tonico had slept with Sinhàzinha? Or was he just trying to impress him? Nhô-Galo swore that Tonico was a bald-faced liar. Usually he did not get involved with married women. But loose women, that was different: he didn't care whether they were being kept or not. Lucky dog, with that elegance of his, the silver-streaked hair, the smooth voice. Nacib wanted very much to be like Tonico: he wanted women to look at him lustfully and to be bitterly jealous over him. He wanted to be loved madly, the way Lídia, Colonel Nicodemos's woman, loved Tonico. She sighed for him, sent him messages, ran after him in the street; but Tonico was sated by such devotion and no longer cared. When it came to concubines, Tonico respected no one's right, except in the case of Gloria—and everybody knew why. But Nacib had never known him to fool around with a married woman.

Nacib, panting from the climb, inserted the key in the lock. The light was on in the front room. Was it a burglar? Or had his new servant forgotten to turn off the light?

He entered quietly and saw her asleep in a chair, smiling. Her long black hair, now washed and combed, fell loose and wavy over her shoulders. Her clothes were ragged but clean; they must have been in her bundle. A tear in her skirt revealed an expanse of cinnamon-brown thigh. Her breasts rose and fell softly in rhythm with her breathing.

"My God!" Nacib stood still, incredulous.

He marveled that such beauty could have been hidden under the dust. Asleep there in the chair—her shapely arm fallen, a smile on her brown face—she looked like a painting. How old might she be? She had the body of a young woman, the face of a little girl.

"My God, what have I got here!" murmured the Arab almost devoutly.

At the sound of his voice, she awoke, startled; but then she smiled, and the whole room seemed to smile. She jumped up and straightened her rags with her hands, simple and bright as a bit of moonlight.

"Why didn't you go to bed, go to sleep?" was all that Nacib found to say.

"The gentleman didn't say anything—"

"What gentleman?"

"You, sir. . . . I did the wash and cleaned the house. Then I was waiting for you and I fell asleep." She spoke in the soft, musical voice of the northeasterners.

The sweet, spicy smell of clove emanated from her—from her hair, perhaps, or from the nape of her neck.

"Can you really cook?"

With lights and shadows playing on her hair, her eyes lowered, a bare foot sliding along the floor as if she were about to start dancing, she replied:

"Yes, sir, I can. I worked for rich folks and they taught me. I like to cook." She smiled, and again everything around her smiled. Nacib dropped into a chair.

"If you really know how to cook, I'll pay you big wages. Fifty milreis a month. Here they pay only twenty—thirty at the most. If the work is too heavy for you, I'll arrange for a girl to help you. Old Filomena would never let anyone help her. She used to say she didn't need a helper, she wasn't dying."

"I don't need one, either."

"And the wages? What do you say?"

"Whatever the gentleman wishes to pay is all right with me."

"We'll see how the food is tomorrow. I'll send the boy here to pick up my lunch. I always eat it at the bar. And now . . ."

She stood waiting, a smile on her lips, a beam of moonlight on her hair, and that scent of cloves.

". . . now go to bed. It's late."

As she left the room, he looked at her legs, the rhythm of her movements, the cinnamon-brown expanse of her thigh. At the door she turned toward him and said:

"Well, good night, sir."

She disappeared down the dark corridor. Nacib thought he heard her say, very softly: "Beautiful man." He rose and almost called her back. No, it was probably just his memory of her saying that at the slave market. Besides, if he were to call her now, he might frighten her. She had an ingenuous air about her; perhaps she was still a maiden. There was a proper time for everything. Nacib took off his coat, hung it on the chair, and pulled off his shirt. Her scent remained in the room, the scent of clove. The next day he would buy her a cotton print dress and a pair of slippers. He would make her a present of them, he would not deduct the price from her wages.

He sat on the bed, taking off his shoes. It had been a full day. Many things had happened. He put on his nightshirt. Some dusky beauty, this new servant of his! And my God, what eyes! And she had a certain color, almost like a sun-tan, that always attracted him. He lay down, put out the light, and fell into a disturbed sleep. He dreamed fitfully about Sinhàzinha. Her nude body, dressed in black stockings, was stretched out on the deck of a foreign ship entering the harbor. Osmundo fled in a bus, while Jesuíno shot at Tonico. Then Mundinho appeared with Dona Sinhàzinha, alive once more. But it was Dona Sinhàzinha with the brown face of his new servant. She smiled at Nacib and held out her arms to him. Before he could reach her, however, she whirled away on the dance floor of the cabaret.

OF FOOD AND FUNERALS

Nacib was awakened by Dona Arminda's loud voice:

"Let's go watch the funerals, girl. You'll enjoy it."

"No, thank you, ma'am. The gentleman hasn't got up yet."

Nacib jumped out of bed: he couldn't miss the funerals. When he came out of the bathroom, he was fully dressed. Gabriela had just placed his breakfast on the white tablecloth: steaming pots of coffee and of milk, fried bananas, yams, cassava, and corn meal with coconut milk. She stood in the doorway to the kitchen and looked at him as if to say:

"The gentleman must tell me what he likes."

With rapture in his eyes, Nacib swallowed mouthfuls of corn meal. His gluttony held him at the table while his curiosity impelled him to hurry; it was time for the funerals. The fried banana was sublime. By a supreme effort he tore himself from the table. Gabriela had tied her hair with a ribbon. Nacib thought how good it must be to bite the back of her brown neck. He left for the bar almost at a run. Gabriela's voice followed him out, singing:

> *"The hill is steep. Take care, my love,*
> *Or down the slope you'll go*
> *And break the thorny branches of*
> *The rosebush down below."*

Osmundo's funeral procession was just entering the square, coming from the avenue along the beach.

"There are barely enough people to carry the coffin," someone remarked.

Only Osmundo's closest friends had the courage to accompany him on his last jaunt through the streets of Ilhéus. To participate in the dentist's funeral procession was almost an affront to Colo-

nel Jesuíno and to society. Ari Santos, the Captain, Nhô-Galo, a
writer on the *Ilhéus Daily,* and a few others, took turns at the
handles of the coffin.

The deceased had no relatives in Ilhéus, but he had developed
many friendships there. A warm-hearted, amiable man, he attended the dances of the Progress Club and the meetings of the
Rui Barbosa Literary Society. He went to family parties and to
the bars and cabarets. Yet he was being borne to the cemetery
like a poor, unknown, friendless devil, without a wreath or a tear.
Osmundo's father had sent a telegram to a merchant in Ilhéus
with whom he had business connections, asking him to take
charge of his son's funeral and saying that he himself would
come on the first ship from Bahia. The merchant had ordered
the coffin and had arranged with some dock workers to bear it to
the cemetery in case no friends showed up. He had not thought it
necessary to spend money on wreaths and flowers.

Nacib had not known Osmundo well. The dentist's regular
hangout was the Café Chic. Sometimes, however, he dropped in
at Nacib's bar. He would have a drink, almost always with Ari
Santos or Professor Josué. They would recite sonnets, read bits
of prose, discuss literature. Occasionally the Arab would sit with
them and listen. Like everyone else, Nacib looked upon the dentist as an agreeable young man; he was reputed to be competent
in his profession, and his clientele was growing. Looking now at
the pitiful funeral, Nacib felt sad. Ilhéus was being unfair, disloyal. Where were those who had eulogized Osmundo's poetic
talent, who had praised his skill and gentleness in the extraction
of molars? Where were his colleagues from the Rui Barbosa Literary Society, his friends from the Progress Club, his cronies from
the bars? They were afraid of Colonel Jesuíno, of the old maids,
of public opinion.

A boy crossed the street in front of the funeral, distributing
handbills. They advertised the performance to be given that very
night by the "famous Hindu magician, Prince Sandra, the century's greatest illusionist, fakir, and hypnotist, acclaimed by European audiences, and his beautiful assistant, Madame Anabela,
a clairvoyant medium and amazing telepathist." One of the
handbills, carried by the wind, fell on the coffin. Osmundo

would not get to meet Anabela or to compete with the others for possession of her body. The funeral was passing in front of the church, and Nacib joined the procession. He would not go as far as the cemetery—he had to prepare for the bus-line banquet to be held that evening—but he felt obliged to walk with the others at least a couple of blocks.

The funeral entered Paralelepípedos Street, although the most direct and shortest route would have been by way of Colonel Adami Street. Why did the procession go out of its way to pass in front of the house where Sinhàzinha's wake was being held? It must have been the Captain's idea. Gloria, wearing a peignoir over her nightgown, watched from her window. The coffin passed under her famous breasts, ill-concealed by the cambric garments.

Children, filled with curiosity, pressed into the doorway of Enoch's school, where Professor Josué replaced Nhô-Galo at one of the handles of the casket. People crowded to the windows and there was a buzz of excited comment. The meager procession moved slowly. Passers-by lifted their hats. Some persons dressed in black were standing in front of the house where Sinhàzinha's body lay. From the window of the house someone shouted:

"Couldn't you have gone some other way? Wasn't it enough that he ruined her life?"

When they reached the cathedral plaza, Nacib turned back. He stopped in for a few minutes at Sinhàzinha's wake. The casket was still open. There were candles and flowers about the room, and a few wreaths. Women were crying. No one had cried for Osmundo.

"We have to wait a little while. Give them time to bury the other one," one of the relatives explained.

The head of the house—the husband of a cousin of Sinhàzinha —paced the hallway. He made no effort to conceal his annoyance. This was an unexpected complication in his life. On the one hand, he was a friend of Colonel Jesuíno and even did business with him. On the other, there was no place but his house where Sinhàzinha's body could lie. In all decency, it could not lie in Jesuíno's house or at the dentist's. His wife was Sinhàzinha's only relative in town; the others lived at Olivença. How, then, could he have refused to let the body be brought there?

"A mess," he muttered.

A night and morning of vexation, to say nothing of expense. Who was going to reimburse him?

Nacib went to look at the corpse. The eyes were closed, the face serene, the hair loose and very smooth, the legs shapely. He turned his eyes away: it was not a time for anyone to be looking at Sinhàzinha's legs. The solemn figure of the Doctor came into the room. He stood for an instant beside the coffin and said softly to Nacib:

"After all, she was a relative of mine." Then, still talking to Nacib but loud enough for everyone to hear: "She had the blood of the Ávilas. A foredoomed blood, the blood of Ofenísia."

Before the astonished eyes of the persons crowding the windows and doorways along the street, Malvina came bearing a spray of flowers gathered in her garden. What was she doing here, at the funeral of a wife shot to death for adultery, this young unmarried woman, this schoolgirl, this daughter of a plantation owner? They reproved her with their eyes and whispered to one another. Malvina smiled at the Doctor, placed the flowers at the foot of the casket, moved her lips in prayer, and left with her head held as high as when she entered.

"That daughter of Melk Tavares has her nerve."

"She's always flirting with Josué, you know."

Nacib gaped in amazement and admiration, and followed her with his eyes. He did not know what had come over him that day. He had started out with a strange feeling of sympathy for Osmundo and Sinhàzinha. He was irritated by the fact that so few persons attended the dentist's funeral and by the complaints of the head of the house where Sinhàzinha's body lay. Father Basílio arrived, shook hands all around, and remarked on the bright sunshine and the end of the rains.

Finally the funeral procession got under way. It was larger than Osmundo's but still pitifully small, with Father Basílio mumbling the prayers, the relatives from Olivença sobbing, the head of the house sighing with relief. Nacib returned to the bar. Why had they not been buried together, with both coffins leaving at the same time from the same house for the same grave? It would have been better that way. Life was rotten, full of hypocrisy; Ilhéus was a heartless town where nothing mattered but money.

"Mr. Nacib," drawled Chico, "your new cook is a knockout!"

"Go to hell!"

As Nacib subsequently learned, Sinhàzinha's coffin entered the gate of the cemetery just as Osmundo's few mourners were leaving. At almost the same instant, Colonel Jesuíno Mendonça, accompanied by Dr. Maurício Caires, knocked at the Judge's door to make his formal appearance. A little later, at the bar, the lawyer ordered a bottle of mineral water.

"Yesterday I really tied one on. At Amâncio's house. He had some wonderful Portuguese wine. . . ."

Nacib withdrew. He did not want to hear about the orgy at Amâncio's. He went to the house of the Dos Reis sisters to learn how they were getting on with the dinner for that evening and found them still excited over the crime.

"She was at church yesterday morning," said Quinquina, crossing herself.

"When you came here, we had just been with her at Mass," said Florzinha with a shiver.

"Such a terrible thing . . . That's why I don't get married."

They took him to the kitchen, where Jucundina and her daughters were hard at work.

"Don't worry about the dinner. Everything is going fine."

"Which reminds me: I found a cook."

"Splendid! Is she good?"

"I found out she can make good corn meal, anyway. I'll know more after lunch."

"Do you want us to go on making appetizers?"

"For a few more days, please."

"Because we have so much work still to do on the tableau."

When the activity at the bar slacked off, he told Lazy Chico to go to lunch.

"Bring my lunch with you when you come back."

At that hour the bar was usually empty. Nacib would count the cash, estimate his expenses, and calculate the profits. Invariably, the first customer to appear after lunch was Tonico Bastos. He would take a rum-and-bitters as a digestive. On that day, they talked about the funerals, and then Tonico told what happened at the cabaret the previous night after the Arab had left: Colonel Ribeirinho drank so much that he had to be almost carried home. On the stairs he vomited three times, all over his clothes.

"He's nuts about the dancer."

"And Mundinho Falcão?"

"He left early. He assured me he has no interest in her, that the road is clear. So then, naturally—"

"You moved in."

"I started my play."

"And she?"

"She's interested, all right. But until she gets the colonel hooked, she's going to act like a saint. I could see right through her."

"And the husband?"

"He's all for the colonel: he learned how rich he is. But he wants me to keep away. The bastard thinks it's wonderful when his wife smiles at Ribeirinho and presses against him on the dance floor, and when she holds his forehead while he throws up. But whenever I come near her he butts right in. He's nothing but a pimp."

"He's afraid you'll spoil his game."

"Me? I just want the leftovers. Let Ribeirinho pay the bills, I'll be satisfied with his days off. As to the husband, don't worry. By this time he must have learned that I'm the son of the political chief here and that he'd better be careful how he acts toward me."

Lazy Chico arrived with Nacib's lunch. Nacib walked from behind the counter, sat down at one of the tables, and tied a napkin around his neck.

"Well, let's see how good the new cook is."

"The new one?" asked Tonico, coming closer.

"She's the prettiest doll you ever saw in your life." Chico rolled the words out lazily.

"And you told me she was a mess, you lying Arab! Hiding the truth from your friend, eh?"

Nacib set out the various dishes that made up his lunch. "Ah!"

he exclaimed, as he inhaled the aroma from the chicken stew, the jerked beef, the rice, the beans, and the banana compote.

Tonico asked Lazy Chico:

"Is she really pretty?"

"Is she!"

Tonico leaned over and sniffed the food.

"And she can't cook, eh? Oh, you deceitful Turk! It makes my mouth water."

Nacib invited him to sit down.

"There's enough for two. Have some."

Eaglebeak opened a bottle of beer and placed it on the table.

"What is she doing?" Nacib inquired of Chico.

"She's gabbing with my old lady. They're talking about spiritualism. That is, Mama is doing the talking, she just listens and laughs. When she laughs, Mr. Tonico, you get weak in the knees."

"Ah!" Nacib exclaimed again, after the first forkful. "Manna from heaven, Mr. Tonico. Now, thank God, I've really got what I need."

"In both bed and board, eh, Turk?"

Nacib stuffed himself. After Tonico's departure, he stretched out, as he did every day, in a deck chair under some trees in back. He picked up a paper from Bahia—nearly a week old—and lit a cigar. He smoothed his mustache with his fingers and felt at peace with the world. His sadness over the funerals had vanished. Later, he would go to his uncle's store and take home a cheap dress and a pair of slippers. He would talk with his cook about the snacks and appetizers for the bar. He had not dreamed that that dust-covered migrant, clothed in rags, could be such a cook. Nor that underneath the dirt lay such charm, such seductiveness. He fell asleep in the peace of the Lord. The breeze from the ocean caressed his mustache.

Although it was not yet five, and the Revenue Board office was therefore still open, Nhô-Galo entered the bar. He was visibly excited and held a copy of the *Ilhéus Daily* in his hand. Nacib poured him a vermouth and was going to tell him about the new cook, but Nhô-Galo spoke first:

"The thing has started!"

"What?"

"Here, in the paper. It just came out. Read it."

There it was, on the front page, a long article in heavy type. The headline stretched across four columns: SCANDALOUS NEGLECT OF THE HARBOR. It was a hard-hitting censure of the local government, of the Mayor ("a useless mediocrity, utterly servile to his political boss, Colonel Ramiro"), and of Alfredo Bastos ("a state assemblyman elected by the people of Ilhéus to defend the sacred interests of the cacao region, but who has completely forgotten those interests and who raises his puny voice only to cry 'aye' and 'hear! hear!' in support of the Governor and his program").

The article made opportunistic use of the grounding of the boat the day before. "The greatest and most pressing problem of the region, the key to its future wealth and civilization or backwardness and poverty, on whose correct solution all local progress depends, is the problem of the sandbar—that is, the problem of the direct shipment of cacao from Ilhéus to foreign countries." For those who, "under special circumstances bearing little relationship to their personal capacities to govern, have grabbed the positions of political power," this fundamental problem did not even exist. The article continued in the same vein and ended with a transparent allusion to Mundinho and his friends: "Fortunately, there are in Ilhéus men of high civic purpose who, in view of the criminal neglect on the part of the local authorities, are disposed to take the problem into their own hands and resolve it. The people, the glorious and public-spirited people of Ilhéus, with their tradition of fearlessness, will know how to judge, punish, and reward."

"Man, the thing is serious."

"It must have been written by the Doctor."

"Sounds more like Ezequiel."

"It was the Doctor. I'm sure. Dr. Ezequiel was drunk yesterday, at the cabaret. . . . There'll be fireworks, all right."

"Fireworks! You're an optimist. It'll be an all-out war."

"As long as it doesn't begin tonight here in the bar."

"Why should it begin here?"

"The bus-line dinner. Have you forgotten? Everybody's coming: the Mayor, Mundinho, Colonel Amâncio, Tonico, the Doctor, the Captain, Manuel of the Jaguars. Even Colonel Ramiro will be here."

"Colonel Ramiro? He doesn't go out nights any more."

"He said he might come. The colonel is a fighter, and now he'll be here for sure; you'll see. The dinner could wind up in a brawl."

Nhô-Galo rubbed his hands together and observed:

"It's going to be fun." He returned to the Revenue Board office, leaving Nacib worried. The bar owner was everybody's friend and had to keep out of political fights.

The waiters who had been hired to serve the dinner arrived and began to push tables together and get things ready. At almost the same time, the Judge, with a parcel of books under his arm, sat down with João Fulgêncio and Josué at one of the sidewalk tables. Gloria was at her window, receiving her usual tribute of silent admiration.

"A scandalous exhibition," said the Judge.

João Fulgêncio laughed and disagreed:

"Gloria, sir, is a social necessity. The government should treat her as a public institution, like the Rui Barbosa Literary Society, the Thirteenth of May Euterpean Society, and the Holy Mercy Hospital. Gloria exercises an important function in the community. By the simple act of appearing at her window and by walking in the street now and then, she raises to a higher level one of the most important aspects of our social life: its sexual aspect. She improves young men's taste for beauty and lends dignity to the dreams of husbands married to homely women—a majority, unfortunately, in our town—and to the performance of their marital duty, which would otherwise be an unbearable sacrifice."

"A splendid defense, my dear fellow," said the Judge, "worthy of him who made it and of her on whose behalf it was made. But, just between ourselves, isn't it really absurd—that much woman for just one man? And such a skinny little man . . ."

"You are apparently assuming that no one else sleeps with her. In this you are mistaken, my dear Judge, mistaken."

"Don't tell me, João! Who would do such a thing?"

"The majority of men, Your Honor. When they lie with their wives they think about Gloria. And they sleep with her."

"Oh, hell, João! I might have known it was just some sort of figure of speech."

"Any way you look at it, the woman's a temptation," said Josué. "She practically grabs you with her eyes."

Someone came up waving a copy of the *Ilhéus Daily.*

"Have you seen it?"

João Fulgêncio and Josué said they had. The Judge took the paper and put on his glasses. Men at other tables, too, were talking about the article.

"What do you think?"

"The lid's off. Anything can happen."

"This dinner tonight ought to be amusing."

"The amazing thing," said Josué, "is that nobody seems to have the nerve to approach her. It's a mystery to me."

Professor Josué was a newcomer to Ilhéus, brought there by Enoch when he founded his school. Although he immediately adjusted himself to the environment—he frequented the Model Stationery Store and the Vesuvius Bar, went to the cabarets, made speeches on occasion, ate late suppers in bordellos—he was not yet wholly familiar with the ways of the town. João Fulgêncio, on the contrary, was an encyclopedia of Ilhéan history and folklore. Accordingly, while the others discussed the article in the paper, he told Josué something that had taken place between Colonel Coriolano and Tonico Bastos shortly before Josué came to Ilhéus.

A PARENTHETICAL STORY WITH A MORAL

This was the story João Fulgêncio told:

Colonel Coriolano brought Gloria to town and installed her in his best house, the one where his family had lived before moving to the state capital. The old maids were scandalized. But Antoninho Bastos, familiarly known as Tonico—husband of a jealous woman, father of two beautiful children, and at once the town's Don Juan and its Beau Brummel, so elegant that on Sunday he wore a vest—was delighted. He immediately began to flirt with the voluptuous mulatto.

This was not a repetition of the idyll of Juca Viana and Chiquinha. Had Josué heard that story? Had he been told the tragicomic details? More tragic than comic; the humor of the Ilhéans was a bit macabre. In the case of Gloria and Tonico there were no walks along the beach or holding of hands on the piers, nor did Tonico push open Gloria's door at night. He only called on her in the afternoon—but frequently, and with little gifts of candy bought at Nacib's bar. Not to mention lingering glances and a little sweet talk. Beyond that, our friend Tonico did not yet go.

Now, Colonel Coriolano and Colonel Ramiro Bastos were political partners. They saw each other constantly. Ramiro was the godfather of one of Coriolano's sons. After lunch, Tonico would often explain to his wife, the supremely fat and jealous Olga, that these ties of friendship and political interest obliged him to call that afternoon at the notorious house. Heaving her huge bust, Dona Olga would reply:

"If you really have to go, Tonico, go; if the colonel wants you to go, don't hesitate on my account. But watch out! If I hear anything about you and that woman, I'll—"

"If you're going to be suspicious, my love, I had better not go. It's just that I promised Coriolano."

Honey-tongued, this Tonico, as the Captain would say. To Dona Olga, poor thing, he was the purest man in the world but also the most attractive; he was therefore pursued by every woman in town—single girls, married women, servants; they were all no better than whores. To reinforce his innate purity in its struggle against the temptations to which he was thus exposed, she tried to maintain careful control over him. If she but knew . . .

With patience and bonbons Tonico was "making the bed" on which he would lie, as he whispered at the stationery store and in the bar. But before Tonico actually lay in the not wholly fig-

urative bed, Colonel Coriolano learned of the visits, of the caramels, and of the amorous glances. One day he appeared unexpectedly in Ilhéus and went in at the front door of Tonico's
house, where his notary's office, full of people at the time, was located.

Tonico Bastos welcomed his friend with loud greetings and
pats on the back, like the extremely cordial fellow he was. Coriolano let himself be fussed over, accepted a chair, sat down,
slapped his mud-soiled boots with his riding whip, and said, without raising his voice:

"Tonico, it has come to my attention that you are hanging
around my ward's house. I value your friendship highly, Tonico.
I remember you as a little boy, the son of my son's godfather.
Therefore I'm going to give you some advice, the advice of an
old friend: stay away from there. I also thought very highly of
Juca Viana, the son of an old poker companion of mine. I knew
Juca, too, when he was a little boy. You remember what happened to him? Too bad, poor boy, but he insisted on fooling
around with another man's woman."

There was an agonizing silence in the office. Tonico stammered:

"But Colonel—"

Toying with the whip, Coriolano continued in the same tone
of voice:

"You're handsome and elegant; you have plenty of women. I'm
worn and old, and my wife has withered, poor soul! I have only
Gloria. I like the girl and I want her for myself alone. This business of keeping women for other men to enjoy was never in my
line."

He smiled at Tonico and added:

"I'm your friend and that's why I'm advising you: stay away
from there."

The notary had turned pale. A deathly silence filled the office.
Manuel of the Jaguars, who had gone there to get a document
executed, declared afterwards that there was the "smell of
corpse" in the air, an odor for which he had a keen nose, for he
had been responsible for many corpses himself during the old
days. Tonico began to make excuses: what the colonel had heard

was nothing but slander, miserable slander by his enemies and by the colonel's. He had gone to Gloria's house merely to offer his services to the colonel's protégée, for she was continually snubbed and insulted by all those narrow-minded people who criticized the colonel for having installed her on St. Sebastian Square in a house where his own family had lived. They turned their faces away from the girl and even spat as she passed. These were the people who were trying to stir up trouble. He had sought only to defy them and to show publicly his esteem for and loyalty to the colonel. He had not touched the girl, nor had he had any such intention. Honey-tongued, that Tonico.

"I know you haven't touched her. If you had, I wouldn't be here talking with you like this; we'd have a different kind of conversation. But I wouldn't want to stake my life on the purity of your intentions. In any case, intentions alone never put horns on anybody. You'd better do like the others: turn your face away from her. That's the way I prefer it. And now that you've been advised, we won't talk about it any more."

He began at once to discuss business, as if nothing had been said, and then he went into another part of the house to say good morning to Dona Olga and to pinch the children's cheeks. From that day on, Tonico Bastos even stopped walking past Gloria's house, and she became still more lonely and unhappy. The town smacked its lips over the incident. "The bed broke down before he could lie on it," they said; and "it sure made a helluva noise when it collapsed," they added. Merciless, these Ilhéans. Colonel Coriolano's warning was heeded not only by Tonico: many others decided definitely not to go beyond their fantasies. On warm nights these fantasies were transformed into dreams, nourished by the vision of Gloria's bosom at the window and of the smile—"moist with desire," as Josué himself so aptly described it in a poem—that spread from her eyes to her lips. And the persons whom this benefited the most, according to João Fulgêncio (as he concluded his narrative), were the wives, the old and ugly wives. As he had said to the Judge, Gloria was a public utility, a social necessity, who raised to a higher level the sex life of the community, so feudal still despite its much publicized and undeniable progress.

THE BANQUET

Despite Nacib's fears, the dinner for the bus line came off in perfect peace and harmony. Jacob the Russian arrived before seven o'clock, as the last customers of the apéritif hour were leaving. He followed Nacib around, rubbing his hands and showing all his teeth in a broad smile. Like Nacib, he had read the article in the paper and was concerned about the dinner's success. They were hot-headed, these Ilhéans. His partner, Moacir Estrêla, was waiting at the garage for the bus bringing the guests from Itabuna—ten persons, including the Mayor and the Judge. And now this damned article sowing discord and suspicion among his guests.

Earlier, when the Captain came for his usual game of backgammon, he confided to Nacib that the article was only the first of a series, and that the series itself was just the beginning of a crusade that would go far beyond newspaper articles. He said there were great days ahead for Ilhéus. Late in the afternoon the Doctor dropped in briefly; his fingers were ink-stained and his eyes shone with pride. He explained that he could stay only a moment, for he had a lot of work to do. Tonico Bastos did not return to the bar; it was reported his father had sent for him.

The first of the guests to arrive were those from Itabuna. They were full of praise for the bus line, which, although the road was not yet completely dry, had made the trip in an hour and a half. They looked with condescending curiosity at the streets, the houses, the church, the Vesuvius Bar, its stock of liquors, and the Ilhéus Cine-Theatre, and decided that Itabuna was better in every respect. In those days the rivalry between the two main towns of the cacao region was beginning to intensify. The Itabunans talked about their immense progress, the amazing development of their area, which a few years before had been only a district (then called Tabocas) of the county of Ilhéus. They engaged the Captain in a discussion of the sandbar problem.

Families on their way to the theatre to attend the magician's first performance looked curiously at the activity in the bar, at the important people gathered there, and at the big T-shaped table. Jacob and Moacir were receiving their guests. Mundinho Falcão arrived with Clóvis Costa, causing a flurry of excitement. The exporter went over to embrace the Itabunans; several of them were men with whom he did business. Colonel Amâncio Leal, with Manuel of the Jaguars at his side, was telling some of the guests that Jesuíno, with the Judge's permission, had left for his plantation, where he would stay until the trial. Every few moments Colonel Ribeirinho looked at the theatre entrance in the hope of seeing Anabela. The conversation became general: there was talk about the funerals, the previous day's crime, business, the end of the rains, the outlook for the crop, and Prince Sandra and Anabela; but everyone avoided reference to the article in the *Ilhéus Daily,* as if each was afraid to start hostilities, or at least wanted no responsibility for doing so.

When, around eight o'clock, they were about to sit down, someone announced from the doorway:

"Here comes Colonel Ramiro with Tonico."

Amâncio Leal went forward to meet them. Nacib became uneasy: the atmosphere grew tense, the laughter sounded hollow, and he detected the outline of pistols under coats. Mundinho Falcão was talking with João Fulgêncio; the Captain approached them. Across the square, one could see Professor Josué at Malvina's gate. Walking slowly, leaning heavily on his cane, Colonel Ramiro Bastos entered the bar, greeting each person as he advanced. He stopped before Clóvis Costa and shook his hand.

"How is the paper, Clóvis? Prospering?"

"It's doing all right, Colonel."

He joined briefly the group composed of Mundinho, João Fulgêncio, and the Captain. He asked Mundinho about his trip to Rio, complained to João Fulgêncio that he had not called on him recently, and joked with the Captain. Nacib was filled with admiration for the old man: he must have been burning with fury inside, but one would never have known it from his manner. He seemed to regard those who were plotting his overthrow as children who lacked judgment but fortunately were too little to be dangerous.

Colonel Ramiro's place was at the head of the table, between the two Mayors. Mundinho sat nearby, between the two Judges. The waiters began to serve the food prepared by the Dos Reis sisters.

At first, no one felt completely at ease. They ate, drank, talked, and laughed, but there was a disquietude in the air as if they were waiting for something to happen. Colonel Ramiro Bastos did not touch the food and barely tasted the wine. His small eyes moved from guest to guest. They grew dark when they fell on Clóvis Costa, on the Captain, and on Mundinho. Suddenly he asked why the Doctor had not come, and expressed regret at his absence. Little by little the atmosphere became more relaxed and cheerful. Anecdotes were exchanged, Anabela's dances were described, and the food was praised.

Finally came the time for speeches. Jacob and Moacir had asked Dr. Ezequiel Prado to speak in behalf of the bus line. The lawyer rose. He had drunk a lot and his tongue was a little thick, but the more Ezequiel drank the more eloquent he became. Amâncio Leal whispered something to Dr. Maurício Caires; doubtless he was asking him to listen very attentively to his fellow lawyer. Ezequiel's political loyalty to Colonel Ramiro had been wavering since the last elections. If he started to talk about the sandbar, it would be up to him, Maurício, to make a crushing reply. But Dr. Ezequiel, greatly inspired, took as his principal theme the friendship between Ilhéus and Itabuna, the sister cities of the region of cacao, now connected also by the new bus line, that "monumental achievement" of enterprising men such as Jacob, "come from the frozen steppes of Siberia to promote progress on these distant Brazilian shores"—a phrase that brought tears to Jacob's eyes, although he actually came from a ghetto in Kiev—and Moacir, "a self-made and honorable man, an example, for all the world to see, of what initiative and hard work can accomplish." Moacir modestly bowed his head amid the resounding cries of assent. Dr. Ezequiel continued in the same vein: he harped on civilization and progress, and foresaw the future of the region, "destined soon to attain the highest peaks of culture."

The Mayor of Ilhéus, tedious and interminable, hailed the people of Itabuna, so well represented there. The Mayor of Itabuna, Colonel Aristóteles Pires, responded with a few words of thanks. Dr. Maurício gave them a full-course oration, with the Bible for dessert. In conclusion he proposed a toast to "that impollute Ilhéan to whom our region owes so much, an elder of insigne virtues, an operose administrator, an exemplary pater-familias, chief, and friend: Colonel Ramiro Bastos." Everyone drank the toast. Mundinho touched glasses with the colonel. No sooner had Dr. Maurício sat down than the Captain was on his feet, glass in hand. He, too, he said, wished to take the opportunity offered by this banquet, which marked another forward step in the land of cacao, to propose a toast to a man who had come among them from the great cities of the south and was here devoting to this region his fortune, his extraordinary energies, his statesmanlike vision, and his patriotism. To this man, to whom Ilhéus and Itabuna already owed so much, whose name was anonymously connected with the bus line and with everything else that the people of Ilhéus had undertaken in recent years, to Raimundo Mendes Falcão, he raised his glass. It was the colonel's turn to touch glasses with the exporter. According to what was told afterwards, Amâncio Leal kept his hand on the butt of his revolver all during the Captain's speech.

Nothing else happened. But, from that day on, it was clear to everyone that Mundinho had assumed the leadership of the opposition and that the fight had begun. Not, however, a fight like those of the early days. Rifles and ambushes, burned-down registry offices and false deeds, were no longer decisive. João Fulgêncio said to the Judge:

"Instead of bullets, speeches. It's better that way."

But the Judge was dubious:

"This will end in bullets. You'll see."

Colonel Ramiro Bastos left early, accompanied by Tonico. Some of the guests started a poker game in the back room; some went to the cabarets; others scattered among the tables in the bar and continued drinking. Nacib moved from group to group and speeded up his employees. The liquor flowed freely. In the midst of all the activity, a boy brought Nacib a note from Risoleta. She wanted to see him that evening without fail; she would wait for him at the Bataclan. The note was signed: "Your little monkey, Risoleta." The Arab smiled. Near the cash register was a package for Gabriela: a cotton dress and a pair of sandals.

When the first session at the theatre ended, a good part of the audience came over to the bar. Nacib had his hands full. Some still talked about the crime of the day before. The women and young people praised the magician. But at nearly all the tables the chief subject of conversation was the article in the *Ilhéus Daily*. The bar was busy until late; it was after midnight when Nacib locked up the cash register and left for the cabaret.

Anabela, seated at one of the tables with Ribeirinho, Ezequiel, and others, was asking for inscriptions in her album. Nhô-Galo, a romantic, wrote: "Thou art, oh ballerina, the incarnation of Art herself." Dr. Ezequiel, stewed to the gills, added in a shaky hand: "Would that I were Art's gigolo." Prince Sandra was smoking through his long, imitation-ivory cigarette holder. Ribeirinho patted him familiarly on the back and boasted about his plantation.

Risoleta was waiting for Nacib. She took him to a corner of the room and told him that she had awakened ill that morning; it was an old ailment that had come back and was driving her crazy, and she had had to call the doctor. She had no money at all, not even enough for the medicine. She had no one else to turn to, she hardly knew anyone else. Nacib had been so kind to her the other night. The Arab muttered something and handed her a bill. She stroked his hair.

"I'll be all right in two or three days. Then I'll send for you."

She left hurriedly. Was she really ill, or was it a little game to get money from him to spend on a supper and wine with some young student or clerk? Nacib felt annoyed: he had expected to sleep with her and, in her arms, to forget the day's sadness, worry, and mad activity. It was the kind of day that got a man down, especially with such a disappointment at the end. He was holding the parcel of things for Gabriela. The lights went down and the dancer appeared with her feather fans. Colonel Ribeirinho called the waiter and ordered champagne.

NACIB AND GABRIELA

He entered the front room and pulled off his shoes. He had spent much of the day on his feet, going from table to table. How good it felt to take off his shoes and socks, wiggle his toes, take a few steps barefoot, and put on a pair of old slippers. Thoughts and images mingled in his mind. Anabela would have finished her number by now and would be at the table with Ribeirinho, drinking champagne. Tonico Bastos had not come to the cabaret that evening. And the prince? His name was Eduardo da Silva and his card said he was an "artist." A pretty high-toned word for a man who trafficked in his own wife's body. Perhaps the prince was just a poor bastard, perhaps Anabela was just a professional associate and meant little or nothing to him. That was his business, his livelihood; he looked as if he had gone hungry more than once. A dirty livelihood, to be sure, but what business is really clean? Why judge and condemn him? He might well be more decent than Osmundo's friends, his companions at the bars, at the Literary Society, at the Progress Club dances—all of them respected citizens, yet afraid to accompany their friend's body to the cemetery. The Captain, on the contrary, was a real man. He was poor, he owned no cacao plantations, he had no income other than his salary as a federal tax collector, but he would stand for his convictions against anybody. He had not been an intimate friend of Osmundo, but there he was at the funeral, holding a handle of the coffin. And how about his speech at the dinner? He had praised Mundinho right in the presence of Colonel Ramiro Bastos.

Nacib shivered when he recalled the dinner. There could have been shooting, and it was just luck that it had ended peaceably. As the Captain said, though, it was just the beginning. Mundinho had money, prestige in Rio, friends in the federal government; he was not a nobody like Dr. Honorato, the elderly, broken-down physician who was supposed to be the leader of the opposition but who was under obligation to Ramiro and sought jobs from him for his sons. Mundinho would certainly upset a lot of people, stir up dissension among the vote-controlling planters, and generally raise hell. If he succeeded, as he promised, in bringing engineers and dredges to open up the harbor, his prestige would be tremendous. He might eventually take over in Ilhéus and drive the Bastoses into oblivion. Besides, the old man was on his last legs. Alfredo remained a state deputy only because he was the colonel's son; but he was just a good baby-doctor, nothing more. As for Tonico, he wasn't meant to command, to accomplish things. Except when it came to women. He didn't show up at the cabaret that evening, no doubt because he wanted to avoid discussions about the article in the paper; he never liked to fight.

Nacib shook his head. He was a friend of men on both sides, of the Captain and of Tonico, of Amâncio Leal and of the Doctor; he drank, played games, talked, and went to bordellos with all of them. The money that he earned came from them. And now there was dissension among them, they were taking sides. On one thing only were they all agreed: it was a husband's right and duty to kill his adulterous wife. Not even the Captain defended Sinhàzinha. Not even the cousin from whose house her body had been taken to the cemetery. Why in the world had the daughter of Colonel Melk Tavares gone there? Nacib was struck by her beautiful face, her silence, her restless eyes. She almost seemed to be bearing a secret, a mystery of some sort. Once, when he saw her with some school chums buying chocolates in the bar, João Fulgêncio had said:

"That girl is different from the others: she has character."

Why should she be different? What did João Fulgêncio, such a distinguished man, mean by "character"? Her father had called on Jesuíno to "give him his embrace," as he told Nacib at the slave market. The daughter—a student, unmarried, not even engaged—had brought flowers to Sinhàzinha's corpse. Why? It was a complicated world, beyond the comprehension of a mere bar owner like himself. Why waste time thinking about it? Let him concentrate on earning enough money to buy a cacao plantation. With God's help he would do it. Then, perhaps, he would look again at Malvina's face and try to solve the riddle. Or, failing this, he could at least provide a house for a concubine like Gloria.

He was thirsty and went to the kitchen for a drink from the water pot. He saw the parcel with the dress and slippers from his uncle's store. He was undecided. It would be better to give them to Gabriela the next day. Or to place the package at the door of her little room in the back yard so she would find it in the morning. As if it were Christmas. He smiled and picked up the package. In the kitchen, he drank water in great gulps; he had drunk a good deal of liquor while helping to serve the dinner.

The moon, high in the sky, shone brightly on the papaya and guava trees in the back yard. The door to the girl's room was open, perhaps on account of the heat. In Filomena's time it had been kept locked. The old woman was afraid of robbers, although the framed pictures of saints were her only treasure. The moonlight invaded the room through the doorway. Nacib went closer. He would leave the package at the foot of the bed; in the morning she would have a big surprise. Then, perhaps, on the following night . . .

His eyes pierced the darkness. A thin streak of moonlight fell across the bed and shone on a part of the girl's leg. Nacib, at once excited, looked closer. He had expected to spend the night in the arms of Risoleta. He had looked forward eagerly to the pleasures she had learned to provide as a prostitute in the big city. Now he could see Gabriela's cinnamon-colored leg outside the cover. He could trace her belly and breasts beneath her torn slip, only partly hidden by the patched coverlet. One breast was half revealed. Nacib strove to see more clearly. A scent of clove hung in the air.

Gabriela stirred in her sleep as the Arab stepped through the doorway. His hand was outstretched, but he did not have the courage to touch her sleeping body. Why hurry? What if she screamed, created a scandal, ran away? He would be left again without a cook, and he could never find another like her. Better leave the package beside the bed. Next day he would stay home longer, gradually gain her confidence, and finally seduce her.

His hand almost trembled as he put down the package. Gabriela started and opened her eyes. She reached for the cover, but somehow (was she flustered?) it slid to the floor. She sat up, smiling timidly. She did not try to cover her breast, now plainly visible in the moonlight.

"I came to bring you a present," stammered Nacib. "I was going to put it by your bed. I just got here."

He was not certain whether her smile really expressed timidity; perhaps it was meant to encourage him. She seemed like a child: her thighs and breasts were exposed as if she knew nothing of the shame and evil associated with the naked body, as if she was all innocence.

"Thank you, sir. May God repay you."

She untied the knot while Nacib ran his eyes over her. Smiling, she held the dress against herself and stroked it with her hand.

"Pretty."

She spied the cheap slippers. Nacib was breathing hard.

"The gentleman is so good."

Nacib's desire filled his breast and tightened his throat. The smell of clove made his head spin. She held up the dress to get a better look at it, revealing again her innocent nudity.

"Pretty. I stayed awake, waiting for the gentleman to give me instructions about tomorrow's meals. It got late and I came and lay down."

"I was very busy." He could hardly get the words out.

"Poor man. Aren't you tired?"

She folded the dress and placed the slippers on the floor.

"Hand it to me, I'll hang it on the nail."

His hand touched Gabriela's and she laughed.

"What a cold hand!"

He could stand it no longer. He took her by the arm and with his other hand grasped her bare breast. She pulled him toward her. The fragrance of clove filled the room. A warmth from Gabriela's body enveloped Nacib, burning his skin. The moon shone on the bed. In a hushed voice, between kisses, Gabriela moaned:

"Beautiful man . . ."

PART TWO § JOYS AND SORROWS OF A DAUGHTER
OF THE PEOPLE IN THE STREETS OF ILHÉUS, FROM
THE KITCHEN TO THE ALTAR (BECAUSE OF RELI-
GIOUS COMPLICATIONS, HOWEVER, THERE WAS NO
ALTAR), AT A TIME WHEN MONEY FLOWED FREELY
AND LIFE WAS CHANGING——WITH MARRIAGES AND
BROKEN MARRIAGES, SIGHS OF LOVE AND CRIES OF
JEALOUSY, POLITICAL DOUBLE-CROSSINGS AND LITER-
ARY LECTURES, ASSAULTS, ESCAPES, NEWSPAPERS IN
FLAMES, AN ELECTORAL FIGHT AND AN END OF LONE-
LINESS, RUFFIANS AND A CHEF DE CUISINE, HOT
WEATHER AND CHRISTMAS FESTIVITIES, STREET PAG-
EANTS AND A SORRY LITTLE CIRCUS, A CHARITY BA-
ZAAR AND DEEP-SEA DIVERS, WOMEN DEBARKING
FROM EVERY SHIP, HIRED ASSASSINS FIRING THEIR
LAST SHOTS, BIG FREIGHTERS IN THE HARBOR AND A
LAW DEFEATED, AND WITH A FLOWER AND A STAR

OR

GABRIELA, CLOVE AND CINNAMON

Lullaby for MALVINA

Sleep on, sleeping maid,
Dream your brave dreams.
Sooner than you know,
You'll sail away forever.

A prisoner in my garden,
With flowers I am bound.
Help! they want to smother me.
Help! they want to kill me.
Help! they want to marry me,
In a house to bury me,
In the kitchen, cooking,
In the rooms, atidying,
At the piano, playing,
At the church, confessing.
Help! they want to marry me,
On the bed impregnate me.

Sooner than you know,
You'll sail away forever.

My husband, lord and master,
Would my life control:
Control the clothes I wear,
Control my scent, my powder,
Control all my desires,
My sleep, my body, even

My very soul.
His the right to kill,
And while I live,
My only right, to weep.

Sooner than you know,
You'll sail away forever.

Help me, take me to a land
Where I can have a lover;
I will not have a master.
Rich or poor, handsome
Or ugly, white or mulatto,
No matter.

Oh! I'll sail away,
With someone or alone,
Blessed or cursed.
I'll sail away
And marry, or
I'll sail away
And live in sin.
I'll work, I'll find myself.
I'll sail away forever.

Sleep on, sleeping maid,
Dream your brave dreams.

THIRD CHAPTER

The Secret of MALVINA
(born for greatness but imprisoned in her garden)

> "Morality grows weak, customs degenerate, alien adventurers intrude upon us . . ." (FROM A SPEECH BY DR. MAURÍCIO CAIRES)

GABRIELA AND A FLOWER

THE FLOWERS in the parks of Ilhéus were bursting into bloom: beds of roses, chrysanthemums, dahlias, daisies, marigolds. The petals of the "eleven o'clock" portulaca opened on time, as punctual as the town-hall clock, splashing the green of the lawns with red. Fantastic orchids grew wild in the nearby forest of Malhado and in the humid woods on Unhão and Conquista hills. But the perfume which hung over the city, pervading the air, did not come from the woods or from the flowers: it came from the storage warehouses, from the wharves and the export houses. It was the smell of dried cacao beans, so strong that it made visitors to Ilhéus dizzy, and so familiar that Ilhéans hardly noticed it.

On the plantations the ripening cacao pods filled the landscape with every shade of yellow. Harvest time was approaching and the crop would be the biggest in the history of the region.

Gabriela was loading an enormous tray with pastries, and another, larger still, with codfish balls, bean-paste balls flavored with onion and palm oil, and other tidbits. Tuísca, waiting to take them, smoked a cigarette butt and repeated all the news he had picked up in the bar which he found especially interesting: the fact that Mundinho owned ten pairs of shoes, the latest soccer scores, a robbery in a dry goods store, and the early arrival of the Great Balkan Circus, with an elephant, a giraffe, a camel, and some lions and tigers. Gabriela pricked up her ears at the mention of the circus.

"Is it really coming?"

"The announcements are tacked up already."

"I once saw a circus. I went with my aunt. There was a man who ate fire."

Tuísca discussed his plans. He would do what he always did when a circus came to town: follow the clown through the streets. Riding backwards on a donkey, the clown would sing out: "What does a clown do?" and the children would yell back: "He runs away with your wife."

The clown would mark Tuísca's forehead with whitewash, and that meant he could go to the night show free. Until the circus left, he would spend all his time there, helping the roustabouts and making himself generally useful.

"One circus wanted to take me along. The manager sent for me."

"To help with the tent?"

Tuísca was almost offended.

"No, as a performer."

"What would you do?"

The little black face lit up.

"I would take care of the monkeys and do tricks with them. I would dance, too. I didn't go, only on account of my Ma."

His mother, Raimunda, was crippled with rheumatism and unable to work any more as a laundress. Her sons—Filo, a bus driver, and Tuísca, a master of many arts—supported her.

"You know how to dance?"

"Haven't you ever seen me? Do you want to see?"

He began to dance. He had dancing in his bones. His feet made up their own steps, his body hung loose, he beat time with his hands. Gabriela watched him for a moment. Then she abandoned her trays and pans, the pastries and tidbits, and raised her skirt. Now they were dancing together, the little Negro and the brown girl, under the sun in the back yard. The world was forgotten. At one point Tuísca stopped dancing and began to drum with his hands on the bottom of an empty kerosene can. Gabriela laughed as she whirled about, her skirt flying, her arms swinging, her hips swaying.

"My God, the trays!"

They hurriedly arranged the two trays, placed the one with the pastries on top of the other, and put them on Tuísca's head. The boy set out, whistling a tune. Gabriela began to whirl again, it felt so good. At the sound of something boiling, she stopped and ran to the kitchen.

By the time she heard Lazy Chico enter his house next door, she was ready. She picked up a covered pot, slipped her feet into her sandals, and started out the door. She was going to take Nacib his lunch and help him in the bar during Chico's absence. She turned back for a moment, plucked a rose from a bush in the back yard, and placed it behind her ear. She could feel the velvety petals against her skin.

It was Felipe the shoemaker—a foul-mouthed anarchist when he blasphemed against the priests but as polite as a Spanish grandee when addressing a woman—who had taught her that bit of coquetry.

"Always in style and always lovely," he said to her. "All the *muchachas* in Seville wear a red rose in their hair."

Despite his many years in Ilhéus, Felipe still mixed Spanish words with his Portuguese. He worked very hard: he repaired saddles and harnesses, made riding crops, put new soles on shoes and boots. In his spare time he devoured red-covered pamphlets and joined in the discussions at the Model Stationery Store. Until recently, he had come to the bar only on Sundays, to play backgammon and checkers. Now he came every day, shortly before noon. At Gabriela's arrival the Spaniard would raise his bushy white head, reveal his perfect teeth in a smile, and exclaim:

"Hail *La Gracia, olé!*"

And he would snap his fingers like castanets.

Many others who had come to the bar only occasionally now became regular customers. The Vesuvius experienced unprecedented prosperity. Reports on Gabriela's appetizers spread through the apéritif crowd and drew customers away from the waterfront bars, to the special consternation of Plínio Araçá, proprietor of the Golden Nectar. Her bean-paste balls were celebrated in prose and verse—in verse because Professor Josué dedicated a quatrain to them in which he rhymed "appetizer" with "gormandizer" and "kitchen" with "bewitchin'."

Nhô-Galo, Tonico Bastos, and the Captain, each in turn, shared Nacib's lunch with him and praised the food ecstatically. Mundinho Falcão borrowed Gabriela for a day when he gave a dinner at his home for a friend, a senator from Alagoas, who was passing through Ilhéus.

Customers brought other customers to the Vesuvius Bar—to drink an apéritif or two, to roll poker dice, and, above all, to munch the exquisitely seasoned appetizers. And many delayed their meals at home in order to spend a few more minutes at the bar, ever since Gabriela herself began to bring Nacib's lunch pot.

Exclamations were heard everywhere in the bar when she entered, with her dancing feet and contagious smile. Her hair was tied in a ribbon. She wore no makeup. She would come in, say good morning as she passed among the tables, and place the pot on the counter. Previously, all the customers except one or two stragglers would have gone home for lunch by that time. But now more and more of them began to linger over their drinks; they gauged the time by Gabriela's arrival and had one last drink after she came.

"Bring me a drink, Eaglebeak."

"Two vermouths here."

"How about another?" The dice rattled in the leather cup and rolled out on the table. "Three kings."

She would help serve the drinks in order to speed the customers' departure; otherwise the food would grow cold in the pot and lose its flavor. Her sandals glided across the cement floor and her hips danced as she walked. As she went in and out among the tables, one customer would utter gallantries, another would look at her with pleading eyes, and the Doctor would pat her hand and call her "my girl." She smiled at all of them, childlike except for her rolling hips. A warmth spread through the bar as if Gabriela's presence made it cozier, more intimate.

From behind the counter, Nacib could see her coming, a rose behind her ear. He would half close his eyes and think of the pot filled with delicious food. By that time of day he was famished and could hardly keep from devouring the little shrimp pies and other appetizers on the trays. Gabriela's arrival would mean an other round of drinks at nearly every table—and more profit. And besides, it was pleasing to his eyes to see her in the middle of the day, to recall the night before and to imagine the night ahead.

Behind the counter he would pinch her, pass his hand up under her skirt, touch her breasts. Gabriela would then laugh softly, pleasurably.

The Captain would call to her:

"Come watch this move, my pupil."

He had called her his pupil, with a falsely paternal air, ever since the day when, with the bar almost empty, he had tried to teach her backgammon. She had shaken her head and laughed; she never succeeded in learning any game but old maid. The Captain would intentionally prolong a game until she arrived and then would call her over at a critical stage:

"Come here and bring me luck."

Sometimes she brought luck instead to Nhô-Galo or Felipe or the Doctor.

"Thank you, my girl," the Doctor would say, patting her hand. "May God make you even more beautiful."

"More beautiful? Impossible!" the Captain would protest, dropping his paternal air.

Nhô-Galo would say nothing, merely look. Felipe, the shoemaker, would praise the rose behind her ear.

"Ah, if I were only twenty again."

He would complain to Josué: why didn't he write a sonnet to that flower, to that ear, to those green eyes? Josué replied that a sonnet was inadequate; he would write an ode, a ballad.

The stroke of twelve-thirty on the clock always came as an unwelcome surprise. They would all get up, leaving fat tips, which Eaglebeak picked up with his dirty, greedy fingernails. They left reluctantly, as if they were being pushed out by the clock. Nacib would sit down in the empty bar to eat. She served him and hovered around the table, opening a bottle of beer and filling his glass. Her brown face lighted up whenever he, stuffed and belching, praised her food. ("Belching is good for the health," he explained.) She gathered up the dishes. Lazy Chico came back and Eaglebeak went to lunch. Gabriela set up the deck chair under some trees behind the bar, said "Goodbye, Mr. Nacib," and returned home. The Arab would light a St. Felix cigar, pick up some week-old newspapers from Bahia, and watch her disappear around the corner of the church with her dancing feet and free-swinging hips. She no longer had the flower behind her ear. He would find it on the deck chair. Had it fallen there accidentally as she leaned over the chair, or had she left it there on purpose? A red rose with a scent of clove.

OF A WELCOME AND UNWELCOME GUEST

Early one day the Captain and the Doctor, both highly elated, appeared at the Vesuvius Bar escorting a man whom Nacib had never seen before. He was in his early thirties and looked like an athlete. Nacib guessed correctly that he was the long-awaited engineer.

"Dr. Rômulo Vieira, of the Ministry of Transportation."

"It's a great pleasure, Doctor."

"The pleasure is mine."

There he was: his face sun-tanned, his hair cropped close, a small scar on his forehead. He gripped Nacib's hand hard. The Doctor was smiling as happily as if he were exhibiting a distinguished relative or a woman of rare beauty.

"This Arab is an institution," said the Captain. "He poisons us with adulterated liquor, cheats us at poker, and knows everybody's business."

"Don't say that, Captain. What will Dr. Vieira think?"

"He knows I'm only joking. Nacib is a gentleman and a scholar and one of my best friends."

The engineer forced a smile and looked with misgiving at the square and the streets, the bar, the motion picture theatre, and the nearby houses, at whose windows inquisitive faces appeared. The men seated themselves at one of the sidewalk tables. Gloria came to her window in morning disarray: her hair was uncombed and she was still moist from her bath. She took a good look at the stranger and ran back to fix herself up.

"Quite a dish, eh?" said the Captain. He told the engineer about Gloria.

Nacib waited on them personally. The beer was barely cool, so he brought some pieces of ice on a plate. The engineer's arrival was a sensational event, although not wholly unexpected. The day before, the *Ilhéus Daily,* in heavy type on the front page, had announced that he was on a ship of the Bahian Line scheduled to arrive on the morrow. The news item ended with this tart prophecy: "The stupid laughter of the fools and mean little men —false prophets who unpatriotically denied not only the coming but even the very existence of an engineer assigned to this task by the Ministry—will be turned into sickly, embarrassed grins. Tomorrow will be a day of deflated arrogance." The engineer came by way of Bahia and landed in Ilhéus at daybreak.

The newspaper hurled insult after insult at those who had opposed the project or had been skeptical about its execution. Yet skepticism, at least, had not been wholly unjustified, for more than three months elapsed between the first announcement of the engineer's imminent arrival and his actual arrival. One day —Nacib remembered it well, for it was the day old Filomena left him and he hired Gabriela—Mundinho Falcão got off an Ita boat and told everybody that there would be an early study and solution of the harbor problem. An engineer from the Ministry would arrive within a few days. The statement created as great a sensation as Colonel Jesuíno Mendonça's crime. It marked the beginning of the political campaign for the elections early the following year.

Mundinho Falcão assumed the leadership of the opposition and took a handful of important people with him. The *Ilhéus Daily,* whose masthead proclaimed it to be "informative and non-political," began to criticize the state government, to taunt the municipal government, and to attack Colonel Ramiro. The Doctor wrote a series of articles—ferocious lampoons—brandishing the engineer's imminent arrival like a sword over the heads of the Bastoses.

In his office building, the entire ground floor of which was used for sacking cacao beans, Mundinho Falcão talked with planters, but no longer solely about sales of cacao and terms of payment.

He discussed politics, proposed alliances, and announced plans; he maintained that the elections were as good as won. The colonels listened and were impressed. The Bastoses had run things in Ilhéus for more than twenty years, always with the backing of successive state administrations. Mundinho, however, reached higher: his prestige derived from Rio, from the federal government. Had he not, despite opposition from the state, obtained an engineer to study the hitherto insoluble problem of the sandbar, and did he not guarantee that it would be solved in a short time?

Colonel Ribeirinho, who had never thought much about the votes he controlled and had always handed them over meekly to Ramiro Bastos, joined the ranks of the new leader and for the first time became active in politics. Full of enthusiasm, he traveled to outlying districts to talk with other plantation owners and with small farmers. Some said that the new political alliance was born in the bed of the dancer, Anabela, whom the exporter had brought to Ilhéus and who there abandoned her partner, the magician, to dance exclusively for the colonel. "Exclusively, in a pig's eye," thought Nacib. Showing exemplary political neutrality, she slept with Tonico Bastos whenever the colonel was off canvassing the villages and hamlets. And she was unfaithful to them both whenever she got a call from Mundinho Falcão, who liked variety in his amours; for it was on him that she really relied to see her through if some misfortune occurred to her in this brutal land.

Among the younger planters, whose commitments with Colonel Ramiro Bastos were of more recent date and had not been sealed with bloodshed, several agreed with Mundinho Falcão in his analysis and solution of the problems and needs of Ilhéus: the building of roads, the plowing back of a part of the tax revenue in the remoter districts—Água Preta, Pirangi, Rio do Braço, Cachoeira do Sul—and a demand upon the British contractors that they finish the building of the rail line connecting Ilhéus and Itapira, a job that was dragging on forever.

"Enough of plazas and parks. We need roads."

They were influenced above all by the prospect of direct shipment abroad, once the sandbar was dredged and large ships could use the port. The local tax revenue would grow and Ilhéus would become a real metropolis. They awaited the arrival of the engineer.

But time went by, week after week, a month, another month, and no engineer came. The planters' enthusiasm began to cool. Ribeirinho alone remained steadfast, holding forth in the bars, promising and threatening. The *Southern Journal,* the Bastoses' weekly, began asking questions about the "phantom engineer, a figment of the imagination of ambitious men with ulterior motives, whose prestige was confined to barroom gossip." Even the Captain, the mainspring of the new movement, was worried, try as he might to hide his concern; he became irritable at backgammon and lost games through lack of concentration.

Colonel Ramiro Bastos went to Bahia against the advice of his friends and family, who considered the trip dangerous at his age. He returned a week later, triumphant. He called his followers together at his house.

Afterwards, Amâncio Leal, in his soft voice, told everyone who would listen that the Governor had assured Colonel Ramiro that no engineer had been assigned by the Ministry to work on the sandbar at Ilhéus. It was an insoluble problem, already thoroughly studied by the state Secretary of Transportation. There was really nothing that could be done about it. The ultimate solution lay in building a new port for Ilhéus at Malhado, to the north of the bar. This was an enormous project, requiring years of preliminary study and millions of contos, plus the whole-hearted co-operation of the federal, state, and local governments. The studies had already begun, but of course they were complicated and difficult and would have to proceed slowly. The people of Ilhéus must try to be patient.

The *Southern Journal* published an article on the proposed new port, praising the Governor and Colonel Ramiro. As for the engineer, it said: "He must have got stuck on the sandbar for good." At Ramiro's suggestion, the Mayor ordered the landscaping of yet another plaza, alongside the new building of the Bank of Brazil.

Every time Amâncio Leal ran into the Captain or the Doctor, he could not resist asking them, with a taunting smile:

"And the engineer—when do you expect him?"

The Doctor would reply stiffly:

"He laughs best who laughs last."

The Captain would add:

"You'll lose nothing by waiting."

"Yes, but how long must we wait?"

Then they would have a drink together and Amâncio would say:

"You fellows pay for my drinks until the engineer gets here. After that, I'll pay for yours."

He wanted to make the same bet with Ribeirinho, but the latter got angry and shouted, so that he could be heard throughout the bar:

"I don't play penny ante. Do you want to bet? Then bet some real money. I'll bet ten contos that the engineer will come."

"Ten contos? I'll put up twenty against your ten, and I'll give you a year's time. What more do you want?" His voice was soft, but the look in his eyes was mean.

Nacib and João Fulgêncio acted as witnesses.

The Captain insistently urged Mundinho to go to Rio and put pressure on the Minister, but the exporter refused; the harvest had begun and he could not get away from his business at that moment. Besides, the trip was unnecessary, for the engineer would certainly come; he was merely being held up by bureaucratic red tape. He did not reveal the real difficulties or the dismay he himself had felt when he learned, through a letter from a friend, that the Minister had backtracked on his promise because of protests from the Governor of Bahia. Mundinho then threw all his influential friends into the breach. One of them spoke to the President of the Republic, but—something Mundinho never discovered—it was the prestige of his brothers Lourival and Emílio which finally tipped the scales. On learning the name of the petitioner and of his kinship with important politicians in São Paulo, the President said to the Minister:

"After all, it's a just request. The Governor is nearing the end of his term, he has made a lot of enemies, and I'm sure he will not be permitted to name his successor. We should not always bow to the will of the state governments."

Mundinho had sweated òut days of terror, almost of panic. If he were to lose now, he would be utterly discredited and mercilessly ridiculed in Ilhéus. He would have to leave town and go back, a beaten man, to live again under his brothers' shadow.

He rarely went to the bars and cabarets; he knew that the skepticism and opposition were turning more and more to ridicule. Even Tonico Bastos, who discreetly tried to avoid the subject of the engineer when any of Mundinho's supporters was present, could not always restrain himself. He and the Captain once got into a loud argument, in which João Fulgêncio finally intervened to keep the peace. It started when, as they sat drinking and talking, Tonico said:

"Instead of an engineer, why doesn't Mundinho bring us another dancer? It would be less trouble for him and more fun for us."

That same evening the Captain went to the exporter's house, without an appointment. Mundinho greeted him a little irritably and said:

"You'll have to excuse me, Captain. I have a visitor, a young woman from Bahia. She arrived on the boat today. To take my mind off business."

"I'll only keep you a minute." (Somehow the Captain was annoyed that Mundinho had had a girl sent from Bahia.) "Do you know what Tonico Bastos said today in the bar? That you're better at bringing women to Ilhéus than engineers."

"Very funny," said Mundinho, laughing. "But don't worry, the engineer will come."

"How can I keep from worrying? Time is passing, and no—"

"I know what you're going to say. But I'm taking appropriate action, Captain. I thought you knew me well enough to assume that."

"Why don't you appeal to your brothers? They have power."

"Never . . . Anyway, it isn't necessary. Today I delivered an outright ultimatum. You can rest assured. And excuse my reception of you."

"It's my fault for coming at an inopportune time." He could hear a woman's footsteps inside.

"By the way, ask Tonico if he prefers blondes or brunettes."

A few days later a telegram came, stating the name of the engineer and the date of his departure for Bahia. Mundinho sent for the Captain, Colonel Ribeirinho, and the Doctor. The Captain took the telegram, stood up, and said:

"I'm going to rub Tonico's nose in it. And Amâncio's."

"The easiest twenty contos I ever got." Ribeirinho raised his hands. "We'll throw a big party at the Bataclan."

Mundinho took back the telegram. He asked them to keep it a secret for a few days longer in order to enhance the effect of an article that would appear in the newspaper after the engineer reached Bahia. Inwardly, he feared a new counteroffensive by the Governor and a new renege by the Minister. A week later, after the engineer, then in Bahia, had wired that he would arrive in Ilhéus by the next ship, Mundinho called the three men together once more and showed them the many letters and telegrams involved in his tough battle against the state government. He had not given his friends the details earlier because he had not wanted to alarm them. But now that they had won, it was well for them to be fully aware of the extent and cost of the victory.

At the Vesuvius, Ribeirinho ordered drinks for everybody, and the Captain, whose good spirits had returned, raised his glass to the health of "Dr. Rômulo Vieira, the liberator of the harbor of Ilhéus." The news spread and was published in the paper; a number of the planters quickly regained their enthusiasm. Ribeirinho, the Captain, and the Doctor quoted portions of the letters to them. The state government had done everything it could to keep the engineer from coming. It had staked all its prestige, all its power. The Governor, because of his son-in-law, had personally gone all out in the struggle. And who had won, the Governor of Bahia or Mundinho Falcão—and without even leaving his office in Ilhéus? His personal prestige had defeated the state government: this was the indisputable truth. The planters nodded their heads, much impressed.

Mundinho and his friends, together with several planters, gathered at the pier to receive the engineer. A large number of townspeople were there out of curiosity. They had heard so much talk and read so much in the paper about the engineer that they wanted to see what he was like; he had become an almost supernatural figure. Even a photographer was on hand, brought there by Clóvis Costa. He herded everybody into a group, with the engineer in the center; then he stuck his head under the black cloth and took forever to snap the picture. Unfortunately, this historic document was lost: the plate was overexposed. The photographer's prior experience had been confined to his studio.

"When are you going to start?" asked Nacib.

"Soon—at least the preliminary studies. I have to wait for my assistants and the necessary engineering instruments. They're coming direct from Rio."

"Will it take long?"

"It's hard to say. A month and a half, two months—I don't know yet."

The engineer manifested interest in other matters.

"The beach is lovely. How's the swimming?"

"Very good."

"But no one's in the water. In fact, no one's even on the beach."

"It isn't the custom here. Only Mundinho, and formerly Osmundo, a dentist who was killed. And only very early in the morning."

The engineer laughed.

"But it isn't forbidden, is it?"

"Forbidden? No. It's just not the custom."

Some girls from the parochial school, taking advantage of a religious holiday, were shopping in the business district and came into the bar for bonbons and caramels. Among them, beautiful and pensive, was Malvina. The Captain introduced them to the engineer.

"Our studious youth—future mothers and housewives: Iracema, Heloísa, Zuleika, Malvina . . ."

The engineer shook their hands, smiling.

"A land of beautiful girls."

"You delayed so long in coming," said Malvina, looking at him with her enigmatic eyes, "we began to think you weren't coming at all."

"If I had known that such pretty girls were waiting for me, I would have come long ago, without even waiting to be appointed." What eyes that girl had! Her beauty lay not alone in her face and shapely figure but seemed to come from inside her.

As the girls went out, Malvina looked back twice. The engineer announced:

"I'm going to take advantage of this sunshine and go for a swim."

"Come back for an apéritif around eleven or eleven-thirty. You'll meet half of Ilhéus."

He was staying at the Hotel Coelho. They saw him go by shortly after, wrapped in a bathrobe, walking toward the beach. They stood up and watched him take off his robe—he was completely naked except for his bathing trunks—run into the water, and start swimming with sure, fast strokes. Malvina, who had gone to sit on a bench at the beach, followed him with her eyes.

OF NACIB'S CONFUSION

He read a few lines in the Bahia paper and enjoyed the fragrant smoke of his St. Felix cigar. He rarely got to smoke all of the cigar or to read very much of the paper. He would soon drop off, lulled by the sea breeze and logy from overeating, and would snore contentedly through his bushy mustache. This half hour's nap under the trees was one of the delights of his life, his good, tranquil life, without complications, without grave problems. His business had never done so well, the patronage of his bar was increasing, he was putting money in the bank, and his dream of a piece of land on which to grow cacao was gaining reality. He had never made a better deal than when he hired Gabriela at the slave market. Who could have guessed that she was such a wonderful cook! Who could have imagined that under the dirty rags there were hidden such grace and beauty, so ardent a body, a fragrance of clove that made your head spin!

On the day of the engineer's arrival, the bar was buzzing with curiosity, introductions, and compliments—"You're an excellent swimmer, Dr. Vieira." Every lunch in Ilhéus was delayed. Just before leaving the bar to return home, Gabriela asked:

"Can I go to the movies tonight with Dona Arminda?"

Nacib took a five-milreis bill from the drawer and said:

"Pay for her, too."

He watched her go, smiling and a little flushed (he had not stopped pinching and feeling her even while he ate). As he puffed his cigar, he reviewed the period since Mundinho's first announcement that the Ministry would send an engineer. Exactly three months and eighteen days. For Mundinho and his friends and for Colonel Ramiro and his supporters, they had been days of worry, agitation, doubt, and hope, with editorial invective, secret conversations, loud arguments, muttered threats, and a climate of increasing tension. There had been days when the bar seemed like a boiler about to explode, when the Captain and Tonico hardly talked to each other, and when Colonel Amâncio Leal and Colonel Ribeirinho barely exchanged greetings.

But for Nacib they had been days of calm, of perfect peace of mind, of gentle joy, perhaps the happiest days of his whole life. His siesta these days was utterly serene. He would awake smiling at the sound of Tonico's voice. The notary always came after lunch for a dram of bitters to aid his digestion and for a few minutes of gossip before opening his office. He and Nacib would soon be joined by João Fulgêncio on his way back to the stationery store. They would talk about Ilhéus and about the world; João was well informed on international affairs, and Tonico knew what every woman in town was doing.

The engineer had been delayed for three months and eighteen days. It was exactly that long since Nacib had hired Gabriela. On the same day that Colonel Jesuíno Mendonça shot and killed Dona Sinhàzinha and Osmundo, the dentist. But it was not until the following day that Nacib learned for sure that she could cook. Sprawled now in the deck chair, the newspaper fallen to the ground, his cigar about to go out, Nacib remembered and smiled. For three months and seventeen days he had eaten food prepared by her; as a cook she had no equal in all Ilhéus. For three months and sixteen days he had slept with her, beginning on that night when the moonlight played on her leg and, in the darkness of the room, one of her breasts slipped out of her torn chemise.

On this afternoon, owing perhaps to the abnormal activity in the bar and to the exciting presence of the engineer, Nacib could not go to sleep, his mind was too full. In the beginning, he had not attached immense importance either to Gabriela's cooking or to her body. True, he soon became so spoiled by the excellence of her cooking that, at Nhô-Galo's birthday dinner, he noted the inferiority of the seasoning and ate almost nothing. Satisfied as he was with her food, he became aware of its full value only when his patronage began to grow, when he had to increase the quantity of the appetizers and pastries, when praises followed upon praises, and when Plínio Araçá, whose business ethics were questionable at best, made Gabriela an offer. As to her body— her abandon in bed, the madness of their sleepless nights—he gradually became dependent on it. At first he had sought her only on nights when Risoleta was unavailable and when he was not sleepy. He would lie with her for want of something better to do. But this indifference did not last long. Without noticing the change, he began to visit the little room in the back yard more frequently. He became irritable with Risoleta's insincere caresses, her whims, her eternal complaints, and even her professional know-how in bed, which she utilized to extract money from him. Finally he stopped seeing her altogether. He did not even answer her notes. And so, for two months now, he had had no woman but Gabriela. Every night he came home from the bar as early as he could and went to her room.

It had been a good time, months of happy living, of lust satisfied, of good, succulent food, of inner contentment. Among Gabriela's virtues, which Nacib went over in his mind during the siesta hour this day, were her love of work and her sense of thrift. How did she find the time and strength to wash clothes, clean house—it had never been so clean—prepare the trays for the bar, and cook Nacib's lunch and dinner! And, with it all, she was fresh and rested at night, humid with desire, not merely giving of herself but also calling on him, never sleepy, never sated. She seemed to read Nacib's thoughts, anticipate his wishes. She provided him with surprises: certain dishes of which he was especially fond, such as manioc mush with crab meat; flowers in a glass beside his picture on a small table in the parlor; and change from money given her for marketing.

Lazy Chico had always brought Nacib's lunch pot when he returned from his own lunch. Half famished, the Arab would wait impatiently, while he and Eaglebeak served the few customers who stayed on into the noon hour. One day Gabriela herself appeared with the pot. She had come to ask permission to attend a spiritualist séance to which Dona Arminda had invited her. While he ate she helped serve the customers, and after that she came every day. That night she said to him:

"It's better for me to take the food. That way you get lunch sooner, and I can help in the bar. You don't mind, do you?"

He soon observed that her presence was another attraction to the customers. They lingered and ordered another drink. The occasional customers began to come every day—to see her, to say things to her, and to touch her hand. After all, what did it matter to him? She was just his cook, with whom he slept without obligation of any kind. She would serve his lunch, set up the canvas deck chair, and leave the rose with her scent on it. Nacib, at peace with the world, would light his cigar, pick up the papers, and drop off to sleep, with the sea breeze caressing his huge mustache.

But on this particular day he could not manage to fall asleep. In his mind he kept going over the previous three months and eighteen days, a period of agitation for Ilhéus and of calm for Nacib. Just the same, he would have liked to nap for at least ten minutes instead of remembering things at random, mostly matters of little importance. He suddenly realized that something was missing; perhaps this was why he could not fall asleep. It was the rose, which fell every day onto the deck chair. He had seen the Judge steal it from behind Gabriela's ear and place it in his buttonhole. The Judge had taken advantage of the excitement over the engineer's arrival. How could he so completely have forgotten his age (he was in his fifties) and the dignity of his office! Nacib had feared some brusque reaction on Gabriela's part, but she acted as if she had noticed nothing. Until recently the Judge had never come to the bar at the before-lunch apéritif hour but dropped in only now and then in the early afternoon, with João Fulgêncio or Dr. Maurício. Now he had apparently changed his habits: there he was, drinking a glass of port and playing up to Gabriela.

Playing up to Gabriela. Yes, Nacib suddenly realized, that was the big thing. Not only the Judge but many others. Why did they linger in the bar well into the lunch hour and thus inevitably get into trouble at home? To see her, smile at her, touch her hand, maybe proposition her. The only proposition Nacib knew about, however, was the one made by Plínio Araçá, and that was directed to the cook, not to the woman. Customers of the Golden Nectar had switched to Nacib's place, and Plínio had offered Gabriela higher wages. But he had made the mistake of entrusting the message to the shoeshine boy, Tuísca, who was faithful to the Vesuvius Bar and loyal to Nacib. And so it was the Arab himself who delivered the message to Gabriela. She smiled.

"No. Tell him no. Unless Mr. Nacib wants me to go."

He took her in his arms—it was night—and wrapped himself in her warmth. And he increased her wages by ten milreis.

"I'm not asking for more money, no," she said.

Now and then he bought her a pair of earrings, a breast pin—cheap little gifts, some of which cost him nothing, for he got them at his uncle's store. He would give these to her at night. She would be touched, humbly grateful, and would kiss the palm of his hand in an almost oriental gesture.

"Mr. Nacib is such a kind man."

Brooches costing one milreis, earrings costing one and a half—with these he thanked her for the nights of love, for the inextinguishable fire. Twice he gave her a cut of cheap dress goods, once a pair of slippers—little enough in appreciation of Gabriela's attentions and kindnesses to him: his favorite dishes, the fruit juices, his shirts so white and well ironed, the rose fallen from her hair to the deck chair. Superior and distant, he treated her as if he were paying her royally for her work and doing her a favor by sleeping with her.

The men in the bar were certainly playing up to her. Maybe

some of them were snooping around St. Sebastian Street in his absence, sending her messages, making proposals. Not all of them would use Tuísca as a messenger. How could he, Nacib, know what was going on? Why did the Judge spend so much time in the bar if not to tempt her? The Judge's paramour, a young half-breed from the country, had contracted an ugly disease and he had dropped her.

When Gabriela had started coming to the bar, he—what a fool!—had been so pleased with the pennies earned on the extra drinks that he had given no thought to the danger, to the daily temptation. He would not stop her from coming, for this would cost him money. But he would have to keep an eye on her, pay her greater attention, buy her better presents, and promise her an increase in wages. A good cook was a rarity in Ilhéus, as no one knew better than he. Many a rich family, as well as owners of bars and hotels, doubtless coveted his employee and would be willing to pay her scandalously high wages. How could he keep the bar going without Gabriela's pastries and appetizers and without her presence at noon? And how could he exist without Gabriela's lunches and dinners with their peppery black gravies, or without her steamed manioc with coconut milk for breakfast?

And how could he live without her, without her bright, timid smile, her cinnamon-colored skin, her smell of clove, her voice whispering "beautiful man," the warmth of her breasts, the fire of her thighs—how could he? My God, what was happening, why this sudden dread of losing her? Why did the sea breeze, like an icy blast, make his fat flesh tremble?

He could never again enjoy food made by other hands, seasoned by other fingers. Never, ah never, could he care so much for, so urgently need, another woman, no matter how white, how well-dressed, or how rich. Why did he feel this fear, this terror at the thought of losing her, this sudden anger at the flower-stealing Judge and the other customers who eyed her, talked to her, and touched her hand? Nacib asked himself anxiously: what was this feeling of his for Gabriela? Wasn't she simply a cook, a pretty, cinnamon-brown mulatto girl with whom he slept for diversion?

Tonico Bastos's voice rescued him from these confusing and terrifying thoughts. But only to plunge him deeper into them a few moments later.

They leaned against the counter and Tonico poured himself a dram of bitters. Nacib, in an effort to cheer himself, said:

"Well, the man finally got here. Mundinho really did it this time and no mistake."

Tonico gave him a dirty look.

"Why don't you mind your own business, Turk! You want some advice? Instead of standing here talking nonsense, take care of what belongs to you."

Was Tonico just trying to avoid the subject of the engineer, or did he know something?

"What do you mean by that?"

"Keep an eye on your treasure. There are robbers about."

"Treasure?"

"Gabriela, stupid. Somebody wants to set her up in a house of her own."

"The Judge?"

"Him, too? I only heard about Manuel of the Jaguars."

Was Tonico just making this up? Manuel was very much on Mundinho's side, so Tonico would naturally speak ill of him. For some reason, though, the old man was in Ilhéus constantly these days; in fact, he hardly ever left the bar. Nacib shivered. Was that cold breeze coming from the ocean? He took the bottle of pure cognac from its hiding place under the counter and poured himself a drink. He wanted to draw Tonico out further, but the notary only said:

"This backward shit-house of a place gets all excited over an engineer, as if he were something from another planet . . ."

OF CONVERSATIONS AND A BURNING

As the afternoon wore on, Nacib became increasingly dejected, as if Gabriela's departure were inevitable, almost as if she had

already gone. He decided to buy her a gift. Once, fooling around
in bed, he had tickled her feet and said: "Get yourself a pair of
shoes." When she came to the bar she wore sandals and at home
she went around barefoot; it wasn't right. She had, indeed, gone
shoeless all her life, even on the long tramp to Ilhéus. Yet her
feet were not deformed: they were only slightly spread and the
big toe stuck out sideways, funnylike. Every remembered detail
filled him with tenderness and longing, as if he had already
lost her.

He was walking down the street with a parcel containing a pair
of yellow shoes—he considered them beautiful—when he observed that a discussion was going on at the Model Stationery
Store. He could not resist: he needed distraction of some sort
and headed for the store. The few chairs in front of the counter
were occupied, and some men were standing. They were probably discussing the engineer and making predictions about the
elections. He hurried. He could see Dr. Ezequiel Prado waving
his arms and, just as he got there, he heard the lawyer's final
words:

". . . want of respect for society and for the people."

Strange! they were not talking about the engineer. They were
discussing the unexpected return to town of Colonel Jesuíno
Mendonça, who had been at his plantation since the shooting of
his wife and the dentist. He had passed in front of the town hall
shortly before and had entered Colonel Ramiro Bastos's house.
It was against this return that the lawyer was protesting: he considered it an affront to Ilhéan dignity and self-respect. João
Fulgêncio laughed.

"Come now, Ezequiel, when have you ever seen the people
here offended because killers were loose in the streets? If all the
colonels guilty of homicide had to stay on their plantations, the
streets of Ilhéus would become deserted, the cabarets and bars
would have to close, and our friend Nacib here would lose his
shirt."

The lawyer disagreed. After all, it was his duty to disagree:
he had been retained by Osmundo's father to help prosecute the
case against Jesuíno. The father did not trust the public prosecutor. He knew that in a crime of this sort, a killing for adultery,

the case against the defendant was never presented very forcefully.

Osmundo's father was a wealthy merchant with powerful connections in Bahia. He had kept Ilhéus in turmoil for a week. Two days after the funerals, he arrived by ship, dressed in heavy mourning. His wife, inconsolable, was under medical care. They had adored Osmundo, their oldest son, and had given him a big party on his recent graduation from dental college. The merchant came to Ilhéus determined to do everything in his power to prevent the murderer from going unpunished. The town soon learned of all this, and many persons were touched by the dramatic figure of the father in black.

Then a curious thing happened. Very few persons had attended Osmundo's funeral, so the father tried to organize a group to visit his son's grave. He ordered wreaths and many flowers; he sent for a Protestant minister in Itabuna; he went to the house of everyone who had had dealings of any sort with Osmundo.

He even knocked on the door of the Dos Reis sisters, with his hat in his hand, his suffering stamped in his dry eyes. Quinquina remembered that one night the dentist had relieved her of a terrible toothache. In the old maids' front room, the merchant told them stories of Osmundo's childhood and what a good, studious boy he had been. He spoke of the boy's distraught mother, of her walking about the house like a demented woman. He cried, and they cried too. So did the old servant who had been standing in the doorway, listening. The Dos Reis sisters showed the merchant their Nativity tableau and spoke well of the dentist:

"Such a fine young man, so polite."

And—who would have believed it!—the pilgrimage to the cemetery was a great success. Among the many who went were Professor Josué, several businessmen, the directors of the Progress Club, and almost the entire Rui Barbosa Literary Society. The Dos Reis sisters were there, standing very erect, each with a spray of flowers. They had consulted Father Basílio: would it not be a sin to visit the grave of a Protestant?

"It is a sin not to pray for the dead," the priest had answered.

Subsequently Father Cecílio, thin and mystical, reproved their gesture. On learning this, Father Basílio said:

"Cecílio is a prig. He likes the punishments of hell more than the joys of heaven. Pay no attention to him. I absolve you, my children."

Around the disconsolate father were gathered Dr. Ezequiel, the Captain, Nhô-Galo, and the dentist's neighbor and swimming companion, Mundinho Falcão himself. There were the funeral wreaths that had been wanting at the burial, and the flowers, flowers in profusion, that had been denied the coffin. A marble slab now covered the grave, inscribed with Osmundo's name, the dates of his birth and death, and—that the crime might not be forgotten—the two words: COWARDLY MURDERED. Dr. Ezequiel had got busy on the case. He had petitioned for the planter's imprisonment, the Judge had denied the petition, and he had appealed to the Superior Court in Bahia, where the matter now awaited decision. It was said that Osmundo's father had promised him fifty contos—a fortune!—if he succeeded in having the colonel put in jail.

The discussion of Jesuíno Mendonça did not last very long. The sensation of the day was the engineer. Ezequiel was unable to infect his listeners with his own well-paid indignation, and finally he too joined in the conversation about the sandbar:

"It serves him right. Maybe it'll knock some of the high-handedness out of the old bandit."

"Don't tell me you're supporting Mundinho Falcão!" exclaimed João Fulgêncio.

"And why shouldn't I?" replied the lawyer. "I stood by the Bastoses for a hell of a long time. I argued several cases for them. And what was my reward? They got me elected to the Municipal Council, which I could accomplish without their help any time I like. My name was proposed for President of the Council; it was practically agreed on. Then they turned around and picked an illiterate like Melk Tavares."

"You're right," said Nhô-Galo in his nasal voice. "Mundinho Falcão has a completely different approach. With him in the government there'll be a lot of changes in Ilhéus."

"The engineer is a nice fellow," remarked Nacib. "The athletic type. He looks more like a movie actor. He'll make a big hit with the girls."

"He's married," said João Fulgêncio.

"Separated from his wife," added Nhô-Galo.

How did they know these intimate details about the engineer? João Fulgêncio explained: the engineer himself had mentioned them after lunch when the Captain brought him to the stationery store. His wife was insane; she was in a sanitarium.

Clóvis Costa had said little, for it was time for the *Ilhéus Daily* to be out on the streets and he was waiting to see and hear the newsboys.

"Do you know," he asked, "who's talking with Mundinho at this very moment?"

"Who?"

"Colonel Altino Brandão. This year he's selling his crop to Mundinho. And he could be making a deal for his votes, too." He changed his tone of voice. "Why the devil hasn't the paper hit the streets?"

Clóvis Costa was right. Sunk in a soft leather chair at Mundinho's office, Colonel Brandão, in boots and spurs, sipped a French liqueur. He was the biggest planter in the region, after Colonel Misael, and controlled the votes of the entire district of Rio do Braço.

"The cacao groves this year are really beautiful, Mr. Mundinho. What you ought to do is come out to the plantation and spend a few days with us. We live very simply, but you'll get plenty of good country food. We've started to harvest. It's an abundant crop, a glorious sight."

The exporter tapped the colonel on the leg.

"All right, I accept your invitation. One of these Sundays—"

"Come on Saturday; the men don't work on Sunday. You can leave on Monday. If you want to, of course, we'd like to have you stay longer."

"That's a deal: I'll be there Saturday. I'm free now to move around a little more; until recently I was tied down with this matter of the engineer."

"They say the young man has arrived."

"It's the truth, Colonel. Tomorrow he'll be out studying the sandbar. Get ready, sir, to see the cacao from your plantations going direct from Ilhéus to Europe and the United States."

"Wonderful, wonderful." He took another sip of the liqueur, watching Mundinho with his shrewd eyes. "First class, fine stuff. Not from here, I suppose?" Without waiting for an answer, he continued: "They're also saying that you're going to be a candidate in the elections. When they told me that, I didn't believe it."

"And why not, Colonel?" Mundinho was pleased that the old man had broached the subject. "Don't you think I'm qualified? Do you think that poorly of me?"

"Me? Think poorly of you? God forbid. You're more than qualified. It's only that . . ." He held the glass to the light. "It's only that, like this liqueur, you're not from here." He raised his eyes to Mundinho, observing him closely.

The exporter nodded his head. He had heard this objection many times. To reply to it had become a sort of intellectual exercise.

"Were you born here, Colonel?"

"Me? I'm from Sergipe: I'm a 'horse thief,' as the kids here call us." He squinted at the sun's reflection on the glass. "But it's been more than forty years since I landed in Ilhéus."

"I've been here only four years, nearly five. But I'm as much of an Ilhéan as you, sir. I expect to live the rest of my life here."

He developed his argument, mentioning the several interests that tied him to the region and the various undertakings he had backed or promoted. He ended with the sandbar and the coming of the engineer.

While Mundinho talked, the planter made a corn-husk cigarette with shreds of rope tobacco. His sharp eyes glanced now and then at Mundinho's face, as if to gauge his sincerity.

"You have much in your favor. Some come here just to make money: they don't think about anything else. You think about everything, the needs of the place. . . . It's a pity you're not married."

"Why, Colonel?" He picked up the bottle, itself almost a work of art, and was about to refill the colonel's glass.

"You'll excuse me, please. This drink is fine stuff. But, to be frank, I prefer a little rum. This liqueur is very deceiving: fragrant, sweetish, as if it were for a woman. And it's really strong as the devil, makes you drunk without your knowing it. But not rum: you know right away. It doesn't fool anybody."

Mundinho took a bottle of rum from the closet.

"As you prefer, Colonel. But why should I be married?"

"Well, if you will permit, I'm going to give you a bit of advice: marry some girl here, one of our daughters. I'm not offering you one of mine; all three are married, and well married, thank God. But there's many a gifted girl here and in Itabuna. That way, everybody will know you're not just on a visit, just to get what you can."

"Marriage is a serious matter, Colonel. First you have to meet the woman of your dreams. Marriage is born of love."

"Or of necessity, no? In the country a worker will marry a stick of wood if it has a skirt on it. Just to have a woman at home, to sleep with and to talk to. A wife is very useful, believe me. She helps even in politics; she gives us children, makes us respectable. And if we want something else, there are always women available."

Mundinho laughed.

"You're asking me to pay a mighty high price for victory. If it depends on my getting married, I'm afraid I'm licked. I don't want to win that way, Colonel. I want to win on my program."

Then he talked with the colonel, as he had with so many others, about the region's problems. With contagious enthusiasm he indicated the solutions and the new perspectives they would open in the future of Ilhéus.

"You couldn't be more right. Everything you've said is like the tablets of the law, pure truth." He was looking at the floor. He had often resented the way the Bastoses neglected the remoter districts of the county. "If people here have any sense, you'll win. Whether the state government will accept you, I don't know. That's a horse of another color."

Mundinho smiled, thinking he had convinced the colonel.

"There's just one thing: you have the truth on your side, but Colonel Ramiro has a large, loyal block of supporters. He has done favors for a lot of people; he has many relatives; he has godfathered a lot of children. Everybody is used to voting for him. Excuse me for suggesting this, but why don't you make a deal with him?"

"What kind of deal, Colonel?"

"That the two of you get together: you with your head and vision, he with his prestige and votes. One of his granddaughters is very pretty. Haven't you met her? The other one is still too young. They are Dr. Alfredo's daughters."

Mundinho kept his patience:

"That's not the issue, Colonel. I think one way—you know my ideas—and Colonel Ramiro thinks another way. To him, government is just paving streets and landscaping the town. I don't see any possible common ground with him. What I've been proposing to you is a program of work, of administration. I'm not asking your votes for myself but for Ilhéus, for the progress of the cacao region."

The planter scratched his head of carelessly combed hair.

"I came here to sell you my cacao, Mr. Mundinho. I sold it well and I'm satisfied. I'm pleased with our talk, too; I've found out how you think." He looked fixedly at Mundinho. "I've been voting with Ramiro a good twenty years. I didn't need him in the early days. When I arrived in Rio do Braço there was nobody there. A few shit-asses came later and I ran them off without anybody's help. But I'm used to voting with Ramiro. He never did me any harm. Once, in a little trouble I had, he took my side."

Mundinho started to speak but the colonel stopped him.

"I don't promise you anything. I never make a promise unless I know I'll go through with it. But we'll have another talk. I promise you that."

He went away, leaving the exporter irritated and sorry he had wasted so much time on him. He said so to the Captain, who had dropped in a few moments after the departure of the master of Rio do Braço.

"The old fool wanted to marry me to one of Ramiro Bastos's granddaughters. I wasted my breath on him. 'I don't promise anything, but we'll have another talk.'" Mundinho imitated the planter's drawl.

"He said he'd come back for more talk? That's an excellent

sign," said the Captain. "My dear fellow, you still don't know our colonels. And above all, you don't know Altino Brandão. He's not a man who pulls his punches. He would have told you to your face that he was against us if that was what he meant. If we can get his support . . ."

The talk at the stationery store continued. Clóvis Costa was getting more and more impatient; it was past four o'clock and the newsboys still had not started crying the *Ilhéus Daily.*

"I'm going to the office and see what the hell has happened."

Girls from the parochial school, Malvina among them, came into the store and interrupted the discussion. They looked through the books of the Red-Rose Library. João Fulgêncio waited on them. Malvina ran her eyes over the bookshelves and examined novels by Eça de Queiroz and Aluísio Azevedo. Iracema approached her and said:

"At home we have *The Crime of Father Amaro.* I started reading it, but my brother took it away from me. He said it wasn't a book for girls." Her brother was a medical student in Bahia.

"Why can he read it if you can't?" Malvina's eyes flashed with their strange, rebellious light.

"Have you *The Crime of Father Amaro,* Mr. João?"

"Yes, we have it. Do you want it? It's a great novel."

"Yes, I'll take it. How much is it?"

Iracema was impressed by her friend's daring.

"Are you really going to buy it? What will people say?"

"What do I care!"

"Will you let me come over to your house and read it?"

"These girls of today," commented one of the men. "They even buy immoral books. And that's why there are cases like that of Sinhàzinha."

"Don't talk nonsense, Maneca," said João Fulgêncio. "You don't understand such things. The book is very good; there's nothing immoral about it. That's an intelligent girl."

"Who is intelligent?" the Judge wanted to know, seating himself in the chair left vacant by Clóvis.

"We were discussing Eça de Queiroz, Your Honor," replied João Fulgêncio, shaking the magistrate's hand.

"A very instructive author." To the Judge, all authors were

"very instructive." He bought books in batches, mixing juris-
prudence and literature, science and spiritualism. It was said that
he read none of them, that he bought them merely to decorate
his bookcase and give an impression of learning and intellectual-
ity. João Fulgêncio would ask him:

"Well, Your Honor, did you enjoy Anatole France?"

"A very instructive author," the Judge would answer imperturbably.

"Didn't you find him somewhat irreverent?"

"Irreverent? Yes, somewhat. But very instructive."

With the Judge's presence, Nacib's apprehensions returned.
Dissolute old man. What had he done with Gabriela's rose? It
was time Nacib got back to the bar.

"Are you leaving, my dear friend?" the Judge inquired.
"That's a good servant girl you have. I congratulate you. By the
way, what's her name?"

Nacib left. Dissolute, cynical old man. Utterly lacking in respect for his high office. And they were talking about an appointment for him on the Court of Appeals.

As Nacib entered the square, he noticed Malvina chatting
with the engineer on the beach avenue. She was seated on a
bench, and Rômulo stood beside her. She was laughing easily,
without constraint. Nacib had never heard her laugh like that.
The engineer was married and his wife was in a hospital for the
insane; Malvina would soon know it. From the bar, Josué also
observed the scene; he could hear the rippling laughter in the
soft afternoon air. The young teacher was miserable and made
no effort to hide his feelings. Nacib sympathized with him. The
Arab thought about Gabriela and about the Judge, Colonel
Manuel of the Jaguars, Plínio Araçá, and the many others who
were making a play for her. Josué himself was among them: he
wrote poetry about her. A complete calm filled the square on this
warm afternoon in Ilhéus. Gloria was leaning out of her window.
Josué, angrily jealous, stood up, facing the forbidden window of
laces and breasts. He lifted his hat to Gloria—a thoughtless and
scandalous gesture.

Malvina was at the beach, laughing. A pleasantly calm afternoon.

Running down the street came that herald of good news and bad, the colored boy Tuísca. He stopped at the bar, all out of breath.

"Mr. Nacib! Mr. Nacib!"

"What is it, Tuísca?"

"They set fire to the *Ilhéus Daily!*"

"What! To the building? To the machinery?"

"No, sir. To the papers. They made a pile in the street and poured kerosene on them. It was a big bonfire, like on the Eve of St. John."

OF NEWSPAPERS AND HEARTS ON FIRE

Employees of the *Ilhéus Daily*, aided by volunteers, brought water in cans and buckets and threw it on the fire. As a result, a few lucky individuals were able to salvage copies of the newspaper, wet but otherwise undamaged. Ashes were scattered over the street and flew in the afternoon breeze. A smell of burned paper filled the air.

Standing on a table brought from the newspaper building, the Doctor, pale with fury, spoke in a choked voice to the crowd that had gathered:

"Our local Torquemadas are trying to destroy freedom of thought, to blot out the light of the printed word with their criminal flames. They are beneath contempt, these obscure obscurantists, these second-rate Neros."

A few persons applauded, and the urchins, having a grand time, yelled, clapped, and whistled. The Doctor was deeply moved. His pince-nez dangling, he extended his arms and said:

"People, oh my people of Ilhéus, land of civilization and liberty! Only over our dead bodies will they ever set up a black Inquisition here to persecute the written word. We shall erect barricades in the streets, tribunes on the corners . . ."

From the nearby Golden Nectar, at a table close to one of the doors, Colonel Amâncio Leal listened to the Doctor's inflamed speech, his one good eye sparkling, and remarked with a smile to Colonel Jesuíno Mendonça:

"The Doctor is inspired today."

"Yes, but I'm disappointed," said Jesuíno. "He hasn't mentioned the Ávilas."

The two colonels had been sitting there for some time. They had seen armed ruffians from the plantations arrive and post themselves at various places near the newspaper building. They had seen these men surround the newsboys as they ran out of the building with papers under their arms, shouting: *"Ilhéus Daily! Get your Daily!* Arrival of the engineer—the government in panic—" But it was the newsboys who were in panic, as the men snatched away their papers.

Some of the ruffians invaded the pressroom and offices and came out with the rest of the edition. As the story was told later, they frightened poor old Ascendino so badly that he soiled himself. He was a teacher of Portuguese who earned a few extra pennies editing Clóvis Costa's articles. He was said to have raised his hands in supplication, crying:

"Don't kill me. I have a family. . . ."

The cans of kerosene were ready, in a truck parked at the sidewalk. The fire blazed; the flames rose high and threatened to spread to the buildings on the street. People stopped to look, uncomprehending. The ruffians fired some shots in the air to insure their getaway and climbed into the truck.

Amâncio and Jesuíno remained seated at their strategically located table. To an individual in the doorway, blocking their view, Amâncio said quietly:

"Please move out of the way."

The man did not hear him. Amâncio seized him by the arm and spoke again:

"I said, get out of the way."

After the truck sped by, Amâncio raised his glass of beer and smiled at Jesuíno.

"A nice, clean job."

"Very successful."

The truck roared through the center of town in the direction of the highway. The driver never slowed down, even at intersections; he just blew his horn. He almost ran down Stevenson, an exporter.

Excited people gathered at the doors of shops and warehouses or walked to the newspaper building. The two colonels remained in the bar. They ignored the curiosity of those around them and of others who were looking at them from the sidewalk across the street. Several persons had recognized among the ruffians men from the plantations of Amâncio, Jesuíno, and Melk Tavares. A certain Whitey had directed the raid; he was a protégé of Amâncio's and a professional hoodlum with a propensity for starting fights in brothels.

Clóvis Costa arrived on the scene as the flames were being brought under control. He pulled out his pistol and posted himself fearlessly at the door of the building. Amâncio remarked contemptuously:

"He doesn't even know how to hold a pistol."

Many friends, including several important persons, came to lend their support. There were so many at one time that they virtually constituted an improvised street rally.

Mundinho came with the Captain and embraced Clóvis Costa. The journalist said to them, as he had to so many others:

"It's one of the hazards of the trade."

That afternoon the person who stopped under Gloria's window to satisfy her thirst for news was not Tuísca, for he was busy commanding the band of urchins in front of the newspaper building; it was Professor Josué, his prudence and respectability cast aside, his face paler than ever. The circles under his eyes were black as crêpe, for his heart was in mourning. He could see Malvina walking on the avenue with the engineer.

Rômulo pointed to the sea; perhaps he was telling her about his profession. The girl listened with interest, laughing now and then. They appeared sublimely unmindful of the town's agitation. The old maids, on the contrary, gathered crowlike at the church door to crowd around Father Cecílio and discuss the fire. Josué passed them as he crossed the square. He approached Gloria's window. Her thick, mulatto lips parted in a smile.

"Good afternoon."

"Good afternoon, Professor. What happened?"

"They burned up today's edition of the *Daily*. Bastos's people. Because of this fool of an engineer who arrived today."

Gloria looked toward the beach.

"You mean the young man who is talking to your sweetheart?"

"My sweetheart? You're mistaken. She's just an acquaintance. In Ilhéus there is only one woman who robs me of sleep."

"And who is that, if one may ask?"

"May I tell you?"

"Don't be afraid."

At the church door, the old maids stared in amazement. On the avenue, Malvina did not even notice.

GABRIELA AND ARMINDA

It was a stray cat, almost wild. Patches of its mud-stained fur had been torn out. One ear was in tatters. It was an inveterate pursuer of female cats, could lick any other tomcat in the neighborhood, and stole food from all the kitchens on the street. Housewives and servants hated it, but it was so agile and wary that no one had ever been able to lay a hand on it.

How, then, had Gabriela made friends with it? Why did it follow her about, mewing, and come to lie in her lap? Perhaps because, whenever it had come around in search of food, she had not chased it away but had thrown it scraps of meat, fish tails, or chicken offal. Gradually it came to trust her, to feel safe with her. Now it spent most of the day in Nacib's back yard, sleeping in the shade of the guava tree. It was no longer so thin and dirty, although it remained as dissolute as ever and continued to prowl the hillside and roofs at night.

When Gabriela returned from the bar and sat down to her own lunch, the cat would come and rub itself against her legs. It purred in gratitude when she reached down and scratched its head or belly.

To Dona Arminda this was a true miracle. She watched in amazement as the animal ate out of Gabriela's hand, let her pick it up, and fell asleep in her arms. Gabriela would hug it against her breasts and press its face against her own, while it mewed softly, its eyes half closed, scratching her lightly with its claws. To Dona Arminda there could be only one explanation: Gabriela was a natural medium, as yet undeveloped and undiscovered, a rough diamond to be polished at the séances until she became a perfect instrument for beyond-the-grave communication. What but mediumistic emanations could subdue so wild an animal?

Seated in Nacib's doorway, the widow was darning socks and Gabriela was playing with the cat. Dona Arminda said:

"Listen, girl, you mustn't miss a single séance. Only the other day Deodoro asked for you. 'Why didn't that sister come back? She had a real good spirit guide. He was standing behind her chair.' That's what he said, word for word. It was a strange coincidence, because I thought the same thing. And take it from me, Deodoro is an expert. You wouldn't think so, him being so young. But he has such a familiarity with the spirits, you have to see it to believe it. He orders them about to suit himself. With his help you might even become a clairvoyant."

"Not me. I wouldn't want to, Dona Arminda. What for? It's best not to disturb the dead, let them be in peace." She scratched the cat's belly and the purring grew louder.

"You're all wrong, my girl. This way, your guide can't counsel you; you can't understand what he says. You go through life like somebody blind, because a spirit is just like a guide for a blind person. He goes along showing you the way, so you can avoid the stumbling blocks."

"No, I haven't any guide, Dona Arminda. What stumblin' blocks?"

"It's not just the stumbling blocks, it's the advice he gives too. The other day I had a hard delivery: Dona Amparo. The baby was crosswise and didn't want to come out. There I was, not knowing what to do, and Mr. Milton began talking about calling the doctor. Who came to my rescue? My departed husband; he accompanies me everywhere, he never leaves me. Up there"—she pointed heavenward—"they learn about everything, even medicine. He kept whispering in my ear and I kept doing what he told me. The result was that the delivery went fine and she had a beautiful baby."

"It must be wonderful to help little babies get born."

"Who's going to give you advice if you don't have a guide? And you need it so bad."

"What do I need it for, Dona Arminda?"

"My child, you're a fool. You don't know how to take advantage of the things God gave you."

"I don't? I take advantage of everything I have. Even the shoes that Mr. Nacib gave me. I put them on to go to the bar. But I don't like them. Slippers are more comfortable. I don't like shoes at all."

"Who's talking about shoes, silly? Can't you see how Mr. Nacib has fallen for you, head over heels, how he drools over you?"

"Mr. Nacib is a kind gentleman. What should I be afraid of? He's satisfied with my work."

Dona Arminda was irritated by such obtuseness.

"There—I pricked my finger. You're an even bigger fool than I thought. Mr. Nacib is able to give you everything. Mr. Nacib is rich! If you ask for silk, you'll get it. If you ask for a girl to help you in the kitchen, he'll hire two for you. If you ask for money— as much as you want—he'll give it to you."

"I don't need it. What for?"

"Do you think you're going to be young and pretty all your life? If you don't make hay while the sun shines, later on it's too late. I'll bet you never ask Mr. Nacib for anything, do you?"

"I ask to go to the movies when you go. What else is there to ask for?"

Dona Arminda lost her composure and threw aside the sock with the darning egg in it. The cat jumped and gave her a dirty look.

"Everything! Everything, girl, that you want. He'll give it to you." She lowered her voice. "If you play it smart, he might even marry you."

"Marry me! What for? He don't have to, Dona Arminda, why would he want to? Mr. Nacib should marry a nice girl from a high-class family. Why should he marry me? He don't have to."

"Wouldn't you like to be a lady? Wouldn't you like to run your own home, and go out walking with your husband, and wear fine clothes?"

"I might have to wear shoes all the time; I wouldn't like that. But maybe I'd like to marry Mr. Nacib so I could spend my whole life cookin' for him and helpin' him." She smiled, made a purring sound at the cat, and touched its cold, damp nose with her own. "But shucks, a man like Mr. Nacib isn't goin' to marry just anybody, like me, who isn't even a virgin. I don't want to think about it, Dona Arminda. Not even if he was crazy enough to want to."

"It's like I tell you, my girl: you just have to play your cards right. Give and then don't give. Leave him with his mouth watering for more. He's already scared, as it is. My Chico tells me the Judge is talking about setting you up in a house of your own. He heard Nhô-Galo say so. Mr. Nacib is worried half sick."

"I don't want it." The smile died on her lips. "I don't like him, I don't. Disgustin' old man, that Judge."

"And here comes another," whispered Dona Arminda.

Trudging up the street with his rustic gait was Colonel Manuel of the Jaguars. He stopped in front of the two women, removed his panama hat, and wiped the sweat from his face with a colored handkerchief.

"Good afternoon."

"Good afternoon, Colonel," responded the widow.

"This is Nacib's house, isn't it? I knew it from the girl." He pointed to Gabriela. "I'm looking for a servant. I'm going to bring my family to Ilhéus. Do you know of any?"

"A servant to do what, Colonel?"

"Hmm . . . to cook . . ."

"It's hard to find one around here."

"How much does Nacib pay you?"

Gabriela raised her ingenuous eyes.

"Sixty milreis, sir."

"He pays well, certainly."

There was a prolonged silence. Dona Arminda picked up her things, said goodbye, and stood listening behind the door of her house. The colonel smiled and said:

"To tell the truth, I don't need a cook. When the family comes, they'll bring one from the country. But it's a pity for a beautiful girl like you to spend her life in a kitchen."

"Why, Colonel?"

"It spoils your hands. If you want to, you can get away from all the pots and pans. I can give you everything: a nice house, a maid, charge accounts at the stores. I like you."

Gabriela stood up.

"What do you say to my offer?"

"I don't want it, thank you, sir. Don't feel bad. I'm happy here. I have everything I want. Excuse me now, please, Colonel."

Dona Arminda raised her head over the low wall in the back yard and called Gabriela.

"Did you ever see such a coincidence? Didn't I tell you? There's two of them want to set you up in a house of your own."

"I don't like him. I wouldn't do it even if I was starvin' to death."

"It's like I tell you: you can have anything you want."

"I don't want nothin'."

She was content with what she had: the cotton dresses, the earrings, the brooch, a bracelet. Not the shoes; they hurt her feet. She was happy with the back yard, the kitchen and its stove, the little room where she slept, the daily fun at the bar with those beautiful young men: Professor Josué, Mr. Tonico, Mr. Ari, and those polite men: Mr. Felipe, the Doctor, the Captain. She was happy with her little friend Tuísca and with the cat she had domesticated.

She was happy with Mr. Nacib, too. It was good to sleep with this big, fat, beautiful young man. It was good to rest her head on his hairy chest or to feel the weight of his heavy leg across her hips. Sometimes his mustache tickled the back of her neck. Gabriela felt a quiver run down her spine; it was so good to sleep with a man. But not with an old man for a house and clothes, only with a young man, like Mr. Nacib.

Dona Arminda, with all that spiritualism, must be losing her mind. What a crazy idea, Gabriela getting married to Mr. Nacib. It was nice to think about, though. To take his arm and go walking down the street. Even with tight shoes on. To go to the movies with him and lay her head on his shoulder, soft as a pillow. To go to a party and dance with Mr. Nacib. A wedding ring on her finger . . .

Why think about it? There was no chance. Mr. Nacib would have to marry a society girl, all fuss, feathers, and perfume, with shoes and silk stockings. A high-class man would want Gabriela only for cooking, cleaning house, and washing clothes. Or to sleep with. But not an ugly old man and not for money. Just because she liked to. On the journey it was Clemente; back home in the country it was Nhôzinho—and Zé de Carmo. In the city, in the rich house where she worked, it was Bebinho, a young student. He used to come quietly, on tiptoe, afraid of his mother. The first was her own uncle, when she was a child. Her old, sick uncle.

BY LAMPLIGHT

Their backs bare under the burning sun, the workers were picking cacao fruit from the trees by means of sickles attached to long poles. The yellow pods fell to the ground with a thud and were gathered up by women and children, who split them open with a short, broad-bladed knife. The heaps of soft cacao seeds, embedded in white pulp, were then deposited in wicker baskets for transport on the backs of donkeys to the fermenting troughs. The work began at daybreak and continued till dusk, with barely enough time out at midday for the workers to gulp down a piece of jerked beef, some manioc meal, and a ripe jack fruit. The women's voices were raised in a doleful work song:

> *"Hard life, bitter gall,*
> *I am a Negro worker.*
> *Tell me, Colonel,*
> *Tell me, please,*
> *When will I harvest*
> *The sorrows of my love?"*

Then the men's voices responded in chorus:

> *"I'm goin' to harvest cacao*
> *In the cacao groves. . . ."*

As soon as the pack train reached the highway, the drivers shouted: "Hey, you damned mule! Get up there, Diamond!" Mounted on his horse and followed by his foreman, Colonel Melk Tavares rode through the groves, inspecting the work. Now and then he would dismount and scold the women and children:

"What kind of loafing is going on here? Hurry up, woman. Take your time when you hunt lice, not when you split cacao."

The knife blows fell more rapidly. The women and children held the knife in one hand and the cacao pod in the palm of the other hand; thus the sharp blade was a continual menace to their fingers. The accelerated rhythm of the song helped to speed up the work:

> *"So much honey in the pods,*
> *So many flowers in the field.*
> *Tell me, Colonel,*
> *Tell me, please,*
> *When will I sleep*
> *In bed with my love?"*

Among the trees, stepping on the dry leaves in the snake-infested paths, the men, too, worked more rapidly as they sang:

> *"I'm goin' to harvest cacao*
> *In the cacao groves. . . ."*

The colonel went about, examining the trees; the foreman shouted at the workers; the hard daily labor continued. Melk Tavares stopped suddenly and asked:

"Who worked this spot?"

The foreman repeated the question, the workers turned their heads to look, and the Negro Fagundes answered:

"It was me."

"Come here."

The colonel pointed to the trees. Among the dense foliage on the highest branches, some pods could still be seen.

"Who's paying you, the kinkajous or me? Do you think it's for them I grow cacao? You lazy bum, all you're good for is going into town and getting drunk."

"Yessuh, I didn't see them."

"You didn't see them because the trees aren't yours—you're not the one who loses the money. From now on, be more careful."

He went on his way. Fagundes raised the long pole, watching the colonel with his soft, kindly eyes. What could he say? He was not a man to swallow insults, but he would never talk back to the colonel. Melk had rescued him once from the police after Fagundes had got drunk and created a disturbance in a whore house. And recently the colonel had taken him into town to set fire to some newspapers and had paid him well for what was, after all, fun rather than work. And the colonel said that the fighting days were coming back, good times for men of courage and sure aim like Fagundes. While waiting, he continued to harvest cacao, tread out the seeds with his feet in the drying trays, sweat at the oven, and get his feet covered with pulp in the fermenting troughs. The fighting days were slow in coming back. That bonfire in town didn't amount to anything. Even so, it was fun: he saw the crowds, he rode in a truck, he fired some shots in the air just to scare the people—and he saw Gabriela. When he passed the bar he heard someone laughing and knew right away who it was. They were on their way to a house where they would stay until the time for action. He spoke to the leader, a young man called Whitey, who replied:

"She's the Arab's cook. A real lump of sugar."

Fagundes slowed his pace to get a look at her.

"Come on," said Whitey angrily. "Don't attract attention. Let's go."

It was a star-filled night when Fagundes got back to the plantation. He heard a concertina wailing chords of loneliness, and he told Clemente what had happened. The light of a small tin lamp cast shadowy images into the gloom among the trees: Gabriela's face, her dancing body, her long legs, her light-stepping feet.

"She looked purty as anything."

"She works for a bar?"

"She cooks for the bar. She works for a fat Turk, with the face of an ox. She was all dressed up and washed, and she had on sandals."

He could barely see Clemente by the lamplight.

"She was laughin' when I passed. Laughin' at some feller, some rich guy, I guess. Know somethin', Clemente? She had a rose behind her ear; I never saw nothin' like it."

A rose behind her ear. Gabriela lost in the lamplight. Clemente withdrew within himself.

"They hid me in the back of the colonel's house. I saw his wife. She's sick, she hardly moves. Looks like a statue of a saint. I saw his daughter, too. She's pretty but she's stuck-up. She walks past you like you weren't even there. But I tell you, Clemente, a girl as pretty as Gabriela, there just ain't no other. What's she got, Clemente? Tell me."

What has she got? He did not know the answer, even though they had slept together all those nights, her head on his chest, during the long journey through the backlands, across the scrub, and finally through the green meadows. He had never learned, he had never understood. She had something; it was impossible to forget her. Was it her cinnamon color? The smell of cloves? Her way of laughing? How should he know? She had warmth, burning on her skin, burning inside, a fire.

"It was a bonfire of paper. Burned up in a minute. I wanted to go see Gabriela and have a talk with her. But there was no way I could. I wish I could have."

The flickering light from the lamp licked at the shadows. Dogs howling, owls hooting, snakes hissing. Both men silently mulling over their longings. The Negro Fagundes picked up the lamp and went off to sleep. In the immense and lonely darkness, the mulatto Clemente recalled Gabriela: her smiling face, her light feet, her brown thighs, her high breasts, her dark belly, her scent

of cloves, her cinnamon color. He took her in his arms, to his bed
of sticks. He lay with her, her head on his chest.

OF THE BALL AND THE ENGLISHWOMAN

One of the most important events in Ilhéus that year was the
inauguration of the new headquarters of the Commercial Association—really its first headquarters, for until then the Association had functioned in the office of Ataúlfo Passos, its president.
He represented several southern business concerns in Ilhéus. The
Association had been in existence for several years, but only
recently had it developed into a progressive, dynamic, influential
factor in the life of the town. The new headquarters, a two-story
building on the street running from St. Sebastian Square to the
waterfront, was not far from the Vesuvius Bar. The Association
engaged Nacib to provide the drinks, snacks, and pastries for the
inauguration. The job was so big that he had to hire two girls
to help Gabriela.

The election of officers preceded the inauguration party.
Heretofore it had been necessary to flatter businessmen into con-
senting to serve. But now the positions were sought after, for they
gave one prestige, strengthened one's credit standing at the
banks, and gave one the right to express opinions concerning the
administration of the local government. Two slates were nomi-
nated, one by the Bastos faction and the other by friends of
Mundinho Falcão. There was a corresponding split on every issue:
the Bastoses on one side, Mundinho on the other. The *Ilhéus
Daily* carried a public statement signed by exporters, importers,
and merchants endorsing a slate headed by Ataúlfo Passos, who
was up for re-election as president, with Mundinho for vice-
president and the Captain for official orator. Other well-known
names completed the list. A similar statement, also signed by important members of the Association but sponsoring a different
slate, appeared in the *Southern Journal.* For president it, too,

proposed the non-controversial Ataúlfo Passos, to whom the Association largely owed its development. For vice-president it proposed Maluf, who came from Syria and owned the largest store in Ilhéus. He was an intimate friend of Ramiro Bastos, on whose lands, many years before, he had made his start with a shack in which he sold provisions. For official orator it proposed Dr. Maurício Caires. In addition to Ataúlfo Passos, one name appeared on both slates, for the modest office of fourth secretary: Nacib A. Saad. The two slates were evenly balanced, and a lively fight was predicted. But Ataúlfo, an able and highly regarded man, declared that he would accept his nomination only if the opposing sides came to an understanding and agreed on a single slate that included names from both factions. It was not easy to convince them. Ataúlfo, however, was tactful. He called on Mundinho, praised his civic-mindedness, his constant interest in the region and in the Association, and told him how honored he felt in having him as a prospective vice-president. But did not Mundinho believe it essential to keep the Association equidistant between the factions, as neutral ground on which the opposing forces could work together for the good of Ilhéus and of the nation? What he proposed was to merge the two slates by creating two vice-presidencies and dividing the other offices between the two factions.

Mundinho readily agreed and was willing even to withdraw his candidacy for vice-president, the nomination having been made without his knowledge. He felt, nevertheless, that he should consult his friends, for, unlike Colonel Ramiro, he was no dictator and made no decisions without hearing and weighing the opinions of his partisans.

"I believe they will be agreeable. Have you spoken to the colonel yet?"

"I wanted to hear you first. I'm going to call on him this afternoon."

With Colonel Ramiro, the matter was more difficult. At first the old man remained adamant and declared angrily:

"He's an outsider, with no roots in the land. He doesn't own a single cacao tree."

"Neither do I, Colonel."

"With you it's different. You've been here more than fifteen years. You're an upright man, the head of a family. You didn't come here to make trouble, you didn't bring a married man here to make love to our daughters, you don't want to change everything as if nothing we've accomplished here is any good."

"Colonel, you know, sir, that I'm not a politician. I don't even vote. I want to live on good terms with everybody, and I deal with one side as well as with the other. But it is a fact that many things must be changed in Ilhéus; we're not living in the old days any more. As a matter of fact, who has brought about greater changes in Ilhéus than you yourself?"

Ramiro, whose anger had been nearing the point of explosion, was appeased by the businessman's rhetorical question.

"Yes, who has made greater changes in Ilhéus?" he echoed. "This place used to be the end of nowhere—run-down, dilapidated—you must remember how it was. Today there's not a town in the state equal to Ilhéus. Why don't they at least wait until I'm dead? I'm just a step from the grave. Why this ingratitude at the end of my life? What have I done wrong, in what way have I offended this Mr. Mundinho whom I hardly know?"

Now the colonel's voice grew tremulous, the voice of an old man.

"Don't think that I'm opposed to change. But why all this hurry, this desperate haste as if the world were coming to an end? There's time for everything." Now he was again the master of the land, the invincible Ramiro Bastos. "I'm not complaining. I'm a fighter and I'm not afraid. This Mr. Mundinho thinks Ilhéus began when he landed here. He wants to ignore everything that happened before, and nobody can do that. He's going to taste bitter defeat, he's going to pay dear for his impudence. First I'll beat him in the elections, then I'll run him out of Ilhéus. And nobody's going to stop me."

"I don't want to get mixed up in that, Colonel. All I want is to settle the matter of the Association. Why involve it in these disputes? After all, the Association is a thing apart: it has to do only with business, with commercial interests. If it becomes a political football, it will be ruined."

"What exactly is your proposition?"

Ataúlfo explained it while the colonel listened, resting his chin on his cane. There was still a trace of anger in his eyes.

"All right, then. I don't want them to say that I ruined the Association. And I think a lot of you. Don't worry, I'll explain it myself to Maluf. Both sides will be exactly the same—is that right?—none of this first and second vice-president business."

"Exactly equal, Colonel. Thank you, Colonel."

"Have you already spoken with this Mr. Mundinho?"

"Not yet. I wanted to hear you first. Now I'll go have a talk with him."

"He may not agree."

"If you, sir, agree, who is he to refuse?"

Colonel Ramiro smiled; he was still first.

Ataúlfo worked out the details of the division without serious difficulty, except that the Captain rebelled at the shift from official orator to librarian, the last office on the list. Ataúlfo argued that the Captain was already the official orator of the Thirteenth of May Euterpean Society and that poor Dr. Maurício was not the orator of any society. Besides, with the substantial budget that had been voted for the library, who but the Captain was sufficiently qualified to choose and purchase the books? The library was to be open to the entire population and would thus be, in effect, the public library of the city of Ilhéus, where both young and old could come to read and learn.

"You're just being kind. How about João Fulgêncio or the Doctor? They're scholars."

"But they're not candidates. The Doctor isn't even a member of the Association, and our good João never accepts appointments to office. You're really the only one. And, of course, no matter whom we elect official orator of the Association, your general recognition as the greatest orator in Ilhéus will certainly never be challenged."

And so Nacib found himself elected fourth secretary of the Commercial Association of Ilhéus and a member of a group that included such important men as Ataúlfo, Mundinho, Maluf, Pimenta the jeweler, Dr. Maurício, and the Captain. They were formally inducted into office at the inauguration of the new headquarters. The ceremonies, with a little champagne and a great

deal of rhetoric, took place in the afternoon in the big hall oc-
cupying the entire ground floor. This is where meetings and
lectures would be held and where the library was to be installed;
the business offices of the Association would be on the second
floor. Nacib had ordered a new suit especially for the occasion.
Wearing a flaming necktie, brightly shined shoes, and a solitaire
ring on his finger, he looked almost like a plantation colonel.

The ball was held in the evening, with a delicious and varied
buffet provided by Nacib. (Plínio Araçá told everybody that
Nacib had taken advantage of his office to charge an exorbitant
sum, but this was untrue.) Drinks of all kinds were served, except
rum. The chairs lined against the walls were filled with tittering
young women, waiting to be asked to dance. Upstairs, in the
brightly lit offices, ladies and gentlemen were munching Gabriela's confections and saying that such a distinguished affair was
unprecedented even in Bahia.

The orchestra from the Bataclan attacked some waltzes, tangos, fox trots, and military polkas. There was no dancing at the
cabaret that night. After all, weren't all the colonels, merchants,
exporters, young businessmen, doctors, and lawyers here at the
Association's ball? The cabaret was sleepily deserted, with one or
two women waiting about.

Old and young ladies whispered together at the dance downstairs. They discussed the dresses and jewels in great detail, gossiped about romantic attachments, and predicted engagements.
In the most beautiful gown of the evening, ordered from Bahia,
Malvina was the subject of lively and malicious comment. By
now everyone in town knew that the engineer was a married
man. To be sure, his wife was incurably insane and confined to a
hospital, but that did not alter the case: he had no right to look
at a single, marriageable girl. What had he to offer her except
dishonor? At the very least he would cause her to be gossiped
about and would kill her chances of ever getting married. They
were inseparable and danced every dance together: they did not
miss a waltz, polka, or fox trot. Rômulo danced the Argentine
tango even better than the deceased Osmundo. Malvina, her face
flushed, seemed wrapped in a dream as she floated lightly in the
engineer's athletic arms. A steady stream of whispers ran through

the row of chairs along the wall, up the staircase, and through the upstairs rooms. Dona Felícia, the mother of the ardent Iracema of front-gate rendezvous, forbade her daughter to be seen with Malvina.

Professor Josué mixed his drinks and talked loud, feigning indifference and gaiety. The sound of music spread across the square and through the window of the room where Gloria lay with Colonel Coriolano, who had attended the cermonies in the afternoon. He did not go to parties—they were for young people.

Mundinho Falcão went downstairs to the dance floor. Dona Felícia pinched Iracema and whispered:

"Mr. Mundinho is looking at you. He's coming to ask you to dance."

Mundinho was the best catch in Ilhéus: an exporter of cacao, a millionaire, a political leader, and a young bachelor.

"May I have the honor of dancing with your daughter?" Mundinho asked.

"With pleasure." Dona Felícia rose slightly from the chair and almost pushed the well-developed, languorous, and affected Iracema into the exporter's arms. He felt the pressure of the girl's breasts and thighs and gently drew her closer.

"You're the queen of the ball," he murmured.

Iracema pressed even closer.

"Poor little me," she said. "No one looks at me."

Dona Felícia sat smiling in her chair. Iracema would be graduated from the parochial school at the end of the year; it would soon be time for her to marry.

Colonel Ramiro Bastos had been represented at the afternoon formalities by his son Tonico. His other son, Dr. Alfredo, had to remain in Bahia at the session of the state legislature. In the evening Tonico escorted Dona Olga to the ball, her bulging body squeezed into a youthful pink dress. They brought their eldest niece, Jerusa, a blond girl with pale blue eyes and a mother-of-pearl complexion. Very restrained and respectable, Tonico did not even look at the other ladies but occupied himself solely in pushing around that mountain of flesh which God and Colonel Ramiro had given him as a wife.

Nacib was drinking champagne, not—as the spiteful Plínio

Araçá maintained—to increase the consumption of an expensive item but to forget his sufferings, to drive away the fear that gripped him, the dread that haunted him day and night. The number of Gabriela's admirers was increasing and they seemed to be closing in on her. They sent her messages, proposals, billets-doux. They offered dazzlingly high wages to the incomparable cook and a furnished house to the incomparable female.

Just a few days ago, when Nacib was feeling less downcast than usual because of his nomination as fourth secretary, a thing happened that showed him how brazen these people were getting. The wife of Mr. Grant, the manager of the railroad, went right to Nacib's house and tried to hire Gabriela. This Mr. Grant was an elderly Englishman, thin and silent, who had lived in Ilhéus since 1910. He was known and addressed simply as Mister. His wife, a tall blonde of free-and-easy and somewhat masculine manner, could not bear to live in Ilhéus and had moved to Bahia some years ago. Of her early days in the town there remained only the memory of her then extremely young figure and of a tennis court that her husband built for her on a piece of ground belonging to the railroad; after her departure it was invaded by weeds. In Bahia she gave big dinners at her house on Barra Avenue, drove an automobile, smoked cigarettes, and (it was rumored) received her lovers in broad daylight. Mister would not leave Ilhéus; he adored the good white rum made there, played poker dice, and unfailingly got drunk every Saturday at the Golden Nectar. On Sundays he went hunting somewhere nearby. He lived in a fine house, surrounded by gardens, with an Indian woman by whom he had a son. His wife came to Ilhéus two or three times a year and always brought presents for the Indian woman, who was grave and silent as an idol. When the boy was six years old, Mrs. Grant took him to Bahia, where she raised him as if he were her own son. On holidays the British flag waved on a flagpole in Mister's garden, for Grant was also Her Gracious Majesty's vice-consul.

His wife had arrived recently in Ilhéus. How did she learn about Gabriela? She ordered some appetizers and pastries from the bar; a few days later she climbed the steep street, knocked on the door of Nacib's house, and, when Gabriela appeared, slowly looked her over.

"You'll do very well."

She was an indecorous woman, of whom vile things were said: she drank like a man, she went to the beach half naked, she adored adolescents, mere boys; it was even whispered that she loved other women. She offered to take Gabriela to Bahia, pay her wages that were impossible in Ilhéus, dress her well, and give her Sundays off. What a nerve, to go right to his house and try to steal his cook!

And had not the Judge now begun strolling in front of Nacib's house, in the afternoons after court hours? How many others dreamed of installing Gabriela in a house and keeping her as a mistress? Some, financially less able, longed only for a night with Gabriela on the beach behind the rocks, a favorite haunt of amorous couples. Every day her admirers became more daring; many even whispered to her in the bar under Nacib's very nose. The sidewalk leading to Nacib's house became increasingly busy. Tonico had something new to tell him every afternoon, and Nhô-Galo warned him:

"The resistance of every woman, even the most faithful, has its limit."

Dona Arminda told him that Gabriela was a fool to refuse so many attractive offers.

"But you're not worried about losing her, are you, Mr. Nacib?"

Not worried! He thought of nothing else. He did not sleep well at night, and he spent his siesta time in the deck chair mulling over his fears. My God, he was even losing his appetite! At the party, while receiving congratulations, embraces, and pats on the back, he tried to drown his worries in champagne. But two questions gave him no peace: what did Gabriela really mean to him, and how far should he go to keep her? He sought the melancholy company of Josué. The professor, fairly drunk by now, was complaining:

"Why the hell don't they have rum at this shitty party!"

Where were his fine words, his rhymed verses?

Two guests caused sensations at the ball. One was Mundinho

Falcão. He soon tired of the easy Iracema (he was not one to steal kisses at front gates or to neck at movie matinees) and, looking about, noticed the blonde with the sky-blue eyes and mother-of-pearl skin.

"Who is she?" he asked.

"Colonel Ramiro's gıanddaughter, Jerusa. Dr. Alfredo's daughter."

Mundinho smiled. The girl, an adolescent beauty, was standing beside her uncle and Dona Olga. Mundinho waited until the music started up again, then went over and touched Tonico on the arm.

"Permit me to pay my respects to your wife and niece."

Tonico stammered out introductions, but soon regained his composure as a man of the world. They made conversation and then Mundinho turned to the girl.

"Do you care to dance?"

She replied with a smile and a nod. Their appearance together on the dance floor caused such excitement that certain couples got out of step turning to look. The whispering among the ladies increased, and people upstairs came down to see.

"So you're the ogre. You don't look like one."

Mundinho laughed.

"I'm a simple exporter of cacao."

It was the girl's turn to laugh, and they continued chatting.

The other sensation was Anabela. It had been João Fulgêncio's idea; he had never seen her dance, for he did not go to cabarets. At midnight, when the festivities were at their height, almost all the lights were extinguished and Ataúlfo Passos announced:

"The well-known artiste from Rio de Janeiro, the ballerina Anabela."

To the applause of the matrons and young women, Anabela danced with her plumes and her veils. Ribeirinho, standing beside his wife, felt triumphant. The men present knew that Anabela's slim body belonged to him, and that for him she danced with neither tights nor plumes nor veils.

The Doctor solemnly affirmed:

"Ilhéus is taking giant strides in the direction of civilization.

Until a few months ago, Art was banned from the salons and
relegated to the gutters. This reincarnation of Terpsichore
could be seen only in the cabarets."

The Commercial Association had rescued Art from the gutter
and introduced it to the best families in Ilhéus. The applause
was deafening.

OF THE OLD WAYS

Mundinho Falcão finally kept his promise and went on a visit
to Colonel Altino's plantation. Not the Saturday previously
agreed on, but a month later and at the insistence of the Captain.
If Altino was won over, the Captain maintained, it would be easy
to get the support of several other planters who had been on the
fence since the engineering studies of the sandbar began.

Undoubtedly the arrival of the engineer—a defeat for the state
government—weighed heavily in Mundinho's favor. Hence the
violent reaction of the Bastoses that resulted in the burning of an
edition of the *Ilhéus Daily*. In the days that followed, a number
of colonels called at the exporter's office to join with Mundinho
and to pledge him their votes. The Captain jotted down figures
and kept a record of the number of votes they could count on.
In view of the political practices of the time, he knew that a close
victory would do them no good. Without a large majority of the
votes, the men they elected as mayor, councilmen, and state and
federal legislators would not be officially recognized. Even with
such a majority, recognition might be difficult to obtain; in this
contingency the Captain relied on Mundinho's friendships in
Rio and on the prestige of the Mendes Falcão family. But they
would have to win by a wide margin, otherwise nothing would be
gained.

Certain groups in Ilhéus were going over more and more to
Mundinho's side. People were alarmed by the burning of the
newspaper. As long as the Bastoses remained in control, they

said, there would always be rule by force and intimidation. But the Captain knew that these merchants, these young men in stores and warehouses, these dock workers, could not swing an election. The important men for this purpose were the colonels, especially the owners of the very large plantations. They were known and respected by everyone; they had, indeed, godfathered the children of half the citizens. They completely controlled the votes and the electoral machinery in their respective districts.

Colonel Altino Brandão's house in Rio do Braço stood near the railroad station. It had a veranda on every side, vines climbing up its walls, a flower garden in front, and fruit trees in the back yard. Mundinho looked at the house with great interest: perhaps the Captain was right in characterizing the colonel as a rare type in Ilhéus—an open-minded man. The tradition of the great manor house, developed in the old days when sugar was king, had not carried over into the era of cacao. The houses of the cacao colonels often lacked the most rudimentary comforts. Some of them were built on stilts, with the pigs sleeping underneath, and those that were on the ground had the pigsty nearby as protection against the large number of deadly poisonous snakes. The pigs, shielded against the poison by their layers of fat, would kill the snakes. The days of violence had left behind a certain austere mode of living. In the towns of Ilhéus and Itabuna, however, this austerity was beginning to disappear: the colonels were building fine houses, some of them real mansions. The pressure on the colonels to live more graciously came chiefly from their sons, college students in Bahia.

"You do us a great honor," said the colonel. In the parlor he introduced Mundinho to his wife. Colored pictures of the couple when they were young hung on the walls.

Afterwards the colonel took him to a luxurious guest room, with a hair mattress, linen sheets, an embroidered bedspread, and a fragrance of lavender incense.

"If it's all right with you, I suggest we get on our horses right after lunch so you'll have a chance to see some of the work going on. We'll spend the night at Águas Claras, go for a swim in the river in the morning, and then ride around the plantation.

We can have a lunch of game of some kind and get back here in time for dinner."

"Splendid. I'd enjoy that very much."

Colonel Altino's Águas Claras plantation, an immense tract of land, was situated about two miles from the village. He also owned a more distant plantation, on which there were still areas of forest to be cleared.

The dishes followed one after another: fish from the river, various kinds of fowl, beef, lamb, and pork. These lunches *en famille* were virtually the same as the dinners served for guests on Sundays.

That afternoon Mundinho watched the workers harvest the cacao. In the evening he and the colonel sat talking by the light of kerosene lamps. Altino told stories about the old days. Some of the workers, seated on the ground nearby, shared in the conversation and recalled details. Altino pointed to a Negro.

"This fellow has been with me about twenty-five years. He showed up here as a fugitive—he'd been a killer for the Badaróses. If he had to serve a year in jail for every man he killed, his whole life wouldn't be long enough."

The Negro smiled, showing his white teeth. He was chewing tobacco. His hands were horny, and his feet were covered with a crust of dried cacao pulp.

"What's the young man goin' to think of me, Colonel?"

Mundinho wanted to talk politics and try to win the rich planter to his cause. But Altino avoided the subject, except for a reference, during the lunch at Rio do Braço, to the burning of the edition of the *Ilhéus Daily:*

"Very bad. That was the sort of thing they did in times that have passed, thank God. Amâncio is an upright man but violent as the devil. I don't understand how he's still alive. He was wounded three times; he lost an eye, and one arm became useless. But he won't change. Melk Tavares, too, was a man you couldn't fool with, to say nothing of Jesuíno, poor fellow. Anybody may find himself in a spot where he has to kill someone. Jesuíno had no alternative. But I see no excuse for the burning of newspapers. Very bad."

He picked some bones out of the fish.

"But, if you'll permit me to say so, you too acted badly."

"Why? Because the newspaper used strong language? You don't win a political campaign by praising your adversaries."

"Your paper hits hard, no question about that. Some of the damnedest articles—it's a pleasure to read them. I heard that the Doctor writes them. That fellow has more brains than all the rest of Ilhéus put together. A real intelligent little man. I like to listen to him talk; he reminds me of a robin. You're right about what you said. What's a newspaper for? To go after the enemy and lay him low. You're absolutely right. I even took out a subscription. But that isn't what I'm talking about."

"What, then?"

"Mr. Mundinho, it was wrong of them to burn the newspapers. I don't approve of that at all. But as long as they did it, right or wrong, you had no choice. Like Jesuíno. Did he want to kill his wife? He did not. But because she put horns on him, he had to kill her; otherwise he would have been no better than a capon or an ox. Why didn't you burn down their newspaper— not the newspapers themselves but the building, why didn't you wreck their press? Excuse me, but that's what you should have done; otherwise people will say that you're a nice fellow and so on, but to govern Ilhéus and Itabuna you have to be tough and fight back."

"Colonel, I'm not a coward, believe me. But as you yourself said, these methods belong to the past. It was exactly in order to change them, to get rid of them, to make Ilhéus a civilized place, that I entered politics. And besides, I have no hired henchmen."

"Well, so far as that's concerned, you have friends you can count on, like Ribeirinho. I myself lined up a few men. I thought: who knows, Mr. Mundinho might want to borrow them."

Nothing more was said about politics. Mundinho did not know what to think. He had the impression that the colonel was treating him as a child, that he was playing with him. That night at the plantation, Mundinho tried to steer the conversation toward politics, but Altino did not respond; all he talked about was cacao. They returned to Rio do Braço the next day after a delicious lunch of several kinds of game—agouti, paca, venison, and another, the most savory of all; Mundinho learned afterwards that it was kinkajou. Dinner that evening, back at the house, was a big affair attended by planters, merchants, the local doctor, the pharmacist, the priest, and everyone else of any importance. Altino had sent for concertina and guitar players and for singers of improvisations. One of them, a blind man, was a marvelous rhymester. At one point the pharmacist asked Mundinho how things were going politically. Without giving him time to reply, Altino said brusquely:

"Mr. Mundinho came here to visit, not to discuss politics." And he changed the subject.

On Monday the exporter returned to Ilhéus. What the devil did Colonel Altino Brandão want? Of his own accord, he had come to him instead of to Stevenson to sell his cacao—twenty thousand arrobas, an excellent piece of business for Mundinho. The colonel was not committed to the Bastoses, yet he did not want to talk politics. The only political suggestion the old man made was utterly absurd: to set fire to buildings, wreck machinery, perhaps even kill people.

"He's not altogether wrong," said the Captain. "That Bastos crowd need a good lesson, something to show them they can't push people around any more. I've thought about it; I even discussed it with Ribeirinho."

"Careful, Captain. Let's not do anything foolish. Our reply to their violence will be the tugs and dredges for the sandbar."

"By the way, when is that engineer of yours going to finish the studies and send for the dredges? I never saw so much delay."

"It's not an easy job. He works at it every day all day long. It can't go any faster."

"He works day and night," said the Captain. "On the sandbar during the day and at Melk Tavares's front gate at night. I'm afraid he's fallen for the colonel's daughter. And vice versa."

"The young man has to have some diversion."

About a week after his visit to Rio do Braço, as Mundinho was leaving a directors' meeting at the Progress Club, he caught sight of Colonel Altino approaching Ramiro Bastos's house. At the window he saw Jerusa. Mundinho lifted his hat and she waved at him. This showed a certain tolerance on her part, or perhaps a sense of humor; for, on the night before, Mundinho's friend Ribeirinho had run one of Bastos's henchmen—an employee of the municipal government—out of Guaraci, a small village near his plantation. The man had been badly beaten, stripped, and obliged to start down the road to Ilhéus naked and on foot. On the way, he obtained some clothing intended for a man twice his size, which he was wearing when he arrived in town.

OF A BIRD'S SAD SONG

Nacib was at his wits' end. Gone were his peace of mind, his happiness, his joy of living. His fat cheeks had lost their jovial look, and he had stopped curling the ends of his mustache, which now drooped over unsmiling lips. All he did was think, think, think—which is certain to get a man down, rob him of his sleep and appetite, cause him to lose weight, and leave him dispirited and melancholy.

Tonico Bastos leaned on the counter and poured himself a dram of bitters. He contemplated ironically the proprietor's gloomy face.

"You look awful, Arab. You're wasting away."

Nacib nodded his head in doleful agreement. His big, staring eyes rested on the elegant notary. His regard for Tonico had been increasing lately. Their friendship had always been somewhat casual: they had merely gone to the cabaret, talked about prostitutes, and had drinks together. But recently a deeper intimacy had developed between them. Of all the daily customers at the apéritif hour, Tonico was the only one who kept his decorum when Gabriela arrived with Nacib's lunch pot and a flower behind her ear. He merely greeted her politely, inquired about her health, and praised her incomparable seasoning. No meaningful glances, no whispered words; he did not even try to hold her hand. He treated her as a lady, beautiful and desirable but unattainable. When Nacib began to sleep with Gabriela, he had feared no one else's competition as much as Tonico's. Was he not the great seducer, the lady-killer?

The world is like that—incomprehensible and full of surprises. Tonico maintained the greatest discretion and respect in the exciting presence of Gabriela. Everybody knew about the relations between the Arab and his servant. But officially she was only his cook, there was no other commitment between them; and so everyone felt free, even in Nacib's presence, to deluge her with sweet talk and to slip little notes into her hand. At first he had read them unheedful, crumpled them, and thrown them away. Now he tore them up angrily; there were so many, and some were even indecent. But Tonico was different from the others. He gave Nacib proof of his true friendship by respecting Gabriela as if she were a married woman, a colonel's wife. And he showed him this consideration even though Nacib never threatened him as Colonel Coriolano had done. Tonico was the only one against whom he had no complaint and to whom he could unburden his aching heart.

"The worst thing in the world is not to know what to do."

"What's the trouble?"

"Can't you see? The other day I even forgot to pay a note when it fell due, so you can see the state I'm in."

"Passion is no trifling matter."

"Passion?"

"Isn't that what it is? Love—the most wonderful and most terrible thing in the world."

Passion. Love. He had been struggling for days against those words, especially during the siesta hour. He was unwilling to measure the depth of his feelings or to accept the reality of the situation. He thought it was only an infatuation, a little more intense and durable than the previous ones. But he had never suffered so much during an infatuation nor experienced such jealousy, such fear, this dread of losing her. It was not the fear of being left without the famous cook in whose magic hands now rested a large part of the bar's prosperity. He did not even think of that any more. His fear derived rather from his inability to imagine a single night without Gabriela and the warmth of her body. Even during her menstrual periods they would lie in her bed and she would rest her head on his chest, the spice of clove filling his nostrils. Those were restless hours of desire contained and stored, to be released on veritable wedding nights, renewed each month. My God, if this was not love, what was it? And if this was love, if life had become impossible without her, what then? "The resistance of every woman, even the most faithful, has its limit." Nhô-Galo, a man of good counsel, had said this. He was another real friend. Not quite so decorous as Tonico, for he sometimes stared long and suppliantly at Gabriela. But he never went beyond that.

"You're right, Tonico, that's what it is. I can't live without her. If she leaves me, I'll go crazy."

"What are you going to do about it?"

"I don't know." Nacib looked utterly miserable. Neither man spoke for a moment.

"Why don't you marry her?" said Tonico suddenly, as if he had divined his friend's innermost, unconfessed thought.

"Are you serious? That's nothing to joke about."

Tonico rose, told him to put the drinks on his bill, and flipped a coin to Lazy Chico, who caught it in the air.

"Well, if I were you that's what I would do."

In the empty bar, Nacib sat thinking. The time was long past when he would go to her room just for a change from Risoleta and the other women; when, as payment, he occasionally gave her a cheap brooch or a rhinestone ring. Now he brought her presents once or twice a week—dress goods, perfume, scarfs, caramels from his bar. But how could these gifts compete with offers of furnished houses, of a life of luxury like Gloria's, a life in which she could buy anything she wanted at the stores and would be better dressed than many a woman with a rich husband! He had to offer her something better, something bigger, something that would dwarf the offers of the Judge and of Manuel of the Jaguars—and now of Ribeirinho, too. For Anabela had left Ilhéus; the place frightened her. She made her decision when she heard about the beating of the municipal employee, which involved Ribeirinho and perhaps foreshadowed a period of violence and danger. She stealthily packed her things, secretly bought a ticket on a Bahiana Line ship, and said goodbye to no one but Mundinho. She went to his house the night before the sailing, and he gave her a conto as a parting gift. Ribeirinho was in the country and learned of her departure only upon his return. He had given her more than twenty contos worth of jewelry, including a diamond ring and a gold locket. Tonico commented in the bar:

"We were left widowers, Ribeirinho and I. Anyway, it's about time Mundinho found someone else for us."

Ribeirinho turned to Gabriela; he had a house all ready, she had only to say yes. He would also give her a diamond ring and a gold locket. Nacib learned of all this from Dona Arminda, who couldn't say enough in praise of Gabriela.

"I never saw anyone so loyal. To resist an offer like that, you really have to love somebody more than yourself. Any other girl, and she'd be gone already, lolling in luxury like a princess."

He had no doubt about Gabriela's feelings toward him. Hadn't she rejected all the offers as if they meant nothing to her? She laughed at them. When someone took her hand or chucked her under the chin, she just smiled and went about her business. She did not hand back their notes, she was not rude, she thanked them for their compliments, but she gave them no encouragement whatever. She never complained, she never asked him for anything. She accepted his gifts, clapping her hands joyfully. And did she not die in his arms every night, ardent, insatiable, calling him "beautiful man" and saying that he was her "ruination"?

"If I were you, that's what I would do." Easy to say when you weren't faced with the problem yourself. But how could he marry a cook picked up at the slave market, a mulatto, without family, without her maidenhead! Marriage was supposed to be with a gifted young lady of good upbringing, respectable family background, and carefully preserved virginity, a girl with a fine trousseau. His uncle, his prim aunt, his sister, his engineer-agronomist brother-in-law—what would they say? What would his rich relatives, the Aschars, big landowners and people of importance in Itabuna, say? And his friends in the bar—Mundinho Falcão, Amâncio Leal, Melk Tavares, the Doctor, the Captain, Dr. Maurício, Dr. Ezequiel? What would everybody in town say? It was an absurdity, something not even to be thought about. Nevertheless, he thought about it.

A man from the country came into the bar, selling birds. In one cage a beautiful, restless black-and-yellow bird whistled a sad, tender song. It was a kind of oriole, called a sofrê * because the first notes of its song suggest the sound of that word. Lazy Chico and Eaglebeak listened to it ecstatically.

One thing he was going to do for sure—put an end to Gabriela's midday trips to the bar. Would it result in loss of business? Too bad. He might lose money, but it would be worse to lose her. Her intoxicating presence was a daily temptation to the men. How could they keep from wanting her, desiring her, sighing for her after she left? Nacib could feel her at the tips of his fingers, in his drooping mustache, in the skin of his thighs, in the soles of his feet. The sofrê seemed to be singing to him, so sad was its song. Why not take it home to Gabriela? Now that she was to be forbidden to come to the bar, she would need other distractions.

He bought the sofrê. He could no longer think straight, he could no longer bear such suffering.

GABRIELA AND A BIRD IN A CAGE

"Oh, how beautiful!" exclaimed Gabriela.

Nacib placed the cage on a chair. The bird was beating against the bars.

"For you—to keep you company."

He sat down and Gabriela curled up on the floor at his feet. She took his big hairy hand and kissed the palm of it. Nacib

---

* A popular pronunciation of *sofrer* (to suffer).

wondered why this gesture reminded him of the land of his fathers, the hills of Syria. Then she leaned her head against his knee and he stroked her hair. The bird had calmed down. It began to sing.

"Two presents at the same time. Such a kind man!"

"Two?"

"The bird and something even nicer: you came home with it. Usually you only come at night."

And he was going to lose her. "The resistance of every woman, even the most faithful, has its limit." Nhô-Galo had meant, of course, that every woman had her price. Nacib's despondence showed in his face, and Gabriela, who had looked up at him as she spoke, noticed it.

"Mr. Nacib is feeling sad. Didn't use to be that way. He used to be happy, smiling. Now he's sad. Why?"

What could he say? That he did not know how to hold her, to tie her to himself forever?

"I have something to say to you."

"Yes, Mr. Nacib."

"There's something I don't like. It's bothering me."

She was alarmed.

"Is the food bad? Didn't I iron your shirts right?"

"Nothing like that. It's something else."

"Then what is it?"

"Your trips to the bar. I don't like them, they don't please me."

Gabriela's eyes opened wide.

"But I go to help, and so your lunch won't get cold. That's why I go."

"I know. But the others don't."

"I see. I never thought about that. It's not nice for me to be in the bar, is it? The others don't like it—a cook in the bar. I didn't think about that."

He seized the opportunity:

"Yes, that's it. Some don't care, but others complain."

Gabriela's eyes turned sad. The sofrê's throat was about to burst, its song was heart-rending.

"What harm did I do?"

Why make her suffer so, why not tell her the truth, tell her of

his jealousy, cry out his love? Why not call her Bié, the affection-
ate nickname that he always gave her in his thoughts?

"Beginnin' tomorrow here's what I'll do: I'll go in the back
way and just serve your lunch. Hardly anybody'll see me."

Why not? In this way he could continue to have her near him
at noon, to feel her hand, her leg, her breast. And wouldn't her
half-concealment put an end to the tempting offers, the honeyed
words?

"Do you like to go to the bar?"

She nodded. How she enjoyed it!—walking in the sunlight with
the pot in her hand, threading her way among the tables, hearing
the remarks, feeling the eyes fixed intently upon her. But not the
old men. Not the colonels' offers of furnished houses. She loved
to feel herself gazed upon, played up to, desired. It was a kind of
preparation for the night: it left her enveloped in an aura of
desire, and in Nacib's arms she would see again all the beautiful
young men—Mr. Tonico, Mr. Josué, Mr. Ari, Mr. Epaminondas
(a store clerk). Could one of them have made the complaint to
Nacib about her? She thought not. It was one of those ugly old
men, no doubt, to spite her for not paying any attention to him.

"All right, you can go. But not to wait on me at the table. You
can remain seated behind the counter."

She would have their glances, anyway, and their smiles; some
would probably come to the counter to speak to her.

"I have to go back," announced Nacib.

"So soon?"

"I shouldn't have come at all."

Gabriela threw her arms around his legs, holding him back. He
had never had her in the daytime, it had always been at night. He
wanted to rise, but she held him, silent and grateful.

"Come here. Yes, right here."

He drew her after him. It would be the first time he had
possessed her in his bedroom, in his own bed, as if she were his
wife and not his cook. When he had pulled off her cotton dress
and her nude body lay invitingly on the bed—her shapely buttocks, her firm breasts—and when she had held his head in her
hands and kissed his eyes, he asked her, for the first time:

"Tell me something: are you very fond of me?"

She laughed in tune with the bird's trill.

"I like you too much."

He had hurt her with that business about going to the bar. Why make her suffer, why not tell her the truth?

"Nobody complained about your going to the bar. I'm the one who doesn't want you to go. That's why I was sad. Everybody talks to you, they make fresh remarks, they hold your hand. They do everything but grab you and throw you on the floor."

She laughed.

"It don't mean anything. I'm not interested in them."

"You aren't? Really?"

Gabriela pulled him toward her, burying his head in her breasts. Nacib murmured: "Bié . . ." And in his language of love, which was Arabic, he said while possessing her: "From now on, you are Bié and this is your bed, here you will sleep. You are not a cook although you cook. You are the woman of this house, the rays of the sun, the light of the moon, the song of birds. Your name is Bié."

"Is Bié a foreign name? Call me Bié, talk to me some more in that language. I like to hear it."

When Nacib had left, she sat in the chair by the bird cage. Mr. Nacib was good, she thought, and he was jealous. She laughed and stuck her finger between the wires of the cage. The frightened bird tried to escape. He was jealous—how silly! She wasn't: if he wanted to lie with another woman, he could. At first he had done so, she knew. He lay with her and with others. She didn't mind. He could go to them if he wanted to. Not to stay, just to lie with them. But Mr. Nacib was jealous. What harm was there if Mr. Josué touched her hand? Or if Mr. Tonico tried to kiss the back of her neck when Mr. Nacib wasn't looking? Or if Mr. Epaminondas tried to date her, or if Mr. Ari gave her candy and took her by the chin? She slept with all of them every night—with them and with those who had come before, except her uncle—as she lay in Nacib's arms. First with one, then with another; most of the time with the boy Bebinho and Mr. Tonico. It was so nice.

And it was so nice to go to the bar, to pass among the men. Life was good, one had only to live it. To warm oneself in the sun, then take a cold bath; to eat guavas and mangoes, to chew peppercorn, to walk through the streets, to sing songs, to sleep with a young man. And to dream of another.

Bié. She liked the name. Mr. Nacib was so big and he could talk a foreign language, but he called her Bié and he was jealous. Funny. She didn't want to hurt him, he was so good. She would be very careful. But when a man got jealous, almost anything could offend him. She might have to stay in the house and never hear men say things to her, or laugh with them, or see the glint she inspired in their eyes. "Please don't ask me to, Mr. Nacib, I couldn't."

The bird was beating against the bars. How many days had it been in there? Not many, certainly, for it was not yet used to it. Who can get used to living in prison, anyway? She was fond of animals and befriended them easily. Cats, dogs, even chickens. In the country she had owned a parrot that could talk; it died of starvation in the drought. She had never wanted a bird in a cage. She felt sorry for the sofrê. She had not said so, in order not to offend Nacib. Its song was so sad, Mr. Nacib was so sad. She did not want to hurt him, she would be very careful: she would say the bird had escaped.

She went to the back yard. Under the guava tree, where the cat was sleeping, she opened the cage. The bird flew out, paused on a branch, and sang for her. What a clear, happy song! Gabriela smiled. The cat woke up.

OF HIGH-BACKED CHAIRS

Heavy, black-leather, high-backed Austrian chairs. They seemed to have been placed there to be seen and admired but not to be sat on. They would have intimidated almost anyone but Colonel Altino. As he looked about, he thought how much he liked this room. The colored portraits on the wall reminded him of those in his own house; there was one of Colonel Ramiro and one of his deceased wife, with a mirror between them. In one corner, a niche with statuettes of saints and, instead of candles, tiny electric lights, blue, green, red. On another wall, small Japanese bamboo mats holding post cards, prints, and pictures of relatives. At the end of the room, a piano covered with a black shawl on which scarlet branches and leaves were embroidered.

When Altino had greeted Jerusa from the sidewalk and had asked if Colonel Ramiro Bastos was at home and could grant him a few minutes, the girl had asked him to step inside. As he stood in the entrance hall which separated the two front rooms, he could hear sounds of activity in one of the rooms—the drawing of window bolts, the removal of chair covers, and the swishing of brooms and dusters. This room was opened only on special occasions, such as the colonel's birthday, the inauguration of a new mayor, or a reception for important politicians from Bahia. Or a visit by a rarely seen but highly esteemed friend.

The door opened and Jerusa appeared.

"Won't you come in, Colonel?"

He had seldom visited Ramiro Bastos's house, and now once again he was admiring the luxurious room, unmistakable evidence of the colonel's wealth and power.

"Grandpa will be right here." Jerusa smiled and left the room with a nod of her head. "What a beautiful girl," he thought. "She is so blond she looks like a foreigner. Her skin is so white it has a bluish cast. That Mundinho is a fool. Why all this fighting when everything could be so easily settled?"

He heard Ramiro's slow footsteps and sat down.

"Well, look who's here! Is this a miracle of some kind?"

They shook hands. Altino was struck by the change in the old man's appearance since he had last seen him. Then, only a few months earlier, he had been a tree trunk of a man, untouched by age, indifferent to storm and wind, planted in Ilhéus to rule forever. Of that strength and firmness he had retained only the dominating look in his eyes. His hands shook slightly, his shoulders were bowed, his step was unsteady.

"You look stronger than ever," said Altino.

"Drawing strength from my weakness. Let us sit down."

Altino sat in one of the straight, high-backed chairs. It might be handsome, but it was uncomfortable. He preferred the deep, soft, blue-leather chairs in Mundinho's office, so comfortable that you just sank in them and wanted to stay there.

"Excuse me for asking, but how old are you now?"

"Eighty-three, I think."

"A beautiful age. May God grant you many more years, Colonel."

"In my family we die late. My grandfather lived to eighty-nine. My father, to ninety-two."

"I remember him."

Jerusa entered the room bearing a tray with small cups of coffee.

"Your granddaughters are becoming young ladies."

"I married late in life, and so did Alfredo and Tonico. Other-wise I would already have great-grandchildren. I might even have great-great-grandchildren."

"I don't think you'll have to wait very long for great-grand-children. Not with such a pretty granddaughter."

"Perhaps not."

Jerusa returned to remove the cups and said:

"Grandpa, Uncle Tonico is here and wants to know if he can come in."

Ramiro looked at Altino.

"What do you say, Colonel? Is your business private?"

"Not for Mr. Tonico, no—he's your son."

"Tell him to come in."

Tonico appeared, wearing a vest and spats. Altino stood up and was enveloped in a cordial embrace. A popinjay, thought the planter.

"Well, Colonel, it makes me very happy to see you in this house. You hardly ever come around."

"I'm only happy in the country. I never leave Rio do Braço and Águas Claras except when I have to."

"What a crop this year, eh, Colonel?"

"God be praised. I never saw so much cacao. Well, I came to Ilhéus and I said to myself: 'I'm going to call on Colonel Ramiro. To talk over some things I've been thinking about.' In the eve-nings out in the country we have plenty of time to think things over. You know how it is, you get something on your mind and then you want to talk about it."

"I'm all ears, Colonel."

"You know that when it came to politics, I never wanted to get involved. Only once, and that was because I had to. You remember, when Mr. Firmo was mayor. They wanted to run things in Rio do Braço."

Ramiro remembered the incident: the Rio do Braço police deputy, one of his men, had fired his first assistant, a protégé of Altino's, and replaced him with an officer of the military police. Altino came to Ramiro's house in Ilhéus to complain. This was about twelve years ago. He wanted the officer removed and his own man reinstated. Ramiro agreed; the police deputy had made the change without his knowledge while he was in Bahia serving in the Senate.

"I'll recall the officer," he promised.

"You don't have to; he came back to Ilhéus on the same train that took him. Seems he was afraid to stay there. I don't exactly know why. I heard that some of the fellows had a little fun with him. I don't think he'll want to go back there. He knows now that authority without the force to back it up is worthless. All you need to do is cancel his appointment and reinstate my man."

And that is what was done. Ramiro recalled the unpleasant conversation. Altino had threatened to break with him and to give his support to the opposition. What did he want this time?

"Well, here I am again. Maybe I'm butting into other people's business. Nobody asked me to come here and preach a sermon. But out in the country I keep thinking about what's going on in Ilhéus. Even when a man doesn't interfere with things, they may interfere with him. Because, in the last analysis, the people who pay the costs of politics are the planters themselves."

"What do you think of the situation?"

"I think it's bad. You've always been respected, you've been the political chief for many years, and you deserve it. Nobody can deny that."

"Somebody is denying it. Not one of our own people. An outsider. He showed up in Ilhéus one day, nobody knows why. His brothers, who are men of integrity, kicked him out of their firm;

they never want to see him again. He has come here and divided those who were united, separated those who were working together. I can understand why the Captain is against me: I defeated his father and threw him out of office. The Captain's opposition to me, therefore, is justified, and for that reason I've always been friendly toward him and I hold him in esteem. But this Mr. Mundinho has no such justification; he should be content with making money here. Why does he want to interfere in politics?"

Altino lit a corn-husk cigarette and studied the electric lighting of the niche.

"Fine illumination. We have some images of saints at home—my wife's idea. We spend a fortune on candles. I'm going to have lights installed like yours. Ilhéus is a land of outsiders, Colonel. The old natives here are just a lot of riffraff—except the Doctor, of course, he's a learned man. We are the real Ilhéans, Colonel, and not one of us was born here. We're all immigrants. When we first arrived here, couldn't the natives have called us just a bunch of outsiders?"

"I don't mean to offend you. I know you sold him your cacao. I didn't know you were friends, and that is why I spoke out. But I don't take it back. What I said is said. His case is completely different from ours. We came here when there was nothing. It was different. How many times did we risk our lives and come close to losing them? Worse than that: how many times did we have to order that other men's lives be taken? Doesn't all that mean anything? Don't compare yourself with him, Colonel, and don't compare me with him either." By sheer will power the aged man spoke in a firm, strong voice, without tremor or faltering. "When did he ever risk his life? He landed here with money and set up an office. He buys and ships cacao. What lives did he take? Where did he get the right to rule here? The right is ours —we won it."

"That's right, Colonel. Everything you've said is right so far as it goes. But it's right by the conditions and needs of an earlier time. We spend our lives working hard, and we don't realize that time is going by and that things are changing. Suddenly we open our eyes and everything is different."

Tonico sat listening. He was alarmed and almost sorry he had entered the room. Out in the hall, Jerusa was giving orders to the servants.

"Where is the difference? I don't understand what you mean."

"I'm going to tell you. It used to be easy to rule. All you needed was force. Today everything has changed. We won control, as you said, by spilling blood. We had to win control in order to get possession of the land and keep it. But we've finished that job. Everything has grown. Itabuna is almost as big as Ilhéus. Pirangi, Água Preta, Macuco, Guaraci are becoming big towns. The region is filled with professional men: agronomists, doctors, lawyers. Everybody wants to get ahead, everybody wants to change things. I wonder if we know how to run this new world."

"And why is it like that—so many doctors, so much progress? Who did it? It was you, Colonel, and your humble servant. It was no outsider. And now, after we've done it all, by what right do they turn against us?"

"We plant cacao seedlings, nurse them into trees, gather and split the pods, collect the seeds in baskets, dry them in pans and ovens, load them on the backs of mules, take them to Ilhéus, and sell them to the exporters. The cacao is dry and fragrant, the best in the world. We did it. But can we make chocolate, do we know how? We had to bring Mr. Hugo Kaufmann from Europe. Whatever Ilhéus has, whatever Ilhéus is worth, is all due to you. God forbid that I should deny it; I'm the first to recognize it. But you've already done all you know how to do—all you can do."

"What does Ilhéus want beyond what we're giving it? What more is there to do? To tell the truth, I don't see these new needs."

"Let me show them to you. Ilhéus is pretty as a garden; but what about Pirangi, Rio do Braço, Água Preta? We opened trails with our gunmen. Now we need roads. They can't be built by gunmen. The worst thing of all is the harbor. Why have you taken a stand against removal of the sandbar, Colonel Ramiro? Because the Governor asked you to? The people are clamoring for it. It would be a great thing for this region if the cacao were shipped from here direct to the whole world, so we wouldn't have to pay shipping costs to Bahia any more. Who pays these costs? The exporters and the planters."

"We have obligations. Each one lives up to his own. Because if he doesn't, he loses respect. I have always lived up to mine, as you well know. The Governor explained the matter to me and I gave my word. Our children will build the port later, beyond the sandbar, up at Malhado. Everything in its own time."

"The time has come, but you don't want to accept the fact. In our days life was different, customs were different. There are so many new things, motion pictures and all, a man hardly knows which way to turn. In the old days, all we had to do to rule was to give orders and fulfill our commitments to the state government. Today that's not enough. You keep your word to the Governor, he's your friend, but that doesn't earn you greater respect. The people aren't interested in that. They want a government that will attend to their needs. Why does Mundinho win so many people to his side?"

"Why? Because he buys supporters, he promises them everything. And there are always scum who go back on their obligations."

"Excuse me, Colonel, but that's not it. What can he promise a man that you can't? A place on the ticket, influence, appointments, prestige? No, Colonel. What he is offering to do and actually doing is to govern in accordance with the times."

"Govern, did you say? When did he win an election?"

"He doesn't have to win one. He built the avenue along the beach, he founded a daily newspaper, he helped to buy the buses, he brought a branch bank from Rio and an engineer for the sandbar. What is all that, if not to govern? You control the Mayor, the Chief of Police, and the officials in the villages. But the man who is really running things, and has been for some time now, is Mundinho Falcão. That's why I came here, because a place can't have two governments. I left my little corner of the world to come and have a talk with you. If things go on this way, there'll be trouble. In fact, it's already begun: you ordered the newspapers to be burned, and one of your men in Guaraci was almost killed. This would have been all right in the old days; it would have been the only way. But nowadays it's all wrong. That's why I came and knocked on your door."

"To tell me what, exactly?"

"That there's only one way out of this situation. At least I see only one."

"What is it? Tell me." The colonel's voice was harsh. They seemed almost like two enemies facing each other.

"Colonel, I've been voting for you and your people for twenty years. I've never asked you for anything. Once only I made a complaint, and I was right. I come here as a friend."

"And I thank you. You may speak as a friend."

"There's only one way—and that is to come to an agreement with him."

"Me? With this newcomer? You know me better than that, Colonel. I never compromised even when I was young and my life was at stake. I'm not going to begin now. I don't want to hear any more about it."

But Tonico intervened. The idea of a compromise sounded good to him. A few days before, Mundinho had visited Altino's plantation. The proposal had undoubtedly originated with him.

"Let the Colonel talk, Father. He came as a friend and you should listen. Whether you accept or not is something else."

"Why don't you take over the sandbar operation? Why don't you invite Mundinho into your party? Why don't you work together with him in everything, with you at the head? No one in Ilhéus wishes you harm. Not even the Captain. But if you follow the course you've chosen so far, you'll lose."

"Have you some concrete proposal, Colonel?" Tonico asked.

"No. A proposal would have to come from Mr. Mundinho, and I didn't even discuss politics with him. I only told him that I saw just one way out: an agreement between both sides."

"And he, what did he say?" asked Tonico.

"He didn't say anything and I didn't press the matter. But if Colonel Ramiro wants to reach an agreement with him, think of the position Mundinho would be in if he didn't accept. If the Colonel extends his hand, how can Mundinho refuse it?"

"You know, I think you may be right." Tonico moved his heavy chair closer to Altino.

Colonel Ramiro's angry voice cut short the dialogue:

"Colonel Altino Brandão, if that is all that brought you here, your visit is ended."

"Father! What are you saying!"

"And you, shut up. If you want my blessing, Tonico, don't even think of a compromise. Colonel, excuse me, I have no wish to offend you, I've always got along well with you. You're the master in this house the same as in your own. Let's discuss other matters, if you wish. But not a compromise. Listen to what I tell you: I may be left alone, even my sons may abandon me and join this outsider. I may be left without a single friend—or with one only, for I'm sure Amâncio won't abandon me—but I won't ever compromise. No one else is going to rule Ilhéus. What was good enough yesterday is good enough today. Even if I have to die with my gun in my hand. Even if I have to order killings once again, God forgive me. There'll be an election a year from now and I'm going to win it, Colonel, even if the whole world turns against me, even if Ilhéus has to become again a land of bandits and killers." He raised his tremulous voice as he stood up: "I'm going to win!"

Altino also rose and took his hat.

"I came with peaceful intentions, but you don't want to hear me. I will not go out of this house your enemy, I have too high a regard for you. But I leave without commitment. I'm under no obligation to you, I'm free to vote as I wish. Goodbye, Colonel Ramiro."

The old man lowered his head; his eyes seemed glazed. Tonico accompanied the visitor to the door.

"My father is hard-headed, stubborn. But perhaps I can—"

Altino pressed his hand and cut him short:

"This way he'll end up alone. With two or three of his most dedicated friends." He looked at the elegant young man; a popinjay, he thought again. "I believe Mundinho is right. Ilhéus needs new people to run it. I'm going to support him. But you, your duty is to stay with your father and obey him. Everyone else has the right to negotiate, to ask him to compromise, to ask him for mercy, even. But not you. There's only one thing for you to do: stay with him even if it costs you your life. That's all anybody expects of you."

Jerusa was standing at the window of the other front room

Altino Brandão lifted his hat to her and walked on down the street.

OF THE DEVIL LOOSE IN THE STREETS

"I swear, you'd think the devil was loose in Ilhéus," said sharp-tongued Dorotéia to the other old maids gathered in front of the church. "Who ever heard of a single girl carrying on like that with a married man!"

"The professor, poor fellow, is nearly out of his mind," said Quinquina. "He's so depressed it makes your heart bleed."

"He's such a fine, sensitive young man," added Florzinha. "A thing like this could make him sick. He's not too healthy as it is."

"And he's not vindictive either. In spite of what that hussy's done he still hangs around her window. He even stops on the sidewalk to talk with her. I said to Father Basílio—"

"What?"

"—that Ilhéus is becoming a depraved city. Some day God will punish it. He'll send a pestilence that will kill every cacao tree."

"What did he say?"

"He got angry. Said I was trying to put a hex on Ilhéus."

"Why did you go and talk to him, of all people? He owns a cacao plantation. Why didn't you speak with Father Cecílio? He is free from sin, poor dear."

"Well, I did. And you know what he said? 'Dorotéia, the devil is loose in Ilhéus and is ruling unopposed.' He's absolutely right."

They turned their faces in order not to see Gloria, who was smiling in the direction of Nacib's bar. To look at her would have been to look at sin itself, at the devil.

In the bar, the Captain triumphantly announced the sensational news: Colonel Altino Brandão, the master of Rio do Braço, a man with a thousand votes, had come out for Mundinho. He had gone to the exporter's office to tell him his decision. Surprised by the colonel's change of heart, Mundinho asked him: "What made you decide in my favor, Colonel?" He supposed it was his progressive program and his irrefutable arguments.

"Some high-backed chairs," replied Altino.

But in the bar they already knew about his unsuccessful interview with Colonel Ramiro and about Ramiro's angry rebuff. The facts, as usual, were being exaggerated. According to one version—born of Tonico's highly excited predictions that Ilhéus was about to revert to the days of open violence—Mundinho sent Altino to Ramiro's house to propose a truce and a compromise, there was a bitter argument, and the old politician ordered Altino to leave his house. The Doctor and Nhô-Galo ran into Colonel Altino on the street and came back with another version. According to them, Ramiro became terribly upset when Altino told him that his defeat was a virtual certainty and that he himself, Altino, was going to vote for Mundinho, whereupon Tonico proposed a humiliating compromise, which Ramiro angrily rejected. Other versions, varying according to the narrator's political sympathies, were bandied about. One thing, however, was certain: after Altino's departure, Tonico hurriedly went for Dr. Demosthenes; Colonel Ramiro had suffered a fainting spell. The day was full of conjecture, discussion, and nervous excitement. When João Fulgêncio came to the bar for the customary afternoon talk, he was asked his opinion.

"I agree with Dona Dorotéia. She has just told me that the devil is on the loose in Ilhéus. She's not quite sure whether he's living in Gloria's house or here in the bar. Where did you hide him, Nacib?"

Not only the devil but all hell was burning inside him. The new arrangement with Gabriela had solved nothing. She would come and stay behind the cash register. It was a fragile barricade indeed against men's desire. Now they drank standing at the counter; they elbowed one another and crowded around as if it was some kind of mass meeting. It was disgraceful! The Judge so far forgot himself as to say to Nacib:

"Get ready, old chap, I'm going to steal Gabriela from you. You'd better start looking for another cook."

"Did she give you any reason for hope, Judge?"

"She will, she will. It's only a question of time."

Manuel of the Jaguars, who seldom came to town until recently, seemed to have forgotten his plantations at the height of the harvest season. He even offered Gabriela a piece of land. The old maid was right. The devil was loose in Ilhéus. He was turning men's heads, and in the end he would turn Gabriela's, too. Only two days earlier, Dona Arminda had said:

"A strange coincidence! I dreamed one night that Gabriela went away. The very next day Colonel Manuel sent word that if Gabriela wished, he would give her a deed to a piece of land, in her name."

Women are weak-minded. There was Malvina, seated on a bench on the avenue, talking with the engineer. Hadn't João Fulgêncio said that she was the most intelligent girl in Ilhéus, with character and everything? And yet she had lost her head and let herself be courted by a married man in plain view of everybody.

Nacib walked to the far edge of the wide sidewalk in front of the bar. Lost in thought, he was startled when he saw Colonel Melk Tavares leave his house and stride towards the beach.

"Look!" Nacib exclaimed.

Some heard him and turned to see.

"He's walking toward them."

"There's going to be a row."

The young woman also saw her father approaching and stood up. He must have just arrived from the country; he was still wearing his boots. The people in the bar left their tables to come outside and watch.

The engineer turned pale when Malvina said to him:

"My father is coming this way."

"What are we to do?"

Scowling and holding his riding whip, Melk Tavares came up to the couple, his eyes fixed on the girl. He completely ignored the engineer. To Malvina he said, in a voice like a lash:

"Go home at once!" The quirt struck sharply against his boot.

He stood watching his daugher as she walked slowly away. The engineer had not moved. His legs were like lead, and his forehead and the palms of his hands were covered with sweat. When Malvina had entered the gate and disappeared from view, Melk raised the quirt and placed the leather tip against Rômulo's chest.

"I heard that you finished your studies of the sandbar and that you sent a telegram asking to be allowed to stay in order to direct the dredging operation. If I were you, I wouldn't do that. I'd send another telegram asking that someone be sent to replace you, and I wouldn't wait around till he got here, either. There's a ship leaving day after tomorrow."

He removed the quirt with an upward movement; the tip lightly grazed Rômulo's face. "Day after tomorrow—that's all the time I'll give you."

He turned his back and looked in the direction of the bar as if to ask why so many of the customers were standing outside. He strode toward them and they sat down again, talking rapidly among themselves and glancing sideways. Melk walked in and slapped Nacib on the back.

"How are things going? Let me have a cognac."

He caught sight of João Fulgêncio and sat down beside him.

"Good afternoon, Mr. João. I hear you've been selling my daughter some bad books. I'll ask you as a favor: don't do it again. Just sell her school books. Other kinds of books put wrong ideas into young people's heads."

Very calmly, João Fulgêncio replied:

"I have books for sale. If a customer wants to buy one, I'll sell it. Bad books? I don't know what you mean. Your daughter buys only fine books, by the best authors. She's an unusually intelligent and capable young woman. You must understand her, you mustn't treat her like just anybody."

"The girl is my daughter, let me decide how to treat her. For certain diseases I know the cures. As for books, good or bad, she won't buy any more."

"That's up to her."

"It's up to me, too."

João Fulgêncio shrugged his shoulders as if to wash his hands of the consequences. Eaglebeak arrived with the cognac. Melk

downed it in one gulp and was about to get up. João Fulgêncio
held his arm.

"Listen, Colonel Melk: talk to your daughter calmly and
with understanding; maybe she'll listen to you. If you treat her
roughly, you may have cause for regret later."

Melk seemed to make an effort to contain himself.

"Mr. João, if I didn't know you, if I hadn't been a friend of
your father, I wouldn't even listen to you. Leave the girl to me.
I'm not in the habit of regretting my actions. But I thank you for
your good intentions."

Slapping the quirt against his boot, he crossed the square.
Josué watched him from one of the tables, and came and sat in
the chair he had vacated, next to João Fulgêncio.

"What is he going to do?"

"Probably something stupid." He rested his kindly eyes on the
professor. "Which shouldn't surprise you, for you're acting pretty
stupidly yourself. Malvina is an unusual person, a young woman
of character. And you all treat her as if she were a fool."

Melk entered the gate of his "modern" house. In the bar the
talk turned back to Altino Brandão, to Colonel Ramiro, to the
political turmoil. Only João Fulgêncio, Josué, and Nacib—who
was out on the sidewalk—had followed the planter with their
eyes.

Melk's wife, frozen with fear, awaited him in the parlor. The
Negro Fagundes was right: she looked like the statue of a morti-
fied saint.

"Where is she?"

"She went up to her room."

"Tell her to come down."

He stood there, striking his boot with the quirt. Malvina came
into the room. Her mother remained in the doorway. Standing
before him, her head held high, tense, proud, resolute, Malvina
waited. Her mother waited, too, with fear in her eyes. Melk
walked up and down.

"What have you to say for yourself?"

"About what?"

"Mind your manners!" he shouted. "I'm your father, lower

your head. You know what I'm referring to. How do you excuse this relationship with a married man? That's all people are talking about in Ilhéus and even out in the country. Don't try to tell me you didn't know he was married—he didn't hide the fact. What have you to say?"

"What's the use of saying anything? You won't understand. I have already told you, Father, more than once: I'm not going to subject myself to a husband chosen for me, I'm not going to bury myself in some planter's kitchen, and I'm not going to be a servant to some doctor or lawyer in Ilhéus. I want to live my own life. When I finish school at the end of the year, I want to go to work in an office."

"You have no say in the matter. You'll do what I tell you to do."

"I'll do only what I want to do."

"What's that?"

"Only what I want to do."

"Shut up! Have you no shame?"

"Don't shout at me. I'm your daughter, not your slave."

"Malvina," said her mother, "don't answer your father that way."

Melk seized the girl's wrist and with his other hand slapped her face. Malvina screamed:

"I'm going away with him—you can be sure of that."

"Oh, my God!" cried the mother, covering her face with her hands.

"You bitch!"

Melk raised and lowered the whip without regard to where he struck her. The blows fell on her legs, buttocks, arms, face, and chest. With blood running from her cut lip, Malvina cried out:

"You can beat me all you want. I'm going away with him."

"No, you are not, even if I have to kill you."

With a shove he pushed her onto the sofa. As she lay there, he raised his arm again and rained blows upon her. The quirt whistled through the air as it rose and fell. Malvina's screams could be heard all over the square.

The mother, in tears, begged fearfully:

"That's enough, Melk, that's enough."

Then, suddenly, she rushed from the doorway and grabbed his hand.

"Don't kill my daughter!"

He stopped; he was panting. Malvina lay sobbing on the sofa.

"To your room! And don't leave it till I say so."

In the bar, Josué was twisting his hands and biting his lips. Nacib felt crushed. João Fulgêncio shook his head. The others were silent. Glória, at her window, smiled sadly.

Someone said:

"He must have stopped beating her."

THE VIRGIN OF THE ROCKS

Black granite rocks rising at the edge of the sea. Waves breaking against them into white foam. Crabs with fearsome claws coming out of their hiding places. During the day, urchins scrambled over the boulders, playing killers-and-colonels. At night one could hear the sound of the water everlastingly lashing the rocks. Sometimes a strange light would be born on the beach, climb up the rocks, disappear in their midst, and appear again on their heights. The Negroes said it was some witchery of the sirens or of tormented water spirits, or maybe even Dona Janaína, the goddess of the sea, taking the form of green fire. Sighs of love rose in the darkness, for poverty-stricken couples and whores with no place of their own made their love couches on the beach, hidden among the rocks. In front of them the wild sea roared, behind them the wild city slumbered.

On this moonless night, a bold, slender figure climbed the rocks. It was Malvina, with her shoes in her hand and a resolute look in her eyes. The hour called for girls to be in bed, dreaming of school, of parties, of marriage. Malvina was climbing boulders and dreaming with her eyes open.

At a certain spot, facing the ocean, a shape like a chair was worn in one of the rocks. Sweethearts often sat there with their feet dangling over the edge. Down below, the breaking waves would stretch their white arms upwards and call to them. Malvina waited there, counting the minutes.

Her father, hard and silent, had come into her room. He took away all her books and magazines and searched for letters. He left her only some Bahia newspapers, her bitterness, and her aching flesh, beaten black and blue. She had hidden the love note ("You are my life found anew, my lost happiness, my dead hopes —you are my world") in the front of her dress. Her mother came with food; she offered advice and talked of dying. Was life worth living between such a father and such a daughter, two clashing prides, two obstinate wills, two raised daggers? She implored the saints to let her die, lest she live to see the tragedy toward which they were headed.

She embraced her daughter. Malvina said:

"Mother, I'm never going to let myself suffer the unhappiness that your marriage has brought you."

"Don't say such things."

Malvina said no more. The time for decision had arrived. She would go away with Rômulo and start a real life.

Her father was as hard as the hardest rock; he might be broken but he would never yield. As a child on the plantation, she had heard stories about the fighting, about the nights when her father commanded bands of armed ruffians on the roads. Later she had seen for herself. Because of a trivial incident involving stray cattle that knocked down a fence and invaded a pasture, her family had broken with their land neighbors, the Alveses. Angry words and offended pride led to gunmen, ambushes, and bloodshed. Malvina saw her uncle Aluísio leaning against the house with blood dripping from his shoulder. He was a handsome man, slender and gay, much younger than Melk. He was fond of horses and cows, he raised dogs; he used to sing in the living room and carry Malvina on his shoulders; he loved life. It was the month of June, but instead of bonfires, firecrackers, and sky rockets, there were gun fights on the roads and ambushes behind trees. Malvina could not remember her mother's face when it was not harried and drawn. It was a face molded by sleepless nights while Melk was out somewhere with his gunmen, and by fear of her husband when he was at home—his shouted orders, his arbitrary and forcibly imposed will. She trembled in his presence. Now she was treating Aluísio's shoulder where the bullet had grazed it. Melk merely said:

"Where are the men?"

"They returned with me."

"What did I tell you?"

Aluísio looked at him with pleading eyes and said nothing.

"What did I tell you? That no matter what happened, you were not to give up the clearing. Why did you?"

Her mother's hand trembled as she applied the dressing. Her uncle was not robust, not made for fighting. He bowed his head.

"You're going back. You and the men. Right now."

"They'll attack us again."

"I want nothing better. When they attack, I'll come up behind with my men and massacre them. If you hadn't run away at the first shot, I would have finished them off by now."

Her uncle agreed reluctantly. Malvina saw him mount his horse and look at the house, the broad veranda, the corral, the barking dogs. One last look. He went off with his men. The others stayed behind, waiting. When the first shots rang out, her father yelled:

"Let's go!"

He returned victorious—he had wiped out the Alveses. Laid across the back of a horse was her uncle's body. He had been a handsome man, full of gaiety.

From whom had Malvina inherited her intense love of life? From whom had she inherited her hatred of subservience, of having to lower her head and speak humbly in Melk's presence? Perhaps from Melk himself. She had learned very young to detest the town and its ways. And her mother's life of humiliation, of trembling before Melk, of submissive agreement to business deals on which she was not consulted. He would come in and say peremptorily:

"Get yourself ready. We're going to Tonico's registry office to sign a paper."

She never even asked the nature of the transaction. Her only privilege was to keep the house, and her only solace was the church. Melk had all the rights, made all the decisions. He frequented the cabarets and brothels, spent money on women, and gambled and drank with his friends in the hotels and bars, while his wife withered away in the house, haggard and meek, compliant in every way, without a will of her own. She had no control even over her own daughter. While still a child, Malvina had sworn that her life would be different. She would not be dominated. At times Melk studied her and wondered. He saw himself in her, in certain mannerisms and in her intense self-affirmation, her desire to live fully.

Melk usually granted Malvina's wishes, but in important matters he imposed his judgment on her and demanded her absolute obedience. When she told him that she wanted to go to high school and then to college, he replied:

"I don't want my daughter to be a scholar. You will attend the parochial school, learn to sew, to figure and read, and to play the piano. That's all you need. No decent woman would set herself up as a scholar; it's an invitation to men to take liberties."

Malvina observed the lives of married women. They greatly resembled her mother's life. The husbands were absolute masters and the wives were reduced to passive obedience. Worse than being a nun. She swore to herself that she would never, never let herself be trapped. Her school chums, daughters of rich fathers, chattered away, while their brothers, in high school or college in Bahia, could do as they pleased and had monthly allowances to help them do it. The only thing the girls had of their own was that short period of adolescence. There were parties at the Progress Club, a few meaningless flirtations, little notes exchanged, furtive kisses in the movies at matinees, sometimes longer ones at the front gate. One day the father would arrive with a friend. It was the end of flirtations: she was engaged. She had no choice. Sometimes a girl married a boy whom she knew and liked, if her parents liked him too. But that made no difference; after the marriage he was her master, he owned her. He had all the rights and was to be obeyed and respected. She was the guardian of the family's honor and of her husband's name, the keeper of the house, the caretaker of the children.

Though Clara was somewhat older and ahead of Malvina in

school, the two girls became close friends. They would laugh and whisper together in the school yard. There had never been a happier, livelier girl than Clara. She was full of healthful beauty, loved to dance the tango, and dreamed of adventure. So passionate and romantic, so rebellious and daring! She married for love, or so she thought. Her husband-to-be was not a planter, not an uneducated man. He was a graduate in law—a "doctor"—and he recited poetry. But it all turned out the same. What had happened to Clara, where was she, where had she hidden her gladness, her fire? Where had she buried her plans, her many dreams? She went to church, took care of the house, gave birth to children. She did not even use makeup—the "doctor" would not permit it.

It had always been thus. And thus it continued to be, as if times had not changed, as if the town were not progressing. At school the girls thrilled to the story of Ofenísia, the Virgin of the Ávilas, who had died for love. She had not wanted the Baron, she had refused the sugar planter. Her brother, Luís Antônio, had brought other suitors, but she dreamed only of the Emperor.

Malvina hated the place, with its gossip and rumors. She hated the life there and tried not to become a part of it. She began to read. João Fulgêncio guided her and recommended books to her. She discovered another world, far beyond Ilhéus, where life was beautiful and women were not slaves. Big cities where she could earn her own living and her freedom. She never looked at the men in Ilhéus. Iracema called her the Bronze Virgin—the title of a novel—because she had no sweethearts. Josué wrote sonnets to her, "dedicated to the indifferent M—"; they were published in newspapers. Iracema would read them aloud in the school yard. One day, when a betrayed husband killed his wife, Malvina exchanged a few words with Josué, and after that they flirted for a short time. Perhaps—who knows?—he might be different. But he wasn't. He soon tried to forbid her to use makeup. He told her she must give up her friendship with Iracema ("Everybody's talking about her, she's no friend for you") and must not go to a party at Colonel Misael's house to which he had not been invited. All this in less than a month.

The only thing she liked about Ilhéus was the new house in which she lived. She had found the design in a Rio magazine.

Her father gratified her wish; it was all the same to him. Mundinho Falcão had brought that crazy unemployed architect from Rio. Malvina adored Mundinho's house. She also dreamed about him. He was really different; he could take her away from Ilhéus to places like those in French novels. To Malvina it was not a question of love, of burning passion. She would love any man who offered her the right to live, who would save her from the fate of every married woman in Ilhéus. It would even be better to grow into an old maid, dressed in black and gossiping at the church door, than to be shot to death like Sinhàzinha.

Mundinho kept away from her as soon as he sensed her interest. Josué revived her hopes, but he soon became demanding and domineering. Then Rômulo arrived on the scene, crossed the square in his swimming trunks, and cut through the waves with powerful strokes. This man really thought differently. And he was unfortunate, he had an insane wife. He talked to Malvina about Rio. What did marriage matter? A mere convention. She could go to work, help him, be his paramour and secretary, go to college if she wished, make herself independent, with only their love to bind them. She knew that everyone gossiped about Rômulo and her, that at school they talked of nothing else. Some of her friends turned their backs; Iracema had been the first. What did it matter? She met the engineer often on the avenue along the beach and they had unforgettable conversations. At the movie matinees they kissed furiously. He told her that since meeting her he had been born again. On certain nights, when Melk was away at the plantation and the house was asleep, Malvina and Rômulo met at the rocks on the beach. They sat in the hollow so popular with sweethearts. The engineer ran his hands over her body, whispering pleas, breathing hard. Why not now, right there on the beach? Malvina wanted to get away from Ilhéus first. After they left she would be his. They made plans for the flight. Ah, how ardently she had lived these past few months!

Beaten and confined to her room, Malvina read in a Bahia newspaper: "Scandal Rocks Italian High Society. Princess Alexandra, daughter of the Infanta Beatriz of Spain and of Prince Vitorio, has left her parents' home and is living alone. She has gone to work as a sales girl in a fashion shop. She took this course of action because her father wanted her to marry the rich

Duke Umberto Visconti de Modrome, of Milan, whereas she is in love with the commoner Franco Martini, an industrialist." It seemed to have been written for her. With the stub of a pencil, she addressed a note to Rômulo on a piece torn from the edge of the newspaper, fixing the time for a rendezvous. Her maid took the note to the hotel and delivered it to Rômulo in person. That night, if he wished, she would be his, for now she was fully determined: she would leave Ilhéus and start living. The only thing that had held her back—and today she realized it for the first time—had been her wish to spare her father. And how he would suffer over this! But she no longer cared.

Seated on the damp rock, her feet hanging over the steep drop, Malvina waited. Her plans were all made, worked out in detail. The waves crashed below, the foam flew. Why didn't he come? He should have got there before her. In her note Malvina had set the exact time. Why didn't he come?

In his room at the Hotel Coelho, with the door locked, Rômulo Vieira lay wide awake, trembling with fear. He had always been a fool where women were concerned. He got himself involved and came out badly. He never learned. He was forever making love to single girls. In Rio he had barely escaped the fury of the hot-headed brothers of a certain Antonieta with whom he had been playing around. The four of them had banded together to teach him a lesson. That was why he had accepted the job in Ilhéus, swearing to himself that never again would he so much as look at a marriageable girl. This job in Ilhéus was a sinecure. He received a good allowance for expenses in addition to his salary, and Mundinho Falcão had promised him a big bonus if he pushed the work through quickly and made a report recommending that dredges be sent at once. He did this and agreed with Mundinho to ask for the job of supervisor of the dredging operation. The exporter had promised him an even greater sum when the first foreign ship entered the harbor. He would also try to get him promoted. What more could he want? Nevertheless, he had again gone and got himself mixed up with an unmarried girl, necking with her in the movies, making impossible promises. The result: he had to send a telegram requesting a substitute, and his conversation with Mundinho had been anything but pleasant. He promised that once in Rio he would not leave the

Ministry in peace until the tugs and dredges were on their way. It was all he could do. What he could not do was remain in Ilhéus and get beaten up in the streets or shot in the middle of the night. So he had locked himself in his room and would not leave it until time to embark. And that crazy girl, wanting to meet him at the rocks. Undoubtedly Melk was still in Ilhéus; he was not needed on the plantation, for the harvest was almost over. She was crazy. He must have a mania for crazy girls, he was always getting involved with them.

Malvina continued to wait high up on the rocks. Below, the waves were calling. That afternoon Rômulo had almost died of fright. She saw it all now. He was obviously not coming. She watched the spume flying. The waters called to her. For an instant she thought of hurling herself to the bottom. It would put an end to everything. But she wanted to live, she wanted to go away, to work, to be somebody; there was a world to be won. What good would it do to die? Into the waves she cast, instead, the plans she had made, Rômulo's attractiveness, his promises and the note he had written her a few days after his arrival. Malvina saw clearly the mistake she had made in thinking that the only way to get away was on the arm of a man, whether husband or lover. Why had she ever thought so? Was she still under the influence of Ilhéus? Why restrict herself by a commitment, by a great obligation? Why not leave on her own two feet, alone? That is what she would do. But not through death's door. She wanted to live and to live ardently, free as the limitless sea. She took her shoes, descended the rocks, and began to sketch a plan in her mind. She felt light as air. The best part of all was that he had not come. How could she live with a coward?

OF LOVE ETERNAL, OR A DOOR AJAR

In the series of sonnets dedicated to M (variously designated as "the indifferent," "the ungrateful," "the haughty," and "the proud") and printed in italics at the head of the widely read column of anniversaries, christenings, deaths, and marriages, in the *Ilhéus Daily,* Josué had vowed repeatedly, in forced rhymes, that his devotion, though spurned, would never end. Many qualities, each more magnificent than the last, characterized the poet's passion; but of them all, the one most loudly trumpeted, in 10-point type, was this endlessness. A labored endlessness, to be sure, with the professor searching for rhymes and counting decasyllables and Alexandrines. His love had grown even greater and, in passionate redundancy, had become not only immortal but also eternal and undying, when finally, in the excitement of the killing of Sinhàzinha and Osmundo, Malvina let down the bars of her pride, and his open courtship began. It was an era of long poems in exaltation of a love that neither death nor the passage of centuries would ever destroy. "Eternal as eternity itself, more immortal than the immortal gods," wrote the teacher-poet.

Out of conviction and also because it made composition easier for him, Josué decided to adopt the doctrines of the celebrated São Paulo Modern Art Week, whose revolutionary echoes finally reached Ilhéus after three years. Now he made his vows to Malvina in modern poetry, freed from the chains of rhyme and meter, as he would say in literary discussions with Ari Santos at the Rui Barbosa Literary Society and with the Doctor, João Fulgêncio, and Nhô-Galo at the Model Stationery Store. And besides, was not Malvina's house in the modern style? Twin souls even in their tastes, he thought.

The extraordinary thing is that his eternity greater than eternity, his immortality greater than the immortality of all the gods together, somehow became greater still, but now in pamphletary prose, as soon as Malvina dropped him and began her scandalous affair with Rômulo. In his broad and understanding breast, Nacib sympathized with the melancholy teacher. Josué's friends at the stationery store and the Literary Society, although perhaps a little less understanding than Nacib, stood solidly with him, too. But, unaccountably, Josué's grief drove him to lean for support on the Castillian and anarchic shoulder of Felipe, the shoemaker. The Spanish cobbler was the only philosopher in town, with fully developed ideas about life, society, women, and priests. He held them all in very low esteem. Josué devoured his red-covered pamphlets, gave up poetry, and began his fecund career as a writer of prose—bombastic, challenging prose. Josué was converted to anarchism, body and soul; he began to hate constituted society, to extol the benefits of regenerative bombs and dynamite, and to cry for vengeance against everything and everybody. The Doctor complimented him on his lofty style. At bottom, all this tenebrous exaltation was directed against Malvina. He declared that he was forever disillusioned with women, especially the beautiful daughters of rich planters, the coveted matrimonial prizes. "They are nothing but little whores." He would spit when they passed by, juvenile in their school uniforms or tantalizing in their fine dresses. But his love for Malvina, ah! it would remain eternal—in exalted prose—and would never perish in his breast. He did not die of despair, but only because he proposed with his pen to transform society and the hearts of women.

Logically enough, the hatred which he now felt for the young ladies in society, and which he rationalized by the confused ideology of the pamphlets, drove him closer to the women of the people. When for the first time he approached Gloria's lonely window—in a splendid revolutionary gesture, the only militant act of his fulminating political career, an act conceived and executed, however, before his conversion to anarchism—he did so for the purpose of bringing home to Malvina the degree of madness to which her shameless meetings with the engineer had driven him. The effect on Malvina had been nil, for she was so absorbed in Rômulo's words that she did not even notice Josué's desperate action; but its repercussion in the community was intense. His rash and indecorous gesture did not become the main topic of conversation only because it was overshadowed by the Malvina-Rômulo affair itself, by the burning of an edition of the *Ilhéus Daily,* and by the beating of the municipal employee.

Felipe congratulated Josué on his courageous act. Thus began their friendship. Josué would take the cobbler's pamphlets to his room over the Vitória Motion Picture Theatre. He scorned Malvina—she was despicable—but he retained for her, nevertheless, an eternal, undying love. He exalted Gloria, a victim of society, ostracized by the community, a woman of defiled purity, undoubtedly violated by force. She was, in fact, a saint. He wrote all this—without mentioning names, of course—in vehement prose that filled several notebooks. He envisioned himself giving Ilhéus its supreme scandal: he would shout from the housetops his respect for Gloria and the desire she aroused in him (his love, of course, was still Malvina's) ; he would talk with Gloria at her window, walk down the street arm in arm with her, take her to his modest little room, and live there with her in sin, a social outcast; and he would hurl this horror in Malvina's face, crying: "See to what depths I have fallen. And you are to blame!"

One day, drinking in the bar, he told Nacib that he was going to do these things. The Arab opened his eyes wide; he believed every word of it. Was not he himself thinking of consigning everything to hell and marrying Gabriela? He did not advise Josué one way or another but merely predicted:

"It will be a revolution!"

That was what Josué hoped for. Gloria, however, smiled and withdrew from the window when he approached the second time. Afterwards she sent her maid with a note, written in a dreadful hand and worse spelling. Moist with perfume, it said at the end: "Excuse the blots." There were, in fact, many such, making the note hard to decipher. He was not to come near the window; the colonel would learn of it, it was dangerous. Especially just now, for the colonel was due to arrive and would stay with her. After the old man had gone, she would let Josué know how they could meet.

It was a new blow to Josué. He now felt the same contempt for women of the people as for society girls. Too bad that Gloria did not read the *Ilhéus Daily,* for in it he spat upon her caution: "I expectorate on women in general, rich and poor, noble and plebeian, virtuous and loose alike. They are all motivated by pure egoism, by utter selfishness."

For a while he did not even look at the window of loneliness. He spent all his time suffering, writing, berating society, spying on Malvina, and, in general, living the life of a rejected lover. The only woman he pursued in this interval was Gabriela. He wrote verses to her in a temporary return to rhyme and offered her his little room, bare of comforts but rich in creativity. Gabriela would smile; she liked to listen to him.

But on the afternoon when Melk punished his daughter, Josué

noticed a sad look on Gloria's face; it expressed pity for the beaten girl, pity for the spurned Josué, and pity for herself in her solitude. He at once wrote her a note and, in the evening, left it on her windowsill.

A few nights later, when quiet had descended on the square and the last late revelers had gone home, Josué went in at the heavy door, which had been left ajar. A mouth crushed his mouth, a pair of arms encircled his thin shoulders and drew him inside. He forgot Malvina and his eternal, undying love.

When daybreak came and with it the time to leave, before the early risers started for the fish market, and when she offered him her avid lips for the final kisses after a night of fire and honey, he told her his plans: to be seen with her in public, arm in arm, and to live with her in his little room over the Vitória. They would be poor in material things but rich in love. He could not offer her a house such as she had, with servants, perfumes, and jewelry, for he was not a planter of cacao, he was just an under-paid teacher. But love—

Gloria did not let him finish his romantic proposal.

"No, my lover, no. It mustn't be like that."

She wanted both love and luxury, Josué and Coriolano. She knew from experience the meaning of want, the bitter taste of poverty. She knew also about the faithlessness of men. She wanted to have him, but secretly, so that Colonel Coriolano would neither learn nor suspect. He was to come at night and leave early in the morning. He was to act as if he did not see her at the window; he was not even to say hello as he passed. It was better this way; it had a taste of forbidden fruit.

"If the old man hears about it, I'm lost. We can't be too care-ful."

She was passionately in love with him. How could he doubt it after that night? But she was also objective and calculating.

"I'm going to make my man forget that mean girl."

"I've already forgotten her."

"Will you come back tonight? I'll be waiting for you."

He had not dreamed of this kind of affair. But what was the use of saying he would not return? Wounded though he was by the shrewdness with which she appraised the risks of love and by the cold skill with which she was making him play second fiddle to the colonel, Josué knew that his return was inevitable. He could not resist that couch of wonder and rapture. Another love had begun.

It was time to leave, to slip out the door, and to snatch a little sleep before he had to face his geography class at eight. She unlocked a drawer and took out a one-hundred milreis bill.

"I would like to give you something, something you can wear to remind you of me all day long. I can't buy it myself, it would look suspicious. You buy it for me."

He tried to refuse in a lofty gesture. She nipped his ear.

"Buy a pair of shoes. For my sake. Don't say no." She had seen the holes in the soles of his black shoes.

"They cost only thirty milreis."

"Then buy some socks, too." She made soft, contented sounds in his arms.

At the stationery store that afternoon, dead tired, Josué announced his definitive return to poetry, but this time sensual poetry: he would sing the pleasures of the flesh. And he added:

"Eternal love does not exist. Even the strongest passion has its span of life. When its time comes, it dies, and a new love is born."

"That's the very reason why love is eternal," concluded João Fulgêncio, "because it is forever renewed. Passions die, love remains."

Gloria, at her window, smiled condescendingly, almost triumphantly, upon the old maids. She no longer envied anyone; her loneliness was ended.

GABRIELA'S SONG

In her piqué dress, with shoes and stockings and everything, Gabriela looked as if she came from a wealthy family. Dona Arminda said:

"There's not a girl in Ilhéus, married, single, or kept, who can hold a candle to you. Not one."

Gabriela twirled in front of the mirror, admiring herself. It was nice to be pretty; the men were crazy about you. They murmured, whispered, pleaded. She liked to hear them—that is, the young ones.

"Mr. Josué wants me to go live with him, can you imagine! He's such a good-lookin' young man, too."

"He's just a school teacher. Poor as a church mouse. Don't even think of it. You can pick and choose to suit yourself."

"I'm not thinkin' of it. I don't want to live with him. Even if he was rich."

"The colonels are thick as flies after you, not counting the Judge. And not counting Mr. Nacib either, who is just about dying."

"I don't know why, I really don't," she said, smiling. "He's so good, Mr. Nacib. He just can't stop givin' me presents. Too many presents. He's not old or nothin'. So many things—what for? He's so good."

"Don't be surprised if he asks you to marry him."

"No need for him to, why should he? He don't have to."

Nacib found that she had a bad tooth; he sent her to a dentist to have a gold crown put on. He himself chose the dentist: a skinny old man with an office on a busy street. (He had not forgotten about Osmundo and Sinhàzinha.) Twice a week, after sending the trays of appetizers to the bar and getting things ready for Nacib's dinner, she went to the dentist in her piqué dress. He was nearly through with the work—what a pity. She liked to walk to his office, swinging her body, looking at the shop windows, strolling through streets crowded with people who brushed against her as she passed. Men tried to pick her up. She saw Mr. Epaminondas in his store measuring out cloth. On her way back she liked to stop at the bar, which at that time of day was filled with customers. Nacib would get angry.

"What did you come here for?"

"Just to see."

"To see who?"

"To see Mr. Nacib."

That was all she needed to say to melt him completely. The old maids would look at her, the men would look at her. Father Basílio, coming out of the church, would say:

"God bless you, my rose of Jericho."

She did not know what that was, but it sounded pretty. Those were good days when she had to go to the dentist. In the waiting room she would start thinking. Mr. Manuel of the Jaguars (what a funny name!), persistent old man, had sent her a message: if she wished, he would put a cacao grove in her name, in black and white at the registry office. If Mr. Nacib weren't so good, and the old man so old, she would accept it. Not for herself—what good would it do her?—but to give to Clemente, he wanted one so badly. Where could Clemente be? Was he still on the plantation of the man with the pretty daughter, the engineer's sweetheart? It was bad of her father to whip her. What had she done wrong? If Gabriela had a grove, she would give it to Clemente. How nice that would be. But Mr. Nacib would not understand, and she was not going to leave him without a cook. If it wasn't for that, she might accept. The old man was ugly, but he spent a lot of time on his plantation, and while he was away Nacib could come for consolation, he could lie with her.

So many things to think about. Sometimes it was nice to think. Not about sad things, not about dead people. But suddenly her mind would turn to those who had died on the journey, including her uncle. Poor old uncle. When she was little he used to beat her. And he came into her bed when she was still just a child. Her aunt would tear her hair and call him names; he would just slap her and push her away. But he wasn't really mean, just so terribly poor that it was hard for him to be good. She liked to think about happy things: the brightly lit city to which she had been taken after her aunt's death, the house of the rich people for whom she had worked. And Bebinho.

Some people liked to think about trouble and misery. How foolish! Dona Arminda had days like that: she would wake up grumpy and would talk a string of grievances, hardships, ailments. Nothing else. When she woke up cheerful, her conversation was like a delicious piece of bread and butter—you can't imagine. She talked about birth, babies. That was nice.

The dentist had finished—what a pity! A gold tooth. Mr. Nacib was a saint. He arranged for the dentist without her even asking. A saint, that's what he was. But so many presents, what for?

Whenever she went to the bar, he scolded her. He was jealous
—how silly!

"What are you doing here? Go on home."

She would start walking toward the house. In her piqué dress,
with shoes and stockings and everything. In front of the church
some children were playing ring-around-a-rosy: Mr. Tonico's little girls, their hair so blond it looked like corn silk; the district
attorney's boys, one with a bad arm; João Fulgêncio's healthy
boys; and the godchildren of Father Basílio. And little black
Tuísca, in the middle of the ring, dancing and singing:

> "The rose was sick in bed,
> The carnation said: 'Oh, my!'
> The rose had a fainting spell,
> The carnation began to cry."

Gabriela had sung that song as a child, before her father and
mother had died, before she had gone to live with her aunt and
uncle. She stopped to listen and to look at the children circling
around. How beautiful the dancing little feet! Her own were
begging to dance, too. She could not resist; she loved to play ring-
around-a-rosy. She tore off her shoes, dropped them on the sidewalk, and ran towards the children. Tuísca on one side of her,
Rosinha on the other. Whirling about, singing and dancing.

> "Palm, palm, palm.
> Dish, dish, dish.
> Circle, circle, circle.
> A crab is a fish."

Singing, circling, clapping hands. Gabriela and the other children.

OF FLOWERS AND VASES

The political struggle affected the election of officers of the
Brotherhood of St. George, a lay organization affiliated with the

cathedral. The Bishop hoped to reconcile the opposing factions, as Ataúlfo Passos had done in the Commercial Association. He would have liked to see Mundinho's devotees and Ramiro's faithful united at the altar of the saintly warrior. But for all his red biretta and high priesthood, he failed.

Mundinho did not take the brotherhood very seriously. He paid his monthly dues and that was all. He told the Bishop that he was ready to vote—if he voted at all—for whomever the Bishop indicated. But the Doctor, with his eye on the presidency, made an issue of the matter and began lining up votes. The devout and devoted Dr. Maurício Caires was a candidate for re-election. And he won, thanks indirectly to the engineer.

The turbulent end of the little romance had intense repercussions in the town. Although no one had heard the dialogue between Melk and Rômulo, at least a dozen versions of it sprang up, all of them extremely unfavorable to the engineer. They even had him down on his knees beside the bench on the avenue, begging for mercy. They made him into a sex monster of unspeakable vices, a frightful threat to the homes of Ilhéus. The *Southern Journal* devoted one of its longest (the whole front page and part of the second) and most grandiloquent articles to the subject. The article quoted the Bible and called attention to the sacredness of family ties, the eminence and exemplary life of the Bastoses, the licentiousness of all members of the opposition beginning with their leader, and the need to safeguard Ilhéus against the moral degeneration that was taking place all over the world.

"Here's a brilliant piece of writing for an anthology of imbecility," said the Captain.

But, as an expression of hot political passion, the article was greatly relished in Ilhéus, especially by the old maids. Dr. Maurício Caires quoted long passages from it in the speech inaugurating his new term as president of the Brotherhood. For example: "Adventurers, come from centers of corruption under the pretext of a desire to 'improve' the community—with projects that are of doubtful value, if not, indeed, utterly useless—have tried, and at least one is still trying, to pervert the incorruptible soul of the people of Ilhéus." The engineer was turned into a symbol of degeneracy, of moral turpitude. Perhaps this was due above all to his cowardly flight: after quaking with fear in his hotel room, he had stolen aboard the ship without even saying goodbye to his friends. If he had fought back, he certainly would have had supporters.

The antipathy that now surrounded him did not extend to Malvina. Of course there was gossip about the carryings-on, about the kisses in the movies and at the gate, and some were even willing to bet that she wasn't a virgin. But, in general, the townspeople felt sympathetic toward her, perhaps because they knew that she had held her head high before her enraged father and, as he whipped her, had screamed at him instead of cringing. When, some two weeks later, Melk took her to Bahia to put her in a boarding school, a number of persons went to the pier to see her off, including even some of her schoolmates at the parochial school. João Fulgêncio brought her a bag of bonbons and said, as he squeezed her hand:

"Courage!"

Malvina smiled, and her cold, haughty look, her statuesque bearing, softened. She had never been so beautiful. Josué did not go to the pier but, standing at the bar, he confided to Nacib:

"I have forgiven her."

He was lively and talkative these days, even though his cheeks were more sunken than ever and there were enormous black circles under his eyes.

Nhô-Galo looked at Gloria's smiling window.

"Professor, you're holding out on us. No one sees you at the cabaret any more. I know every tart in town and I know with whom each of them is having an affair. None of them with you. Where is Your Excellency getting those bags under his eyes?"

"From studying and working."

"Studying anatomy. I'd like that kind of work, too." His impudent eyes turned from Josué to the famous window.

Nacib, too, was suspicious. Josué not only displayed an exaggerated indifference toward Gloria but had stopped his kidding around with Gabriela. Something was going on, all right.

"That engineer hurt Mundinho's chances."

"None of that matters in the least. Mundinho is sure to win. I'll bet on it."

"It's not so sure as all that. But even if he wins, the government won't recognize his election—you'll see."

Colonel Altino's adherence to Mundinho's cause and his break with the Bastoses had impelled others to follow his lead. The announcements came one after another over several days: Colonel Otaviano of Pirangi, Colonel Pedro Ferreira of Mutuns, Colonel Abdias de Souza of Água Preta. One got the impression that, if the prestige of the Bastoses had not crumbled altogether, it had at least suffered a severe jolt.

But Ramiro's birthday, which occurred a few weeks after the Rômulo incident, proved the unreliability of such an impression. Never had the occasion been celebrated with such to-do. The town was awakened by fireworks set off in front of the colonel's house and the town hall. The Bishop himself sang Mass. The church was crowded, not only with women but also with most of the members of the Brotherhood of St. George. Father Cecílio, in his ardent, effeminate voice, preached a sermon in praise of the colonel. Planters from all over the region came to town; so did Aristóteles Pires, the Mayor of Itabuna.

It was a show of strength, and it continued through the day. In the parlor with the high-backed chairs, the colonel received visitors in unending succession. Amâncio Leal ordered free beer for everybody in the bars and announced that the elections would be won, whatever the price. Even some members of the opposition, the Doctor among them, went to offer Ramiro Bastos their congratulations. The colonel stood up to receive them, as if to show that he enjoyed vigorous health as well as prestige. In truth, however, he had declined a great deal recently. Only a short time ago he had looked like a man advanced in years but still strong and tough; now he was an old man with trembling hands.

Mundinho Falcão did not go to the Mass or to the colonel's house. Instead, he sent a large bouquet of flowers to Jerusa with a note on which he had written: "I ask you, my young friend, to present my best wishes to your grandfather. Though we are in opposite camps, I am one of his many admirers." It was a huge success. All the young ladies in Ilhéus became greatly excited. That gesture struck them as the acme of urbanity, something hitherto unheard of in a land where political opposition signified mortal enmity. What nobility, what refinement! Colonel Ramiro himself, on reading the card and seeing the flowers, remarked:

"He's a clever one, that Mr. Mundinho! If he sends me his embrace through my granddaughter, I cannot refuse it."

The idea of a compromise was briefly entertained. Tonico, with the card in his hand, felt new hopes. But nothing came of it, and the strife grew even more bitter.

The day's festivities were to close with a ball that evening in the town hall auditorium. The snacks and pastries for the ball had been ordered from Nacib, and Jerusa had personally explained to Gabriela exactly what she wanted. (Afterwards she had said: "Your cook is a beauty, Mr. Nacib, and so charming.") The drinks had been ordered from Plínio Araçá; old Ramiro wished to please everyone.

Jerusa hoped that Mundinho would attend the ball. She did not go so far as to invite him, but she hinted to the Doctor that the exporter would be welcome. Mundinho did not go. A new woman for him had arrived from Bahia, and he was devoting the evening to her.

This and the day's earlier developments were discussed in the bar. Nacib participated in the discussions, but without enthusiasm. None of the happenings in town, whether political or social—not even the news about one of the buses turning over on the road and injuring four persons, one of whom subsequently died—could take his mind off his problem. The idea casually suggested by Tonico, that he marry Gabriela, had taken root. He saw no other solution. His love for her possessed him completely. He needed her as he needed water, food, and a bed to sleep in. The bar needed her, too. All this prosperity—money piling up in the bank, the cacao grove coming ever closer—would evaporate if she left. By marrying her he would eliminate his fear and insecurity; what greater good could anyone ever offer him?

He could even put her in charge of a kitchen with three or four cooks and open a restaurant, a plan he had been nurturing for some time. The Greek couple, it was rumored, had the same idea and were looking for a good location. Mundinho Falcão often said that Ilhéus needed a good restaurant. The food at the hotels was terrible, and bachelors had to choose between the food of second-rate boarding houses and a service that sent out dinner containers with food that was always cold by the time it arrived. Transients, who were numerous after a ship came in, could not find a decent eating place. Where could one give a big, formal dinner? Mundinho had said that he might be willing to put up part of the capital himself. If he could be sure of Gabriela to run the kitchen, Nacib would go ahead and open a restaurant.

But how could he be sure? Stretched out in his deck chair at the siesta hour—the hour of his greatest martyrdom—with his cigar bitter and unlit, a bad taste in his mouth, his mustache drooping, Nacib racked his brains. Only recently, Dona Arminda, the freckle-faced mulatto Cassandra, almost scared the life out of him. Gabriela had felt tempted by a proposition for the first time. With almost sadistic pleasure, Dona Arminda described in detail the girl's vacillation on receiving the offer from Colonel Manuel of the Jaguars. A cacao grove yielding two hundred arrobas was not to be sneezed at—who wouldn't vacillate! Nacib and Dona Arminda did not know about Clemente; nor, as a matter of fact, did they really know much about Gabriela.

For a few days Nacib nearly went crazy, and more than once he was on the point of proposing marriage. But then Dona Arminda herself told him that Gabriela had refused the colonel's offer.

"I never saw the likes of her. She deserves a wedding ring, that girl."

Nacib remembered Nhô-Galo's dictum: "The resistance of every woman, even the most faithful, has its limit." The colonel's offer had apparently fallen short of the limit of Gabriela's resistance, but not by much, for it had tempted her. What if, in addition to a grove of cacao trees, Colonel Manuel were to offer her a house on a quiet street with a deed in her name? A woman loves to have a house (or houses) of her own; just look at the Dos Reis sisters, who refused a pile of money for their houses. And Manuel of the Jaguars was quite able to make such an offer.

On his plantation, money was used for kitty litter, as the expression went, and with this year's bumper crop he would be richer than ever. He was building a regular palace in Ilhéus for his family. It had a tower from which you could see the entire town, the ships in the harbor, and the railroad. And he was so crazy about Gabriela that, with the folly of an old man in love, he would pay any price for her.

Whenever she saw Nacib, Dona Arminda repeated her opinion that Gabriela deserved marriage, and early every afternoon at the bar Tonico would ask him:

"How about it, Arab, have you decided to take my advice?"

In his heart he had decided. He was procrastinating only for fear of what people would say. Would his friends approve? And what about his uncle, his aunt, his sister, his brother-in-law, and his rich relatives in Itabuna, those proud Aschars? And yet, why should he concern himself about these people? His relatives in Itabuna, sitting pretty on their great pile of cacao, didn't seem to know he existed. He owed his uncle nothing, and as for his brother-in-law, he could go to hell. And his friends, customers of the bar, his partners at backgammon and poker, had any of them by chance—except Tonico—considered his feelings? Didn't they play around with Gabriela and try to make her before his very eyes? How much respect did he owe them?

On that day in the bar, before lunch, there was a lot of discussion about politics and the sandbar. Bastos's followers were spreading a rumor that the engineer's report had been filed away and that the sandbar project was buried for good. Many believed this. They could no longer see the engineer out in a boat, probing the sandbar with his instruments. Moreover, Mundinho Falcão had embarked for Rio. Ramiro's partisans were radiant. Amâncio Leal proposed another bet to Ribeirinho: twenty contos that the tugs and dredges would never come. Again Nacib was called to serve as witness.

Tonico seemed cheerful once more as he dropped in at the bar after lunch for his daily dose of bitters. He had resumed his patronage of the cabarets and had taken up with a Ceará girl with black braids.

"Life is beautiful."

"You've got a right to feel happy."

Tonico, who was cleaning his fingernails with a toothpick, agreed:

"Yes, boys, my cup runneth over. The girl from Ceará is hot stuff, the plans for the sandbar went down the drain—what more can I ask?"

It was fear of the Judge rather than of Colonel Manuel of the Jaguars that finally impelled Nacib to act on his decision about Gabriela. Tonico asked:

"And you, Arab, why are you always so sad these days?"

"You know why. What am I going to do?"

"You're going to get even sadder. I have bad news for you."

"What?" There was alarm in Nacib's voice.

"The Judge, my dear fellow. He has taken a house on Quatro Mariposas Alley."

"When?"

"Yesterday afternoon."

"For whom?"

"For whom do you think?"

The silence that followed was so deep one could hear the buzzing of the flies. Lazy Chico, returning from lunch, reported:

"Miss Gabriela said to tell you she's going out and will be back soon."

"What is she going out for?"

"Don't know, no, sir. I think to buy some things she needs."

Tonico smiled. Nacib asked him:

"When you talk about me getting married, are you serious? Do you really mean it?"

"Of course I do. I already told you, Arab, if it were I—"

"I've been thinking about it. I've just about decided."

"Wonderful!"

"But there are some problems. You can help."

"Here, let me embrace you! Congratulations! You lucky Turk, you!"

After the embrace Nacib, still ill at ease, continued:

"She hasn't any papers. No birth certificate. She doesn't know when she was born or what her father's last name was. Her parents died when she was small, she doesn't know anything about them. Her uncle's name was Silva, but he was her mother's brother. She doesn't know how old she is. She doesn't know anything. What am I going to do?"

Tonico moved his head closer and said:

"I'm your friend, Nacib. I'm going to help you. Don't worry about the papers. I'll fix everything up in the registry office: a birth certificate, complete names for her and for her father and mother. There's just one condition: I want to be best man at the wedding."

"You're invited right now." Suddenly Nacib felt himself free again. All his joy returned and he felt the warmth of the sun and the coolness of the gentle sea breeze.

João Fulgêncio walked in.

"Have you heard the news?" exclaimed Tonico.

"What about?"

"Nacib is getting married."

João Fulgêncio, always so calm, seemed startled.

"Is that true, Nacib? Who is the lucky bride, may I ask?"

"Who do you suppose? Guess," said Tonico, smiling.

"Gabriela," said Nacib. "I'm fond of her and I'm going to marry her. I don't care what anybody says."

"All anyone can say is that you have a noble heart and that you're a decent man. My congratulations."

João Fulgêncio looked troubled as he embraced Nacib. The Arab asked:

"Am I doing a sensible thing? Do you think it'll turn out all right?"

"Nobody should give advice in such matters, Nacib. Whether it will turn out well, who can tell? I hope it will; you deserve it. Only—"

"Only what?"

"There are certain kinds of flowers—have you ever noticed?— that are beautiful and fragrant as long as they grow in the garden. But if you put them in vases, even silver vases, they wilt and die."

Tonico cut in:

"Nothing of the sort, Mr. João! Forget the poetry. It's going to be the gayest wedding in Ilhéus."

João Fulgêncio laughed and said:

"Just foolish talk on my part, Nacib. I wish you well with all my heart. It's a gesture of great nobility, this step of yours. The act of a civilized man."

"Let's drink a toast," said Tonico.

Nacib felt the ocean breeze and heard the song of the birds in the bright sunlight.

OF DREDGES AND A BRIDE

As soon as Nacib and Gabriela became engaged, he sent her to stay with Dona Arminda. It would not look right for her to continue sleeping under the same roof with her fiancé.

"Why not?" asked Gabriela. "It doesn't matter."

Yes, it did matter. Now that she was engaged to be his wife, their respectability must not be compromised. When he had asked for her hand, she had hesitated:

"What for, Mr. Nacib? You don't have to."

"Don't you accept, then?"

"Accept? Yes, I accept. But you didn't have to. I like you without it."

He hired two servants: one to do the house cleaning and the other, a young girl, to learn how to cook. Afterwards he would think about employees for the restaurant. He had the house painted and bought new furniture. His aunt helped him to choose a trousseau for the bride. Dresses, slips, shoes, stockings. After their first surprise, his uncle and aunt had been very gracious. They had even offered to take Gabriela into their home as a guest. But he had not accepted; how could he do without her all that time! Only a low wall separated his back yard from Dona Arminda's; Gabriela jumped over it like a mountain goat, her legs flying, and spent the nights with him. His sister and brother-in-law ignored the wedding completely. The Aschars of Itabuna sent a present, a lampshade made of sea shells—a conversation piece.

The wedding was the liveliest ever held in Ilhéus. Nacib had many friends and acquaintances, and they were all there, even the ones who had not been invited. They saw Gabriela, ravishing in her sky-blue dress, enter the parlor on the arm of Tonico, who was clothed as if for a state occasion. Her eyes were lowered and she was smiling timidly. They saw Nacib awaiting her in a navy-blue suit and patent-leather shoes, with his mustache splendidly curled and a carnation in his lapel. The Judge pronounced them man and wife: Nacib Aschar Saad, thirty-three years old, businessman, born in Ferradas, registered in Itabuna, and Gabriela da Silva, twenty-one years old, at home, born in Ilhéus and there registered. After the ceremony the Judge said something to the effect that he wished happiness to the man and woman whom true love had united on a level higher than that of social convention and class distinction. After giving up hope on Gabriela he had acquired a new paramour, for whom he had rented a house on Quatro Mariposas Alley.

So many people came that they filled not only the house but also the sidewalk outside. Even Plínio Araçá, Nacib's arch-rival in business, was there; he brought champagne. The only women present, however, were Dona Arminda; Tonico's wife, who served as a witness; her niece, the blond Jerusa; the Captain's wife, so simple and good; the Dos Reis sisters, smiling all over; and João Fulgêncio's wife, a happy mother of six. And Gloria, who remained on the sidewalk. Other women considered the wedding a little too irregular.

The tables were heavily laden and liquor flowed freely. A religious ceremony would have made the occasion even more joyful, but none could be held, for Nacib—as everybody then discovered—was technically a Moslem. Only technically, for in Ilhéus he had lost Allah and Mohammed. He had not, however, found Jehovah and Christ. This did not prevent Father Basílio from coming and giving Gabriela his blessing:

"May you blossom forth with children, my rose of Jericho." Then, turning to Nacib: "And I'm going to baptize them whether you like it or not."

"It's all right with me, Father."

The party would no doubt have continued into the night, if at dusk someone had not shouted from the sidewalk:

"Look, the dredges are coming!"

There was a rush to the street. Mundinho Falcão, back from Rio, had come to the wedding, bringing flowers for Gabriela— red roses—and a silver cigarette case for Nacib. He dashed outside, a smile on his face. Headed toward the sandbar were two tugs drawing four dredges. Someone shouted "viva," many others responded, and the guests began to say goodbye. Mundinho was the first to do so; he left in the company of the Captain and the Doctor.

The festivities were transferred to the piers on the waterfront. Only Josué, Felipe, and the ladies stayed behind a little longer. When at last Dona Arminda said good night and left the newlyweds alone in the house, with bottles and dishes scattered about, Nacib turned to his wife.

"Bié."

"Mr. Nacib."

"Why do you call me Mister? I'm your husband now, not your employer."

She smiled, took off her shoes, and, in her bare feet, began to put things in order. Nacib took her hand.

"You mustn't any more, Bié."

"Mustn't what?"

"Walk in your bare feet. You're a lady now."

She looked startled and distressed.

"I can never go barefoot any more?"

"No."

"Why not?"

"Because you're a lady now, a woman of means, of position."

"No, I'm not, Mr. Nacib. I'm just the same as I was before."

"Don't worry, I'll teach you." He took her in his arms and carried her to bed.

The multitude at the docks applauded and yelled. Someone found skyrockets somewhere. As night fell, they rose into the sky and illuminated the path of the dredges. Jacob the Russian became so excited that he started to talk in an unknown language. The tugs blew their whistles as they came across the bar.

Plaint on Behalf of
GABRIELA

Oh, Sultan, what have you done
With my blithesome girl?

I gave her a royal palace,
A throne of precious stones,
Shoes with gold embroidered,
Emeralds and rubies,
Amethysts for her fingers,
Gowns of diamonds,
Slaves to serve her,
Beside me 'neath
My canopy;
And I called her queen.

Oh, Sultan, what have you done
With my blithesome girl?

She wanted only fields,
To gather flowers.
She wanted just a glass,
To see her face.
She wanted only sun,
To feel its warmth.
She wanted only moonlight,
To lie in its beams.
She wanted just to love
And to be loved.

Oh, Sultan, what have you done
With my blithesome girl?

To a royal ball
In a regal gown
I took your blithesome girl.
She talked with scholars
And smiled at a princess.
She danced foreign dances,
Drank rare wines,
And tasted fruit
From distant lands.
She lay in the arms of the King
And became a queen.

Oh, Sultan, what have you done
With my blithesome girl?

Send her back to her kitchen,
To the guavas in the yard,
To her rustic dancing,
To her cotton print,
To her green slippers,
To her honest laughter,
To her lost childhood,
To her innocence,
To her sighs in bed.
Why would you change her?

Color of cinnamon,
Sweet smell of clove.
Oh, Sultan, what have you done
With my Gabriela's love?

FOURTH CHAPTER

The Moonlight of GABRIELA

("What is she, that all our swains commend her?")

> "The transformation that has taken place in Ilhéus is far-reaching and profound. It embraces not only the harbor and the town; customs, too, have changed and the character of our men has evolved." (FROM THE SUMMATION BY DR. EZEQUIEL PRADO AT THE TRIAL OF COLONEL JESUÍNO MENDONÇA)

OF AN INSPIRED BARD AND HIS MUNDANE NEEDS

"THIS IS Dr. Argileu Palmeira, an eminent and inspired poet, a bright star in the firmament of Bahian letters," said the Doctor with a touch of pride in his voice.

"A poet, hmm." Colonel Ribeirinho looked at him suspiciously; most of these so-called poets were nothing but a bunch of high-class moochers. "It's a pleasure."

The inspired bard was a tall, stout, light-skinned mulatto in his fifties, with leonine hair and a broad smile that revealed several gold teeth. He wore striped pants and, despite the heat, a black wool jacket and a vest. His general attitude was that of a senator visiting his rural constituents. Evidently accustomed to the suspicion exhibited by uncultured countryfolk toward the Muses and their elect, he drew a card from his vest pocket, cleared his throat loudly to attract the attention of everybody in the bar, and said to the colonel in a resonant but modulated voice:

"Bachelor of letters *and* bachelor of juridical science. Lawyer with two academic degrees. Prosecuting attorney of the district of

Mundo Novo, in the interior of Bahia. Your servant, my dear sir."

He bowed and extended the card to the astonished Ribeirinho. The planter searched for his glasses in order to read:

DR. ARGILEU PALMEIRA

Bachelors
of
Letters
and of
Juridical Science

AUTHOR OF SIX BOOKS ACCLAIMED
BY THE CRITICS

Prosecuting Attorney   *Poet Laureate*

MUNDO NOVO, BAHIA   PARNASSUS

Ribeirinho, confused, rose from his chair.

"That's fine, Doctor. . . . At your service sir. . . ."

Reading over the planter's shoulder, Nacib, too, was impressed and nodded his head emphatically.

"Yes, sir. He's really somebody."

The bard did not like to lose time; he placed his large leather brief case on the table and opened it. For a country town, Ilhéus was comparatively large and there were many persons he had to call on. He took out first a bundle of tickets to his lecture.

The illustrious dweller on Parnassus was, unfortunately, subject to the material exigencies of life in this mean and sordid world, where the stomach prevails over the soul. He had therefore developed a strong sense of the practical, and whenever he went on a lecture tour he worked each locality systematically in order to wring every possible milreis from it. He was especially thorough in the richer towns, such as Ilhéus: he tried to build up

reserves to offset the inadequacy of his receipts in the more backward places, where very often a prospective customer greeted
him with abusive language or slammed the door in his face.
Fortified by an astounding amount of gall, he never accepted defeat even after such discouragement. He damned the torpedoes,
returned to the attack, and generally managed to sell the hostile
party at least one ticket.

His salary as prosecuting attorney was barely sufficient for the
basic needs of his large and ever-increasing family—or, more
precisely, families, for there were at least three of them. The eminent bard observed the statutory laws of the nation only so far
as absolutely necessary. They were suitable perhaps to the common run of mortals but were inappropriate and unduly restric-
tive to exceptional individuals like himself. The law on marriage
and monogamy, for example. How could a true poet, a free spirit,
subject himself to such shackles? He never married, although he
had been living for about twenty years, in what might be called
his main office, with the once sprightly but now aging Augusta.
For her he wrote his first two books, *Emeralds* and *Diamonds*
(all his books bore names of precious stones), and in return she
gave him five robust children.

A cultivator of the Muses cannot cultivate one Muse alone.
Moreover, a poet has to renew his founts of inspiration. And
Argileu Palmeira renewed his zealously: a woman in his path
soon became a sonnet in his bed. For the mulatto housemaid
Raimunda, a beautiful adolescent when he first knew her and
now the mother of three of his children, he fashioned *Turquoises*
and *Rubies*. He wrote *Sapphires* and *Topazes* for the widow
Clementina, who bore him Hercules and Aphrodite. In each of
these celebrated volumes, of course, there were verses to various
lesser Muses. There may also have been children other than
those he acknowledged, all ten of whom, to the great dismay of
the priests, were baptized with names of Greek gods and heroes.
Ten vigorous Palmeiras of assorted ages, twelve heroic mouths to
feed (for the widow had two by her first husband)—and they all
had inherited their father's (or stepfather's) prodigious appetite. He liked to travel, but it was chiefly because of his children

that he made these literary tours during the court holidays. He took along a stock of his books in an enormous black trunk, which taxed the strength of the sturdiest porter.

"Only one ticket? Just for yourself, sir? You must take the madam, too. And your children, how old are they? The younger one is fifteen? Then he's already amenable to the influence of poetry and to the ideas presented in my lecture—extremely educational ideas, suitable to the shaping of young minds."

"Isn't there anything at all off-color in your lecture?" asked Ribeirinho. He was thinking of Leonardo Motta, who came to Ilhéus once a year and, without even peddling tickets, drew packed houses with his frank talks about life in the backlands. "No spicy stories about local customs?"

"What do you take me for, my dear sir? Nothing but the highest morality, the most noble sentiments."

"I didn't mean to criticize. In fact, I sort of like the other kind. To tell the truth, it's the only kind of lecture I can stand." He was getting flustered again. "What I mean . . . don't be offended . . . what I mean to say is, lectures like that are amusing, wouldn't you say? I'm just a man from the country, I haven't much learning, and most lectures put me to sleep. I only asked on account of the missus and the girls. Because if it was the wrong kind I couldn't bring them." Then, to put an end to the matter: "Four tickets. How much are they?"

Nacib bought two tickets. The lecture was to take place the following evening in the town hall auditorium. The introduction was to be made by Dr. Ezequiel Prado, a classmate of Argileu at law school.

Now the poet entered upon the second and more difficult phase of his operation. Hardly anyone refused to buy tickets. But books were something else. Many turned up their noses at the pages filled with verses in small type. Even those who decided to buy, out of interest or politeness, felt awkward when, to their inquiry as to the price, the author replied:

"Whatever you wish. Poetry is not something one sells. If I didn't have to pay for paper, printing, and binding, I would distribute my books free, by the handfuls, as the poet within bids me do. But—who can escape the base materialism of life? This volume, which contains all my latest and finest poems, acclaimed throughout the country from north to south and enthusiastically received by the critics in Portugal, had to be published at my own expense, and it was an expense beyond my poor means. To be utterly frank with you, sir, I have not yet been able to pay the bills. The price is whatever you wish it to be, my dear friend."

These were good tactics when dealing with an exporter of cacao or a big planter. Mundinho Falcão gave him one hundred milreis for a book and bought a ticket. Colonel Ramiro Bastos paid him only fifty for a book but made up for it by buying three tickets and inviting him to dinner. Argileu always provided himself in advance with detailed information about the market he intended to exploit. Thus, he had learned about the political rivalry in Ilhéus and had come armed with letters of recommendation to Mundinho, Ramiro, and other important figures in both factions.

For many years the corpulent bard had been patiently, and sometimes intrepidly, selling his books. On the basis of this experience he could tell almost immediately whether a prospective purchaser was going to make his own decision and pay an absurdly high price, or whether he needed to be prodded with a specific figure.

"Twenty milreis, and I'll add my autograph."

If the potential buyer continued to resist, he would become magnanimous and go the limit:

"Because I sense your interest in my poetry, I'm going to let you have it for ten—so that you may not be deprived of your share of dreams, of illusions, of beauty!"

Ribeirinho, holding a copy of the book, scratched his head and consulted the Doctor with his eyes as to how much he should pay. The whole thing was a damned nuisance, money thrown away. He put his hand in his pocket and drew out another twenty milreis; he was doing it for the Doctor. Nacib did not buy a copy; Gabriela could barely read, and as for himself, he had more than enough poetry with the verses that Josué and Ari Santos spouted in the bar. Felipe refused to buy a copy; he was very drunk.

"You excuse me, poet, sir. I read only prose and a certain kind of prose." He emphasized the "certain." "Novels, no! Fighting prose, the kind that moves mountains and changes the world. Have you ever read Kropotkin?"

The illustrious poet hesitated. He was familiar with the name and he wanted to say yes, but thought it wiser to resort to a grand phrase:

"Poetry is above politics."

"And I crap on your poetry, my dear sir," the cobbler said in Spanish, pointing his finger. He spoke unmixed Spanish only when he was very excited or very drunk. "Kropotkin is the greatest poet of all time. The only thing greater than Kropotkin is dynamite. Long live anarchy!"

He had arrived at the bar already drunk and had continued his drinking there. This happened once every year. Only a few knew that it was his way of commemorating the death of a brother, shot against a wall in Barcelona twenty years before. His brother had been a militant anarchist, hotheaded and fearless. Felipe gathered together the dead man's books and pamphlets and left Spain; he was afraid of arrest on suspicion because, although not himself a fighter for anarchism, he was his brother's brother. Every year since then, on the anniversary of the shooting, he closed his shop, got drunk, and swore to return to Spain with bombs and avenge his brother.

Eaglebeak and Nacib led the Spaniard to the private poker room where he could drink all he wanted without annoying anyone. Felipe turned on Nacib and said:

"What have you done, you infidel Saracen, to my red flower, to my Gabriela? She had merry eyes, she was a song, a joy, a holiday. Why did you steal her, why did you take her away and put her behind bars? You filthy bourgeois . . ."

Eaglebeak brought him a bottle of rum and placed it on the table.

The Doctor explained to the poet the reasons for the Spaniard's condition and apologized for it. Felipe was ordinarily a very polite person, a decent citizen, but once a year . . .

"I understand perfectly. Even persons in the highest circles go on a little bender now and then. I myself am not a teetotaler: I take a little drop occasionally."

Now the conversation had turned to a subject with which

Ribeirinho was familiar. Feeling more at ease, he launched into a discourse on the several kinds of Brazilian rum. An excellent brand, known as Ilhéus Sugar Cane, was made right there. Most of it was shipped to Switzerland, where they drank it like whisky. Mister (the Doctor explained to Argileu that Mister was the English manager of the railroad) would drink no other brand. And he was a connoisseur.

Ribeirinho's discourse was often interrupted. With the approach of apéritif time, the customers began to arrive and each in turn was introduced to the bard. Ari Santos embraced him fervently. He knew him well by name and had read a great deal of his poetry; this visit to Ilhéus would be a historical landmark in the annals of the town's cultural life. The poet drooled with pleasure and thanked him. João Fulgêncio studied the card and put it carefully in his pocket. After selling a copy of his book to Colonel Manuel of the Jaguars and an autographed copy to Ari, Argileu sat down at one of the tables with Nhô-Galo, the Doctor, João Fulgêncio, Ribeirinho, and Ari, to sample the famed Ilhéus Sugar Cane.

As he sipped his drink among his new-found friends, his manner became more informal and he proved an excellent conversationalist. He told funny stories in his booming voice, laughed loudly, and talked about local affairs as if he had lived there for years. But every time a new customer came in, he stopped, took tickets and a book from his brief case, and waited for an introduction.

After a while, at the suggestion of Nhô-Galo, they established a kind of code to save time and make his work easier. When the victim was somebody likely to be good for both a book and tickets, the Doctor was to make the introduction; if he was good for tickets but no book, Ari would introduce him; and if the prospect was single, poor, or miserly, and therefore likely to buy only one ticket, Nhô-Galo was to introduce him. The poet did not like the idea.

"People can fool you. You should see some of the unlikely characters I've talked into buying a book. After all, the price is optional."

He was quite frank in that jovial company, augmented now

by the arrival of Josué, the Captain, and Tonico Bastos. Nhô-Galo assured him:

"You can trust us, my dear fellow. We know everybody's income, tastes, and degree of illiteracy."

An urchin came into the bar and passed out handbills advertising a circus whose opening performance was scheduled for the following day. The poet shuddered.

"No, I won't have it! Tomorrow is the day for my lecture. I chose it because both of the movie houses are showing children's pictures tomorrow. And now, out of a clear blue sky, this damned circus falls on top of me."

Ribeirinho tried to comfort him:

"But aren't your tickets sold and paid for in advance? You have nothing to worry about."

"Do you expect me to address empty chairs? To read my verses to half a dozen people? My dear sir, I have a name to uphold, a name known and, I may say, honored in the entire Portuguese-speaking world."

"It's just a cheap little circus," said Nacib, standing next to the distinguished table. "It's coming here from Itabuna. They have no animals or famous artists. Only the kids will go."

The poet had to leave; Clóvis Costa had invited him to lunch. He asked the Doctor (to whose office he had gone immediately upon debarking) if he would accompany him on his door-to-door visits during the afternoon.

"Certainly, with the greatest pleasure. I'll walk over to Clóvis's house with you and I'll pick you up later."

"Why not have lunch with us, old man?"

"I wasn't invited."

"But I was invited and I invite you. Lunches under these circumstances, my dear chap, are generally pretty good. They're usually better than what you get at home, and they're always better than hotel food, which not only is inedible but is served in such homeopathic portions that you never feel filled."

As they left, Ribeirinho said:

"This double bachelor—you can keep him. He goes along gobbling up everything: money from tickets, money from books, luncheons. . . . I'll bet he eats like a boa constrictor."

"He's one of the greatest poets in Bahia," declared Ari.

João Fulgêncio took the card from his pocket.

"His card is certainly unique. 'Bachelors'—really, now! And he gives Parnassus as one of his addresses. Forgive me, Ari, but even without having read his poetry I'm sure it's no good."

Josué turned the pages of *Topazes*—the copy bought by Colonel Ribeirinho—and read a few verses aloud in a singsong voice.

"It has no life. Obvious, anemic little rhymes. As old-fashioned as if the evolution of poetry stopped ten years ago. There's no excuse for writing this sort of thing nowadays."

"Don't talk like that; it's sacrilege," said Ari excitedly. "Listen to this divine sonnet, João Fulgêncio." In a declamatory tone he began to read: " 'The Boom of the Waterfall.' "

But he got no farther than the title, for the Spaniard came into the room, falling over tables, and said in a thick voice:

"Filthy Saracen, bourgeois, where is Gabriela? What have you done to my red flower?"

Now it was a young mulatto girl, an apprentice cook, who brought Nacib his daily lunch pot. Felipe, stumbling over chairs, wanted to know where he had buried Gabriela's great joy. Eaglebeak tried to lead him back to the poker room. Nacib made a vague gesture with his hands as if to ask everyone's pardon—nobody knew exactly for what. Perhaps for Felipe's condition; perhaps for the absence of Gabriela's charm, her cheerfulness, her flower. The bar seemed to have lost its warmth and intimacy. Tonico broke the silence:

"Do you know the title of the lecture?"

"No, what is it?"

" 'Tears and Longing.' "

"Good title," said Ribeirinho. "We'll be bored to tears and longing to go home."

OF MRS. SAAD'S CONFORMITY AND NONCONFORMITY

Tuísca looked at the tent pole and shook his head; it was not much taller than the mast of a fishing boat. A smaller or poorer circus was unimaginable. The canvas was as full of holes as the dress of the crazy beggarwoman Maria the Gimme. It was not much larger than the fish market, which it barely hid from view on the open ground at the waterfront. Had it not been for his traditional loyalty to circuses as an institution, Tuísca would have taken no interest whatever in the Three Americas Circus. He remembered the Great Balkan Circus; it had a huge tent, wild animals in cages, four clowns, a dwarf and a giant, trained horses, and trapeze artists. Everyone in town had gone to see it. Tuísca had not missed a performance. Now he shook his head.

Several loves were nurtured in his warm little heart: devotion to his mother Raimunda, who did laundry and whose rheumatism was a little better these days; his secret passion for golden-curled Rosinha, the daughter of Tonico Bastos; his affection for the Dos Reis sisters; his idolatrous love for his brother Filo, a bus driver. And, of course, his special feeling for circuses. No circus raised its pavilion in Ilhéus without his support and collaboration: he followed the clown through the streets, helped the roustabouts, ran errands, and bossed an enthusiastic claque of urchins. He was untiring and indispensable. He did not love circuses merely as amusement, spectacle, and adventure: he found in them the fulfillment of his destiny. And the only reason he had not already gone off with one of them was Raimunda's rheumatism. She needed the income he earned in his various occupations—as conscientious shoeshine boy, persuasive salesman of the Dos Reis sisters' fine confections, discreet bearer of love notes, and, in the bar, occasional waiter or assistant bartender.

He sighed at the extreme poverty of the Three Americas Circus. Its last remaining animal, a toothless old lion, had been presented to the local government of Conquista in gratitude for transportation furnished and because the circus could no longer feed it. "A Greek gift," the Mayor had said. At every stopping place, one or more of the artists deserted; they did not even try to collect their back wages. The cast was reduced to the manager's family: his wife, his two married daughters and their husbands, his unmarried teen-age daughter, and a vaguely related man who sold the tickets and bossed the roustabouts. The seven of them took turns in the ring as jugglers, acrobats, sword-swallowers and fire-eaters, tightrope walkers, magicians, "human pyramids," and so on. The old manager was the clown and magician, and he played on a handsaw while his three daughters danced. The entire cast played parts in *The Clown's Daughter*, presented during the second half of the show; it was a mixture of slapstick and melodrama, a "hilarious but emotional tragicomedy that moves the distinguished audience to both laughter and tears." God only knows how they ever got to Ilhéus. They hoped to earn enough there to pay their boat fares to Bahia, where they would try to join a more prosperous outfit. In Itabuna they had almost been forced to beg. The three daughters, although the unmarried one was still a minor, earned the train fares to Ilhéus by dancing in a cabaret.

Tuísca was their heaven-sent savior. He took the humble manager to the Chief of Police (to obtain a waiver of the customary tax), to João Fulgêncio (to have the programs printed on credit), to Mr. Cortes of the Vitória Motion Picture Theatre (for a loan, rent-free, of the old chairs that had been gathering dust in storage since the remodeling of the theatre), and to the ill-famed Rot-Gut Bar on Sapo Street (to hire, under his supervision, some roustabouts from among the good-for-nothings that hung out there). In addition, he played the servant in *The Clown's Daughter*, for the artist who had previously played the role had abandoned both his career and his back wages for a job as grocery clerk in Itabuna.

"You should've seen the man when he told me to say the lines after him and I got every word right the first time. And he hasn't seen me dance yet."

"Tuísca, you are sure goin' to become a real actor," said Gabriela. "Tomorrow I'll be there, in the first row. I'm goin' to invite Dona Arminda. And I'm goin' to try to get Mr. Nacib to go, too. He ought to get away from the bar a little bit. When you come on, I'll clap my hands so hard they'll swell up."

"Mama is goin', too. She can get in free. Maybe when she sees how it is, she'll let me go away with them. The only thing is, this isn't a very good circus. They're hard up for money. They cook their food right there so they won't have to spend money at the hotel."

"Every circus is good. It can be fallin' to pieces and it's still good. Tomorrow I'll be there, clappin' hands. And Mr. Nacib too, you'll see."

That evening, the eminent bard Argileu Palmeira dined at the Captain's, made some other calls, sold several more books, and headed for the bar. He found Ilhéus altogether charming. The circus—he glimpsed the miserable little tent near the waterfront —was obviously no competition. After the movies a large group surrounded the poet, and the talk in the bar lasted far into the night. Argileu proved himself a drinker of extraordinary capacity. He called white rum "the nectar of the gods" and "the backlander's absinth." Ari Santos recited some of his own verses and won the distinguished visitor's praise:

"Profound inspiration. Correct structure."

Josué was urged to recite and did so. Modernistic poems, to shock the visitor—which they failed to do.

"Beautiful! I do not myself worship at the futuristic shrine, but I applaud talent wherever I find it. Such vigor, such imagery!"

Josué succumbed. Who was he to challenge the opinions of so famous a writer? Josué thanked him and asked permission to recite one of his latest poems. More than once during the long session, Gloria appeared at her window and looked impatiently toward the bar. She saw and heard Josué standing and declaiming strophes filled with breasts, buttocks, nude bellies, sinful kisses, and copulation—incredible orgies. Even Nacib applauded. The Doctor mentioned the name of Teodoro de Castro, and Argileu raised his glass.

"Teodoro de Castro, the great Teodoro. I bow before the singer of verses to Ofenísia. I drink to his memory." They all drank. The bard recited some of Teodoro's lines, with changes here and there:

> *"Graceful, reclining at her window,*
> *Ofenisia in the moonlight crying—"*

" 'Sobbing,' " corrected the Doctor.

Between toasts, they talked about Ofenísia and the Emperor,

about Sinhàzinha and Osmundo, and about other famous lovers. Then the funny stories began. How Nacib laughed! The Captain paraded his inexhaustible repertory. The august bard was no mean storyteller himself. His resonant voice broke out in guffaws that shook the plaza and died among the rocks on the beach. In the back room there was a lively, five-handed poker game. Amâncio Leal was playing for high stakes with Dr. Ezequiel, Maluf, Ribeirinho, and Manuel of the Jaguars.

Nacib arrived home utterly exhausted. He threw himself into bed. Gabriela awakened, as she did every night.

"Mr. Nacib, have you heard the news?"

Nacib yawned, his eyes on the outline of her body between the sheets, that body of mysteries daily reborn. A tiny flame of desire flickered in the midst of his fatigue and drowsiness.

"I'm dead tired. What happened?"

He stretched out, throwing one leg across Gabriela.

"Tuísca is an actor now!"

"Actor? What are you talking about?"

"In the circus. He's going to act."

Nacib's tired hand wandered up her body.

"Act? In the circus? I don't know what you're talking about."

"How could you know?" Gabriela sat up in bed, the news was so sensational. "He was here after dinner and told me." She tickled Nacib to wake him up.

"You want something?" He laughed lasciviously. "Well, you're going to get it."

But she was more interested in Tuísca and the circus.

"Mr. Nacib could very well come tomorrow with Dona Arminda and me. To see Tuísca. You could leave the bar for just a little while."

"Can't tomorrow. Tomorrow you and I are going to a lecture."

"A what, Mr. Nacib?"

"A lecture, Bié. A famous man is here, an author. You just ought to hear the poetry he writes. He's terrific. Imagine, he's a college graduate twice! Everybody was hanging around him today; the way he talked and recited poetry, it was wonderful. He's going to give a lecture tomorrow at the town hall. I bought two tickets, for you and me."

"What's a lecture like?"

Nacib twisted his mustache.

"Ah, it's great stuff, Bié."

"Better than the movies?"

"Finer."

"Better than a circus?"

"You can't compare them. Circuses are for kids."

"What do they do? Is there music and dancin'?"

"Music and dancing!" He laughed. "You have a lot to learn about things, Bié. It's not like that at all."

"Then what makes it better than the movies or a circus?"

"I'll explain it to you; pay attention. There's a man, a poet, who talks about something."

"Talks about what?"

"About anything. This one is going to talk about tears and longing. He talks and you listen."

Gabriela opened her eyes wide.

"He talks and we listen. Then what?"

"Then? He stops talking and everybody claps."

"Is that all? Nothin' else?"

"That's all. But the thing is, what he says."

"And what does he say?"

"Beautiful things. Sometimes the way they talk, it's hard to understand what they mean. That's when it's best."

"Oh, Mr. Nacib," she remonstrated. "The man just talks and folks listen. And Mr. Nacib says it's better than the movies or a circus, imagine such a thing! Mr. Nacib, an educated man!"

"Listen, Bié. You're not just a servant any more. You're a lady. Mrs. Saad. You must let that sink in. There's going to be a lecture. A poet is going to talk; he's marvelous. All the upper crust of Ilhéus will be there. We can't pass up an important thing like this to go to a cheap, half-assed circus."

"Can't we, Mr. Nacib? Can't we really? Why not?"

Her anxious voice touched him. He caressed her.

"Because we can't, Bié. What would everybody say? Nacib, that idiot, that ignoramus, passed up the lecture to go to a dirty little circus. And afterwards everybody in the bar discussing the man's lecture and me talking about the circus."

"I see. Mr. Nacib can't go. What a pity! Poor Tuísca! He would like so much for Mr. Nacib to be there. I promised. But Mr. Nacib can't possibly go. I'll tell Tuísca. And I'll clap hands for both Mr. Nacib and myself." She laughed and pressed herself against him.

"Bié, listen. You have to remember that you're a lady. You have to live and behave like the wife of a businessman, not like just some ordinary woman. You have to go to these affairs where you meet the cream of society. So you can begin to learn and catch on to things. You're a lady now."

"You mean I can't?"

"Can't what?"

"Go to the circus tomorrow? I'll go with Dona Arminda."

He removed his hand from her body.

"I've already told you that I bought tickets for both of us."

"The man talks and folks listen. I don't like that. I don't like the cream of society, either. People all dressed up, awful women. The circus is so much fun! Let me go, Mr. Nacib. I'll go to the lecture some other day."

"Can't be done, Bié." He was caressing her again. "They don't have lectures every day."

"Circuses neither."

"You can't miss the lecture. People are already asking why you don't go anywhere. Everybody's talking. It's not right."

"But I like to go places—the bar, the circus, around the streets."

"You just want to go where you shouldn't, that's all you want to do. When are you going to get it into your head that you're my wife, that I married you, that you're the lady of a well-to-do, established businessman? That you're no longer—"

"Mr. Nacib is angry. Why? I didn't do anything."

"I want to turn you into a fine lady, in the top circles. I want everybody to respect you and to behave correctly towards you. I want them to forget that you were a cook, that you walked barefoot, that you arrived in Ilhéus as a migrant, and that they used to treat you with familiarity in the bar. That's what I want, do you understand?"

"I've got no knack for those things, Mr. Nacib, I haven't. They make me sick. I was born a penny and I can't pass for a nickel. What can I do?"

"You can learn. Those other women, all stuck up, who do you think they are? Just girls from the farms, but they learned."

They fell silent. Nacib was about to drop off, his hand resting on Gabriela's body.

"Let me go to the circus, Mr. Nacib. Just tomorrow."

"You're not going. I've already told you. You're going with me to the lecture. And that's all there is to it."

He turned over in bed with his back toward her and pulled up the sheet. He missed her warmth, for he was accustomed to sleeping with one leg thrown across her. But he had to show her that her stubbornness annoyed him. How much longer would Gabriela refuse to conduct herself like a member of Ilhéus society— that is, like the wife of Mr. Nacib A. Saad, who had money in the bank, enjoyed ample credit, owned the best bar in town, knew all the important people, and was an officer of the Commercial Association. He was even being mentioned for a directorship in the Progress Club. Yet his wife never left the house except to go to the movies with Dona Arminda or for a walk with him on Sunday. As if nothing had changed in her life, as if she were still that Gabriela without a surname whom he found at the slave market, as if she were not Mrs. Gabriela Saad. It had been a struggle to make her stop bringing his lunch to the bar; she had cried. It was hell to get her to wear shoes. It was almost impossible for her to remember not to talk loudly at the movies, not to be familiar with her servants, not to laugh with every one of his customers whom she happened to run into. She still wanted to wear a rose behind her ear when they went out for a walk together. And she preferred a cheap little circus to a literary lecture.

Gabriela curled up, perplexed. Why was Mr. Nacib angry? She missed the weight of his leg across her body. And the usual caresses, the fun they always had in bed. Was he angry because Tuísca had become an actor without consulting him? Tuísca was a part of the bar: he shined shoes there and helped out on busy days. No, it wasn't Tuísca he was cross with; it was her. Why didn't he want her to go to the circus? He wanted to take her to listen to a man talk in the big auditorium at the town hall. She didn't like that. At the circus she could wear old shoes that would let her toes spread out. At the town hall she would have to wear a silk dress and tight new shoes. All that showing-off, those women who looked down their noses at her, who laughed at her —she didn't like that, no, she didn't. Why was Mr. Nacib so insistent? She liked to go to the bar, but he didn't want her there. He was jealous—it was funny. She no longer went there, she wanted to please him, she didn't want to hurt him. But why make her do a lot of dull, stupid things? And Mr. Nacib was so good, too. Why then did he get angry and turn his back just because she asked to go to the circus? He was always telling her that she was Mrs. Saad. No, she wasn't—she was the same Gabriela as always. She didn't like high society, no, she didn't. Yes, she liked the beautiful upper-class young men, all right. But not when they were gathered together in some important place. Then they became so serious, they never smiled or said funny things to her. She loved the circus; nothing else in the world was so much fun. And especially now, with Tuísca in it.

Sleeping restlessly, Nacib threw his leg across her. Then he became quiet. She felt the accustomed weight. She did not want to hurt him.

The next morning, as he went out, he said:

"I'll be home about six-thirty. We'll eat and get dressed for the lecture. You must look absolutely elegant tonight. I want you to make all the other women jealous."

He had bought her silk dresses, shoes, hats, even gloves. He had given her expensive rings, real beads, and bracelets. He wanted her to be as well dressed as the richest lady in Ilhéus; fine clothes would erase her past and hide the stove burns on her arms. But the fine clothes rarely left the closet. When she was at home she wore a cotton dress and slippers or went barefoot, busy with the cat and the kitchen. What did she need with two servants? The kitchen girl was little help and the housemaid was no help at all—Gabriela dismissed her. She agreed to send the laundry to Raimunda, but only because she wanted to help Tuísca's mother.

She didn't want to displease him. Both the lecture and the circus were for eight o'clock. Dona Arminda told her that the lecture would not last longer than an hour. And Tuísca would appear only in the second half of the show. It would be a pity to miss the first part, with the clown and the girl on the tightrope. But she didn't want to displease him.

Dressed like a princess, her shoes pinching, Gabriela walked through the streets of Ilhéus on Nacib's arm. He was wearing his blue wedding suit. The Arab climbed ungracefully up the steps of the town hall and greeted friends and acquaintances on the way in, while the ladies looked Gabriela over from head to toe, whispering and smiling among themselves. She felt awkward, confused, timorous. In the lobby many men were standing about and talking; the ladies were seated inside. Nacib took Gabriela to the second row of seats, had her sit down, and then left to join in conversation with Tonico, Nhô-Galo, and Ari. She sat there, not knowing what to do. Dr. Demosthenes's wife, seated near her and wearing a fur cape (in that heat!), glanced haughtily at her through a lorgnette and turned to talk to the district attorney's wife. Gabriela surveyed the hall; it was beautiful and so bright that it hurt your eyes. She turned to Dr. Demosthenes' wife and inquired loudly:

"What time does it end?"

The people around her laughed. This put her even more ill at ease. Why had Mr. Nacib made her come?

"It hasn't started yet."

At last, a huge man in a stiff shirt, accompanied by Dr. Ezequiel, mounted the platform, where there were two chairs and a table with a carafe and a glass. Nacib had taken his seat next to Gabriela. Everyone applauded. Dr. Ezequiel arose, cleared his throat, and filled the water glass.

"Ladies and gentlemen, today is a red-letter day on the calendar of the intellectual life of Ilhéus. Our cultured city is proud and thrilled to have here tonight the inspired poetic imagination of Argileu Palmeira, noted . . ."

And he took off from there. The man talks and the people listen. Gabriela was listening. Now and then people clapped hands, and she did, too. She thought about the circus; it must have started. Fortunately it always started at least half an hour late.

Before her marriage she had gone twice to the Great Balkan Circus, with Dona Arminda. It was supposed to start at eight but did not really begin until after eight-thirty. She looked at the big clock on the wall. Its loud ticking provided a diversion. Dr. Ezequiel was talking eloquently. She could not make out the words, but his voice was smooth and soothing. Punctuated by the ticking of the clock and the sound of its moving hands, the voice made her drowsy. A burst of applause interrupted her nodding. Wide-awake now, she asked Nacib:

"Is it over?"

"The introduction, yes. The lecture is going to begin now."

The huge man in the stiff shirt stood up and was greeted with applause. He removed a big sheaf of paper from his pocket, laid it on top of the table, smoothed it with his hand, cleared his throat, as Dr. Ezequiel had done but more forcefully, and took a swallow of water. A voice like thunder rocked the hall.

"Gentle damsels, blossoms from the flower beds of this garden which is Ilhéus; virtuous ladies who have come out from the sacred seclusion of your homes to hear and applaud me; distinguished gentlemen, you who have built on the shores of the Atlantic this great Ilhéan civilization . . ."

And he was off, pausing now and then to drink water, to clear his throat, and to wipe the sweat with a handkerchief. It seemed as if he would never stop. His voice would resound through the hall, then it would suddenly soften and out would come another poem:

"A mother's tears over the corpse of her little child, called to heaven by the All-Powerful—the most sacred of tears. Listen: 'Tears, Maternal Tears.' "

With him it was more difficult to doze. Sometimes Gabriela stopped looking at the clock and her eyes began to close, but then suddenly the poem came to an end and the voice boomed out again. Aroused with a start, she would ask Nacib:

"Is it almost over?"

"S-s-sh."

But he, too, was getting sleepy, as Gabriela well perceived. During long poems, despite his efforts to appear attentive, Nacib's eyelashes fluttered and his eyes sometimes closed. Roused by

the applause, he would join in it and remark to Dr. Demosthenes's wife beside him:

"What talent!"

Gabriela watched the hands of the clock: nine o'clock, nine-
ten, nine-fifteen. The first part of the circus must be nearing its
end. Even if it started as late as eight-thirty, the first half would
be over by nine-thirty. True, there was an intermission after that;
perhaps she could still get there in time to see Tuísca perform.
The only thing was, it looked as if this talker would never finish.
Jacob the Russian was asleep in his chair. Mister, who had
taken a seat near a door, had long since disappeared. There was
no intermission; the whole performance was non-stop. A more
unentertaining thing she had never been to. The huge man
drank some water.

"I'm thirsty," said Gabriela.

"S-s-sh!"

"When will it be over?"

The lecturer was turning over sheet after sheet of paper. He
spent an awful lot of time on each one. If Mr. Nacib wasn't
enjoying it, either, and was nearly falling asleep, why had he
come? It was crazy. And he *paid* to come. He even got angry and
turned his back because she preferred the circus. She couldn't
understand.

Prolonged applause and scraping of chairs. Everybody was going up to the dais. Nacib took her. People shook the man's
hand, spoke words of praise:

"Excellent!"

"Marvelous!"

"What a gift!"

"I enjoyed it immensely," said Nacib.

He had not enjoyed it, he was lying. Gabriela knew when he
enjoyed something. Why was he pretending? They exchanged
greetings with acquaintances. The Doctor, Josué, Ari, and the
Captain crowded around the man. Tonico, with Dona Olga,
lifted his hat as he approached them.

"Good evening, Nacib. How are you, Gabriela?" said Dona
Olga, smiling. Tonico stood by circumspectly.

This Mr. Tonico, beautiful as anything, the most beautiful

man in town, was a sly rascal. In Dona Olga's presence he seemed
like a church saint. But the minute Olga was out of the way, he
became honey-tongued, tender; he would press against Gabriela,
call her gorgeous, blow kisses to her. He had taken to walking
past her house and, if she was at the window, he stopped to talk.
Ever since her marriage, he addressed her as goddaughter.* He
was the one, he told her, who persuaded Nacib to marry her. He
brought bonbons, made eyes at her, took her hand. A beautiful
man, beautiful as anything.

Nacib and Gabriela were in a hurry—he, because the bar
would soon be crowded; she, because of the circus. He did not
take her all the way home but left her halfway up the deserted
street. He had barely turned the corner when she started back,
almost running. It would be hard for her to avoid being seen
from the bar. She did not want to go by way of Unhão, for the
road was too lonely. So she went along the beach. Mr. Mundinho
was just entering his house and paused to look at her. Walking
quickly, she reached the waterfront. The circus was very small
and almost without lights. She held the money tightly in her
hand, but there was no one selling tickets. She lifted the tent flap
and went in. The second part had begun, but she did not see
Tuísca. She sat on one of the cheap benches and watched. This
was something really worth seeing. Soon Tuísca appeared; he
was dressed as a slave and looked funny. Gabriela clapped her
hands. She could not contain herself and cried out:

"Tuísca!"

The boy did not hear her. The play was about a clown who
was unhappy because his wife had left him. But there were funny
moments in it, and Gabriela laughed at all of them. She heard a
voice behind her and felt a man's breath on the nape of her neck.

"What are you doing here, goddaughter?"

It was Mr. Tonico.

"I came to see Tuísca."

"If Nacib learns of it—"

"He doesn't know. I don't want him to know. Mr. Nacib is
so good."

---

* Because the Portuguese word for "best man at a wedding" also means
"godfather."

"Don't worry, I won't tell him."

The show ended all too quickly. How wonderful it had been!

"I'll escort you home."

On the way out, he said:

"Let's walk by way of Unhão. We'll go over the hill so as not to pass near the bar."

They walked quickly. Soon they left the lampposts and street lights behind them. Mr. Tonico's voice was seductive. The most beautiful man in town.

OF CANDIDATES AND DEEP-SEA DIVERS

The people never tired of watching the deep-sea divers. In their diving suits and helmets they looked like beings from another planet. Almost every day for the past several months, they had gone down into the waters over the sandbar, there where the river and ocean met. When they first started diving, the whole population assembled on the point at Unhão to watch at closer range. With exclamations of wonder they followed every step of the operation: the preparations, the submerging, the throbbing pumps, the swirling waters, the air bubbles. Store clerks left their counters, laborers left their sacks of cacao, cooks abandoned their kitchens, seamstresses their sewing, Nacib his bar. Some people rented rowboats and circled about the anchored tugs. The engineer in charge, a red-faced bachelor (Mundinho had asked the Minister to appoint an unmarried man), shouted orders.

Dona Arminda was struck with amazement at the monstrous figures:

"They invent the darndest things! When I tell my husband about it at the séance, he's liable to call me a liar. Poor dear, he didn't live to see it."

"I didn't think it was true, no, I didn't," confessed Gabriela. "To go to the bottom of the ocean! I didn't believe it."

The close-packed crowds continued to fill the point at Unhão under the hot sun. The end of the harvest was approaching. The cacao was drying in the trays and ovens, filling the exporters' warehouses and the holds of the small ships of the Bahiana, Costeira, and Lloyd lines. When one of the ships entered or left the harbor, the tugs and dredges moved away from the sandbar until it had passed. The work was progressing rapidly. The divers were the great sensation of the season.

Gabriela explained to Dona Arminda and Tuísca:

"They say the bottom of the ocean is more beautiful than the land. They have everything down there, you can't imagine. There are hills bigger than Conquista, fishes of all colors, and meadows for them to graze on; flower gardens prettier than the one at the town hall. There are trees, and plantations, and cities with no people in them—and sunken ships."

Tuísca was dubious:

"There's nothin' but sand under the water around here."

"Silly. I'm talkin' about the open sea, way down deep. A young man told me. He was a student. He read hundreds of books and knew about everything. In a house where I worked, in a city. He told about the strangest things." She smiled as she remembered.

"What a coincidence!" exclaimed Dona Arminda. "I dreamed about a young man knocking on Mr. Nacib's door. He had a fan in his hand and he hid his face behind it. He was asking for you."

"Saints preserve us, Dona Arminda! It sounds like a ghost."

All Ilhéus was engrossed in the port project. In addition to the divers, the dredging machines caused wonder and admiration as they tore away at the bar, widening and deepening the channel. It was like an upheaval, an earthquake, as if they were over-turning the very life of the city, changing it forever.

The dredges and tugs, power shovels and engineers, divers and technicians changed the balance of political forces in Ilhéus. The already shaken prestige of Colonel Ramiro Bastos was threatened with total collapse by this new blow. According to the Captain, Colonel Ramiro Bastos lost ten votes every time the machine bit into the sand.

The political struggle had become more bitter since the arrival of the equipment at dusk on Nacib's and Gabriela's wedding day.

That evening had been one of turmoil. Mundinho's partisans crowed victory, and Ramiro's men growled threats. There was a big fight at the cabaret. Dora Apple-Ass was struck in the thigh by a bullet when Whitey and his hoodlums came in and started shooting out the lights. They apparently intended to beat up the engineer in charge of the project and force him to leave Ilhéus; but in the confusion the Captain and Ribeirinho were able to spirit that ruddy-faced gentleman away, after he had demonstrated his enjoyment of the fracas by breaking a bottle of whisky over the head of one of the hoodlums. According to Whitey himself, the attack had been hastily and inadequately organized.

On the following day, the *Ilhéus Daily* cried out to heaven that the former masters of the region, facing inevitable defeat, were resorting to the methods of twenty and thirty years before. Behold them unmasked: they would never be more than bandit chiefs. But they were mistaken if they thought they could cow the able engineers and technicians who had been sent by the government to open a channel through the sandbar, thanks to the efforts of that worthy promoter of progress, Raimundo Falcão, efforts that were successful despite the unpatriotic opposition of the gangsters in power. No, they would frighten no one. Those who were working for the development of the cacao region rejected such methods. But if they were driven to them by their filthy adversaries, they would know how to retaliate. No other engineer was going to be run out of Ilhéus. This time their threats and pretexts would fail. The editorial caused a sensation.

Gunmen came into town from the plantations of Altino Brandão and Ribeirinho. For a while the engineers never walked in public unless accompanied by these strange bodyguards. The notorious Whitey, with a black eye, was seen with ruffians supplied by Amâncio Leal and Melk Tavares, including a Negro by the name of Fagundes. But, aside from a few brawls in houses of prostitution and in dark alleys, nothing serious occurred.

More and more planters switched their allegiance to Mundinho. Colonel Altino's prediction proved true: Ramiro Bastos was being deserted. His sons and friends grasped the situation. They now pinned their hopes on the state government, which might refuse to recognize any victory of the opposition. They talked about this in Colonel Ramiro's house—he, his two sons (Dr. Alfredo was in Ilhéus at the time), and his two most devoted friends, Amâncio and Melk. It was suggested that they set up the election in the old way—that is, that they take control of the electoral boards, the voting places, and the record books. An election made to order. This would work all right in the smaller country districts, but in the two important towns of Ilhéus and Itabuna such methods involved certain risks. Alfredo reported that the Governor had assured him that Mundinho and his people would never obtain official recognition even if they won the elections by overwhelming odds. He was not going to let the richest and most prosperous region in the state fall into the hands of an opposition group led by an ambitious opportunist like Mundinho. The idea was absurd.

The old colonel sat listening, his chin resting on his gold-headed cane. His eyes, from which the light was fading, narrowed. That kind of victory was no victory at all, it was worse than defeat. He had never needed to resort to such measures. He had always won at the ballot box. To be really beaten by his adversaries and then win a hollow victory through fraud—it was unthinkable. Yet here were Alfredo and Tonico, Amâncio and Melk calmly discussing just that, unconscious of the deep humiliation to which they were subjecting him.

"We won't need to do that. We're going to win by getting the votes."

Mundinho's announcement of his candidacy for federal congressman was encouraging. The big danger would have been for him to seek the mayoralty. He had made himself popular and had gained prestige. His election as mayor would have been a practical certainty.

To become a congressman, however, Mundinho would have to be elected by that part of the seventh electoral district that consisted of Itabuna, Ilhéus, and Una. The population of Una was very small, but Itabuna now had almost as many voters as Ilhéus. The unopposed boss there was Colonel Aristóteles Pires, who owed his political career to Ramiro Bastos.

"Aristóteles will vote the way I tell him."

Moreover, the federal congressmen were not usually dependent on municipal politics, and except for candidates in capital cities, their election was, as a rule, a mere formality. They owed their office to the Governor's commitments and to federal influence. The present congressman for Ilhéus, Itabuna, and Una (the other seventh-district congressman was elected by Belmonte and Canavieiras) lived in Rio and had come to Ilhéus for one brief visit since the last elections. He was a physician, a protégé of a federal senator. Mundinho had no chance of unseating him. Even if Mundinho won in the town of Ilhéus, he would lose in Itabuna and Una; he would lose also in the rural parts of the county, for the elections there were rigged.

"He's up the creek without a paddle," concluded Amâncio.

"But he's got to lose by a big majority," said Ramiro. "He's got to be swamped. I want him to lose even here in Ilhéus."

The Captain would run for mayor, and Ezequiel Prado for state assemblyman. Ramiro scoffed at the lawyer's candidacy. Alfredo would certainly be re-elected. Ezequiel would do for court trials, land grabs, and speeches on holidays. As a candidate for public office he was very much discredited by his heavy drinking and scandalous affairs with women. Moreover, as in the case of Mundinho, he had to have votes from a large area.

"He poses no threat," declared Amâncio.

"The traitor! It'll serve him right."

The Captain's election was dependent only on the votes of the county of Ilhéus. Ramiro himself admitted that he was a dangerous adversary. He would have to be defeated in the small outlying districts, for in the town proper he could probably win. His father, Cazuzinha, who had been overthrown by the Bastoses, had become a legend in Ilhéus as an upright man and an exemplary administrator. The first street to be paved had been paved by him; it was still called Stone Street. He had been responsible also for the first plaza and the first park. Loyal to the point of fanaticism, he had remained faithful to the Badaróses and had spent everything he owned to combat the Bastoses. People still cited him as an example of kindness and dedication. The Captain, who had inherited from Cazuzinha a fondness for romantic and heroic gestures, not only benefited from the legend surrounding his father's memory but was himself very much liked. Though born in Ilhéus, he had lived in big cities and had an air of culture. And he was a powerful orator.

"A dangerous candidate," confessed Tonico.

"He makes friends easily and is highly regarded," agreed Melk. "It depends on who our candidate is."

The candidacy was not offered to Amâncio, for he always refused political office. Instead, Ramiro proposed Melk. Was he not already President of the Municipal Council? But Melk refused.

"Thank you very much, but I wouldn't want it. In my opinion, the candidate shouldn't be a planter."

"Why not?"

"The people want a better educated man. They say that the planters don't have enough time to give to the job and that they don't understand it very well, anyhow. I have to admit they're right. We certainly don't have much spare time."

"That's the truth," said Tonico. "The people are always hollering for a more capable mayor. It should be a man from town."

"Who?"

"Why not Tonico?" proposed Amâncio.

"Me? God forbid! I'm not meant for that sort of thing. If I go in for politics at all, it's only on account of Papa. God save me from becoming mayor! I'm perfectly happy in my own little corner."

Ramiro shrugged his shoulders. The suggestion was not worth discussing. If Tonico was mayor, the only thing he would accomplish would be to fill the town with prostitutes.

"I see just two possibilities," he said, "either Dr. Maurício or Dr. Demosthenes."

"Dr. Demosthenes came here less than four years ago," objected Amâncio. "Even more recently than Mundinho. He could never win against the Captain."

"I still think he'd be better than Maurício. He's a prominent physician; he's pushing ahead with the building of the hospital. Maurício has many enemies."

They discussed the two men and decided on the lawyer, although his well-known love of money, his exaggerated and hypocritical puritanism, his sanctimoniousness, and his pious attachment to priests in a land of little religion made him somewhat unpopular. Dr. Demosthenes was not well liked, either; he was pretentious, smug, opinionated.

"A very good doctor, but harder to swallow than a dose of castor oil," said Amâncio, reflecting local opinion. "Maurício has enemies, but there are a lot of people who like him. He's a good speaker."

"And he's loyal." Ramiro had lately come to learn the value of loyalty.

"Even so, he could still lose."

"We have to win. And win here in Ilhéus. I don't want to appeal to the Governor for help of any kind. I want to win on my own." He seemed almost like a spoiled child. "If I have to depend on the prestige of others to maintain my position, I'd rather give up."

"Right," said Amâncio. "But to put it over, we'll have to use our boys and scare the hell out of a few people."

"Do whatever has to be done."

Then they began consideration of names for the Municipal Council. Traditionally, the opposition elected one councilor. Traditionally, also, it was old Honorato, an oppositionist in name only, who owed favors to Ramiro. He was at times more pro-government than any of his colleagues.

"This time they haven't included him in the slate."

"The Doctor will be elected. That's almost certain."

"Let him. He's a good man. And alone on the Council, what opposition can he put up?"

Colonel Ramiro had a weakness for the Doctor. He admired his learning, his knowledge of the history of Ilhéus; he liked to hear him talk about the past and to listen to his stories about the Ávilas. He would lend distinction to the Council and, after a while, would probably vote with the others as Honorato had done. Even at that hour, when the shadow of defeat hovered in the room, Ramiro remained the grand seigneur, magnificent, generously leaving one seat for the opposition and designating the most noble of his adversaries to fill it.

"Don't worry, Ramiro," said Amâncio. "I'm going to get busy. As long as God gives me life, no one in Ilhéus is going to have a laugh at your expense. You won't lose. Leave it to us—Melk and me."

In the meantime, during that hot summer, Mundinho's friends were also busy. Ribeirinho went from district to district; he said he was going to cover the entire region. The Captain visited Itabuna, Pirangi, and Água Preta. When he got back, he advised Mundinho to go to Itabuna without delay.

"In Itabuna not even a blind man will vote for us."

"Why not?"

"Have you ever heard of a popular government? Well, they have one there. Colonel Aristóteles has everybody in the palm of his hand, from the planters to the beggars."

Mundinho ascertained the truth of this statement for himself when he visited the neighboring town. He was, to be sure, very well received there. A number of persons waited at the railroad station on the day of his arrival, but they were disappointed; Mundinho came by the highway in his new automobile, a sensational black car which aroused great curiosity as he drove through the streets. His business friends honored him with luncheons and dinners and took him to the cabaret, to the Planters' Club, and even to the churches. But they would not discuss politics with him. When Mundinho explained his program, they agreed that it was excellent.

"If I weren't committed to Aristóteles, I'd vote for you."

The hell of it was, they were all committed to Aristóteles. On the second day of his visit, Colonel Aristóteles stopped by the hotel to call on him. Mundinho was not in, so he left a friendly invitation for the exporter to come and have coffee with him his office. Mundinho decided to accept.

Colonel Aristóteles Pires was a big, bronzed man, with a pockmarked face and an easy, contagious laugh. A planter of average wealth, harvesting his fifteen hundred arrobas, his authority in Itabuna was indisputable. He was a born administrator and he had politics in his blood. No one, not even the big planters, had ever thought of challenging his leadership.

He had started out on the side of the Badaróses, but he perceived before anyone else their imminent political decline. He abandoned them before it would have been ugly to do so.

Nevertheless, they tried to kill him. He escaped by a hair; the bullet struck one of his men. The Bastoses, in gratitude, made him the local magistrate of what was then called Tabocas, a village near Aristóteles's lands. In a short time, the miserable little place began to transform itself into a real town.

Some years later, he raised the issue of the separation of Tabocas and its environs from the county of Ilhéus. He wanted to transform it into the county of Itabuna. Almost everyone liked the idea, but Colonel Ramiro Bastos became furious, and a break almost occurred between the two men. Who did Aristóteles think he was, Ramiro demanded, to want to cut up Ilhéus and steal an enormous part of its area? Aristóteles, apparently humble and more devoted than ever, sought to convince him. The then Governor had told Aristóteles that he would approve the decree only if Ramiro's consent was obtained. What would Ramiro lose? The creation of the new county was inevitable, whether they wanted it or not. The colonel might postpone it, but he could not prevent it. Instead of opposing the idea, why didn't Ramiro appear as its sponsor? He, Aristóteles, had no aims other than to support Ramiro. The only difference was that instead of being the chief of one county, Ramiro would control two. Ramiro finally let himself be won over and attended the inaugural festivities of the new county seat. Aristóteles lived up to his promise: he continued to support Ramiro, in spite of a secret grudge resulting from the humiliations to which the colonel had subjected him. And Ramiro continued to treat him as if he were still the young local magistrate of Tabocas.

A man with ideas and initiative, he threw himself into the task of improving Itabuna. He rid the place of ruffians and paved the main streets. He did not concern himself much with plazas and parks, but he gave the town good lighting and a fine sewerage system, opened roads to the smaller settlements, brought in experts on the pruning of cacao trees, founded a producers' cooperative, provided commercial facilities, and made the young city the metropolis of the whole vast region of the interior all the way to the backlands.

Mundinho found him studying the plans for a new bridge

across the river to connect the two parts of the town. He seemed to be waiting for the exporter and rang for coffee.

"I have come here, Colonel, to congratulate you on your town. Your achievements are most impressive. And to talk politics. I don't like to be indiscreet, so if the subject doesn't interest you, please say so at once."

"Sure, it interests me. Politics is my hobby. If it wasn't for politics, I'd be a rich man. It has cost me plenty, Mr. Mundinho. I'm not complaining. I enjoy it. It's my weakness. I have no children, I don't gamble, I don't drink. Women—well, now and then I piss outside the chamber-pot a little." He laughed infectiously. "Politics for me means administration. For others it means business and prestige. But not for me."

"I believe you completely. Itabuna is the best proof."

"What gives me satisfaction is to see Itabuna grow. We're going to outstrip Ilhéus one of these days, Mr. Mundinho. I don't mean the town itself, because Ilhéus is a port. But the county. Ilhéus is a good place to live in, but here is the place to work."

"Everybody has spoken highly of you to me. Everyone respects and esteems you. You have no opposition."

"There are a few persons who don't like me, although they won't say why. Haven't they called on you yet?"

"Yes, they have. Do you know what I told them? Let those who want to vote for me do so, but I'm not going to serve as a basis of opposition to Colonel Aristóteles. Itabuna is lucky to have him."

"I learned about it. I learned about it right away. And I thank you." He laughed again, his wide, bronze face radiating cordiality. "For my part, I've been following your own activities. And applauding them. When will the work on the sandbar be finished?"

"A few more months and we'll be able to export directly to any place in the world. The work is proceeding as rapidly as possible. But there's a lot yet to be done."

"This business of the sandbar has caused a lot of talk. It's liable to get you elected. I've been studying the subject, and I'm going to say something to you: the real solution is not to clear the sandbar but to build a port at Malhado. You can dredge all you want, but the sand will fill it up again. What will really solve the problem is the construction of a new port for Ilhéus at Malhado."

If he expected Mundinho to argue with him, he was mistaken.

"I'm perfectly aware of that. The definitive solution is the port at Malhado. But do you think the government is willing to build it? And how many years do you figure it would take to get it into service after the construction began? The port at Malhado is going to be a tough battle, Colonel. And in the meantime, should the cacao continue to have to be transshipped at Bahia? Who pays for this? We, the exporters, and you, the planters. Don't think that I regard the dredging of the sandbar as the final solution. Those who oppose me with arguments in favor of a new port little realize that I agree with them. But until we have the port, let's at least have a bar that can be crossed. As soon as the work on the sandbar is finished, I'm going to start fighting for the new port. Meanwhile, one of the dredges will remain permanently in Ilhéus to keep the channel open."

"I see." He was thoughtful, unsmiling.

"I want you to know something: I'm in politics for exactly the same reasons you are."

"A lucky thing for Ilhéus. So is your private business activity, which I hope will spread some day to Itabuna. In a way, it already has; I'm thinking of your financing of the bus line."

"Ilhéus is my center of action. But, whether I'm elected or not, I intend to expand my business a great deal, especially in Itabuna. One of the things that brought me here was to look into the possibility of opening a branch office. I've decided to do it."

They were drinking coffee, which Aristóteles savored along with the news.

"Very good. Itabuna needs enterprising people."

"Well, we have talked, Colonel. I've told you all I had to say. I haven't come to solicit votes. I know that you're hand in glove with Colonel Ramiro Bastos. It's been a great pleasure to see you."

"Why all the hurry? You just got here. Who told you that I was hand in glove with old Ramiro?"

"Everybody knows it, Colonel. In Ilhéus they say that your votes will guarantee the re-election of Dr. Alfredo Bastos to the state Assembly and Dr. Vitor Melo to Congress."

Aristóteles laughed as if he were enjoying himself enormously.

"Have you got a little more time to spare? I'd like to tell you a few things. It'll be worth your while."

He shouted for the servant and ordered more coffee.

"This fellow Dr. Vitor, the congressman, is the fattest man you ever saw. The government proposed him, the colonel accepted him, so what was I going to do? There was no one else to vote for, even if you wanted to. The opposition in Ilhéus and Itabuna came to an end with the death of Mr. Cazuza. All right. Well, this doctor, after he was elected, came here to Itabuna. He was in a hurry. When he saw the town, he turned up his nose. He thought everything was ugly. He asked what the devil I was doing that I didn't plant parks and why didn't I do this and that. I replied that I was a mayor, not a gardener. He didn't like it. To tell the truth, he didn't like anything. He didn't even want to see the roads or the sewerage system, nothing. He didn't have time. I asked for funds for various things. I wrote him letter after letter. Did he get those funds allotted? He did not. Did he answer any of my letters? He did not. As a great favor, a Christmas card once a year. They say he's going to run again. He won't get any votes in Itabuna."

Mundinho was going to speak, but the colonel laughed and continued:

"Colonel Ramiro is all right in his own way. It was he who made me the local magistrate here more than twenty years ago. He tells everybody that I owe what I am to him. Do you want to know the truth? He was able to overthrow the Badaróses only because I sided with him. Another thing they say is that I abandoned the Badaróses because they were losing. I left them when they were on top, winning. They were going to lose, true, because they were no longer fit to govern. Politics to them was only a means to accumulate land. At that time, Colonel Ramiro stood in relation to them as you do to him now."

"You mean to say—"

"Wait a minute; I've almost finished. Colonel Ramiro agreed

to the separation of Itabuna. If he hadn't agreed to it, it would have been delayed while the government shilly-shallied. Because of that, I've supported him. But he thinks it's because I'm committed to him. When you began to stir things up in Ilhéus, I started thinking. Yesterday, when you arrived here, I said to myself: he's going to be approached by that gang of loafers; let's wait and see what he does." He laughed his easy laugh. "Mr. Mundinho Falcão, if you want my votes, they are yours. I don't ask you for anything in return; this is not a deal. Just one thing: remember Itabuna, too. The cacao region is all one. Don't neglect us, the way Dr. Vitor does."

Mundinho was so surprised he could only say:

"Together, Colonel, we will accomplish great things."

"For the time being, let's keep the news to ourselves. When it gets close to election, I'll make the announcement."

It proved impossible, however, for him to delay the announcement as long as prudence and wisdom dictated, for a few days later Colonel Ramiro asked him to come to Ilhéus to receive a copy of the pro-government slate of candidates. Aristóteles talked with his most influential friends and took the bus to Ilhéus.

For him, Colonel Ramiro did not open the parlor with the high-backed chairs. He handed him a paper with the names. The first name was Dr. Vitor Melo, for congressman. Aristóteles read the list slowly, as if he were spelling it out. He handed back the sheet.

"I'm not going to vote for this Dr. Vitor again, Colonel. He's not worth a damn. I asked for so many things and he did nothing."

Ramiro spoke in an authoritative tone, as one who reprimands a disobedient boy:

"Why didn't you come to me with your requests? If you had asked him through me, he could not have refused. The fault is yours. As to voting for him, he's the government's candidate and we are going to elect him. The Governor is committed to it."

"It's his commitment, not mine."

"What do you mean?"

"I already told you, Colonel: I won't vote for that fellow."

"And for whom will you vote, then?"

"For Mundinho Falcão."

The old man stood up, leaning on his cane, very pale.

"Are you speaking seriously?"

"It's as I tell you."

"Then get out of this house," he cried, pointing his finger at the door, "and quickly!"

Aristóteles did not get angry. He left calmly and went straight to the office of the *Ilhéus Daily,* where he said to Clóvis Costa:

"You can put it in the paper that I've switched to Mr. Mundinho."

Jerusa found her grandfather slumped in a chair.

"Grandpa! What happened? What's the matter?" She screamed for her mother, for the servants, for a doctor.

The old man got hold of himself and said:

"No, I don't need a doctor. Send for Amâncio. Quickly."

The doctors put him to bed and made him stay there. Dr. Demosthenes explained to Alfredo and Tonico:

"He must have had a great emotional upset. I don't want him to have another. His heart won't stand it."

Amâncio Leal arrived. The news had reached him just as he was sitting down to lunch. He had rushed away, leaving his family alarmed. About the time he entered Ramiro's room, the *Ilhéus Daily* appeared on the streets with a banner headline the full width of the front page: ITABUNA SUPPORTS THE PROGRAM OF MUNDINHO FALCÃO.

Aristóteles, in company with the exporter, was returning in a boat from a visit to the dredges and tugboats at the sandbar. He had seen the divers go down into the waters and had watched the machines eating sand like fabulous animals of some sort. He laughed his easy laugh. "Together we'll build a great port at Malhado," he said to Mundinho.

The bullet struck him in the chest as he and Mundinho were walking through the vacant land near Unhão on their way to Nacib's bar. He had just said: "I don't drink—"

A Negro was running toward the hill, chased by two citizens

who had witnessed the shooting. The exporter held the Mayor of Itabuna as warm blood began to stain his shirt. A crowd started to gather.

Cries could be heard in the distance:

"Catch him! Catch the murderer! Don't let him get away!"

THE MAN HUNT

The excitement that afternoon was greater even than on the day Sinhàzinha and Osmundo were murdered. Perhaps not since the end of the struggles of more than twenty years before had anything stirred the town and all the surrounding region so deeply. In Itabuna it was like the end of the world. A few hours after the shooting, automobiles from there began to arrive in Ilhéus; the afternoon bus came in overloaded, and two trucks filled with hired ruffians unloaded their passengers. It looked as if a war was about to start.

"The Cacao War. It will last thirty years," predicted Nhô-Galo.

Colonel Aristóteles Pires was taken to the still unfinished hospital of Dr. Demosthenes, where only a few bedrooms and the operating room were in service. The leading local surgeons gathered around the wounded man. Dr. Demosthenes, a political friend of Colonel Ramiro, did not wish to assume responsibility for the operation. Aristóteles's condition was serious, and what would be said if the man died under his hands? The operation was performed by Dr. Lopes, a surgeon of high standing—black as midnight and a fine person—with the assistance of two colleagues. When the doctors from Itabuna arrived, rushed there by relatives and friends of the victim, Dr. Lopes had finished the operation and was washing his hands with alcohol.

"Now it depends on him. On his resistance."

The bars were full, the streets were crowded, and there was a general nervousness in the air. The entire edition of the *Ilhéus*

Daily telling of the sensational interview with Aristóteles was quickly snatched from the hands of the newsboys at ten tostões a copy. The Negro who fired the bullet had hidden in the woods on Unhão Hill. He had not been identified. One of the witnesses to the shooting, a bricklayer working nearby, stated that he had seen the man several times with Whitey, hanging around street corners and at the Big Noise, a low-class cabaret. The other witness, who had chased the assassin and almost got shot, had never seen him before but described the way he was dressed, in a pair of cheap store pants and a checkered shirt. No one had any doubt about the identity of the instigators, and their names were mentioned in a low voice.

Mundinho remained at the hospital during the operation. He sent his car to Itabuna to bring Aristóteles's wife and dispatched a series of telegrams to Bahia and to Rio. Some of Altino Brandão's and Ribeirinho's henchmen, who had been kept in town ever since the arrival of the dredges, were beating the woods on the hill under orders to bring back the Negro, dead or alive. The local police questioned Mundinho, and two men were sent off to search the neighborhood. The Captain, also at the hospital, charged in a loud voice that Ramiro, Amâncio, and Melk were the instigators. The Chief of Police refused to take his statement, for he had not witnessed the crime, but asked Mundinho if he joined in the Captain's accusations.

"What's the use?" said the exporter. "I'm not a child. I know that the Lieutenant"—the Chief was a lieutenant in the military police—"won't do anything about it. The important thing is to catch the would-be killer, and we'll do that ourselves. He'll tell us who armed him."

"You are insulting me, sir."

"Insulting you? Pretty soon I'm going to kick you out of Ilhéus. You can start packing your bags." Mundinho sounded almost like a colonel of the old days.

In his bar, Nacib hurried from table to table listening to the talk. João Fulgêncio declared:

"No upheaval in society occurs without bloodshed. This crime is a symptom of change, and because it was botched, it will actually hasten the change. If the man had been killed outright, opinions in Itabuna might have been divided. But after this, Aristóteles's prestige will really grow. It's the end of the long reign of Ramiro the Gardener. And we're not going to be subjects of Tonico the Well-beloved. Now begins the reign of Mundinho the Lighthearted."

People whispered also about Colonel Ramiro's state of health, in spite of his family's attempts to maintain secrecy. Tonico and Alfredo had not left his side. It was rumored that the old man was dying, but this was denied later in the evening by the Doctor and Josué.

Though an important leader in Mundinho's campaign, the Doctor had been invited, along with Ari and Josué, to a dinner at Ramiro's house in honor of the poet. He had accepted; his political opposition, even his scathing articles in the *Ilhéus Daily*, had not altered his friendly relations with the Bastoses. On that day he, the bard, and Josué had gone on a junket to a coconut plantation owned by Dr. Helvécio, a lawyer, where they ate a delicious stew of small fish and coconut milk. They spent the whole afternoon there, then rushed back to the hotel in time for the poet to put on his necktie. By then, the crime had been committed. On their way from the hotel to Ramiro's house, Josué called their attention to the unusual activity in the streets, but they attached no special significance to it. Meanwhile, Ari Santos, at the bar, assumed that the invitation had been cancelled and did not go.

The dinner was far from gay. The members of the family appeared tense and apprehensive—probably, thought the guests, because of the colonel's illness. His sons had not wanted him to come to the table but he insisted on it, though he ate nothing. Tonico was strangely quiet. Alfredo could not keep his mind on the conversation. His wife, who was directing the serving maids, had circles under her eyes as if she had been crying. It was Jerusa who sparked the conversation, nudging her father to respond when he was addressed, and talking with the poet and the Doctor, while Ramiro imperturbably questioned Josué about his pupils at Enoch's school. Now and then the talk died down and Ramiro or Jerusa would start it up again. On one of these occasions the young woman and the bard engaged in a dialogue that subsequently provided great amusement in the bars.

"Are you married, Dr. Argileu?" the girl asked affably.

"No, miss," replied the poet in his thunderous voice.

"A widower? Poor man. It must be sad for you."

"No, miss, I am not a widower."

"You are still a bachelor? It's time you were married, Dr. Argileu."

"I am not a bachelor, miss."

Confused and ingenuous, Jerusa kept on:

"Well, then, what are you, Dr. Argileu?"

"A cohabitant, miss," he answered, lowering his head.

It was so unexpected that Tonico, who had been quiet and glum, burst out laughing. Ramiro looked at him severely. Josué had to struggle to keep from laughing, too. Jerusa looked down at her plate, while the bard continued eating. The Doctor saved the situation by telling one of his stories about the Ávilas.

Amâncio Leal arrived just as the dinner was ending. The Doctor felt that something unusual was happening. Amâncio, visibly surprised to find him there, remained silent and waited. The whole family waited. Finally, Ramiro could contain himself no longer and asked:

"Did you hear the result of the operation?"

"It looks as though he's going to pull through."

"Who?" asked the Doctor.

"Haven't you heard?"

"We came almost straight here from Dr. Helvécio's plantation."

"They shot Colonel Aristóteles."

"In Itabuna?"

"Here in Ilhéus."

"Why?"

"Who knows!"

"Who shot him?"

"Nobody knows. Some hoodlum, it seems. He got away."

"What a terrible thing!" said the Doctor. "He's a very good friend of yours, isn't he, Colonel?"

Colonel Ramiro bowed his head. The dinner ended gloomily. In the parlor the poet recited a few verses to Jerusa. The silence of the others was so heavy that Josué and the Doctor decided to leave. The well-fed bard wanted to stay; he was enjoying his cognac. But the other two were insistent and he left with them, complaining:

"What was the hurry? Such distinguished people . . ."

"They wanted to be alone."

"What the devil's up, anyway?"

They got the details when they reached the bar. The Doctor rushed off to the hospital. The illustrious bard grumbled:

"Why the devil did they have to go and kill people on the day when they were giving me a dinner? Couldn't they have picked some other time?"

"It was an emergency," explained João Fulgêncio.

People kept coming and going in the bar. They brought news about the big hunt organized to bring back the Negro, dead or alive. The hill was surrounded and the men were beating the woods. More men from Itabuna arrived and swore they would not return without the bandit's head—to display in the streets of Itabuna. People came from the hospital; they reported that Aristóteles was sleeping and that Dr. Lopes said it was too early to make a prognosis. The bullet had pierced a lung.

Nacib stood near his house and watched the men stationed at the foot of the hill. He explained to Gabriela and Dona Arminda:

"They tried to kill Colonel Aristóteles, the Mayor of Itabuna. But they only wounded him. He's in the hospital; his life is hanging by a thread. They say the man who did it works for Colonel Ramiro Bastos, or maybe for Amâncio or Melk, which is the same thing. He's hiding on the hill, but he won't escape. There are more than thirty men hunting him. And if they catch him—"

"What will happen? Will they take him to jail?"

"Take him to jail! By the way they're talking, I think they're going to cut off his head and take it to Itabuna. They've already chased the Chief of Police off the job."

This was the truth. The Chief and one policeman had shown up at Unhão, coming from the direction of the waterfront where the Negro had done the shooting. Armed men were guarding the road up the hill. The Chief wanted to go by, but they would not let him.

"Nobody can pass here," said a petulant young man with a pistol in his hand. Near him stood five ruffians with rifles.

"Who are you, sir?" asked the Chief. He was wearing his uniform and his insignia of a lieutenant.

"I'm the Municipal Secretary of Itabuna. Américo Matos is my name, if you want to know it."

"And I am the Chief of Police of Ilhéus. I'm going to arrest the criminal."

"Arrest him? Don't make me laugh. If you want to arrest somebody, you don't have to climb the hill. Go arrest Colonel Ramiro, or that rat who calls himself Amâncio Leal, or Melk Tavares, or their boy Whitey. You don't have to go up the hill, there's plenty of work for you in town."

The Chief made a slight gesture and the ruffians raised their guns. The young man said:

"Chief, you better go away if you don't want to get killed."

The lieutenant glanced about; the policeman had disappeared.

"You'll be hearing from me," he said and turned about-face.

All the roads up the hill were being guarded. There were three of them, two on the side of the port and one on the ocean side, where Nacib's house was located. More than thirty armed men, ruffians from Itabuna and Ilhéus, were scouring the hill, beating the dense undergrowth, breaking into huts and searching them. The rumors in town were flying thick and fast. Someone would appear in the Vesuvius Bar from time to time with an additional bit of news; the latest was that the police were guarding Colonel Ramiro's house, where he, his sons, and his most devoted friends, including Amâncio and Melk, had barricaded themselves. This was pure invention, for a few minutes later Amâncio himself came into the bar, and Melk was on his plantation. The reported death of Aristóteles made the rounds twice. According to one story, Mundinho had called on Colonel Altino Brandão for more men and had sent a car to fetch Ribeirinho.

Amâncio Leal's entrance into the bar caused a certain sensation. As always, in his soft voice, he said: "Good evening, gentle-men," called for a cognac, and inquired if anyone wanted to join him in a game of poker. No one did. He walked among the ta-bles exchanging remarks with acquaintances. Everyone felt that the colonel was daring the crowd to accuse him of the shooting. No one even mentioned the subject. Amâncio said good night and went up Adami Street in the direction of Colonel Ramiro's house.

The men on the hill continued to beat the woods, searched every hut, ferreted every gully. More than once they came within a few feet of the Negro Fagundes.

He had dashed up the hill with the revolver still in his hand. Ever since Aristóteles—who had been pointed out to him at the port by Whitey—had come ashore, he had waited for the right moment to shoot. When the colonel and Mundinho started through the vacant land near Unhão Hill, almost deserted at that hour, he decided the time had come and fired at the man's heart. He saw the colonel falling and fled. A man started after him but he frightened him off with a shot. He hid among some trees and chewed a piece of tobacco. He was going to earn big money. At last the bloodshed was starting again. Clemente knew of a piece of land for sale. They dreamed of planting a little grove of their own. If the fighting got hot, a man like himself, Fagundes, with plenty of courage and good marksmanship, could soon be well fixed. Whitey had said to meet him at the Big Noise soon after dark before the place got busy. Around eight o'clock. Fagundes was not worried. He rested awhile, then started walk-ing to the top of the hill with the intention of going down the other side when it was dark enough. He would then be on the beach, not far from the Big Noise. He walked calmly past several small houses and even spoke to a woman who was making lace. He went into the woods, found a sheltered spot, and lay down to think and to wait for nightfall. He could see the beach from where he was. The twilight lasted a long time. Fagundes raised his head a little and saw the sun spreading a blood-red fan over the horizon. He thought about the coveted bit of land and about Clemente, poor fellow, still unable to forget Gabriela. Clemente did not know, as he himself had learned in town, that she was now married and a rich lady. Slowly the shadows grew. The hill was silent.

When he started down the hill, he spied the men. He almost ran into them. He retreated into the bushes. From there he could see them entering houses. Their number increased. They divided into groups. He heard snatches of their conversation. They wanted to catch him, dead or alive, to take to Itabuna. He scratched his head. Was the man he had shot that important? By now the man must be stretched out, surrounded by flowers. Fagundes was alive, he did not want to die. There was a piece of land that was going to be his and Clemente's. The shooting had just started; there was a lot of money to be earned.

The men, in groups of four or five, were headed toward the woods, into which the Negro retreated further and further. The undergrowth was dense and the thorns tore at his pants and shirt. His pistol was in his hand. He remained still a few minutes, squatting in the bushes. He soon heard voices.

"Somebody went through here."

He waited anxiously. The voices went away, and he penetrated deeper into the thick woods. His leg was bleeding from a thorn scratch. An animal jumped out and fled, and Fagundes discovered a deep hole half concealed by branches. He got down into it just in time. The voices came close again.

"There was somebody here. Look."

"Damned thorns!"

It was almost night now. At moments the voices were so close that he expected to see a man break through the fragile screen of branches and enter the hole. Through the leaves he could see a firefly winking. He was not afraid, but he began to feel impatient. At this rate he would be late for his appointment. He heard other bits of conversation: they talked about cutting him up with a knife, and they wondered exactly who had hired him. He was not afraid, but he didn't want to die. Not just then, when the fights were beginning again and there was that piece of land for him and Clemente to buy.

No more voices. The darkness fell rapidly as if tired of waiting so long. Fagundes also was tired of waiting. He crawled out of his hole and peered about cautiously. There was no one around.

Perhaps they had given up because of the darkness. He rose to his feet and looked around. He could see nothing but the trees close by; the rest was blackness. But he knew exactly where he was. In front of him, the ocean; behind him, the port. He would go straight ahead, come out near the beach, circle around the rocks, and find Whitey, who would not be at the Big Noise yet. He wanted to collect his well-earned money; he even deserved a bonus on account of having been chased. On his right, the light from a lamppost marked the end of the road up the hill. Beyond it, a few weak lights from houses. He started walking. He had barely taken two steps, pushing the branches aside, when he saw the first flashlight coming up the road. The sound of voices rode on the breeze. They were coming back with flashlights.

The first of them reached the top where the houses were and asked people if they had seen the Negro.

"We want to take him alive so we can torture him."

"We're going to take his head to Itabuna."

To torture him. He knew what that meant. If they caught him alive, they would kill him bit by bit to make him reveal the name of the man who had hired him. One time, in the backlands, he and some others had killed a farm hand that way, trying to find out where somebody was hiding. They had cut him to bits with a sharp dagger. They had cut off his ears and gouged out his eyes. Fagundes didn't want to die that way. He grasped his pistol again. That man he shot must really have been important. If he got out of this alive, he would demand a big bonus.

Suddenly a beam of electric light cut through the darkness and hit the Negro full in the face. A cry:

"There he is!"

Men started running up. He bent down quickly and entered the woods. In coming out of the hole he had broken some branches and it would no longer serve as a hiding place. His pursuers drew closer. The Negro dashed forward, bent low like a hunted animal, while the thorns tore at the flesh on his back. The descent was steep and the woods thicker, with trees now instead of bushes. His bare feet struck against stones. The noises behind him told him that there were many men. This time they had not broken up into groups but were searching together.

They were close—getting closer all the time. The Negro found it difficult to break through the undergrowth. Twice he fell, now with injuries all over his body, his face bleeding. He heard blows of a machete cutting through the tangled growth and a voice saying:

"He can't get away. In front is the precipice. Let's surround him." The men scattered.

The way down was getting steeper. Fagundes was on his hands and knees. Now he was afraid. He could not escape. And in that spot it would be hard to shoot, to kill two or three as he wanted to do, so that the others would kill him with a hail of bullets. The kind of death for a man like him. Between strokes of the machete, a voice shouted:

"Start getting ready, killer, we're going to chop you up with a knife."

He trembled. With great difficulty he dragged himself along the ground. He was not afraid of dying. A man is born to die when his time comes. All he hoped for now was a clear space where he could wait for them with his gun in his hand. To kill and be killed. So that he would not be tortured like that poor fellow in the backlands.

And suddenly he found himself at the edge of the precipice. He would have fallen if he had not grabbed onto a tree. He looked down; it was impossible to see anything. He moved sideways to the left and discovered a steep incline. The undergrowth was less dense here. The sound of the machete grew weaker. His pursuers were now in the thick woods bordering the precipice. He started slipping and sliding down the incline in a desperate effort to escape. He did not feel the thorns tearing at his flesh. What he felt were points of daggers in his chest, in his eyes, in his ears. The incline came to an abrupt end about six feet above the ground at the bottom of the hill. He grabbed some branches and let himself drop. He could still hear the machete. He fell almost soundlessly on top of the thick vegetation. He stood up. Before him was the low wall of a back yard. He jumped over it. A cat took fright and ran up into the hill. He waited in the shadow of the wall. There were lights in the back of the house. He raised his pistol and crossed the yard. He saw a lighted kitchen. And Gabriela washing dishes. He smiled. She was the prettiest woman in the world.

HOW MRS. SAAD BECAME INVOLVED IN POLITICS, IN VIOLATION OF HER HUSBAND'S TRADITIONAL NEUTRALITY, AND OF THAT LADY'S ADVENTUROUS NIGHT

The Negro Fagundes laughed, although his face was swollen from the poisonous thorns and his shirt was stained with blood.

"They're goin' to spend the night lookin' for the black man, and the black man's sittin' right here talkin' with Gabriela."

Gabriela laughed, too, and poured him another drink of rum.

"What are you supposed to do now?"

"There's a fella called Whitey. You know him?"

"Whitey? I heard the name once. Quite a while ago, in the bar."

"You go talk with him. Ask him where I should meet him."

"Where will I find him?"

"He said to meet him at the Big Noise at eight o'clock. It's a good place for dancin'. On Sapo Street. He probably left there by now, though. What time is it?"

Gabriela went to look at the clock in the front room.

"It's after nine. What if he isn't there?"

"If he isn't there?" He scratched his head. "The colonel's out on the plantation, and his wife ain't right in the head, so it's no use goin' to his house."

"Which colonel?"

"Mr. Melk. You know Colonel Amâncio? Blind in one eye?"

"I know him plenty. He goes to the bar a lot."

"Well, he'll do. If you don't find Whitey, look for Colonel Amâncio and he'll take care of everything."

It was lucky the kitchen helper did not sleep in. Gabriela took the Negro to the little room in the back yard where she used to sleep. He said:

"What about another drink?"

She gave him the bottle of rum.

"Don't take too much."

"Don't worry yourself. Just another drop so I won't think what almost happened. Get killed with a bullet, I don't mind. You die fightin' and you die happy. Tortured with a knife, I don't want that, no. I saw a man die like that. It ain't pretty to look at."

Gabriela wanted to know more:

"What did you shoot the man for? What harm did he do you?"

"To me, he didn't do none. It was for Colonel Melk. Whitey ordered me to, what could I do? Everybody's got a trade, and this is mine."

"But the man didn't die. I bet you don't get paid nothin', wait and see."

"I thought I killed him for sure. It wasn't his day to die, I guess."

She cautioned him not to make any noise, not to light a light, and not to leave the little room. The man hunt on the hill continued. The frightened cat, running swiftly through the brush, had thrown the pursuers off the track. They were scouring every foot of the woods. Gabriela put on a pair of old yellow shoes. It was a little after nine-thirty by the clock; at that hour no married woman would go out alone into the streets of Ilhéus. Only prostitutes. The thought never occurred to her. Neither did she stop to think what Nacib's reaction would be if he learned of it, nor what those who saw her might say. The Negro Fagundes had been good to her on the journey. He had carried her sick uncle on his back for a while before he died. When Clemente knocked her down, he had jumped to defend her. She wasn't going to let him fall into the hands of those ruffians. It was bad to kill and she didn't like it. But it was the only thing Fagundes knew how to do. He never learned anything else.

She stepped out, locked the street door, and took the key. She had never been on Sapo Street, which lay over by the railroad tracks. She walked down to the beach. She could see the busy bar, so crowded that many customers were standing. Nacib was moving from table to table. On Rui Barbosa Square she changed her course and headed for Seabra Plaza. There were a few people in the street, some of whom glanced at her curiously. Two men spoke to her. Acquaintances of Nacib's, customers of the bar. But they were so absorbed with the afternoon's crime that they gave her no further thought. She reached the railroad tracks and came to the slums, where whores of the lowest class were walking the streets. They looked at her with curiosity. One of them took her by the arm.

"You're new around here, I never seen you before. Where you from?"

"From the backlands," she replied automatically. "Where is Sapo Street?"

"Up ahead. Where you goin'? To Mé's house?"

"No. To the Big Noise."

"You ain't goin' there! You got nerve. I wouldn't go there myself. Especially not today. They're raisin' hell. Turn to the right and you'll find it."

She turned right at the next corner. A Negro took hold of her.

"Where you goin', snooty?" He looked her in the face, found her pretty, and pinched her cheek with his strong fingers. "Where you live?"

"Far from here."

"That don't matter, snooty. Come on, let's make a baby."

"I can't now. I'm in a hurry."

"You scared I'll cheat you? Look here." He put his hand in his pocket and pulled out some small bills.

"No, I'm in a hurry."

"I'm in a hurry, too."

"Let me go. I'll come back soon."

"How do I know?"

"I swear."

"I'm gonna wait for you."

"I'll meet you right here."

She hurried away. As she approached the Big Noise, on a poorly lit street, she could hear the music of a tambourine and a guitar against a background of loud talk, bursts of laughter, and screams. A drunk seized her and tried to hug her. She pushed his elbow upwards until he lost his balance and fell against a lamppost. She went in. A man called to her:

"Over here, baby. How about a drink?"

An old man was playing a guitar and a boy was thumping the tambourine. Some of the women looked old; they were heavily made up and several were drunk. Others were extremely young mulatto girls. One, with loose hair and a thin face, looked no more than fifteen. A man tried hard to get Gabriela to sit with him. The women, both the old and the young, looked at her suspiciously. The owner of the place, a one-legged mulatto, came toward her, his wooden leg thudding the floor as he walked. A man dressed like a sailor, probably just off a Bahiana boat, put his arm around her waist and murmured:

"Are you free, sweetheart? I'll go with you."

"No, I'm not free."

She smiled at him; he was an agreeable young man and smelled of the sea. He said: "What a pity," squeezed her a little against himself, and went off to look for another girl. The one-legged man came and stood in front of Gabriela.

"Where have I seen your face before?"

She asked him:

"Is there a fellow here called Whitey? I want to talk to him. Somethin' important."

One of the women heard the question and called out:

"Edith! Madame here is lookin' for Whitey."

Laughter rang out in the room, and the very young, thin-faced girl jumped up.

"What does that cow want with my Whitey?" She came toward the door, her hands on her hips.

"You're not goin' to find him tonight," a man said, laughing. "He's got his hands full."

The young girl, with her dress above her knees, posted herself in front of Gabriela.

"What do you want with my man, you piece of horse shit?"

"I just want to talk to him."

"Just to talk to him!" She spat. "I know your kind, you dirty-ass. You want to sleep with him. All the cows around here want to sleep with him."

The girl was surely no more than fifteen, perhaps younger. Gabriela thought of her uncle, she did not know why. An older woman said:

"Cut it out, Edith. He don't even look at you."

"Leave me alone. I'm gonna teach this cow . . ."

She raised her hands toward Gabriela's face, but Gabriela seized her thin wrists and forced her arms down.

"You cow!" screamed Edith and lunged at Gabriela. Every-body in the dive stood up; there was nothing they liked more than to see women fight. But the one-legged proprietor came be-tween the two women. He pushed the young girl to one side.

"Get outa here before I bust you in the face!" He took Gabri-ela by the arm and led her outside. "Tell me somethin': aren't you the wife of Mr. Nacib, who owns the Vesuvius Bar?"

She nodded her head affirmatively.

"Well, what the devil are you doin' here? You got a thing for Whitey?"

"I don't even know him. But I have to talk to him. Somethin' very important."

The one-legged man studied her for a moment.

"Some message? Somethin' about what happened today?"

"Yes, sir. It's important, very important."

They went down one street, then another, until they came to a dark alley. The one-legged man, walking a short distance ahead of her, stopped in front of a house with the door ajar. He knocked as if to give warning and went inside.

"Follow me."

A disheveled woman appeared, dressed only in a chemise.

"Who's this, Peg Leg? New stuff?"

"Where's Teodora?"

"She's in her room. She don't want to be disturbed."

"Tell her I have to talk to her."

The woman measured Gabriela from head to toe. As she turned to go, she said:

"They've already been around."

"The police?"

"Some tough guys. Lookin' for you know who."

After a whispered conversation at the door of a bedroom, she returned with Teodora, a bleached blonde, who asked:

"What do you want?"

Peg Leg took her aside and whispered in her ear while both of them looked at Gabriela.

"I don't know where he is. He came by here just a little while ago. He asked for some money and then left in a rush. If they'd found him, they'd have killed him."

"Where did he go?"

"I swear to God I don't know."

Peg Leg and Gabriela returned to the street and he said to her:

"If he ain't here, nobody knows where he is. Chances are he's left town, in a canoe or on horseback."

"Isn't there some way to find out? It's important."

"I don't know none."

"Where does Colonel Amâncio live?"

"You mean Amâncio Leal?"

"Yes."

"Near the public school. D'you know where that is?"

"Over by the beach. I know. Thanks very much."

"I'll go with you part way."

"You don't have to."

"To see that you get out of these alleys, otherwise you might not get there."

As they walked, Peg Leg asked a lot of questions. She answered vaguely, not really telling him anything. He accompanied her as far as Seabra Plaza. The lights were still on in Colonel Ramiro's house, and a few people were standing about, watching it inquisitively. Gabriela walked through the nearly deserted streets, reached the public school, and located Amâncio's house. It had a blue iron gate, as the proprietor of the Big Noise had told her. The house was silent and dark. A late moon had risen, illuminating the wide beach and the coconut palms on the road to Malhado. She clapped her hands.* In vain. She tried again. The

---

* A method used in Brazil by a person in the street to attract the attention of someone inside a house when there is no bell at the gate.

neighborhood dogs started barking and others farther off took up the chorus. Gabriela cried: "Anybody home?" Again she clapped her hands, until they hurt. Finally there was a stirring in the back of the house. Someone turned on a light and called out:

"Who is it?"

"A friend."

A mulatto appeared, bare from the waist up, a pistol in his hand.

"Is Colonel Amâncio in?"

"What do you want with him?" He eyed her suspiciously.

"Somethin' very important."

"He ain't home."

"Where is he?"

"What you wanna know for? What you want with him?"

"I already told you."

"You never told me nothin'—just that it was important. Is that all?"

What could she do? She had to risk it.

"I have a message for him."

"Who from?"

"From Fagundes."

The man stepped back, then came forward and looked at her closely:

"You tellin' the truth?"

"The honest truth."

"Look at me good. If it ain't the truth . . ."

"Quick, please."

"Wait here."

He went in the house and put out the light. After a few minutes he returned. He had put on a shirt.

"Follow me." He stuck the pistol in his belt, with the handle showing. They started walking. He asked her only one question:

"Did he escape?"

She replied with a nod of her head. They entered the street on which Colonel Ramiro lived and stopped in front of the well-known house. On the corner, near the town hall, two policemen looked at them and took a few steps in their direction. The man with the pistol knocked on the door. Through the open windows came a murmur of voices. Jerusa appeared at the window and was so startled when she saw Gabriela that the latter smiled to reassure her. So many persons had been surprised to see her that night. Fagundes most of all.

"Will you please call Colonel Amâncio? Tell him it's Altamiro."

The colonel came quickly to the door.

"Something happen?"

The policemen were approaching. The mulatto noticed them and did not answer. Seeing Amâncio, one of the policemen asked:

"Anything the matter, Colonel?"

"Nothing, thank you. Go back where you were."

After they had left, the man with the pistol said:

"This girl here, she wants to speak to you. From Fagundes."

Amâncio had not noticed Gabriela until then. He recognized her at once.

"It's Gabriela, isn't it? You want to speak to me? Come in, please."

The man entered also. From the entrance hall Gabriela could see the dining room. She saw Tonico and Dr. Alfredo there, and others. Amâncio waited, but she pointed to the man.

"The message is for you only, sir."

"Go on inside, Altamiro. Speak up, my child," he said in his soft voice.

"Fagundes is at my house. He sent me to tell you. He wants to know what to do. And it has to be soon, because in a little while Mr. Nacib will be comin' home."

"At your house? How did he get there?"

"He escaped down the hill. Our back yard is right at the foot."

"That's true; it hadn't occurred to me. And why have you hidden him?"

"I know Fagundes a long time—from the backlands."

Amâncio smiled. Tonico, curious, came into the hallway.

"Thank you very much. I'll never forget it. Come with me."

Tonico returned to the dining room. She followed with Amâncio. She saw the family gathered there. Old Ramiro, in a rocking chair, was pale as death, but his eyes were as bright as those of a young man.

Dishes, coffee cups, and beer bottles littered the table. Seated in one corner of the room were Dr. Alfredo, his wife, and Jerusa. Tonico was standing, glancing at Gabriela obliquely. Dr. Demosthenes, Dr. Maurício, and three other colonels were seated. The kitchen and the patio in back were full of armed men. More than fifteen of them. The maids were serving them food in tin plates. Amâncio said:

"You all know her, don't you? Ga . . . Dona Gabriela, the wife of Nacib, the bar owner. She has come here to do us a favor." Then, turning to her as if he were the head of the house, he said: "Sit down, please."

Thereupon everyone said good evening to her. Tonico gave her a chair. Amâncio went over to the old colonel and spoke to him in a low voice. Ramiro's face lit up and he smiled at Gabriela.

"Bravo, my girl. From this day on, I am forever in your debt. If you need me at any time, you have only to come here—if you need me or any of mine." He pointed to the members of his family. They were in the corner of the room, three of them seated and one standing. It looked like a portrait. Only Dona Olga and the youngest granddaughter were missing. "I want you all to know," said Ramiro, "that if Dona Gabriela ever asks anything of us, we will do it. It will be our obligation and our privilege. Come, Amâncio."

He arose and went with Amâncio to another room. The man with the pistol said good night and left. Gabriela sat there, not knowing what to do, what to say, or where to put her hands. Then Jerusa smiled and spoke to her:

"I talked with you once, do you remember? At the time of grandfather's birthday celebration." Jerusa wondered if she was being indelicate in speaking of an occasion when Gabriela was still the Arab's cook.

"Yes, I remember. I made enough pastry to choke an ox. Was it good?"

Tonico spoke up:

"Gabriela is an old friend of ours. She's our goddaughter—Olga's and mine. I was best man at her wedding."

Dr. Alfredo's wife deigned to smile. Jerusa inquired:

"May I serve you some dessert? Will you have a liqueur?"

"Thanks—don't bother."

She accepted a cup of coffee. Amâncio's voice came from the other room, calling Dr. Alfredo. The assemblyman returned in a few moments and beckoned to Gabriela.

"Will you come with me, please?"

When she entered the other room, Ramiro said:

"My daughter, you have done us a great favor. Only, I wonder if we can place ourselves even more in your debt. Do you think it possible?"

"If it's something I can do."

"We have to get the Negro out of your house—without anybody knowing. It can only be done early in the morning, before daybreak. He must remain hidden until then. Excuse me for insisting on this, but not even Nacib must know about it."

"He'll come home as soon as the bar closes."

"Don't say anything to him. Let him go to sleep. At three o'clock—three o'clock sharp—you get up and go to the window. See if you can see some men in the street; Colonel Amâncio will be with them. If the men are there, open the door and let Fagundes slip out. We'll take care of him."

"You're not goin' to arrest him? Do him harm?"

"You can rest assured. We're going to keep the others from killing him."

"All right, then. Now I must leave, if you'll excuse me. It's late."

"You mustn't go alone. I'll send someone with you. Alfredo, take Dona Gabriela home."

Gabriela smiled.

"I don't know, sir—at night alone on the street with Dr. Alfredo. If someone saw us together, what would they think? What would they say? Tomorrow Mr. Nacib would hear about it."

"You are right, my daughter." He turned to his son. "Tell your wife and Jerusa to get ready. The three of you will take the girl. Hurry."

Alfredo opened his mouth to say something, but Ramiro repeated:

"Hurry!"

Thus it was that on that evening Gabriela was escorted home by an assemblyman, his wife, and his daughter. Alfredo's wife walked in silence, burning up inside. But Jerusa gave Gabriela her arm and talked about a thousand things. Fortunately, Dona Arminda was not at home; it was séance night. A few curiosity seekers were heading up the street, for the man hunt on the hill was still in progress.

Nacib came home shortly after midnight and stayed at the window awhile, watching the men come down from the hill There was a rumor that the Negro had fallen off the precipice Finally, Nacib and Gabriela went to bed.

Not for a long time had she been so caressing and ardent, so giving of herself and so demanding of him. Lately—he had even complained about it—she had been withdrawn, elusive, as if she was always tired. She never refused him when he wanted her, but she no longer sought to stimulate him when he was tired, tickling him and insisting on making love. On nights when he came home exhausted and dropped silently into bed, she would only laugh and let him go to sleep, with his heavy leg thrown across her. Whenever he sought her, she would give herself smilingly, calling him beautiful man and moaning in his arms, but the old wildness was gone. Now it was like a pleasant game; before, it had been a frenzy of love-making, a coming into life and a dying, a mystery unveiled nightly and nightly renewed. He had even complained to his old confidant, Tonico. The notary explained to him that this is what happened in all marriages: love became calmer, the sweet love of a wife, more prudent and less frequent: it was no longer the demanding and lascivious love of a paramour. A good explanation, perhaps, but it did not console him.

Tonight, however, she was her former self once more. She was a raging bonfire, an inextinguishable flame, an ashless fire of sighs and moans. Her skin burned into his. Even when they were not in bed, Nacib always felt her presence—in his heart, in the soles of his feet, in the scalp of his head, in the tips of his fingers. He thought that it would be heavenly to die in her arms. He fell happily asleep, his leg across Gabriela's tired hip.

At three o'clock, Gabriela peeped through the window in the

front room and saw Amâncio leaning against a lamppost, smoking. Some thugs were standing farther down the street. She went
to get Fagundes. As she passed the bedroom door she observed
that Nacib was restless in his sleep, feeling the absence of her
body. She entered the room and placed a pillow under the restive
leg. Nacib smiled. He was such a good man!

"God will repay you some day," said Fagundes in farewell.

"Buy the piece of land with Clemente."

"Let's go," said Amâncio. "Hurry!" And to Gabriela: "Once
again, thank you."

Fagundes looked back as he left and saw her at the door.
There was nobody else in the world like her, nobody.

OF THE JOYS AND SORROWS OF MATRIMONY

That night of elemental forces unleashed in bed, that unforgettable night—with Gabriela consuming herself as in a fire, and
Nacib coming to life and dying in her sweet and terrible flame—
had melancholy consequences.

Nacib thought it meant a return to happy turbulence after the
long stretch of smooth, dull sailing, a hiatus caused by small and
silly misunderstandings. Tonico had attributed the first change to
the fact of matrimony, to subtle and complex differences between
the love of a wife and that of a mistress. It could be true, but
Nacib had his doubts. Why had the change not come about soon
after their marriage? The nights of magic had continued for
some time; again and again they had caused him to oversleep
and to arrive late at the bar. The change became noticeable
when the misunderstandings began. Gabriela must have felt a
good deal more anger than she showed.

Perhaps he had demanded too much of her. He had not taken
her nature sufficiently into account and had virtually forced her
to give up deep-rooted habits. Lacking the patience to train her
gradually, he had tried to change her overnight into a lady of the

upper circles, of the cream of Ilhéan society. She wanted to go to the circus and he dragged her to a tedious, soporific lecture. He tried to keep her from laughing at everything as she was wont to do. He reprimanded her at every turn, for trifles, in his desire to make her act like the wives of the doctors, lawyers, colonels, and merchants. "Don't talk so loud, it's not nice," he would whisper to her in the movies. "Sit up straight, don't stick out your legs, keep your knees together." "Not those shoes. Put on the new ones, what do you have them for?" "Put on a decent dress." "Today we're going to visit my aunt. Watch how you behave." "No, you can't do that tonight. We have to go to the meeting of the Rui Barbosa Literary Society"—which meant she had to listen to the interminable recitation of poems and essays that she could not understand. "Dr. Maurício is speaking tonight at the Commercial Association. We have to be there"—which meant she had to listen to the Bible from beginning to end. "We're going to call on Dona Olga. I know she's a pain, but remember, Tonico was our best man." "Why don't you wear your jewelry? What did I buy it for?"

He must have hurt her, though she did not show it in looks or manner. She simply asked him, a little sadly perhaps, why he wanted her to do these things, and sometimes she asked him please not to make her do them. But she did them: she obeyed his orders, she followed his instructions. Afterwards, she would not mention the subject. She merely became more passive in bed, as if his insistence of making her a lady and their little conflicts of will—they were never quarrels—had dampened her ardor, suppressed her desire, cooled her passion. When he sought her, she opened to him like the corolla of a flower. But no longer hungry and thirsty for love. Only on that night, when he came home after the fatiguing day on which Colonel Aristóteles was shot, had she been as before, perhaps even more passionate. Afterwards, she had returned to the still waters, the tranquil smile, the giving of herself willingly and passively, while he took the initiative. Purposely, he let three days pass without seeking her. She awoke when he came in, kissed him on the face, snuggled her hip under his leg, and went back to sleep, smiling. On the fourth day, he could stand it no longer and blurted out:

"You don't even care."

"I don't care about what, Mr. Nacib?"

"Me. I come home and it's the same as if I didn't."

"Do you want something to eat? A cold drink?"

"The hell with that! You no longer even caress me. You used to pull me to you."

"Mr. Nacib comes in tired. I don't know if he wants me. He turns over and goes to sleep. I don't want to annoy him."

She was twisting a corner of the sheet, her eyes lowered. Nacib had never seen her look so sad, and he was touched. So it was not to annoy him, not to increase his fatigue, to let him rest after his hard day's work. His Bié . . .

"What do you think I am? I can come home tired, but I'm always ready for love. I'm no old man or anything."

"When Mr. Nacib crooks his finger at me, don't I come close to him at once? When I see he wants something?"

"But it's not the same. You used to be a burning torch, a furious wind. Now you're a gentle breeze."

"Don't you like the way I am any more? Have you become tired of your Bié?"

"I like you more all the time, Bié. I can't live without you. You are the one who acts weary."

She kept her eyes on the sheet.

"It's not because of anything. I like you a lot, too. You can believe me, Mr. Nacib. But it's just that I've been feelin' worn out, that's why."

"And whose fault is that? I hired a servant to clean house and you discharged her. I got a girl to help you in the kitchen and you still do all the cooking. Do you want to do everything as if you were still a servant?"

"Mr. Nacib is so good, he's more than a husband."

"Sometimes I'm not. I scold you. I thought maybe that was why you were acting this way. But it's for your own good that I pick on you. I want you to make a good impression on people."

"I like to do what Mr. Nacib wants. But there are some things I just don't know how, no, I don't. No matter how hard I try, I just can't do them. Please be patient with your Bié. You have much to forgive me for."

He took her in his arms. She put her head on his chest. She was crying.

"What have I done to you, Bié? Why are you crying? I won't speak of it any more. I didn't mean to hurt you."

With eyes lowered, she wiped the tears with the back of her hand, and once more she leaned her head against his chest.

"You didn't do anything. I'm the one who's mean. Mr. Nacib is so good."

And again she greeted him with passion on his arrival home, and again they had sleepless nights together. At first he was thrilled. She drove away all his drowsiness and fatigue. Her own fatigue, on the other hand, was apparent and was increasing. One night he said to her:

"Bié, this has got to stop."

"What, Mr. Nacib?"

"You're killing yourself with too much work."

"No, I'm not, Mr. Nacib."

"You can hardly go through with it, at night." He smiled. "Isn't that so?"

"Mr. Nacib is a strong man."

"I'm going to tell you something: I've leased the floor over the bar. As soon as the tenants get out, I'm going to clean the place, paint it, and fix it up as a restaurant. I think we can open by the first of the year. Mr. Mundinho even wants to have an interest. If I agree, he'll send to Rio for a lot of things: an icebox, some kind of fancy stove, and unbreakable dishes and glasses. I'm going to accept his offer."

Gabriela clapped her hands happily.

"I'm going to get two cooks. From Sergipe, maybe. You'll be in charge. All you'll have to do is choose the dishes and show them how to season them. You'll never do any cooking except at home for me; and when you finish teaching your helpers, I don't even want you to do that, except maybe the seasoning. And tomorrow you're going to hire a cleaning woman, you hear me?"

"What for, Mr. Nacib? I'm only tired because I was helpin' Dona Arminda with her housework."

"Why?"

"She's been sick, you know. I couldn't let the poor thing do everything all by herself. But she's better now. I don't need a cleanin' woman. I really don't want one."

He did not argue or insist. His thoughts were concentrated on the restaurant. The floor it would occupy had been a movie theatre before Diogenes built the Ilhéus Cine-Theatre. Then it was divided into offices and rooms for bachelors. The two largest offices were occupied by operators of a numbers game. The owner of the building, Maluf the Arab, wanted to rent all of it to one tenant if possible, and preferably to Nacib, who already occupied the ground floor. He gave the other tenants a month's notice to move. Nacib had a long talk with Mundinho Falcão. The exporter was all for the idea, and they discussed a partnership. He took a magazine out of his desk drawer and showed Nacib pictures of refrigerators, freezers, and all kinds of amazing things used in foreign restaurants. They were going to have a fine place, better than any in Bahia even. During those days, full of so many plans, Nacib forgot about Gabriela's lassitude.

Tonico came in as usual after the siesta, a little before two, for his daily dose of bitters to aid digestion (he stopped paying for it after serving as best man at the proprietor's wedding), and inquired in a low voice:

"How are things at home?"

"Better, except that Gabriela is very tired these days. She simply won't have a cleaning woman. Wants to do all the work herself and help her neighbor, besides. At night she's always dead tired."

"You must be careful not to force her nature. If you insist on hiring a cleaning woman against her wishes, you'll upset her. And you don't seem to understand, Arab, that a wife is not a loose woman. A wife's love is more decorous. Aren't you the man who wanted to make Gabriela into a respectable lady? Begin in bed, my friend. If you want to have a hot time, there are plenty of other women in Ilhéus. Too many, in fact. And some of them are out of this world. You've practically turned into a monk. You don't even go to the cabaret any more."

"I don't want any other woman."

"And then you complain that your wife is tired!"

"She needs a maid. It doesn't even look good for my wife to be doing housework."

Tonico tapped him on the shoulder.

"Leave it to me: I'll get her to hire a maid. Leave it to me."

"I'd appreciate it. She listens to what you tell her. You and Dona Olga."

"You know who's really fond of Gabriela? Jerusa, my niece. She always speaks of her. She says Gabriela is the prettiest woman in Ilhéus."

"She really is," sighed Nacib.

Tonico started to go and Nacib said jokingly:

"You've been leaving early these days. Something's going on. A new woman, eh? Are you keeping secrets from your old friend?"

"Some day I'll tell you all about it."

He went out in the direction of the port. Nacib thought about the restaurant. What would be a good name for it? Mundinho had suggested The Silver Fork. A pointless name; what did it mean? He preferred Commerce Restaurant, a name of distinction.

OF GABRIELA'S SIGHS

Why did he have to marry her? It wasn't necessary. Things were lots better before. But Mr. Tonico, with his eye on her, used his influence with Mr. Nacib, and Dona Arminda, who adored matchmaking, kindled the flame. Mr. Nacib wanted to because he was afraid of losing her, afraid she might go away. That was dumb of Mr. Nacib. Why should she go away when she was so happy where she was? He was afraid she would exchange the kitchen and him for a house of her own, offered her by some planter. With charge accounts in the stores. Some awful old man who wore boots, carried a pistol in his belt, and had money in his pocket. Those were the good days, when she used to go to the bar with Nacib's lunch. A rose at her ear, a smile on her lips. She flirted with everyone and she could sense their desire. They winked at her, said things, touched her hand, and even her breast sometimes. Mr. Nacib was jealous—how funny.

Mr. Nacib would return at night and she would be waiting. She would sleep with him and with all the other young men at the same time, just by thinking about them and wishing it. He would bring her presents: things from the open-air market, cheap things from his uncle's store. Brooches, bracelets, rhinestone rings. He brought her a bird, which she set free. Tight shoes, which she didn't like at all. She used to walk in sandals, her hair tied with a ribbon. She liked everything: the back yard with its trees—cherry, guava, papaya; her gold tooth; the walks through the street. She liked to gab with Tuísca, to dance for him and to get him to dance; to sing in the morning as she worked in the kitchen; to go to the movies with Dona Arminda; and to go to the circus whenever one set up its tent in the vacant lot. Those were the happy days. When she was not Mrs. Saad, just Gabriela. Just Gabriela.

Why did he have to marry her? It was awful being married, she didn't like it at all. The closet full of dresses. Tight shoes, more than three pairs. Even jewels. One of the rings was worth a lot of money; Dona Arminda found out it cost nearly two contos. What was she going to do with all that stuff? She couldn't do any of the things she liked. She couldn't play merry-go-round in the square with Tuísca and Rosinha. She couldn't go to the bar with Mr. Nacib's lunch. She couldn't laugh with Mr. Tonico, Josué, Mr. Ari, Mr. Epaminondas. She couldn't walk barefoot on the sidewalk in front of the house. She couldn't run on the beach, with her feet in the water and the wind blowing through her loose hair. She couldn't laugh whenever she felt like it, wherever she was. She was Mrs. Saad, so she mustn't do such things. It was bad to be married.

She never wanted to offend or hurt him. Mr. Nacib was good, the best in the whole world. He loved her, he really did, he was crazy about her. Such a big man, proprietor of a bar, with money in the bank. It was funny! None of the others had loved

her; they wanted only to lie with her, take her in their arms, kiss
her mouth, pant on her breast. None of them, without exception:
old or young, handsome or ugly, rich or poor. Without exception? Except Clemente. Perhaps Bebinho, too, but he was just a
boy, what did he know about love. Mr. Nacib, ah! he knew about
love. She, too, felt something for him inside herself, different
from what she felt for the others. As for the others, without
exception, without a single exception—not even Clemente, not
even Bebinho—she had wanted only to lie with them. When,
smiling to herself, she thought now of someone like Tonico or
Josué, Epaminondas or Ari, she thought only of being in bed
with the young man, moaning in his arms, biting his mouth, enjoying his body. She felt all of this toward Nacib also, and more
than this: she was fond of him, she liked to be with him, to hear
him talk, to cook spicy dishes for him to eat, to feel his heavy leg
across her at night. She liked him in bed. But not just in bed, not
just for that. For the other things, too. And for these other things,
she liked only him. To her, Mr. Nacib was everything: husband
and employer, the family she had never had, father and
mother, the brother who had died shortly after birth. Mr. Nacib
was everything, all she possessed. It was bad being married. It was
lots better before. The ring on her finger had in no way changed
her feelings toward Mr. Nacib. Only, now that she was married,
she was always arguing with him, displeasing him, hurting him.
She didn't like to hurt him, she didn't like it at all. But how
could she help it? Everything that Gabriela loved was forbidden
to Mrs. Saad. Everything that Mrs. Saad should do was something
Gabriela hated. But she would finally do it in order not to displease Mr. Nacib, because he was so good. The forbidden things
she would do on the sly, without his knowledge, in order not to
upset him.

It was lots better before. She could do everything then. She
danced and sang, and was happy all the time. Nacib was jealous,
but it was a bachelor's jealousy and it quickly disappeared—in
bed. Now there was a sorrow for every joy. For example, she had
to go and visit high-class families. She felt so ill-at-ease, dressed in
silk; her feet hurt, and she had to sit for hours on a hard chair.
Without opening her mouth, so she wouldn't say something

wrong. Without laughing, as if she were made of wood. She didn't like it, she didn't like it at all. What good were all those dresses, shoes, jewels, rings, necklaces, and solid gold earrings, if she couldn't be Gabriela? She hated being Mrs. Saad.

Now that it was too late, why had she agreed to it? Not to displease him? Perhaps afraid of losing him some day? She had made a mistake in agreeing to it. And worst of all, in order to be Gabriela, to retain something of herself, to live her own life, she did things behind his back. And he sometimes learned about them. Her friend Tuísca never even came to see her any more. He adored Nacib, and with good reason. When his mother, Raimunda, was sick, Nacib would send money to her house for food. Mr. Nacib was good. Tuísca thought she should be Mrs. Saad, not Gabriela. That was why he no longer came, because she still often acted like Gabriela and hurt Nacib. Her friend Tuísca, even he didn't understand.

No one understood. Dona Arminda was amazed, said it was evil spirits that prevented her from trying to improve herself. Who ever heard of a person who had everything and still wanted to act like a nobody? Even Tuísca couldn't understand it, much less Dona Arminda.

And at this time, especially, what was she to do? The Christmas festivities were approaching: Nativity scenes, street pageants— she loved all that. In the backlands, she had been a shepherdess in one of the pageants. It didn't amount to much, they had no lanterns even, but it was so much fun! These days she went frequently for dress fittings to Dora the seamstress, whose house was the last one at the top of the street on which Nacib and Gabriela lived. Rehearsals were beginning there for a pageant of The Three Kings, with shepherdesses, lanterns, and everything. Dora said:

"To carry the king's flag, I want nobody but Dona Gabriela."

The seamstress's three helpers agreed. Gabriela's face lit up and she clapped her hands joyfully. But she didn't dare tell Nacib. She went at night, secretly, to rehearse. Every day she intended to speak to Nacib, but always put it off. Dora was making her a satin dress with shining beads and spangles. A shepherdess in The Three Kings, dancing in the streets, carrying the banner,

singing songs, leading the most beautiful pageant in Ilhéus—
this is what she was born for. Mrs. Saad couldn't appear as a
shepherdess in the parade. Gabriela continued to rehearse in
secret. She was determined to see it through. It would displease
Nacib, it would hurt him. But what could she do? Ah! what
could she do?

OF THE CHRISTMAS FESTIVITIES

As Christmas approached, preparations were made for pageants of The Three Kings, graduation parties, church festivals,
and charitable bazaars on the plaza in front of the Vesuvius Bar.
The town was filled with brash, exuberant students, home for
the holidays from the schools and colleges in Bahia. Dancing
parties in the rich homes and belly-bumping sambas in the houses
of the poor on the hills. Drunken sprees and brawls in the
cabarets and street-corner saloons. Junkets to Pontal and picnics
at Malhado and on Pernambuco Hill, from where one could see
the dredges at work. Courtships, engagements. Young people
with newly won degrees in law, medicine, engineering, and
agronomy, wearing their graduation rings and receiving congratulations in the presence of their misty-eyed parents. Young
lady teachers, graduated right there at the parochial school.
Father Basílio, happy as a lark, baptizing his sixth godchild,
delivered by the grace of God from the womb of his housekeeper,
Otália. Ample material for the gossiping old maids.

There had never been a year with so joyful an ending. The
crop had been much greater than anyone could have imagined.
Champagne flowed in the cabarets. A new batch of women arrived on every ship, and the students competed with the young
businessmen and traveling salesmen for their favors. The colonels
flashed big bills and paid for everything, paid with an open
hand. Colonel Manuel's new house, almost a palace, was inaugurated with a big party. There were many new houses and new

streets, with the beach avenue extending now toward the coconut groves of Malhado. Ships arrived from Bahia, Recife, and Rio, loaded with merchandise to meet the increasing demand for greater comfort in the homes. Store after store with bright, attractive show windows. The town was growing, changing.

At Enoch's school, the first examinations under federal supervision were held. The man to whom this little political plum was awarded—that is, the supervisor—arrived from Rio and immediately announced that he would give a lecture. The pupils at Enoch's school sold tickets. Many people went, for the supervisor was a well-known writer for the government newspaper. After an introduction by Josué, he launched into his subject, "The New Currents in Modern Literature from Marinetti to Graça Aranha." It was tremendously dull, and only four or five persons understood it: João Fulgêncio, Nhô-Galo, the Captain, and, to a limited extent, Josué. Ari understood but disagreed. Comparisons were made with the well-remembered Dr. Argileu Palmeira and his thunderous voice. There was a lecturer for you! No comparison. To say nothing of the fact that the young man from Rio couldn't even drink. Two swigs of good local rum and he was pie-eyed. Dr. Argileu, on the other hand, could stand up against the most competent toss-pots in Ilhéus. He could drink like a fish and orate like Rui Barbosa. Talk about talent . . .

Nevertheless, the evening had its diverting aspect. For Gloria, asighing no longer at her lonely window, came into the hall. She was drenched with perfume and, in a lace gown from Bahia, was clearly the best-dressed woman in the audience. She fanned herself, looking for all the world like a respectable matron—not in years, for she was young, but in her bearing, her grave manner, the demureness of her glance, her extreme dignity. As she walked down the aisle in her magnificent and now appeased carnality, a buzz arose among the ladies. Dr. Demosthenes's wife lowered her lorgnette and snorted:

"The hussy!"

Dr. Alfredo's wife—her husband was a state assemblyman, not so important as a federal congressman but important just the same—stood up when the glorious Gloria politely placed her coveted buttocks on the chair next to hers. The offended lady, dragging Jerusa with her, went and sat farther away. Gloria smiled as she gathered her skirts about her. The empty seat next to her was quickly taken by Father Basílio—to such mortification was he driven by Christian charity! The married men stole furtive glances at her and envied that lucky dog Josué. For, despite the great precautions, everyone in Ilhéus knew about the schoolteacher's mad affair with Colonel Coriolano's mistress. Not quite everyone: Colonel Coriolano did not yet know.

Josué arose, pale and thin, to introduce the speaker. He wiped the non-existent sweat from his face with a silk handkerchief, a present from Gloria—by whom, incidentally, he was dressed from head to toe, from the fragrant brilliantine in his hair to the polish on his shoes—and described the journalist from Rio as a "fulgurant talent and prototype of the new generation, the futurists." He eulogized the young man, but mostly he excoriated the hypocrisy prevalent in antecedent literature and in Ilhéan society. Literature was for singing the beauties of life, the joy of living, the bodies of beautiful women. Without hypocrisy. He took occasion to recite a poem inspired by Gloria—a shockingly immoral poem. Gloria, feeling flattered, applauded vigorously. Dr. Alfredo's wife wanted to get up and leave; she did not do so only because Josué had finished and she wanted to hear the speaker of the evening. No one understood the speaker, but at least he was not immoral.

On the whole, people were only mildly shocked, perhaps because Ilhéus was becoming—in the words of Dr. Maurício, a candidate for the mayoralty and a champion of moral austerity— "a paradise for women of ill fame, a place of corrupt customs from which the sobriety, the chastity, the decency of olden days are disappearing." In any case, how could one be troubled by Gloria's presence at a public lecture when the news spread, and was soon confirmed, that Malvina had disappeared? Students arrived by every boat from Bahia. The only one that did not arrive was Malvina, who had been a student with the Sisters of Mercy.

Some thought at first that her father, Melk Tavares, had extended her punishment by depriving her of her vacation. But when Melk unexpectedly went to Bahia and returned alone, somber-faced and looking ten years older, the truth came out. Malvina had taken advantage of the confusion caused by the departure of students for the holidays and had disappeared without a trace. Melk called in the Bahian police, but they could not find her. He then communicated with the police in Rio de Janeiro. Everyone thought she had gone to Rio to live with Rômulo Vieira. No other motive could be found for her sensational flight. It was a juicy morsel for the old maids. Unfortunately, news soon arrived that the engineer, on being questioned by the police in Rio, had satisfied them that he did not know Malvina's whereabouts and in fact had heard nothing of her since his return from Ilhéus. It was a complete mystery. Almost everyone predicted, however, that the girl would soon return, filled with repentance and seeking her father's forgiveness.

João Fulgêncio did not agree:

"Malvina will never beg forgiveness and she'll probably never come back. That girl knows her own mind, and it's a good one. She'll go far—literally and figuratively."

Many months later, at the height of the following year's harvest, it was learned that Malvina was working in an office in São Paulo, studying at night, and living alone. Her mother took a new lease on life, but never left the house after that. Melk refused to listen to anything about the girl:

"I have no daughter."

But all this came to pass later. At that year-end, Malvina's disappearance was considered scandalous. Dr. Maurício used it in his vigorous pre-campaign speeches to support his contentions about current morality.

Although the elections would not be held until May, the lawyer lost no opportunity to harangue the people. But he persuaded few. The new ways were penetrating everywhere, even into the homes. Especially now, with the arrival of the students on holiday. All these young men sided with the Captain. They even gave him a dinner in Nacib's bar, at which a third-year law student acclaimed him as "the future Mayor, who will rid Ilhéus of its backwardness, its ignorance, and its small-town mentality, a man who understands and will promote the progress that is just beginning to shed the rays of civilization on the capital of cacao." The student who said this was a son of Colonel Coriolano, one of Ramiro's most loyal followers. Worse still was the case of Amâncio Leal's son, who stood up against his father in endless arguments:

"It's no use, Father. Don't you see how things are? My godfather Ramiro is the past; Mundinho Falcão is the future." The boy was a student of engineering in São Paulo, and all he talked about was highways, machinery, and progress. "You're right in sticking with Colonel Ramiro. You have reasons of sentiment and affection that I respect. I understand your point of view; you should try to understand mine." He associated with the engineers and technicians working on the sandbar. He even put on a diving suit and went down to the bottom of the channel.

Amâncio listened, put up arguments, and let himself be beaten. He was proud of his son, a brilliant and dedicated student.

"Who knows, perhaps you're right. Times have changed. Only, I started out with Ramiro. You weren't even born. I was just a youngster and he was a grown man, but we always stood by each other. We shed a lot of blood together, and together we got rich. I'm not going to abandon him now, when the man is in trouble and near death."

"You're right, sir. And I am, too. I like my godfather, but if I were voting I would vote for the other side."

Those were happy days for Amâncio. Early in the morning he would leave the house to go to the fish market, just as Berto, his son, was coming in from an all-night spree. They would talk awhile together. This son, his oldest, was a great joy to him. He took occasion to give the boy a bit of advice:

"You're mixed up with Florêncio's wife." Florêncio was an elderly colonel who had married, in Bahia, the young fiery daughter of a Syrian couple; she had languorous eyes. "You enter his house at night, through the back door. There are so many other women in Ilhéus, in the cabarets. Aren't they enough for you? Why do you get mixed up with a married woman? Florêncio wasn't born to be cuckolded. If he learns about it . . . I don't want to have to provide you with a bodyguard. Put an end to it, Berto. I'm afraid for you." He was laughing to himself: that son-of-a-gun of a boy of his, putting horns on poor old Florêncio.

"It's not my fault, Father. She practically seduced me. I'm not made of wood. But don't worry. She's going to Bahia for the holidays. Tell me, Father, when will there be an end in Ilhéus to this business of killing a woman who deceives her husband? I never saw such a place! A fellow can't slip out of a house at four o'clock in the morning without every window on the street opening and everybody sticking his head out."

Amâncio gazed at the boy with his one good eye, filled with tenderness.

"Son-of-a-gun . . ."

He visited Ramiro every day without fail. The old man was directing the campaign, with Amâncio, Melk, Coriolano, and a few others as his lieutenants. Alfredo took advantage of the Assembly's holiday recess to travel through the interior and call on influential voters. Tonico was useless; he could not get his mind off women. Amâncio would listen to Ramiro talk and give him encouraging news, not all of it quite true. He knew they would lose. To keep himself in power, Ramiro would have to depend on the government to block his adversaries by refusing to recognize their election. But the old man would not permit such an eventuality even to be mentioned. He considered his position unshakable and maintained that he had the people with him. As proof he cited the case of Nacib's wife coming at night, braving the streets, to save their names and Melk's; she did this so that they would not become publicly involved in the attempt on Aristóteles's life, which certainly would have happened if the Negro had been caught by the men from Itabuna. Their non-involvement was especially important in view of the treachery of the state Justice Department in appointing a special prosecutor to take charge of the investigation.

"In my opinion, Amâncio, the Negro would have died rather than talk. He's a decent, loyal Negro. Too bad he missed."

Aristóteles recovered his health and even put on a little weight after leaving the hospital. He declared that Itabuna would vote unanimously for Mundinho Falcão. He went to Bahia, where he was interviewed by the press. The Governor was unable to keep the Justice Department from taking up the case. Mundinho had aroused many persons in Rio, where the crime made a deep impression. A congressman of the opposition told the federal legislature that the wild and woolly days in the cacao region had returned.

Lots of noise, but no arrests. The case was difficult. The criminal was rumored to be a ruffian by the name of Fagundes who, together with a certain Clemente, worked by contract on Melk Tavares's lands. But there was no proof. Nor was there proof of the complicity of Ramiro, Amâncio, or Melk. The case was finally filed away, along with the special prosecutor. But the harm had been done.

"Damned bastards!" said Ramiro, referring to the Justice Department.

They had even wanted to discharge the Chief of Police. Ramiro had had to send Alfredo to Bahia to demand that he be kept in his job. Not that the police chief was any good—a big, lazy coward who crapped from fear when he faced the men from Itabuna. But, if they fired the lieutenant, it would be he, Ramiro, who would lose face.

He talked daily with Amâncio, with Tonico, with Melk. It was his one hour of activity, of real living, for now he spent much of the time in bed. He was skin and bones, but the light shone in his eyes whenever he discussed politics. Dr. Demosthenes also came every day to see him, and now and then listened to his heart and took his pulse.

Although forbidden by the doctor to do so, Ramiro left the house at night—just once—to go to the inauguration of the Dos Reis sisters' Nativity tableau. He could not miss that. And who, in the whole town, did not go! The house was crowded.

Gabriela had helped Quinquina and Florzinha with their final preparations: she cut out pictures and pasted them on cardboard, and she made tissue-paper flowers. At Nacib's uncle's house she found some magazines from Syria; this is how a number of Mohammedans and oriental pashas and sultans happened to get into the tableau, to the great delight of João Fulgêncio, Nhô-Galo, and Felipe the cobbler. Joaquim built some hydroplanes out of light cardboard and hung them over the manger. They were that year's great novelty.

To preserve their neutrality (the crèche, Nacib's bar, and the Commercial Association were the only neutral grounds during the electoral campaigns), Quinquina begged the Doctor to speak at the inauguration and Florzinha made a similar appeal to Dr. Maurício. Both orators showered the spinsters' silvery heads with beautiful phrases. The Captain also spoke to them in secret, soliciting their votes and promising them official aid if he was elected. People came from afar to see the grand spectacle: from Itabuna, from Pirangi, from Água Preta, and even from Itapira. Whole families. From Itapira came Dona Vera and Dona Angela, who clapped their hands ecstatically and said:

"How marvelous!"

The fame not only of the tableau but also of Gabriela's cooking had reached that distant city. With the room full of people, Dona Vera dragged Gabriela off into a corner and asked her for detailed recipes of some of her special sauces and dishes.

From Água Preta came Nacib's sister and brother-in-law. They did not call on Nacib and Gabriela. At the inauguration party, Nacib's sister gave her timid sister-in-law, seated awkwardly on a chair, an insultingly disdainful once-over. When Gabriela smiled at her, she turned her back. Gabriela was soon avenged by Dona Vera, whom Nacib's sister was trying to flatter with little laughs and attentions. After introducing Dona Angela, Dona Vera said:

"Your sister-in-law is charming. So pretty and well-mannered. Your brother was lucky, he made a fine marriage."

Old Ramiro avenged her even more when he entered the room with his halting step. The crowd made way for him to pass and left room for him in front of the tableau. He spoke with the Dos Reis sisters. He complimented Joaquim on his work. But then Ramiro spied Gabriela and dropped everybody to go over to her. He pressed her hand warmly.

"How are you, Dona Gabriela? I haven't seen you in a long time. Why don't you come to call? One day I want you and Nacib to come to my house for lunch."

Jerusa, at her grandfather's side, smiled and talked to Gabriela. The agronomist's wife trembled with fury. And finally Nacib, too, avenged Gabriela. He did it deliberately; Mr. Nacib was so good. It happened when he came to get her and they were leaving together arm in arm. As they passed close by his sister and

brother-in-law, Nacib said in a voice loud enough for them to
hear:

"Bié, my little wife, you're the most beautiful woman here."

Gabriela lowered her eyes. She felt sad, not because of her
sister-in-law's scorn, but because, with his sister in town, Nacib
would never let her join in the pageant of The Three Kings,
dressed as a shepherdess and carrying the banner.

She had put off speaking to him about it until nearer the end
of the year. In the meantime she joyfully attended the rehearsals,
which were directed by the young man, smelling of the sea, whom
she had met at the Big Noise on the night of the hunt for
Fagundes. He had been a sailor but now worked on the docks in
Ilhéus. His name was Nilo. A spirited young man and an expert
director. He taught her the steps and how to hold the banner.
Sometimes the others danced well into the morning—on Saturdays, until daybreak. But Gabriela always came home right after
the rehearsal, in case Mr. Nacib returned early. She had decided
not to speak to him until shortly before the pageant was to take
place. In this way, if he did not give his consent, at least she
would have enjoyed the rehearsals. Dora was getting worried:

"Have you spoken to him, Dona Gabriela? Do you want me to
speak to him?"

Now it was all over, impossible. With his sister in town, eager
to see him ashamed of Gabriela, Nacib would never consent to
her parading through the streets, bearing the standard with Baby
Jesus on it. And he was right. With his sister in Ilhéus it was impossible. He was right. To displease him that much, hurt him
that much, she just couldn't . . .

OF THE SHEPHERDESS GABRIELA, OR MRS. SAAD AT THE BALL

"What would my sister say, and her jackass of a husband?" No,
Gabriela, he could never let her do a thing like that.

What would the people of Ilhéus say, especially his friends at the bar, the ladies of good family, and Colonel Ramiro, who had distinguished her so? Impossible, Gabriela; he never heard of anything so absurd. Bié must realize that she is no longer a poor servant girl with no family, no name, no date of birth. Can you imagine Mrs. Nacib Saad leading a street pageant, with a crown of gilt cardboard on her head? Can you imagine a woman of social distinction swinging her hips and dancing along the street, dressed in blue and red satin, carrying a banner, and followed by twenty-two other shepherdesses carrying lanterns? Impossible, Bié, what a crazy idea!

Sure, he would like to see the pageant; he would applaud the paraders when they stopped in front of the bar and he would order a round of beer for them. Who didn't like the pageant of The Three Kings? It was beautiful, he didn't deny it. But had she ever seen a distinguished married woman in the pageant? Don't come giving him Dora as an example, because it was just on account of things like that that her husband left her and she was obliged to work at her sewing machine for others. And besides, his snooty sister was in town, and that brother-in-law, all puffed up with his college graduation ring. Impossible, Gabriela, let's not talk about it any more.

She bowed her head in agreement. He was right, she could not offend and humiliate him in the presence of his sister and brother-in-law. He took her and sat her on his lap:

"Don't be sad, Bié. Smile for me."

She smiled, but inside she was crying. She cried that afternoon over the satin dress, so beautiful it was, blue and red, the loveliest combination of colors. She cried over the golden crown with a star on it. She cried over the banner with the colors of their group, with Baby Jesus and his lamb sewn in the middle. She was not consoled by the present Nacib brought her when he came home that night: an expensive embroidered scarf with a fringe.

"For you to wear at the ball," he said, "the New Year's party. I want Bié to be the most beautiful woman there."

The main subject of conversation in Ilhéus was the ball planned by the girl and boy students for New Year's eve at the Progress Club. The local seamstresses could not handle all the orders, and dresses were arriving from Bahia. In the tailor shops, men's white linen suits were being tried on. All of the tables were reserved well ahead of time. Even Mister was going; he was taking his wife, who had come to spend Christmas with him, as she did every year. Instead of the usual parties in the homes, all of Ilhéan society was going to gather at the Progress Club for the great ball.

On the same night the pageant would parade through the streets—without Gabriela. She would be at the ball in her lace mantilla, silk dress, and tight shoes. She would sit there in silence with her eyes lowered, not knowing how to act. Who would carry the banner? Dora was heartbroken. Nilo, the young man who smelled of the sea, did not hide his disappointment. Only Miquelina seemed pleased; perhaps she would be chosen to carry the banner.

Gabriela forgot her unhappiness for a little while and stopped crying when a carnival show was set up on the vacant land at Unhão. The Chinese Carnival it was, with a Ferris wheel, a merry-go-round, a whip, and a crazy house. Shiny bright metal and a flood of light. It caused so much talk that Tuísca, who had been so remote of late, could not resist and came around to discuss the event.

Nacib said to her:

"On the day before Christmas I won't stay at the bar; I'll just look in on it. We'll go to the carnival in the afternoon and to the charity bazaar at night."

That was more like it. She went on all the rides with Mr. Nacib—twice on the Ferris wheel. The whip was tremendous fun, it gave you a little chill under your navel.

She came out dizzy from the crazy house. Tuísca, wearing shoes—he, too!—and new clothes, rode everything free for having helped post bills all over town.

At night they went to the bazaar on the square in front of the Church of St. Sebastian. Tonico and Dona Olga came by, and Nacib left Gabriela with them for a few minutes while he looked in at the bar to see how things were going. Girl students were selling things in the stalls, and Ari Santos, sweating profusely, was conducting an auction for the benefit of the church.

"A dish of sweets donated by the gracious Miss Iracema," he shouted. "Made with her own hands. How much am I offered?"

"Five milreis," bid a medical student.

"Eight," said a clerk.

"Ten," offered a law student.

Iracema had many beaus, who competed with one another for rendezvous at her front gate, and now for her dish of sweets. When the auction started, people came from the bar to watch and participate. The plaza was filled with families, sweethearts exchanging signals, and smiling couples arm in arm.

"A tea set, donated by Miss Jerusa Bastos. Six cups, six saucers, six cake plates, and other pieces. How much am I offered?"

Ari Santos held up a small cup.

The girls eyed one another in rivalry, for each hoped that her gift to St. Sebastian would fetch the highest price. Their suitors and fiancés bid generously. Sometimes colonels would lock horns over an item. The excitement increased as their bids climbed to one hundred and two hundred milreis. In a bidding duel with Ribeirinho, Amâncio Leal paid five hundred milreis for six napkins. That was really throwing money away, but money flowed freely in Ilhéus. The marriageable girls gave encouraging looks to their sweethearts and would-be sweethearts, and watched to see how they behaved when the auctioneer put up their gifts. Iracema's dish of sweets went for eighty milreis. It was bid in by Epaminondas, the youngest partner in Soares & Bros., a dry-goods store. Poor Jerusa, without a sweetheart. Somewhat aloof, she did not encourage the young men of Ilhéus. There were whispers of a sweetheart in Bahia, a fifth-year medical student. If her family did not enter the bidding—her uncle Tonico and Dona Olga, or some friend of her grandfather—her tea set would probably not be sold at all. Iracema smiled victoriously.

"How much am I offered for the tea set?"

"Ten milreis," said Tonico.

Gabriela bid fifteen, with Nacib once more at her side. Colonel Amâncio, who would certainly have raised the bid, was no longer there; he had left for the cabaret. Ari Santos, on the platform, was sweating and shouting:

"Fifteen milreis. Do I hear more?"

"One thousand milreis."

"What was that? Who said that? Please don't joke."

"One thousand milreis," repeated Mundinho Falcão.

"Ah! Mr. Mundinho. Fine. Miss Jerusa, will you please deliver the tea set to the gentleman? One thousand milreis, my friends, one thousand milreis! St. Sebastian will be eternally grateful to Mr. Mundinho. As you know, this money goes to build a new church on the same spot, an enormous church to replace the present one. Mr. Mundinho, I'll take the money. Thank you very much."

Jerusa stepped up, took the box containing the tea set, and handed it to the exporter. The girls who had lost first place discussed his mad gesture. What did it signify? This Mundinho was engaged in mortal combat with Jerusa's family; newspapers had been burned, murder attempted. He defied old Ramiro, challenged his powers, gave him heart attacks. Yet here he was paying one thousand milreis, two crisp bills of five hundred each, for half a dozen cheap china cups put up at auction by his enemy's granddaughter. He must be crazy. But all of them, from Iracema to Diva, sighed for him. He was a rich bachelor, handsome, elegant, and widely traveled; he went constantly to Bahia, owned a house in Rio. . . . The girls knew about his affairs with women—with Anabela and with others brought from Bahia and from the south; sometimes they would see one of them, elegant and free, strolling on the beach avenue. But he never courted Jerusa or, for that matter, any of the other unmarried girls in Ilhéus. In fact, he hardly looked at them.

"It wasn't worth that much," said Jerusa.

"You see, I'm a sinner. In this way, through your influence, I'll get in good with the saints, I'll win a place in heaven."

She smiled and, after a moment's hesitation, asked:

"Are you going to the ball?"

"I don't know yet. I may have to spend New Year's eve in Itabuna."

"I hear they're going to have a big celebration there. But so are we."

"I hope you enjoy yourself and I wish you a happy new year."

"The same to you . . . if we don't meet again before then."

Tonico Bastos was watching them. He couldn't understand the fellow. Tonico still hoped for a last-minute compromise that would save the Bastoses' prestige. He greeted Mundinho with a smile. The exporter smiled back and left; he was going home.

On the day before New Year's, Mundinho went to Itabuna, lunched with Aristóteles, and attended the opening of the cattle fair, an important new event that would attract the cattle trade of the whole region. He made a speech, was applauded, got in his car, and returned to Ilhéus. Not because of Jerusa but because he wanted to spend the evening with his friends at the Progress Club.

The ball was a splendid affair. People said that nothing like it could be seen anywhere else, except of course in Rio. True, the crêpes de Chine, taffetas, velvets, and jewels could not wholly hide the rusticity and lack of refinement of some of the ladies, just as the thick wads of five-hundred-milreis bills in the colonels' pockets could not conceal their awkward manners and rough speech. But more important than the colonels and their ladies were the young people who planned and took charge of the party. They had painstakingly decorated the club with paper streamers and artificial flowers. Some of the boys wore tuxedos in spite of the heat. The girls laughed, fluttered their fans, flirted, and sipped cool drinks. Virtually everyone of importance was there—even João Fulgêncio, who hated balls. Champagne flowed in abundance.

Jerusa smiled when she spied Mundinho Falcão in conversation with Nacib and the good Gabriela, whose left shoe pinched her big toe so terribly that she could hardly remain standing. Despite her discomfort, she looked delightfully pretty. Even the haughtiest ladies, even Dr. Demosthenes's wife, admitted that the mulatto girl was the belle of the ball.

"An ordinary little nobody, but very pretty."

She was a daughter of the people lost in a jumble of incomprehensible talk, of unattractive sumptuousness, and of envies, vanities, and gossip that did not interest her. In a little while the pageant of The Three Kings, with the gay shepherdesses and the embroidered banner, would be in the streets. It would halt in front of houses and bars, and the paraders would sing, dance, and invite themselves inside. The doors would be opened to them, they would dance and sing in the front rooms, they would sip liqueurs and eat sweets. On this New Year's eve and again at Epiphany, more than ten pageants would come from Unhão, from Conquista, from Cobras Island, and from Pontal across the river, to frolic in the streets of Ilhéus.

Gabriela danced with Nacib, with Tonico, with Ari, and with the Captain. She twirled about gracefully, but she did not love to dance these dances. Moving around in the arms of a gentleman. A dance to her was something else: a samba ring, a fast maxixe, a lively *coco* dance such as they did in the backlands. Or even a polka to the tune of a concertina. Argentine tangos, waltzes, fox trots she didn't like. Especially when her shoes pinched.

The party was very gay. Only Josué seemed glum. He stood at the window and looked outside, a glass in his hand. The sidewalk and street in front of the building were crowded with people watching the ball through the windows. Gloria was in the crowd. Standing beside her, as if by chance, was Coriolano; he was tired and eager to go to what he called *his* party, i.e., Gloria's bed. But Gloria lingered on the sidewalk and looked at Josué's thin face in the window. Champagne corks were popping at the tables. Mundinho Falcão, in much demand by the girls, danced with Jerusa, Diva, and Iracema, and asked Gabriela to dance, too.

Nacib joined a group of men. He did not like to dance. Two or three times during the evening, he went around the floor with Gabriela; then, each time, he left her at a table with João Fulgêncio's wife. Under the tablecloth, Gabriela pulled off her shoe and rubbed the aching toe. She struggled to keep from yawning. Other ladies came, sat at the table, and started talking animatedly with Mrs. Fulgêncio. Condescendingly, they would say good evening to Gabriela and ask how she was. She remained there, silently staring at the floor. Tonico, like some priest performing a complicated rite, steered Dona Olga through an Argentine tango. Boys and girls, frolicking and laughing, danced mainly in the rear hall, which they had declared out of bounds for the older people. Nacib's sister and her husband danced superciliously. They pretended not to see Gabriela.

About eleven o'clock, when the crowd out in front had dwindled to only a few people—Gloria and Coriolano had long since left—one could hear sounds of music coming from the street: ukeleles and guitars, flutes and tambourines. And voices singing songs of The Three Kings. Gabriela raised her head. No mistake about it: it was Dora's pageant.

The paraders halted in front of the Progress Club. The dance orchestra stopped playing and everybody ran to the windows and front doors. Gabriela hastily forced her foot into her shoe and was one of the first to reach the sidewalk. Nacib joined her there. His sister and brother-in-law were standing close by, still pretending they did not see her.

Shepherdesses with lanterns. Miquelina carrying the banner. Nilo, the ex-seaman, with a whistle between his lips, directing everything. From Seabra Plaza, at the same time, came a group doing the traditional ox pageant, with its three principal characters—the "ox," the cowherd, and the hillbilly. People in both groups were dancing. The shepherdesses sang:

> *"I'm a pretty shepherdess,*
> > *I've braved the night's dark danger*
> *To come and pray with kings*
> > *To a little Babe in a manger."*

The participants in the pageant did not invite themselves in, for the affair at the Progress Club was too formal, too swanky, for that. But Plínio Araçá, at the head of some waiters, brought out bottles of beer and passed them around. The ox stopped dancing a minute to drink.

Then they all resumed their dancing and singing. Miquelina, in the center, held the banner and swung her thin hips. Nilo blew his whistle. Guests from the ball crowded the sidewalk. The young people laughed and clapped hands in time to the singing, whose tempo was livelier than the words might suggest:

> *"I'm a pretty shepherdess*
> > *All made of gold and light,*
> *And with my song I'll lull*
> > *The Babe to sleep this night."*

Gabriela could see nothing but the pageant of The Three Kings: the shepherdesses with their lanterns, Nilo with his whistle, and Miquelina with the banner. She could not see Nacib, she could not see Tonico, she could not see her sister-in-law with her nose in the air. The ox pageant had already started moving. Nilo blew his whistle and the shepherdesses took their positions. He blew it once more and they began to dance. Miquelina was waving the banner in the night air.

> *"The shepherdesses go now*
> *To sing and dance elsewhere . . ."*

"Oh!" exclaimed Nacib's sister. For Gabriela had kicked off her shoes, run to the front, and snatched the banner from Miquelina's hands. Her body whirled, her hips swung, her liberated feet set the dancing pace. The pageant started off down the street.

Jerusa looked at Nacib; he was almost crying with shame. And then she too stepped out, took a lantern from a shepherdess, and began to dance. A young man joined in, then another. Iracema took Dora's lantern. Mundinho Falcão took Nilo's whistle. Mister and his wife started dancing. João Fulgêncio's wife, the happy mother of six children, got into step. Other ladies, too; and the Captain, and Josué, and everybody. At the tail end were Nacib's sister and her agronomist husband. At the front, Gabriela with the banner in her hand.

FROM THE ARISTOCRATIC OFENÍSIA TO THE PLEBEIAN GABRIELA, WITH DIVERS EVENTS AND THEFTS OF MONEY

Many exciting and even scandalous events occurred early that new year. For one thing, the students considered it their duty to transform the simple inauguration of the Commercial Association's library into a big celebration.

"All these kids want to do is dance," complained Ataúlfo.

The Captain, however, who had organized the library with João Fulgêncio's help, saw in the students' idea an excellent opportunity to advertise his candidacy for mayor. And besides, as he told Ataúlfo, the students did not wish merely to amuse themselves. This was immediately apparent in the earnest speech, made by Ribeirinho's son, a second-year medical student. He indicated the immense significance to Ilhéus of this, its first real library. (The one at the Rui Barbosa Literary Society consisted of only one small bookcase, filled mostly with poetry.) It was a type of celebration hitherto unknown in Ilhéus. The students organized a literary soirée in which several of them took part, along with outstanding personalities such as the Doctor, Ari Santos, and Josué. The Captain and Dr. Maurício made speeches, the former ostensibly as librarian of the Association and the latter as its official orator, but both really as candidates for the mayoralty. Young ladies of Ilhéan society, including girls from the parochial school, gave poetry readings. Some were ill at ease, others were quite self-assured. Diva, who possessed a clear and agreeable voice, sang a lyrical number. Jerusa played a piece by Chopin on the piano. Verses by Bilac, Raimundo Correia, and Castro Alves—and of course some by Teodoro de Castro in praise of Ofenísia—resounded through the hall; so did poems by Ari and Josué, recited by the authors themselves. To the school inspector from Rio, it was all a ludicrous caricature of culture, exactly what one would expect in a provincial town. But the people of Ilhéus found it stimulating and charming.

"Delightful," commented Quinquina.

"Really worthwhile," agreed Florzinha.

The artistic program was followed, naturally, by dancing. And so ended the celebration. Subsequently, to run the library, the Association brought from Belmonte the poet Sosígenes Costa, who was to exercise a notable influence on the cultural life of the community.

Apropos of culture and literature, and especially of Teodoro's verses, one must not overlook the publication of a small book consisting of chapters from the Doctor's magnum opus, *A History of the Ávila Family and of the City of Ilhéus*. It was printed right there in Ilhéus on João Fulgêncio's press by the master hand of Joaquim. Not with that title, however; as he was publishing only the chapters referring to Ofenísia and her controversial affair with the Emperor, Dom Pedro II, the Doctor modestly labeled it *A Historic Love Affair,* with a subtitle in parentheses *(Echoes of an Old Polemic)*. Eighty pages, in 7-point type, of erudition and conjecture, in a prose style reminiscent of the sixteenth century. There was the romantic story in all its details, with abundant quotations from other authors and from Teodoro's verses. The booklet crowned with glory the venerable head of the illustrious Ilhéan. True, a critic in the state capital declared the slim volume unreadable and "asinine beyond imagination." But this critic was a mean and envious man, a half-starved newspaper hack, a composer of mordant epigrams against the glories of Bahian literature. On the other hand, from Novo Mundo, where he was busy starting a fourth family, the eminent bard Argileu Palmeira sent to a newspaper in Bahia six panegyrical pages on the passion of Ofenísia, "an early and exalted instance of the concept of free love in Brazil." Another curious observation, though hardly a literary one, was made by Nhô-Galo in conversation with João Fulgêncio at the stationery store:

"Have you noticed, João, that the physique of our Ofenísia has changed? She used to be as skinny as a piece of jerked beef. In this little book she's put on some weight. Read page fourteen. Do you know whom she looks like now? Gabriela."

João Fulgêncio gave his intelligent, kindly laugh.

"Who in the whole town hasn't fallen in love with her? If she were running for election as mayor, she could beat either the Captain or Maurício, or both of them together. Everybody would vote for her."

"The women would be against her, if they had the right to vote."

"Not all of them by any means. There's something unique about Gabriela. Take what happened at the New Year's ball, for example. Who was it that drew everybody to the street and started them dancing? I believe she has the kind of magic that causes revolutions and promotes great discoveries. There's nothing I enjoy more than to observe Gabriela in the midst of a group of people. Do you know what she reminds me of? A fragrant rose in a bouquet of artificial flowers."

The days following the publication of the Doctor's little volume, however, were days of Ofenísia and not of Gabriela. The noble Ávila and her passionate sighs for the royal beard enjoyed a new wave of popularity. She was talked about in the homes at dinner, in the Progress Club (currently in a constant succession of lively spur-of-the-moment parties and tea dances), in the buses, in the trains, in the bars, and among the young girls and college students in their now habitual strolls along the beach avenue. Ofenísia's name was heard even in the cabarets, in connection with a Spanish girl recently arrived in Ilhéus. She had large, black eyes and a hooked nose, and hung out in the El Dorado, a new cabaret near the waterfront. She loved Mundinho, but the exporter was fully occupied with a chanteuse whom he had brought back from Rio on his last trip there. Observing the Spanish girl's sighs and languishing glances, some joker nicknamed her Ofenísia. The name stuck and followed her even after she left Ilhéus for the diamond fields of Minas Gerais.

Important inaugurations occurred in rapid succession during the early months of the new year. One was the opening of the El Dorado, which belonged to Plínio Araçá and provided stiff competition to the Bataclan and the Trianon, for all its entertainers and women came from Rio. Dr. Demosthenes's new hospital was also inaugurated, with the blessing of the Bishop and a speech by Dr. Maurício. After the inauguration, by a strange coincidence which escaped the attention of Dona Arminda, the first patient in the operating room to which Aristóteles had been taken was the notorious Whitey. He had a bullet in his shoulder, the result of a brawl at the Big Noise. A vice-consulate of Sweden was established and, at the same address, the agency of a Swedish steamship company with a long, unpronounceable name. Sometimes, in Nacib's bar, one would see a bean-pole of a gringo drinking Ilhéan white rum in the company of Mundinho Falcão. He was the Swedish vice-consul and agent of the steamship company. A colossal new hotel, five stories high, was being built.

A somewhat less important event, except perhaps in its impli-

cations, was the temporary change of the *Southern Journal* from
a weekly to a daily. It was now devoted almost exclusively to politics. In every issue it lambasted Mundinho Falcão, Aristóteles,
and the Captain. The *Ilhéus Daily* answered the charges. It also
published a statement by the students calling for the election as
mayor of whichever candidate would publicly commit himself to
extend the highway as far as Pirangi and to build a municipal
high school, a sports stadium, and a home for the old and the
indigent. In the following issue, the Captain promised all this
and more.

An early date was announced for the opening of Nacib's restaurant. Several of the upstairs tenants had already moved out.
Only the numbers-game office and the two store clerks had not
yet found new quarters; Nacib kept after them. Through his silent partner, Mundinho, he ordered various things from Rio.
The crazy architect designed the interior of the restaurant. The
Arab was happy again. Not with that complete happiness of the
early days with Gabriela, before he began to fear he would lose
her. Such a possibility no longer worried him, but for him to become completely happy she would have to make up her mind
once and for all to comport herself like a lady. He no longer complained of her lukewarmness in bed. He felt pretty tired himself
these days, for he worked very hard at the bar. He had become
accustomed to the conjugal type of love, less impulsive, more
tender and tranquil. But what he refused to accept was her passive refusal to become a member of society. This, in spite of the
fact that she had made a hit in the episode of the pageant on
New Year's eve. At a moment when Nacib felt that all was lost,
that wonderful thing had happened; even he had joined the
dancing in the street. And had not his sister and brother-in-law
come to call on them afterwards to get acquainted with Gabriela?
Why, then, did she continue to go around the house dressed like
a pauper? Why did she wear slippers, play with the cat, cook,
clean house, sing folksongs, and laugh loudly with everybody she
talked to?

He was counting on the restaurant to get her into line. Tonico
said it probably would. Two or three kitchen helpers were to be
hired for the restaurant, and this would put Gabriela in the posi-

tion of proprietor's wife and lady, who merely supervised the kitchen and took care of the seasoning. It would bring her into daily contact with high-class customers.

The thing that bothered him most was that she did not want a cleaning woman to help her. The house was small, but even so there was plenty of work. Gabriela insisted on doing everything. The kitchen helper complained that she would not let her help with the cooking. The girl merely washed dishes, stirred the pots, and trimmed the meat. Gabriela herself prepared all the food.

The terrible blow fell on a quiet afternoon when he was enjoying perfect tranquillity of spirit, pleased with the good news he had just received that the numbers-game people were moving out. He now had only to speed up the departure of the two clerks. Soon the equipment from Rio would arrive. He had a brick-mason and a painter already lined up to transform the dirty, partitioned space upstairs into a jewel of a place—a well-lighted dining room and a kitchen modern in every respect but one: Gabriela insisted on a large, brick, wood-burning stove. Everything else had been worked out with the mason and the painter to his complete satisfaction. Well, it was on this afternoon that he caught Eaglebeak redhanded taking money out of the till. It was no great surprise, for he had been suspicious of Eaglebeak for some time. Nevertheless, Nacib lost his head and struck the boy.

"Thief! Robber!"

Oddly enough, he did not think of firing him; he just wanted to teach him a lesson. But Eaglebeak, knocked to the floor by the blows, started to insult him:

"The thief is you, you shitty Turk! Cheating on brands. Padding charge accounts."

He had to slap him a few more times, but still did not intend to fire him. He picked Eaglebeak up by the shirt front and hit him hard in the face.

"To teach you not to steal."

He let him go. The boy ran out from behind the counter, crying and yelling:

"You lousy bastard, why don't you go home and beat your wife?"

"Shut up, or I'll really hit you."

"Come on!" shouted Eaglebeak, heading for the door. "You Turkish cuckold, son of a bitch! Why don't you take care of your wife? Don't your horns hurt you?"

Nacib went after the boy and managed to grab him.

"What did you say?"

"Nothing, Mr. Nacib. . . . Let me go. . . ."

"What is it you know? Tell me, or I'll bust you wide open."

"It was Lazy Chico who told me."

"Told you what?"

"That she's deceiving you with Mr. Tonico."

"With Tonico? Tell me everything, quickly." He held him so tightly that he tore the boy's shirt.

"Every day, after he leaves here, Mr. Tonico sneaks into your house."

"You're lying, you miserable creature."

"Everybody knows about it and laughs behind your back. Let me go, Mr. Nacib."

He loosed his hold and Eaglebeak ran out. Nacib was stunned, blind, deaf, unable to move, unable to think. This was how Lazy Chico found him when he returned from the ice plant.

"Mr. Nacib!"

Mr. Nacib was crying.

He took Lazy Chico to the poker room in the back and made him tell all he knew. Nacib listened, with his hands over his face. Chico rattled off names and details. Right from the time he had hired her at the slave market. Tonico was recent, started just after the wedding. Nacib tried not to believe it. Why couldn't it be a lie? He had to have proof, see with his own eyes.

When he arrived home, she woke up smiling and kissed him on the cheek. He managed to drag out a few words:

"I'm very tired."

It was torture that night to lie in the same bed with her. He turned over on one side and put out the light. He stayed away from the warmth of her body, lying on the edge of the bed. She snuggled close and tried to get her hip under his leg. He did not sleep all night. He wanted to question her, to learn the truth from her own lips, and to kill her right there as a good Ilhéan should. He wondered if after killing her he would still suffer. His pain was limitless, a vast empty feeling inside. As if his soul had been drained out of him.

The next day he went early to the bar. Eaglebeak did not show up. Lazy Chico kept out of his way and worked without looking at him. A little before two o'clock, Tonico came in, drank his bitters, and noted that Nacib seemed in a bad humor.

"Any trouble at home?"

"No. Everything's fine."

He waited fifteen minutes by the clock after Tonico's departure. Then he took his pistol out of the drawer, stuck it in his belt, and started for home. Shortly after, Lazy Chico appealed agonizingly to João Fulgêncio:

"Help, Mr. João! Mr. Nacib has gone to kill Dona Gabriela and Mr. Tonico Bastos!"

"What are you talking about?"

He told him in a few words, and João Fulgêncio took off in the direction of Nacib's house. He had hardly turned the corner at the church when he heard Dona Arminda screaming. Then he saw Tonico, naked from the waist up and with his coat and shirt in his hand, running barefoot in the direction of the beach.

OF HOW NACIB BROKE AND DID NOT BREAK THE UNWRITTEN LAW, OR HOW MRS. SAAD BECAME GABRIELA AGAIN

When Nacib discovered them, Tonico was sitting on the edge of the double bed and Gabriela lay stretched out on it. Both were nude. She was smiling; Tonico's eyes were heavy with lust.

Why didn't Nacib kill them? The unwritten law, long established and scrupulously observed in Ilhéus, required that the honor of a deceived husband be washed clean in the blood of his betrayers. Nacib had the recent example of Colonel Jesuíno Mendonça before him. His gun was in his belt. Yet he did not kill them.

If people thought he was afraid, they were mistaken. He was no coward, as he had proved on more than one occasion. Nor did he lack sufficient time. Gabriela remained on the bed, and Tonico stammered out:

"Don't kill me, Nacib! I came here just to give her some good advice."

Nacib did not even remember that he had a pistol. He hit Tonico with his heavy fist. Tonico was knocked off the edge of the bed but jumped up, grabbed his clothes, and dashed out into the back yard. He jumped the low wall and pulled on his pants while running through Dona Arminda's house. Why didn't Nacib shoot him? There was time and to spare, with no chance of missing.

Why, instead of killing Gabriela, did he only beat her? He hit her repeatedly, leaving black and blue marks all over her cinnamon body. Neither of them spoke. She did not scream or even sob, but wept silently. She was still on the bed and he was still beating her when João Fulgêncio arrived. She covered herself with the sheet.

They were mistaken if they thought he did not kill her because he loved her too much. At that moment Nacib did not love her. He did not hate her either. He beat her mechanically, as if to relax his nerves from the tension of suffering. He was empty, like a vase without a flower. He felt a pain in his heart as if someone were slowly pushing a dagger into it. He felt neither hate nor love. Just pain.

The reason he didn't kill them was that it was against his nature to kill. All those terrible stories he told about Syria were just talk. He could beat her without mercy, as if he were collecting an overdue bill. But he could not kill her.

He obeyed silently when João Fulgêncio took him by the arm and said:

"That's enough, Nacib. Come with me."

At the door of the room he stopped a moment and, without turning around or raising his voice, said:

"I'll come back tonight. I don't want to find you here."

João Fulgêncio took Nacib to his own house. As they entered, he made a sign to his wife to leave them alone. They sat down in the book-filled room. The Arab held his head in his hands. He did not speak for a long time and then asked:

"What should I do, João?"

"What do you want to do?"

"I'm going away. I can't stay in Ilhéus after this."

"Why not?"

"You know why not. I'm a cuckold. My life here would be miserable."

"Are you going to abandon her?"

"Didn't you hear what I said? Why do you ask me that? Just because I didn't kill her, you think I'll stay married to her? Do you know why I didn't kill her? Because I never could kill anything, not even a chicken. I could never kill a wild animal, even."

"I think you acted very properly. To kill on account of jealousy is barbarous. It still happens only in Ilhéus. Or among uncivilized people. You did the right thing."

"I'm going away. . . ."

João Fulgêncio's wife came to the door and said:

"João, there's somebody here looking for you. Mr. Nacib, I'm going to get you a cup of coffee."

Nacib did not touch the coffee. He felt neither hunger nor thirst, just pain. João Fulgêncio reappeared, took a book from a shelf, and said:

"I'll be back in a minute."

He returned to find Nacib in the same position, staring vacantly. He sat down beside him and laid a hand on his leg.

"I think you would be foolish to go away."

"Why should I stay? To be laughed at?"

"No one is going to laugh at you."

"Not you, because you're kind. But the others. . . ."

"Tell me something, Nacib: if instead of being your wife, she were only your mistress, would it be so important, would you still want to go away?"

Nacib weighed the question.

"She was everything to me. That's why I married her."

"I know. You may remember that I warned you."

"You warned me?"

"I said there are certain flowers that wilt if you put them in a vase."

Nacib remembered. He had attached little importance to the remark. Now he understood: Gabriela was not made for marriage and a husband.

"But if she were only your mistress," continued the book dealer, "would you leave Ilhéus? Maybe you'd suffer; we suffer because we love, not because we're married. But would you go away?"

"If she were only my mistress, no one would laugh at me. The beating I gave her would be enough. You know that as well as I do."

"Well, then, I want you to know that in the eyes of the law that's all she ever has been. So there's no reason why you should go away."

"I married her, with a judge and everything. You were there yourself."

João Fulgêncio opened the book he had taken from the shelf.

"This is the Civil Code. Listen to what it says in chapter six, article 219, first paragraph. It's the law relating to families, the part about marriage. What I'm going to read refers to cases of annulment. Listen: it says that a marriage is null *ab initio* when there is substantial error as to one of the parties."

Nacib listened without great interest; he understood nothing of what João Fulgêncio was trying to tell him.

"Your marriage is voidable, Nacib. You can become unmarried whenever you wish and it will be as if you had never married in the first place, just cohabited."

"How's that? Explain it to me so I'll understand."

"Let me read it to you," said João. " 'Substantial error is said to exist when there is error as to the identity, honor, and good reputation of one of the parties, and this error, when later discovered, is such as to render cohabitation unbearable to the deceived spouse.' I remember that when you announced your engagement you said that she didn't know her family's name or her own date of birth—"

"Nothing. She knew nothing."

"—and that Tonico volunteered to provide the necessary papers."

"He drew them up in his office."

"Well, then, your marriage is voidable, for there was substantial error as to one of the parties. I thought about this when you got here. Then Ezequiel came to talk about something and I took the opportunity to ask him about it. I was right. You have only to prove that the documents were false and you're no longer married. And you never were married. You only lived together."

"But how can I prove that?"

"You have to talk with Tonico and the Judge."

"I'll never talk to that bastard again."

"Do you want me to handle it for you? That is, to talk to Tonico? Ezequiel can handle the legal work, if you wish. He even offered to."

"He already knows about it?"

"Don't worry about that. Do you want me to take care of things?"

"I don't know how to thank you."

"All right, then, I'll see you later. You stay right here." He put his hand on Nacib's shoulder. "Read a book—or cry, if you feel like it. Crying is nothing to be ashamed of."

"I'll go out with you."

"No, sir. Where would you go? You stay here and wait for me. I won't be long."

It was not so easy as João Fulgêncio had expected. Ezequiel refused to talk with Tonico and arrange the thing amicably:

"What I want is to put that character behind bars. I'm going to get his license revoked on the grounds of falsification of documents. He, his brother, and his father have gone around saying terrible things about me. He's going to have to get out of Ilhéus."

João Fulgêncio finally succeeded in winning him over. They went to the notary's office together. Tonico was still pale and looked at them uneasily. With a sickly smile, he tried to make a joke of the matter:

"If I hadn't got out fast, the Turk might have gored me with his horns. I was scared to death."

"Nacib is my client and I ask you to speak of him with respect," demanded Ezequiel very gravely.

The lawyer explained the proposal. Tonico refused categorically. How could there be grounds for an annulment? The documents, even though false, had been accepted as genuine. Nacib had been married for about five months and had made no complaint. And how could he, Tonico, confess publicly to the falsification? They were no longer living in the days of old Segismundo, who sold birth certificates and land deeds to everybody.

Ezequiel shrugged his shoulders and said to João Fulgêncio: "What did I tell you?"

"Tonico, this can be arranged somehow," said João Fulgêncio. "Let's go and talk to the Judge. We'll find some way of getting around the situation so that the falsification of documents will not become public. Or, at least, so that you won't appear guilty. It can be stipulated that you acted in good faith, that you were deceived by Gabriela. We'll make up some kind of story. After all, this so-called civilization of Ilhéus was founded on false documents."

But Tonico continued to resist. He didn't want to become involved.

"Involved you already are," said Ezequiel, "right up to your neck. One of two things: either you agree and come with us to the Judge and help us arrange everything amicably and quickly, or I'll enter suit this very day on behalf of Nacib for annulment of his marriage by reason of substantial error owing to documents falsified by you—falsified in order to marry off your paramour, whose favors you continued to enjoy, to a good and ingenuous man whom you called your friend. You enter the case from two angles: falsification and adultery. And with premeditation as to both of them. It's a beautiful case."

Tonico was struck almost dumb:

"Ezequiel, for God's sake, do you want to disgrace me?"

João Fulgêncio added:

"What will Dona Olga say? And your father? Have you thought about that? The scandal will kill him."

"My God, why did I get mixed up in this! I only fixed up the papers to help. I had nothing to do with her at that time."

"Come with us to see the Judge; it's best for all concerned. If you won't, I give you fair warning that the whole story will come out tomorrow in the *Ilhéus Daily*. I'll write it myself."

"But, João, we've always been friends."

"I know. But you took advantage of Nacib. If it had been some other man I wouldn't care. I'm his friend too, and Gabriela's. You took advantage of both of them. Either you agree or I'll cover you with shame, I'll hold you up to ridicule. With the political situation as it is, you won't even be able to stay in Ilhéus."

All of Tonico's resistance vanished. The prospect of scandal horrified him. He was in deadly fear of what Dona Olga and his father would do if they found out. The best thing would be to swallow the bitter pill: to go to the Judge and confess the falsification of the papers.

"I'll do whatever you want. But, for God's sake, let's straighten out this matter of the documents as smoothly as possible. We're all friends."

The Judge was highly amused at the whole thing.

"Well, Mr. Tonico, such a great friend of the Arab's and cuckolding him behind his back? I, too, had my eye on the girl, but after she married I gave up the idea. A married woman I respect."

Inwardly, his feeling was like that of Ezequiel's: it was with some reluctance that he agreed to grant the annulment quietly and to let Tonico appear as an honest and trustworthy public servant. He would have preferred to indict him. He was not fond of Tonico, for he suspected that the gallant notary had slept with Prudência during the two-year period when she was the magistrate's mistress. Moreover, he liked Nacib and wanted to help him. As they were leaving, the Judge inquired:

"And what about Gabriela? What will she do now, eh? Now that she's free and uncommitted. If I weren't already so well fixed . . . Incidentally, she must come to see me. Everything depends on her, because if she doesn't agree . . ."

Before returning home, João Fulgêncio went to see Gabriela. Dona Arminda had taken her in. She agreed to everything, she wanted nothing, she did not even complain of the beating.

"Mr. Nacib is so good. I didn't want to hurt Mr. Nacib."

Thus it came about that by means of an action for annulment of marriage, which traveled its legal course from initial petition to final judgment in an extremely short time, the Arab found himself again (or still) a bachelor. He had and had not been married; he had and had not been cuckolded; and so, in not killing his betrayers, he had and had not broken the unwritten law. In a sense, this cruel law had been outwitted *ex post facto*.

Thus it happened, too, that Mrs. Saad became again what she had always been—Gabriela.

OF GABRIELA'S LOVE

The case was under discussion at the Model Stationery Store. Nhô-Galo said:

"I always liked Nacib and now I like him even more. At last Ilhéus has a civilized man. And a genius, for only a genius could have conceived so brilliant a solution."

The Captain asked:

"João Fulgêncio, how do you explain Gabriela? From what you tell me, she really loves Nacib. You say the break-up is a lot harder on her than on him. Yet she betrayed him. How come? If she loved him, why did she do it?"

João Fulgêncio looked out on the busy street, saw the Dos Reis sisters wrapped in their mantillas, and smiled.

"I don't know the answer, Captain. Gabriela is a mystery, and a mystery is by definition inexplicable."

"A beautiful body and the soul of a bird," said Josué. "Sometimes I wonder if she has a soul at all." He was thinking of Gloria.

"The soul of a child, perhaps," the Captain speculated.

"Of a child? Maybe. Of a bird? No, Josué, that's nonsense. Gabriela is generous and pure. She's impulsive; she lacks foresight and adaptability. You can state her good and bad qualities without much trouble. But explain her? Never."

Gabriela sat in Dona Arminda's house, sewing and thinking. She was still black and blue. That morning, before Nacib's servant arrived, she had jumped over the wall, entered his house, and swept and cleaned it. Mr. Nacib was so good! He beat her because he was angry. She was to blame. She should never have accepted his proposal of marriage. She accepted it because she wanted to walk arm in arm with him in the street, with a wedding ring on her finger. She was afraid of losing him, maybe, afraid he might marry somebody else and send her away. She did wrong, she should never have agreed to marry him. Till then, she had been wonderfully happy.

He had the right to kill her if he wanted to. A married woman who deceives her husband deserves to die. Everybody said so, even Dona Arminda. She deserved to die. He was good; he only gave her a beating and put her out of his house. Then the Judge asked her if she had any objection to undoing the marriage, as if it never happened. He warned her that she would have no right to any part of the bar, to any money of his in the bank, or to the house on the steep street. It was up to her. If she refused, the matter would be delayed in court and nobody could tell how it would end. But if she agreed . . . And she did agree, immediately. Nevertheless, the Judge explained again that it would be as if she had never been married. This was fine, she said, because then Mr. Nacib would have no reason to suffer so. She didn't care about the beating. Even if he had killed her. She wouldn't have died hating him, because he was right. But what she felt bad about was being put out of the house and not being able to look at him, smile at him, listen to him talk, feel his heavy leg across her hip, his mustache tickling her neck, his hands caressing her body, her breasts, her buttocks, her thighs, her belly. Mr. Nacib's chest was like a pillow. She loved to sleep with her face nestled in the hair on the broad, friendly bosom. And to cook for him and hear him praise the delicious food. But she didn't like shoes. Or visits to fine families. Or parties, or expensive clothes, or real jewels costing a pile of money. These things she didn't like, no, she didn't. But she loved Mr. Nacib, the house on the steep street, the back yard with its guava trees, the kitchen, the parlor, the bedroom.

The Judge told her that in a few days she would no longer be married and would never have been. Would never have been—how funny! It was the same judge who had married them, the same one who, before that, wanted to set her up in a house. Now he spoke of it again. He was a nice man but he was old; she didn't want him. If she was no longer married and never had been, why couldn't she go back to Mr. Nacib's house, to the little room in the back yard, and take care of the kitchen, the laundry, and the house-cleaning?

Dona Arminda said that Mr. Nacib would never look at her again, or say good morning, or talk to her. But why should he act like that if they weren't married and never had been? In a few more days, the Judge said. Then she could go back to Mr. Nacib. She didn't mean to offend him, to hurt him. But she did offend him because she was married, she hurt him because she lay in bed with somebody while she was married. One day she had realized that he was jealous. Such a big man—it was funny. She had been careful after that, very careful, because she didn't want him to suffer. It was the silliest thing: why did men suffer so much when a woman with whom they lay, lay also with another man? She couldn't understand it. If Mr. Nacib wanted to, he could have gone to lie with another girl and sleep in her arms. She knew that Tonico lay with others; Dona Arminda told her that he had lots of other women. But, if it was fun to be in bed with him, why insist that she be the only one? She didn't get it. She liked to sleep in a man's arms. Not just any man but a nice young one, like Clemente, like Tonico, like Mr. Nilo, like Bebinho—and ah! like Nacib. If the man wanted it too, if he looked at her asking for it, if he smiled at her, if he pinched her, why refuse him, why say no? If both of them wanted to, why shouldn't they? It was good to be in bed with a man, to hear him gasp and feel his body quiver. She understood that Mr. Nacib had a right to be angry with his wife for lying with another man, for there was a law against it; only the husband had a right to lie with others, not the wife. But how could she help it? When she felt like it she did it, without even remembering that it was forbidden. Anyway, in a few days the marriage would be undone, it would be undone forwards and backwards, so why should Mr. Nacib go on being angry?

She loved many things with all her heart: the morning sun before it got too hot; white sand and the sea; circuses, carnivals, and movies; guavas and pitanga cherries; flowers, animals, cooking, walking through the streets, talking, laughing. Above all, beautiful young men; she loved to lie with them, moaning, kissing, biting, panting, dying and coming back to life. With Mr. Nacib among others. But in his case there was something more. She liked to fall asleep in his arms and dream about the sunshine, the cat, the sand on the beach, the moon in the sky, the food to be cooked. Feeling the weight of Mr. Nacib's leg across her. She loved him very much, too much. She missed him. She hid behind the door to watch him when he came in at night. He would arrive very late, sometimes drunk. She wanted so much to be with him again, to have him lay his handsome head on her breast, to hear him babble words of love in a foreign tongue, to hear him murmur "Bié!"

It was all because she went to bed with Tonico. Why should this be so important, why should it make Mr. Nacib suffer so? It didn't take anything from her, it made her no different, she loved him just the same and she couldn't love him more. She doubted if there was another woman in the world who loved a man as much as she loved Mr. Nacib. No matter whether the woman wanted to live with the man or to lie with him, no matter whether she was his wife, his mother, his sister, his daughter, or just his woman, she couldn't possibly love him as much as Gabriela loved Mr. Nacib. All this fuss just because he found her with another man. Dona Arminda said that Mr. Nacib would never take her back. She wanted at least to cook for him. Where would he eat? And the bar—who would prepare the snacks and appetizers? And the restaurant that was about to be opened? She wanted to cook for him at least.

And she wanted—oh, how she wanted—to see a smile on his kind, beautiful face. She wanted him to take her in his arms and call her Bié. She wanted to feel his mustache on the side of her neck. No other woman in the whole world missed and sighed for the man she loved as Gabriela missed and sighed for Mr. Nacib.

The discussion in the Model Stationery Store continued.

"Fidelity is the greatest proof of love," said Nhô-Galo.

"It's the only yardstick for measuring the magnitude of a love," added the Captain.

"Love is not to be proven or measured," said João Fulgêncio. "It's like Gabriela. It exists, and that is enough. The fact that you can't understand or explain something doesn't do away with it. I know nothing about the stars, but I see them in the heavens; and my ignorance in no way affects either their existence or their beauty."

OF LIFE'S SURPRISES

That first night at the house without Gabriela. The agonizing humiliation, the realization that it was not a dream, that the impossible, unimaginable had really happened. The empty house, filled with memories and emotions. He could see Tonico sitting on the edge of the bed. Anger and sorrow assailed him, and the knowledge that all had ended, that she was not there, that she belonged to another, that she would never be his again. He felt utterly worn out. The night seemed eternal. That deep pain, that emptiness. He didn't know what to do; he saw no reason to go on living and working. He sat up on the edge of the bed; sleep was impossible. The night, just begun, would last his whole life through. Gabriela's scent of clove permeated the mattress and the sheets; it filled his nostrils. He could not bear to look at the bed, for when he did he saw her lying there; he saw her erect breasts, the curve of her hips, the velvet shadow of her thighs, the V of her groins; he saw the cinnamon color of her skin, with purple patches left on her shoulders and breasts by his sucking kisses. The light of day was gone forever, the gloom in his bosom would last as long as he lived. His mustache drooped over a mouth that would never smile again, never!

But a few days later he did smile, as he listened to Nhô-Galo in the Vesuvius Bar reviling the priests. The first few weeks had been difficult. Everything, everyone reminded him of Gabriela. He looked at the counter and saw her standing there, a flower behind her ear. He looked at the church and saw her in sandals, walking toward him. He looked at Tuísca and saw her dancing. While the Doctor talked about Ofenísia, Nacib heard only Gabriela's voice. When the Captain and Felipe played checkers, her crystal laughter ran through the bar. In his house it was even worse: he saw her everywhere, working at the stove, sitting on the doorsill in the sunshine, eating guavas under the trees, pressing the cat's face against her own, revealing her gold tooth in a smile, waiting for him on moonlit nights in the little room in the back yard. He was unaware of a peculiar aspect of these memories: none of them related to the time during which they were married (or during which they lived together, for, as he explained to everybody, it wasn't marriage, just cohabitation). His memories of Gabriela made him suffer but at the same time they were sweet. Now and then, however, he saw her in the other man's arms. This vision was like a stab in the chest; it wounded his pride as a male—not, of course, his honor as a husband, for he had never been her husband. The first weeks without her left him drained, empty, dead inside. From his house to the bar, from the bar to his house. Now and then he went for a chat with João Fulgêncio.

One day his friends took him almost by force to the new cabaret. He drank too much. But he had prodigious resistance and did not get completely drunk. He went back the following night. He met Rosalinda, a blonde from Rio, utterly unlike Gabriela. He began to live again, and slowly to forget. The hardest part was to sleep with another woman. Lying there, between them, was Gabriela, smiling, putting her arms around him, snuggling her hip under his leg, laying her head on his chest. No other woman had her scent, her warmth. Even so, she began to fade from his thoughts. Rosalinda reminded him of Risoleta, expert in the art of love. He sought her every night now, except when she was due to sleep with Colonel Manuel of the Jaguars, who paid for her room and board at Maria Machadão's house.

One night a player was needed to make up a poker game. Nacib took a hand and played until late at night. He began once more to sit down at the tables and talk with his friends. He played checkers and backgammon, discussed politics, laughed at jokes and even told some of his own. He no longer saw Gabriela in the bar. Once again he could fall asleep in his own bed, aware now only of the lingering scent of clove. He had never before been invited to so many lunches, dinners, suppers at Machadão's place, and gay outings with women to the coconut groves at Pontal. It was as if he were better liked than before, as if he were more highly respected.

He couldn't understand it. He had broken the law. Instead of killing her, he had beaten her and let her go. Instead of shooting Tonico, he had only hit him. He had imagined that people would make his life a living hell. That's what they did to Dr. Felismino; they refused to speak to him, referred to him as a "tame ox," and virtually forced him to leave Ilhéus, all because the doctor had not killed his wife and her lover, had not fulfilled the law. There was, to be sure, a difference: he, Nacib, annulled his marriage. But he never expected the situation to be understood and accepted. He had visions of an empty bar, of his friends refusing to shake his hand, of jeering laughter, of Tonico being patted on the shoulder and congratulated as he sneered at Nacib. None of this had happened. Just the opposite. People rarely mentioned the subject to him, and whenever, in passing, it was referred to, they expressed admiration of his adroitness, his cleverness, the way he had got out of the predicament. They laughed and jeered, yes, but at Tonico. The notary now took his daily bitters at the Golden Nectar, where even the proprietor, Plínio Araçá, needled him about the trick Nacib had played on him, the blow Nacib had given him, and Tonico's ignominious flight. The affair was related in both prose and verse, for Josué composed an epigrammatic poem about it. Nobody said anything about Gabriela, either good or bad, as if she were beyond comment or no longer existed. After all, a kept girl has a right to amuse herself a little. She was not married, the matter was unimportant.

Gabriela continued to live with Dona Arminda. Nacib had not

seen her again. He learned from the midwife that she was working in Dora's prosperous dressmaking shop. And from others
he heard about the many offers she was receiving. Plínio Araçá
sent word to her to name her own wages. Manuel of the Jaguars
was prowling around her again. Ribeirinho, too. The Judge was
willing to get rid of his present mistress and set Gabriela up in a
house of her own. Even Maluf, apparently so austere, was said
to be a candidate. A funny thing: nothing tempted her, neither
houses, nor charge accounts, nor cacao groves, nor hard cash. She
continued to sew for Dora.

The bar suffered heavy losses. The kitchen helper's cooking
was insipid. The appetizers were being provided once more by
the high-priced Dos Reis sisters—and as a personal favor at that.
Thinking of the restaurant, Nacib sent to Sergipe for a cook, but
she had not yet arrived. He hired a chap named Valter to take
Eaglebeak's place; the young man had no experience and no
talent for waiting on customers. The effect on business was bad.

For a time, Nacib had not concerned himself with the restaurant. The two clerks had moved out upstairs while he was still in
that first desperate phase, when thoughts of Gabriela's absence
were the only reality filling the emptiness of his days. After the
upper floor had remained unoccupied for a month, Maluf presented a bill for the rent. Nacib paid it, and this forced him to
think about the restaurant. Even so, he kept putting the matter
off. One afternoon Mundinho Falcão sent a message asking him
to come to the exporter's office. He was received with a display of
great friendship. Mundinho had not been in the bar for some
time; he had been traveling in the interior, campaigning.

"Well, how are things going, Nacib? Still prospering?"

"Getting by." And then, to get the matter over with, he said:
"You must have heard what happened to me. I'm a bachelor
again."

"They told me about it. What you did was splendid. You behaved like a European—a man from London or Paris." Mundinho looked at him with kindly feeling. "But tell me something, just between the two of us: it still hurts a little inside,
doesn't it?"

Nacib was startled. Why did he ask such a question?

"I know how it is," continued Mundinho. "Something happened to me, not exactly the same thing but similar in a way. That's why I came to Ilhéus. In time, the wound healed. But now and then it still hurts. Like when it's going to rain, isn't it?"

Nacib assented, feeling comforted. He was sure that Mundinho, too, had been betrayed by a woman he loved. But had there been a marriage and annulment? He almost asked the question. He felt himself in good company.

"Well, my dear fellow, I want to talk to you about the restaurant. It should have been opened by now. It's true, the things ordered from Rio haven't come yet, but they'll show up any day now. They've already been shipped, on one of the Ita boats. I didn't want to bother you about this—you were feeling depressed —but, after all, it's two months more or less since the last tenants moved out upstairs. It's time we were getting busy. Or have you given the thing up?"

"No, sir. Why would I want to give it up? It was only that at first I couldn't think. But now everything is under control."

"All right, then, let's go ahead. Have the remodeling done and get the place ready for the new equipment. Let's see if we can open on April first."

"Don't worry."

Nacib returned to the bar and sent for the brickmason, the painter, and an electrician. Again full of enthusiasm, he went over the remodeling plans with them. He thought of the money he would make. If all went well, inside of a year he could buy the cacao grove of his dreams.

In the whole episode, only his sister and her husband had behaved badly. They came to Ilhéus as soon as they heard the news. The sister said: "Didn't I tell you so?" The brother-in-law, with his graduation ring on his finger, acted as if the whole subject was repulsive—almost as if it gave him indigestion. He joined his wife in running down Gabriela. Nacib remained silent; he wished they would go away.

His sister rummaged through the closets. She examined the dresses, the shoes, the chemises, the skirts, the scarfs. At one point she said:

"This is brand new—it's never been worn. I'll take it for my self."

Nacib growled:

"Leave it alone. Don't touch those things."

"Listen to that!" exclaimed Mrs. Saad de Castro. "Are these the clothes of some saint?"

They returned to Água Preta. His sister's covetousness reminded Nacib of all the money he had spent on dresses, shoes, jewelry. He could return the jewelry and get most of the price back. The dresses could be sold in his uncle's store. So could two pairs of shoes; they had never been worn. That's what he would do. But after a while he forgot.

On the day following his talk with Mundinho, however, he put the jewelry in his pocket and made two bundles of the dresses and shoes. Then he went to the jewelers, and from there to his uncle's store.

OF THE GLASS SNAKE

At the end of the day, when the shadows turned into ghosts in the forests and cacao groves, and night fell slowly as if to prolong the day's labor, Fagundes and Clemente finished their planting. The Negro smiled and said:

"Everything's in the ground now. Four thousand cacao plants to make the colonel richer."

"And for us to buy a piece of land three years from now," added the mulatto Clemente cheerlessly. He had lost his taste for smiling.

Melk's men had brought Fagundes back at daybreak in a canoe. He listened in silence to Melk's recriminations:

"I thought you really knew how to shoot. You're not worth a damn." Melk paid him his meager compensation and added: "I hired you to kill the man, not to wound him. I really shouldn't give you anything."

Fagundes said only:

"His day to die just hadn't come, Colonel. Everybody's got his day, fixed for him up there." He pointed heavenward.

Under their contract Clemente and Fagundes had to fell ten acres of forest land, clear it by burning, cultivate it, plant four hundred cacao seedlings per acre, and take care of them for three years. Among the seedlings they planted manioc, corn, sweet potatoes, and aipim. These scanty crops would provide their sustenance for the next three years. At the end of that period, for each surviving cacao tree the colonel was to pay them one and one-half milreis. Clemente dreamed of using this money for a piece of land that they would cultivate together. What land could they buy with so little money? Just a small patch of bad soil. Fagundes thought that unless there was a good deal more shooting for him to do, it would be difficult, very difficult, for them to buy even a small piece of land. They could barely live on the manioc and corn, the sweet potatoes and aipim. They would have no money with which to go to town, raise a little hell, fire some shots in the air, and get a woman to sleep with. They would have to draw part of the money in advance. At the end of three years they would receive the balance, perhaps less than half the total contract price.

The colonel looked somber; he, too, had lost his taste for smiling. Fagundes knew the reason. Everyone on the plantation knew; they learned about it in Cachoeira do Sul. His daughter, the haughty girl that Fagundes had seen, had run away from school to chase after a married man. Women were the devil: they upset everybody's life. If it wasn't a man's wife, it was his daughter or his sister. Look at Clemente with his head bowed, killing himself with work and then sitting half the night on a stone at the door of his mud hut, looking up at the sky. He had been doing this ever since he learned from Fagundes that Gabriela was married to the proprietor of a bar and was now a lady with a wedding ring on her finger, a gold tooth, and servants of her own.

Fagundes and Clemente had burned away the brush and fallen trees. Terrified animals ran before the flames: wild pigs, peccaries, pacas, deer, large lizards, guans, and a world of snakes—bushmasters, rattlesnakes, pit vipers. And afterwards, when the two men cultivated the soil, they had to be constantly on the lookout for snakes that lay hidden, coiled, and ready to strike. A moment's carelessness might have been fatal.

After they began to plant the tender seedlings, the colonel sent for Fagundes. He stood on the veranda, slapping the side of his boot with his riding whip—the same whip he had used on his daughter. He looked at the Negro with eyes that had become thoughtful and sad since Malvina's disappearance, and said in a voice of distilled hate:

"Start getting ready, black man. One of these days I'm going to take you to Ilhéus again."

Would it be to shoot the fellow that his daughter loved? And maybe the girl, too? She was proud, looked like a saint in a picture. But he, Fagundes, would not kill a woman. Or were the fights starting up again? He laughed and said:

"I won't miss this time."

"It's for the elections. We're going to win, even if we have to do it with guns."

Good news after so long a period of calm. He resumed planting with renewed ardor. The sun beat down on his back like a whip. At last they finished. Four thousand cacao seedlings covered the ground where the terrifying virgin forest had stood.

Carrying their hoes on their shoulders, Clemente and the Negro talked as they trudged toward their hut. The twilight was dying and night was falling, bringing with it the werewolves, the souls of men murdered in ambush, and the ghost of a priest's mistress in the form of a headless mule. The shadows filled the cacao groves, and the owls opened their nocturnal eyes.

"One of these days the colonel is sendin' me to Ilhéus again," said Fagundes. "That's the place for havin' fun. There's so many women at the Big Noise you can't count 'em—each one purtier than the other. I'm goin' to have myself a time." He patted his protruding navel. "My belly's goin' to turn white from rubbin' against so many white women."

"Why is he sendin' you to Ilhéus?"

"I told you the other day. The colonel says there's goin' to be an election and we gotta win it with bullets. I'm ready now, just waitin' for orders."

Clemente turned pensive, mulling over an idea. Fagundes said:

"This time I'm comin' back with money. There ain't nothin' better than elections. Plenty to eat and drink and a big party after your side wins. And money comes rollin' into your pocket. You can count on it: this time I'm goin' to bring home the mil· reis to buy us a piece of land."

Stopping in a shadow, his face darkened, Clemente said:

"You could ask the colonel to take me, too."

"What do you wanna go for? You ain't a fightin' man."

Clemente started walking again. Fagundes repeated:

"What for?" Then he remembered. "To see Gabriela?"

Clemente's silence was his answer. The shadows grew. Soon the headless mule would come up from hell and run loose in the woods; her hoofs would strike sparks from the stones, and flames would belch from her neck.

"What's the use? Won't do no good. She's a married woman."

"Just to see her. Just once, to see her face. To hear her laugh —learn me how to laugh again."

"You got her planted in your mind. You don't think about nothin' else. Even when you talk about gettin' a piece of land, it's just to be talkin'. Especially since you heard she was married. What you wanna see her for?"

A glass snake came out of the grass and started down the road. In the scattered shadows, its beautiful body sparkled like a miracle. Clement caught up with it, lowered his hoe, and chopped it into three pieces. With another blow he smashed its head.

"What you do that for? 'Tain't poisonous, don't hurt nobody."

"It's too pretty—that's harm enough."

They walked in silence for a short distance. Fagundes spoke first:

"We hadn't ought to kill a woman, even if the bitch ruins our life."

"Who said anything about killin'?"

He could never do it; he had neither the courage nor the

strength for it. But he was capable of giving ten years of his life, of abandoning all hopes of a piece of land, to see her again, just once, and to hear her laughter. She was a glass snake. She wasn't poisonous but she sowed affliction just by going among men—mysteriously, like a miracle. Deep in the woods the owls were calling to Gabriela.

OF THE TOLLING OF THE BELLS

In the end, no gunmen came down from the plantations. Not Melk's, or Jesuíno's, or Coriolano's, or Amâncio Leal's; not Altino's, or Aristóteles', or Ribeirinho's.

The electoral campaign took on aspects previously unheard of in Ilhéus, Itabuna, Pirangi, Água Preta, and the rest of the cacao region. Formerly the candidates, sure of election, did not even bother to campaign. Or, at most, they would call on the more powerful colonels, those with the most land and the largest number of cacao trees. This time things were different, for no one was sure of being elected. Previously, the elections had been decided by the colonels, acting under the orders of Ramiro Bastos. Now everything was mixed up. Even if Ramiro still ran things in Ilhéus, it was his enemy Aristóteles who ruled in Itabuna. Both of them supported the state government; Mundinho had prevented a break between Aristóteles and the Governor. Which side would the government support after the elections?

In the bars, in the Model Stationery Store, in the gatherings at the fish market, opinions were divided. Some asserted that the government would continue to back Ramiro Bastos and would recognize his candidates even if they were outvoted. Wasn't the old colonel one of the main supports of the status quo? Others believed that the government would recognize the winners at the polls, regardless. The Governor was nearing the end of his term and his successor would need their support. If Mundinho won, they said, the new Governor would recognize him in order to have Ilhéus and Itabuna on his side. The Bastoses were no good any more; they were like cane trash, fit only to be thrown out. Still others thought that the government would try to please both sides. It would refuse to recognize Mundinho and would let the physician in Rio continue to enjoy his subsidy as a federal congressman; also, Alfredo Bastos would remain in the state legislature. At the same time, it would recognize the Captain, whose election as Mayor of Ilhéus no one doubted. The Mayor of Itabuna, naturally, would be Aristóteles's candidate. They predicted that the government would offer Mundinho the seat in the Senate which would become vacant upon Ramiro's death. After all, the old man had already celebrated his eighty-third birthday.

"He'll live to a hundred."

"He sure will. Mundinho will have to wait a long time for his seat in the Senate."

In this way the government would have the support of both sides and would consolidate its position in the southern part of the state.

"They'll get in bad with both sides, that's what they'll do."

While the people conjectured and argued, the candidates of the two factions intensified their efforts. They visited voters, made trips to outlying communities, attended christenings, gave presents, and made speeches at rallies, which were held every Sunday in Ilhéus, Itabuna, and the smaller towns. The Captain had already made more than fifty speeches. His throat was sore and he was hoarse from repeating his thunderous tirades and his promises of improvements and reforms worthy of the memory of his father, the beloved Cazuza de Oliveira. Dr. Maurício was equally active. While the Captain was speaking in Seabra Plaza, Maurício recited the Bible in Rui Barbosa Plaza. Declared João Fulgêncio:

"I know the Old Testament by heart just from listening to Maurício's speeches. If he wins, boys, we'll have compulsory Bible reading in the public square, led by Father Cecílio. Poor Father Basílio; all he knows about the Bible is that the Lord said: 'Be fruitful and multiply.'"

But while the Captain and Dr. Maurício Caires campaigned

only in the county of Ilhéus, Mundinho, Alfredo, and Ezequiel campaigned also in Itabuna, Ferradas, Macuco, and other places in the cacao zone, for they had to win votes in the entire region. Dr. Vitor Melo was appalled by reports reaching him in Rio. He cursed the damned insurgents who were upsetting his applecart, abandoned the bored ladies whose nerves he treated in his elegant consultation room, deserted the French girls at the Assírio and the chorus girls of the revues, and took an Ita boat for Ilhéus. Before leaving, he complained to Emílio Mendes Falcão, one of his colleagues in the Republican party and in Congress:

"Who is this namesake of yours, Mundinho Falcão? He's running against me in Ilhéus. Do you know him?"

"He's my youngest brother."

The congressman from the cacao zone became alarmed. If Mundinho was Emílio's and Lourival's brother, then his own election and, worse yet, his recognition by the government were in real danger. Emílio went on:

"He's a madman. He abandoned everything here and went off to bury himself in that hole. He says he wants to get elected to Congress just so he can come here and heckle me." He laughed and asked: "Why don't you switch to another electoral district? Mundinho is a holy terror. He'll probably win."

How could he switch now? He was the protégé of a senator, his uncle on his mother's side, and he had been handed that sinecure in Congress when a vacancy occurred in the seventh electoral district of the State of Bahia. All the others were already preempted. And who would want to swap with him in order to run against a brother of Lourival Mendes Falcão, a coffee king to whom even the President of the Republic listened? He embarked hastily for Ilhéus.

João Fulgêncio agreed with Nhô-Galo: the greatest good that Congressman Vitor Melo could have done for his own candidacy was not to have come to Ilhéus at all. He was the most repulsive of men—"a human emetic," in the words of Nhô-Galo.

His speeches, delivered in a nauseating, effeminate voice, were hard to understand and were punctuated by medical terms. "They smell like formaldehyde," said João Fulgêncio. He wore

queer-looking coats with a belt in the back and would have been
taken for a homosexual if he had not been such a woman-chaser.

"He is Tonico Bastos raised to the third power," said Nhô-
Galo.

All this while, Tonico was in Bahia on a junket with his wife,
hoping that Ilhéus would forget his sad adventure. He did not
want to get mixed up in the electoral campaign; the opposition
might decide to exploit his experience with Nacib. In fact, someone pasted on the wall of his house a crayon drawing of him running in his shorts and yelling for help, with a crude limerick underneath:

> *Tonico had hoped on the sly*
> *With another man's wife to lie;*
> > *Though the "wife" in the bed*
> > *Was really unwed,*
> *Tonico got socked in the eye.*

Another candidate for punishment on account of his sexual
activities was Dr. Vitor Melo. With his Don Juan manner and his
experience with nervous lady clients on the couch in his office, he
made advances to every pretty woman he saw. At a party in the
Progress Club, he narrowly escaped a beating at the hands of
Moacir Estrêla of the bus line. The congressman was dancing
with Moacir's good-looking wife, who had begun to frequent the
Club in keeping with her husband's recent prosperity. The lady
suddenly left her partner in the middle of the floor and exclaimed in a loud voice:

"Fresh!"

She told her friends that the congressman had tried to get his
leg between hers while holding her tightly against himself, as if
instead of dancing he wanted to . . . The *Ilhéus Daily* carried
the story, written by the Doctor's chaste but aggressive pen, under the heading: COWARD IGNOMINIOUSLY THROWN OUT OF
CLUB. He had not exactly been thrown out. Alfredo Bastos had
saved him from Moacir by taking him away. Tempers were running high. Colonel Ramiro himself, on learning of this and other
shameful incidents, confessed to his friends:

"Aristóteles was right. If I had known sooner, I wouldn't have quarreled with him and lost Itabuna."

In Nacib's bar the congressman got involved in another altercation. The little man lost his head in an argument and said that Ilhéus was a land of illiterate boors. This time it was João Fulgêncio who saved him—from the wrath of Josué and Ari Santos, who felt personally insulted and wanted to thrash him.

Nacib's bar had become a Mundinho stronghold. As a partner of the exporter and an enemy of Tonico, the Arab (a native-born Brazilian and a registered voter) had jumped into the campaign. At the largest of the rallies, to everyone's surprise, he got up and made a speech. It was just after a speech by Dr. Ezequiel in which the lawyer broke all his own records for drunken inspiration. After listening to Ezequiel, something hit Nacib inside. He could not restrain himself and asked for the floor. His speech was an unprecedented success, perhaps because, having begun in Portuguese and then finding himself at a loss for fine words, he had switched to Arabic and let loose a stream of high-speed, unintelligible eloquence. The applause was prolonged and deafening.

"It was the sincerest and most inspired speech of the whole campaign," declared João Fulgêncio.

All this agitation came to a sudden stop on a lovely morning of bluish-white brilliance. The gardens of Ilhéus exhaled their fragrance, and the birds trilled for joy at so much beauty. Colonel Ramiro Bastos was in the habit of arising very early. The oldest servant in the house—she had been with the Bastoses about forty years—always served him a small cup of coffee. Then he would sit in his rocking chair, think about the elections, and make his calculations. He was almost resigned to the idea that the only way he would remain in power was by the government's recognition of his candidates alone and its repudiation of any of his opponents who might be elected. That morning, the servant waited for him to come for his cup of coffee. He did not appear. She became alarmed and woke Jerusa. Together they went into his room and found him dead in bed, his eyes open, his right hand clutching the sheet. A sob burst from the girl's breast, and the servant screamed: "My godfather is dead!"

The *Ilhéus Daily*, with a heavy black border, eulogized the colonel: "At this hour of grief and mourning, all partisanship ceases. Colonel Ramiro Bastos was one of Ilhéus's great men. The city, the county, and the region are indebted to him for much of what they have. Were it not for him, the progress on which we pride ourselves and for which we continue to strive would not exist." On the same page, among the many other obituary notices —inserted by, among others, the Bastos family, the Mayor, the Commercial Association, the Brotherhood of St. George, the Amâncio Leal family, and the Ilhéus-Conquista Railroad—there was one by the Ilhéus Branch of the Democratic Party inviting all its adherents to attend the funeral of the "unforgettable public figure, loyal adversary, and exemplary citizen." It was signed by Raimundo Mendes Falcão, Clóvis Costa, Miguel Batista de Oliveira (the Captain), Pelópidas de Assunção d'Ávila (the Doctor), and Colonel Artur Ribeiro (Ribeirinho).

Alfredo Bastos and Amâncio Leal stood in the parlor with the high-backed chairs, in which the colonel's body lay in state, and received the condolences of the multitude that filed past all morning and afternoon. Tonico was advised by telegram. At midday, Mundinho Falcão, bringing an enormous wreath, entered the house, embraced Alfredo, and, filled with emotion, pressed Amâncio's hand. Jerusa was standing near the coffin, her pearly cheeks wet with tears. Mundinho approached her; she raised her eyes, broke into sobs, and ran from the room.

At three o'clock in the afternoon there was not room for another person inside the house. The street was jammed with people all the way to the Progress Club and the town hall. From Itabuna came a special train and three busloads of mourners. Altino Brandão arrived from Rio do Braço and said to Amâncio:

"It was better this way, don't you think? He died before defeat, still in command, as he liked to be."

The Bishop came, accompanied by all the priests. The nuns and the pupils of the parochial school were lined up behind the Mother Superior, waiting for the start of the funeral procession. Waiting also were the teachers and students of the public school and of Enoch's, Dona Guilhermina's, and other private schools, as well as members of the Brotherhood of St. George, headed by Dr. Maurício in his red robe. Mister, dressed in black, was there. So were the tall Swede of the steamship agency, the Greek couple, exporters, planters, merchants (all business houses were closed in sign of mourning), and the populace in general, down from the hills and from Pontal and Cobras Island.

Gabriela, accompanied by Dona Arminda, made her way with difficulty to the parlor filled with wreaths and people. She managed to get close to the coffin, raised the silk handkerchief that covered the dead man's face, and gazed upon it for a moment. She remembered that at the inauguration of the Dos Reis sisters' tableau, the colonel had singled her out and treated her with friendship and respect in full view of her then sister- and brother-in-law. She leaned over the white, waxlike hand and kissed it. She embraced Jerusa, and the girl clung to her neck, sobbing. Gabriela, too, was crying, as were many other persons in the room. All the church bells were tolling.

At five o'clock the funeral procession got under way. The street could not contain the multitude, which spilled over into the plaza. The speeches at the grave had already begun—they were given by Dr. Maurício, Dr. Juvenal, a lawyer from Itabuna, the Doctor, representing the opposition, and the Bishop—while a part of the procession was still climbing Vitória Street to reach the cemetery. That night the movie houses and cabarets remained closed and the bars were empty. The town seemed as deserted as if everyone in it had died.

OF THE (OFFICIAL) END OF GLORIA'S LONELINESS

A secret liaison is a dangerous and complicated business. It requires patience, intelligence, quick-wittedness, and unflagging alertness. The parties must guard against the carelessness that naturally creeps in with the passage of time and with the imperceptible increase in their sense of security. At first they take exaggerated precautions, but then the precautions are gradually relaxed and ultimately abandoned. The affair loses its clandestine character, drops its mantle of mystery, and after a time the secret is being discussed by everyone. This is what happened to the affair between Gloria and Josué.

Whether it was infatuation, passion, love, or a passing fancy—the classification depended on the speaker's degree of culture and good will—the relationship between the teacher and the mulatto girl was known to the whole town and its outlying districts. It was talked about even on the distant plantations over toward the Baforé Range. Nevertheless, in the initial days, the greatest precautions had seemed insufficient to the lovers, especially to Gloria. She had explained to Josué the two basic and cogent reasons why they must keep the people of Ilhéus in general, and Colonel Coriolano Ribeiro in particular, ignorant of the cause of the bliss that shone in her face. The first reason derived from the colonel's uncommendable record of violence. He was extremely jealous and could never forgive a mistress's infidelity. So long as he kept her in luxury like a queen, he demanded the exclusive right to her favors. Gloria remembered that Coriolano's men had severely beaten Chiquinha and her lover, Juca Viana, and had shaved their heads. She wanted to avoid all risk of such treatment, especially in view of Josué's delicate physique. The second reason was that she did not want to lose, along with her hair, the comforts of her splendid house, the charge accounts at the stores, the servant who did all the work, the bottles of perfume, and the money that she kept locked in her drawer. And so Josué was to enter her house only after the last night owl had gone home and was to leave before the appearance of the first early riser. He was to ignore her completely outside of those few hours when on her creaking bed they ardently and voraciously avenged themselves of such restrictions.

Such strict secrecy can be maintained for a week or two. Then carelessness sets in, inattention, inadvertence. A little earlier yesterday, still earlier today, and Josué found himself entering the forbidden house while the Vesuvius Bar was still full of customers, right after the closing of the Ilhéus Cine-Theatre or even sooner. Another five minutes' sleep one morning, ten more the next, and before long he was going directly from Gloria's house to his classroom. A few whispered confidences by Josué to Ari Santos, Nhô-Galo, Nacib, and João Fulgêncio—"What a woman!" "Don't tell anybody, for God's sake, but . . ." "Nacib, she's divine!"—and soon everyone knew about the teacher and the colonel's woman.

Josué's indiscretion was perhaps excusable. How could his heart contain a passion that filled it to bursting! How could he wait till a set time before entering paradise! In any case, he was no less discreet than Gloria. She abandoned her window and strolled about the square so that she might see him and smile at him. She went to the stores and bought him neckties, socks, shirts, even shorts. She took one of Josué's old suits to Petrônio, the best and highest-priced tailor in town, for this master crafts-man to use as a pattern in making a new suit of blue serge as a birthday surprise for her lover. She appeared in the town hall auditorium to applaud him when he introduced a lecturer. She was the only woman in a sparse audience of six persons at the Sunday morning meetings of the Rui Barbosa Literary Society and, on her way there, passed insolently through the midst of the old maids coming out of ten o'clock Mass. The sisters Quin-quina and Florzinha, the sharp-tongued Dorotéia, and the in-censed Cremildes talked with Father Cecílio about Gloria's new devotion to literature:

"She'd do better to come and confess her sins."

"Somebody should write a letter to the newspaper. . . ."

The height of madness was reached one Sunday afternoon when, with the square crowded, Josué was spied through Gloria's open window shutters, walking about in his shorts. The spinsters loudly protested: this was too much, a decent person could no longer walk on the street.

Nevertheless, that bit of depravity (Dorotéia's word for it) did not cause a scandal. There were more important things for the people of Ilhéus to talk about. For example: after Colonel Ra-miro Bastos's funeral, people wanted to know who would take his place, who would step into the dead leader's shoes. Some thought it natural and just that the leadership pass to his son, Dr. Alfredo Bastos, for he was a state assemblyman and former mayor. His faults and his virtues were weighed. He was not a brilliant or especially energetic man. He was not a born leader. He had been an honest, hard-working mayor, and he was now a mediocre legislator. He was a really competent doctor and the first to practice pediatrics in Ilhéus. He was married to an insufferable, priggish woman who never let anyone forget her supposedly noble blood. On net balance, people reached somewhat pessimistic conclusions about the future of the government party in Ilhéus if it came under Alfredo's leadership.

Only a few, however, really expected Alfredo to be Ramiro's successor. The large majority coalesced around the dangerous and disturbing figure of Colonel Amâncio Leal. Although Ramiro's name and fortune belonged to his sons, Amâncio was his political heir. He had been Ramiro's alter ego, indifferent to appointments for himself but sharing in all the decisions: the only person whose opinions the departed ruler had heeded. It was rumored that the two friends had planned to unite their families by the marriage of Jerusa with Berto as soon as the boy finished his studies. Ramiro's old servant declared that she had heard the colonel speak of this a few days before his death. It was also known that the Governor had offered Amâncio the state senate seat left vacant by his friend's death.

What would be the future of the party and of the cacao region in Amâncio's violent hands? It was hard to say, for the man was unpredictable. His friends praised him for two outstanding qualities: his courage and his loyalty. Others censured him for his stubbornness and intolerance. All agreed, however, in forecasting a turbulent end to the electoral campaign then in progress, for Amâncio would almost certainly resort to violence.

With such fascinating matters before them, how could the people of Ilhéus take much interest in the case of Gloria and Josué, which had been going along for months without incident? Only the old maids, now envious of the perpetually jubilant look on Gloria's face, continued to talk about them. Nothing but a dramatic or colorful incident of some sort, interrupting the lovers' monotonous bliss, could reawaken the Ilhéans' interest in the affair. If Coriolano learned about it and pulled off one of his stunts —ah! then there would be something worth talking about, something exciting.

But, as things turned out, nothing very exciting occurred. It happened one evening about ten o'clock, just after the movies had closed. The Vesuvius Bar was full; Nacib was going from table to table announcing the early opening of the Commerce Restaurant. Josué had crossed Gloria's doorsill more than an hour before. He had thrown caution to the wind; he cared nothing for the moralistic opinions of the families or of certain individuals, such as Dr. Maurício. Indeed, who did?

There was a sound of tables and chairs scraping when Coriolano appeared in the square, shabbily dressed, walking toward the house where his family formerly lived and where his mistress was now enjoying herself with the young teacher. Was he armed? Would he whip them? Would he shoot them? Coriolano inserted his key in the lock. The excitement in the bar increased. Nacib walked to the entrance. Everyone was listening, waiting to hear screams, perhaps the sound of shots. Nothing like that happened. Not a sound came from Gloria's house.

Several long minutes passed. The customers looked at one another. Nhô-Galo held on to Nacib's arm. The Captain proposed that a group go over to prevent a possible tragedy. João Fulgêncio opposed the idea:

"It isn't necessary. Nothing's going to happen; I'll bet on it."

And nothing did happen, except that Gloria and Josué came out of the house and started walking arm in arm along the beach avenue, to avoid passing in front of the crowded bar. A little later the servant began to bring out Gloria's things and to pile them up on the sidewalk: trunks and bags, a guitar, and a chamber pot, which was the only amusing detail in the whole incident. She then sat down on the largest trunk and waited. The door was barred from the inside. Shortly afterwards, a porter came and took the things away. It was then after eleven o'clock and few customers remained in the bar.

Something much more exciting occurred a few days later when

Amâncio Leal called on Mundinho. After the funeral the planter had returned to his plantation, where he remained for several weeks. The electoral campaign had bogged down with Ramiro's death, as if the government party had died with its leader and the opposition were left without adversaries. After a time Mundinho and his friends became active again, but without their old enthusiasm and drive.

One day Amâncio Leal got off the train and walked straight to the exporter's office. It was a little after four in the afternoon; the business center was crowded with people. The news spread quickly all over town, even before the interview ended. A knot of idlers gathered on the sidewalk in front of the building; they stretched their necks to look into Mundinho's office through the windows.

The colonel shook his opponent's hand, sat down in the comfortable armchair, and declined a liqueur, a glass of rum, and a cigar.

"Mr. Mundinho, I've been fighting you with all my strength. It was I who ordered the newspapers burned." His soft voice, the look in his one good eye, the clearly enunciated words, all seemed the result of long reflection. "It was also I who ordered Aristóteles to be shot."

He lit a cigarette and continued:

"I was prepared to turn Ilhéus upsidedown. It wouldn't have been the first time." He paused in recollection. "My men were alerted and ready to come to town. My men and my friends' men. To break up the elections." He looked at the exporter with his good eye and smiled. "An expert trigger man, a fellow I've known for years, was assigned to get you."

Mundinho listened very gravely. Amâncio puffed on his cigarette.

"You have Ramiro to thank for being alive. If he hadn't died, you'd be the one in the cemetery. But God didn't want it that way . . ."

He fell silent, thinking perhaps of his lost friend. Mundinho, somewhat pale, waited.

"Now it's all over. I stood against you because Ramiro was not just my friend, he was like a father to me. I never bothered to ask who was right. What for? If you were against him, I was against you. If he were still alive, I'd stand with him against the devil." A pause. "My oldest son was here during the holidays."

"I met him. We talked two or three times."

"I know. He used to argue with me that you were right. But I wasn't going to change on that account. Neither did I try to force the boy. I want him independent, using his own head. That's why I work and make money. So that my sons won't need anyone, so they can take whatever stand they please."

He fell silent again, smoking. Mundinho did not move.

"Then Ramiro died. I went to the country and started thinking. Who's going to take his place? Alfredo?" He dismissed Alfredo with a gesture. "He's a good man—cures children's diseases. And he's his mother's image; she was a saintly woman. Tonico? I don't know who he takes after. They say Ramiro's father was a ladies' man. But not scummy like Tonico. I kept thinking, and I saw only one man in Ilhéus to take my friend's place. And that man is you. I came here to tell you. As for me, I'm through; I won't fight you."

Mundinho remained silent a few moments longer. He thought about his brothers, his mother, and Lourival's wife. When his clerk had announced Colonel Amâncio, Mundinho had taken his pistol out of the drawer and slipped it into his pocket. He was prepared for anything except the colonel's extended hand. Now he was the new leader of the land of cacao. He felt, however, neither happy nor proud. He no longer had anyone to contend against. At least not until times changed once again and he himself, like Ramiro Bastos, was no longer fit to rule.

"Colonel, I thank you. I, too, fought you and Colonel Ramiro without any personal animosity. I admired the colonel. But we didn't agree about the future of Ilhéus."

"I know that."

"We, too, had our men ready—and one of them was assigned to take care of you, sir. I didn't know your prospective assassin as well as you knew mine, but he was an old and trusted associate of one of my friends. Now, like you, I'm through with all that. And listen, Colonel: that woman-chaser, Vitor Melo, will not be re-elected to Congress. Ilhéus needs to be represented by

someone from here, someone who's interested in its progress. But
it doesn't have to be me. It can be anybody you wish. You pick
him and I'll withdraw. I'll even recommend him to my friends.
Dr. Alfredo? You yourself? I see you best in Colonel Ramiro's
old seat in the state senate."

"No, I don't want it, Mr. Mundinho, but thank you. I don't
want anything for myself. If I vote, it'll be for you. I would
have voted for that louse Dr. Vitor only for Ramiro's sake. But
I'm through with politics. I'm going to stay in my corner. I just
came to tell you that I'm not going to fight you any longer.
There'll be no more politics in my house, unless my son wants
to get mixed up in it after he graduates. But I have a request
to make of you, sir: don't persecute Ramiro's sons or his friends.
The boys don't amount to much, that I know. But Alfredo is an
upright fellow. And Tonico is to be pitied. Our friends are loyal
men who stood with Ramiro when things were tough. That's all
I wanted to ask you. For myself I want nothing."

"I have no intention of persecuting anyone; that's not the way
I do business. As a matter of fact, what I'd like to discuss with
you is the best way to avoid hurting Dr. Alfredo."

"The best thing is for him to return to Ilhéus and practice
medicine. That's what he really likes. And now, with his father's
death, he's very rich; he doesn't have to stay in politics. As for
Tonico, leave him with his notary's office."

"What about Colonel Melk? And the others?"

"That's between you and them. Melk has become very depressed since that trouble with his daughter. It's quite possible
that he'll do as I've done: drop out of politics entirely. I have to
leave, Mr. Mundinho, I've already taken up too much of your
time. From now on, count on me as a friend. But not for politics.
When the election is over, I want you to come out one day to
my little plantation. We'll do some hunting."

Mundinho accompanied him to the top of the stairs. Soon
after, he too went out. He walked alone down the street, barely
acknowledging the numerous and extremely cordial greetings of
his admirers.

OF PROFIT, LOSS, AND A CHEF DE CUISINE

João Fulgêncio tasted an appetizer and spit it out.

"Second-rate merchandise, Nacib. Cooking is an art, as I'm sure you know. It requires knowledge, but even more it requires natural talent. This new cook of yours just hasn't got it. She's a charlatan."

The others at the table laughed, except Nacib; he was worried. Nhô-Galo tried again to get an answer to a previous question; why had Coriolano been satisfied with just throwing Gloria and Josué out of the house instead of dealing with them as he had with Chiquinha and Juca Viana?

"Why? Because of the bus line, the library of the Commercial Association, the dances at the Progress Club. Because of his son about to be graduated. Because of the death of Ramiro Bastos. Because of Mundinho Falcão."

He stopped, and then, as Nacib got up to attend to another table, he added:

"Because of Malvina. Because of Nacib."

The closed windows of Gloria's former house struck a melancholy note in the square. The Doctor reflected:

"I must confess that I miss seeing her framed in the window. We had got used to the picture."

Ari Santos remembered the breasts held high as in an offering; he sighed. She had gone with Josué to spend a few days in Itabuna. After her return, on what windowsill would she lean, where would she display her breasts and smiles, her heavy lips and sparkling eyes?

"Nacib!" called out João Fulgêncio. "You have to take steps, my dear fellow, urgent steps. You must change cooks and you must rent Coriolano's house so that we can put Gloria back in it. Otherwise, oh illustrious son of Mohammed, this bar will go to pot."

Nhô-Galo suggested a subscription by customers to pay the rent on the house and a big party to re-install Gloria's carnal magnificence.

Nacib laughed, but he was worried. He held his head in his hands, perhaps to make sure he still had a head—he had lost it so often these past months. During the first week or two after his discovery of Gabriela's infidelity, he neglected the bar and virtually forgot his plans for a restaurant. This was quite understandable. Less understandable was the fact that afterwards he still was unable to concentrate on business.

Now, however, everything had apparently returned to normal. The wound in his breast had healed; he no longer cornered Dona Arminda to learn about Gabriela and the proposals she received. The customers gathered as before, played checkers and backgammon, talked, laughed, drank beer, and sipped their apéritifs before lunch and dinner. But they weren't drinking so much and spending so much as in Gabriela's time. The cook he had brought from Sergipe at his own expense proved a dismal flop. She cooked only unimaginative dishes, which were nevertheless full of grease and too highly seasoned. Her desserts were too sweet. The appetizers for the bar were a mess. And the woman was a nuisance, always complaining about the work and insisting that she needed helpers. On top of it all, she was a scarecrow, with warts and hair on her chin. It was obvious she would never do; not even for the bar, let alone the restaurant.

Appetizers whetted the customers' thirst; now they rarely ate them and so they drank less. The bar did not lose many customers, thanks to Nacib's popularity; but the over-all consumption of drinks declined and, with it, the profits. Many customers now took only one drink, and some no longer came in every day. And this at a time when people were spending freely in the stores and cabarets. He had to do something about it. He would fire the cook and get another, no matter what it cost. But, as he knew from experience, he wouldn't be able to find one in Ilhéus. He talked over his problem with Dona Arminda, and the midwife had the nerve to say to him:

"What a coincidence, Mr. Nacib. I was just thinking that, after all, the best cook for you would be Gabriela. I can't imagine any other who would do."

He could hardly contain his temper. This Dona Arminda was getting crazier all the time; forever going to séances and talking with dead people. She told him that old Ramiro appeared at Deodoro's place and made an emotional speech in which he forgave all his enemies, beginning with Mundinho Falcão. Damned old screwball! Every day now she came back to the subject: why didn't he hire Gabriela as a cook? As if he could even think of such a thing.

He had recovered, all right; so much so that he could listen unperturbed when Dona Arminda praised Gabriela's continence and industry. She worked day and night, sewing linings on dresses, making buttonholes, hemstitching blouses: tedious work for Gabriela, for, as she herself said, she was born to work with a skillet, not a needle. She had made up her mind, however, that she wouldn't cook for anybody but Nacib, in spite of the tempting offers that poured in on her from every direction—offers of jobs as cook or as mistress. Nacib would listen to Dona Arminda almost indifferently, for he was only slightly flattered by Gabriela's belated fidelity. Then he would shrug his shoulders and enter his house.

He was cured: he had succeeded in forgetting her—the woman, not the cook. When he recalled the nights spent with her, it was with the same languorous feeling with which he remembered Risoleta's skill, and the long legs of Regina, the one before her, and the kisses stolen from his cousin Munira during a holiday in Itabuna. Without an ache in his heart, without hate, without love. But he sighed for the cook and her wonderful fish stews.

His recovery from the emotional blow had cost him a lot of money. For weeks he went to the cabaret every night; he gambled at roulette and baccarat and bought champagne for Rosalinda, the Rio blonde. She wheedled five-hundred-milreis bills from him as if he were a cacao colonel keeping her as a mistress and not just her lover in a bed paid for by Manuel of the Jaguars. Taking stock of his affairs, he got an idea of the amount of money he had squandered on her. Thereupon he dropped her in favor of Mara, a little Indian girl from Amazonas. She was a less spectacular, more modest conquest, who was satisfied with beer and a few presents. But Mara was not being kept by any one man; she practiced her profession in Machadão's place and on many nights was busy. Nacib would then assuage his disappointment with sprees at the other brothels or at the cabarets.

During this period of wild living he put no money in the bank. He paid his bills, but dissipated his profits. In the old days he went to the cabaret once or twice a week and slept with some woman who liked him. These diversions had cost him very little. Even after he was married, despite his many gifts to Gabriela, he had been able to set aside a few contos each month toward the future cacao grove. He decided to end his ruinous debauchery. He could do it easily now, for he was no longer tortured by Gabriela's absence, by dread of being alone. His leg no longer sought to rest across her rounded hip.

Nacib's financial situation and prospects were not altogether black. The poker room in the back, what with money so abundant that year, yielded good profits. Now, with the resumption of friendly relations between Amâncio Leal and Melk on the one hand and Ribeirinho and Ezequiel on the other, the room was in use every night, with the game sometimes lasting till daybreak. They played for high stakes and the house kitty grew fat.

And soon there would be the restaurant, in which Mundinho was investing his money and Nacib his work and experience. It was sure to be profitable, for there was no competition. The food in the hotels was atrocious. After dinner the restaurant could be used for poker, blackjack, and other card games, which the colonels preferred even to the roulette and baccarat of the cabarets.

The biggest problem was the lack of a cook. The top floor was painted and partitioned into dining room, pantry, and kitchen; the tables and chairs were ready; so were the stove, the sink, and the urinal for customers. Everything the best. The equipment from Rio had arrived, including a machine for making ice cream and a freezer that manufactured its own ice—

items never before seen in Ilhéus. The bar customers were struck dumb with admiration. Soon everything would be ready; only the cook was missing. On the day when João Fulgêncio, the supreme authority, severely criticized the appetizers, Nacib decided to consult Mundinho on the subject.

The exporter took a keen interest in the restaurant; he liked to eat well. He, too, Nacib learned, had offered Gabriela fabulous wages to cook for him. After a discussion with the Arab, he suggested that they send to Rio for an experienced restaurant cook. It was the only solution. Nacib demurred: those cooks from Rio didn't know how to prepare Bahian dishes, and besides, they cost a lot of money. Mundinho, however, was charmed with his own idea: a chef clad in white, with a tall cap on his head, coming out of the kitchen to talk with customers and recommending special dishes to them. He sent an urgent telegram to a friend in Rio.

During the apéritif hours many customers climbed the stairs to gaze with wonder at the large dining room lined with mirrors and at the immense stove, the freezer, and all the other marvelous things. Nacib, busy with the final and complex details, returned to his former mode of life: he seldom went to the cabaret any more and slept with the Amazon girl only when he had time and she was free. As soon as the chef arrived from Rio, he would set the date for the formal opening of the Commerce Restaurant.

The chef arrived by way of Bahia. On the same ship was Mundinho Falcão, who had gone to the state capital at the invitation of the Governor to discuss the political situation and especially the approaching elections. He had taken Aristóteles with him and they returned victorious. The Governor had yielded to them on every point: Vitor Melo would be abandoned to his fate, and Dr. Maurício too. Alfredo withdrew his candidacy for state assemblyman and was replaced by Dr. Juvenal of Itabuna, who did not have a chance. In fact, the electoral campaign was over; what had been the opposition was now the government.

Nacib was dumbfounded when he saw the chef: a pudgy little creature with a pointed, waxed mustache and effeminate mannerisms. Tremendously self-important, as arrogant as a grand duke, as demanding as a beautiful woman. His wages were fantastic.

"This is no cook," said João Fulgêncio. "He must be at least the President of the Republic."

The chef's pronounced accent revealed his Portuguese birth, but many of his disparaging remarks were uttered in French. Nacib felt inferior because he didn't understand them. The chef called himself Fernand—not Fernando. His card, which João Fulgêncio carefully put away with that of the "Bachelors" Argileu Palmeira, read simply: "Fernand, Chef de Cuisine."

Followed by some of the bar customers, Fernand climbed the stairs with Nacib to see the restaurant. He shook his head at the sight of the stove.

"*Très mauvais.*"

"What?" said Nacib helplessly.

"Lousy," translated João Fulgêncio.

The chef demanded an iron, coal-burning stove. As soon as possible. He set a time limit of one month, otherwise he would leave. Nacib begged for two months, for he would have to send to Bahia or Rio for it. His Excellency granted the request with a superior gesture and ordered Nacib to send at the same time for a large number of kitchen utensils, which he described. He characterized Bahian cooking as repulsive to a cultivated stomach, thereby at once creating profound ill will. The Doctor leaped to the defense of taro-and-shrimp stew and other local dishes.

"A conceited little jackass," he murmured.

Nacib felt intimidated. He would start to say something and the chef de cuisine would freeze him with a haughty, critical look. If the man hadn't come from Rio and at such a high cost, and still more important, if it hadn't been Mundinho's idea, Nacib would have told him to go to hell, along with his fancy-named dishes and French words.

To try him out, Nacib asked him to begin by preparing his meals and the appetizers for the bar. Once again the Arab held his head, for Fernand ordered outlandishly expensive ingredients. He insisted on canned olives, canned fish, canned hams. The appetizers cost nearly as much as they sold for. And they were heavy. What a difference, my God, between Fernand's meat patties and the ones Gabriela used to make! His were doughy and stuck to your teeth and the roof of your mouth. Hers were agreeably piquant and fragile; they melted on the tongue and called for another drink. Nacib shook his head.

He invited João Fulgêncio, Nhô-Galo, the Doctor, Josué, and the Captain to a luncheon prepared by the great chef: salad with mayonnaise, vegetable soup, chicken à la Milanaise, filet mignon, and french fried potatoes. Not that the food was bad—it wasn't. But how could one compare it to the flavorful, fragrant, pungent, colorful local dishes! How could it be compared to Gabriela's cooking! Josué spoke of her "poems" of shrimp and palm oil, of fish and coconut milk, of meat and pepper. Nacib wondered how it was all going to end. Would the customers accept these strange dishes, these white sauces? He and his friends ate without knowing what they were eating, whether it was fish, meat, or chicken. The Captain summed it up in a phrase:

"It's fine food but it's no good."

As for Nacib, the only non-Bahian dish with which he felt at home was Syrian kibba. What to do? There the man was, earning a princely wage, swollen with insolence and importance, and cackling away in French. He had cast some meaningful glances at Lazy Chico, and the boy had threatened to knock his block off. Nacib feared for the future of the restaurant. Nevertheless there was great public curiosity about the chef; he was spoken of as an important figure who had run famous restaurants. Stories were made up about him, especially about his cookery lessons for the girls who had been hired to help him. The poor things understood nothing. The cook from Sergipe nicknamed him The Bantam Capon.

At last everything was ready. The inaugural luncheon of the Commerce Restaurant was announced for a Sunday. Nacib invited all the notables of Ilhéus—except Tonico Bastos. The chef de cuisine planned a fancy menu.

Nacib thought about Dona Arminda's suggestion. There was really no cook like Gabriela. But of course it was out of the question.

OF THE COMRADE IN BATTLE

When the moon came up and cut through the blackness of the night, the seamstresses turned into shepherd girls. Dora became a queen and her house a sailboat. Nilo's glowing pipe was a star; in his right hand he carried a king's scepter and in his left hand sheer joy. When he came in, he tossed his cap, in which were hidden the winds and the storms, on top of the old mannequin. Then the magic began. The mannequin came to life—a one-legged woman in an unfinished dress, wearing a sailor cap on her headless form. Nilo seized her by the waist and they danced about the room. The mannequin looked funny as she twirled on her one leg. The shepherdesses laughed. Dora would smile like the queen that she was.

Down from the hill came more girls, and Gabriela would come up from Dona Arminda's house. But they were no longer mere shepherd girls: they were priestesses of the voodoo gods. Every night Nilo came with his gift of joy and set it free in the room. In the poor little kitchen, Gabriela created great riches of bean paste, shrimp, and manioc meal. The festive rites were about to begin.

Dora and Nilo, Nilo and Dora. But, indeed, which of the shepherdesses did Nilo not mount? They were holy mares. Nilo was transformed into all the gods—Ogun and Xangô, Oxossi and Omulu; for Dora he was the great god Oxalá. Gabriela was Yemanjá, goddess of the sea. The house sailed away in the moonlight, over the hill. The songs were the wind, the dances the oars, Dora the figurehead on the prow, Nilo the captain directing the crew.

The crew came from the waterfront: the Negro Terêncio, a bongo-drum player; the mulatto Traíra, a famous guitarist; young Batista, a ballad singer; and Mário Cravo, an eccentric peddler of holy images and, as a sideline, a market-place magician. Nilo blew his whistle and the room became a voodoo ground, a nuptial bed, a rudderless boat sailing in the moonlight. Every night Nilo let loose his joy. He had music in his feet, songs in his mouth.

Sete Voltas was a thunderbolt, a flaming sword. All swagger, danger, and fascination. When he showed up with Nilo, his body swaying, a razor in his belt, the shepherdesses bowed before him. A magic king, a voodoo god, a holy horseman come to mount his steeds.

Gabriela, the horse of Yemanjá, galloped across plains, through valleys, over mountains, and down to the bottom of the ocean. Dancing, singing, horse and rider. Into the waves she cast gifts for the goddess of the sea—a comb, a vial of perfume—and begged a favor: Nacib's kitchen, his stove, the little room in the back yard, his hairy chest, the tickle of his mustache, and his heavy leg across her rump.

When the guitar stopped, the storytelling began. Nilo had been shipwrecked twice, he had looked death in the face. But he was clear as spring water. Sete Voltas was a bottomless well, a deadly secret, who had tattooing on his chest and a notch on the handle of his razor for every man he had killed. The women in the tattoos never let him forget the loneliness of his months in prison. He had recently killed a man. Policemen and detectives were looking for him in Bahia, in Sergipe, in Alagoas, in the voodoo grounds, in the market places and fairs, in the corners of the docks, in the waterfront dives. Even Nilo treated him with respect, for no one could stand against him. On the docks in Bahia his intimate friends, including gamblers, voodoo priests, and four women, awaited his return. He planned to keep out of sight until the police forgot about him. Meanwhile he was available to the entranced young girls who came to Dora's house.

On Sunday afternoons, Negroes and mulattos gathered in the yard behind the house to watch or engage in *capoeira,* the curious fight contest of the region. Sete Voltas played the one-string instrument that usually accompanies *capoeira* and sang:

> *"Comrade in battle,*
> *Together let's wander*

> *The wide world over.*
> *Comrade, ah, comrade!"*

He handed the instrument to Nilo and entered the *capoeira* ring. With cartwheels and sudden thrusts of the feet and elbows, all in rhythm, he outpointed his opponents and remained alone and victorious on the field of battle.

On the beach, among the rocks, Sete Voltas was puzzled by Gabriela's moods, like waves of a stormy sea. She was the sweetness of the world, the light of day, the secret of night. But her sadness persisted; it resounded among the rocks, spread over the sand, and flowed into the sea.

"Why you such a sad woman?"

"I'm not a sad woman. I'm just sad now."

"Don't want no sadness around me. I got a happy saint. Lemme kill the sadness with my razor."

"You can't."

"Why not?"

Because what she wanted was a stove, a yard with guava, pitanga cherry, and papaya trees, and such a kind man.

"Ain't I enough? There's women ready to kill and die for this colored boy. You ought to thank your lucky star you got me."

"No, you're not enough. Nobody's enough."

"Like somethin' you can't get outta your mind?"

"Like that."

"So?"

"So it's bad."

"Like no taste in your mouth any more?"

"Just bad."

One night she went with him. The night before it had been Miquelina, and on Saturday, Paula, with breasts like doves. Now it was his eagerly awaited turn with Gabriela. In Dora's house, Nilo lay in the hammock with the queen in his arms. Their boat was about to set sail.

But Gabriela was crying. She lay on the sand at the edge of the sea. The moon shed its gold on her, the breeze wafted her scent of cloves.

"You cryin', woman." He touched her face with his razor hand. "Why? Women don't cry when they with me—they laugh 'cause they're happy."

"It's all over, now it's all over."

"What's all over?"

"Thinkin' that one day—"

"What?"

That she might return to the stove, to the back yard, to the little room, to the bar. Wasn't Mr. Nacib going to open a restaurant? Wouldn't he need a good cook? Dona Arminda had told her not to worry; only Gabriela could take charge of such a big kitchen and handle the job right. But instead of hiring her, Mr. Nacib brought a cook from Rio, a silly little stuffed-doll of a man who talked like a foreigner. The restaurant would open in three days. There was no hope now. She wanted to go away from Ilhéus. To the bottom of the ocean.

Sete Voltas was freedom renewed every day at dawn. He was an offering and a decision. He was pride and a gift. He struck like lightning, he nourished like rain, a comrade on the field of battle.

"A Portugee, you say?"

The comrade in battle stood up. The wind cooled as it touched him, the moonlight turned pale in his hands, the waves came to lick his feet.

"Don't cry, woman. No woman cries when she's with Sete Voltas."

"What can I do?"

For the first time in her life she was a poor, sad, helpless creature with no desire to go on living. Neither the sunshine, nor the moonlight, nor the cold water, nor a man's body, nor the warmth of a voodoo god could make her laugh or put the joy of living in her empty breast. Empty of Nacib, so good, so beautiful.

"You can't do nothin'. But Sete Voltas can do somethin'."

"I don't see how."

"If the Portugee disappears, who's gonna cook? On the day of the blowout if he ain't there, they gotta send for you. Well, he's gonna disappear."

Sometimes he was as dark as a moonless night and as hard as the rock facing the sea. Gabriela trembled.

"What are you goin' to do? Kill him? I don't want that."

When he laughed, it was like the day breaking, like St. George in the moon, like land spied by a castaway, like the anchor of a boat.

"Kill the Portugee? He done me no harm. I'll just send him away in a hurry. I won't hurt him, except a little bit if he won't go."

"You're really goin' to do it? Really?"

"A woman with me is for laughin', not cryin'."

Gabriela smiled. The comrade in battle narrowed his blazing eyes and decided it was better so. He could continue on his way, freedom in his breast, his heart unfettered. She was the only one in the world who could tie him to that small port, who could bend and tame him. He had thought this night of telling her his love, of surrendering to her. But it was better like this, better for her to sigh and cry for another man. Sete Voltas could go away now, wander the wide world over. . . .

She took him by the hand and pulled him to herself in gratitude. A boat on a quiet sea, sailing in a bay, an island covered with cane brakes and pepper plants. The comrade in battle sailing on the high-prowed vessel. Ah, comrade! The pain of losing her was burning in his breast. But he was a god of the voodoo, with pride in his right hand and freedom in his left.

OF A DISTINGUISHED SON OF ILHÉUS

On the day before the formal inauguration of the Commerce Restaurant, Nacib could be seen in his shirt sleeves running like a crazy man down the street in the direction of Mundinho Falcão's office, with his big belly bouncing above his belt. As he reached the door of the federal tax-collector's office, the Captain managed to grab him by the arm and halt his mad dash.

"What's the matter, man? Where are you going in such a hurry?" Amiable and friendly by nature, the Captain had become even more so since the announcement of his candidacy for mayor. "Has something happened? Can I help you in any way?"

"Vanished! Vanished!" gasped Nacib.

"Vanished? What's vanished?"

"The cook."

It did not take long for the whole town to hear about the mystery: the great chef de cuisine from Rio, Monsieur Fernand (as he liked to be called), had disappeared overnight. He had made an appointment for a meeting in the morning with the two waiters and the kitchen helpers to go over the plans for the day, but he had not shown up. No one had seen him.

Mundinho Falcão sent for the Chief of Police, explained the situation, and urged a thorough investigation. The official was that same lieutenant with whom Mundinho had clashed after the attempted murder of Aristóteles. Now he was all servility and addressed Mundinho as "Doctor."

In the Model Stationery Store, João Fulgêncio and Nhô-Galo were discussing the mystery. The cook, from his mannerisms and the way he used his eyes, was definitely a homosexual. Had there been some sort of sex crime? He had made advances to Lazy Chico. The Chief of Police interrogated the young waiter, who became indignant:

"I go with women! I don't have anything to do with that fairy. The other day I nearly socked him one. He made believe he didn't know what for."

Perhaps he had been a victim of robbers. Ilhéus was host to numerous thieves, crooks, and pickpockets, unsavory characters who had fled from Bahia and other centers and who had now replaced the colonels' gunmen in the human landscape of the town. The Chief and his men searched the port, Unhão and Conquista hills, Pontal, and Cobras Island. Nacib mobilized Nhô-Galo, Felipe, Josué, the waiters, and various customers. They combed the city without result.

João Fulgêncio thought that the man had probably run away:

"My theory is that our gay friend simply packed his things and left of his own accord. He found our sexual climate antipathetic, he learned that the small demand for what he had to offer was being adequately served by Machadinho and Miss Pirangi, so he felt forlorn and decided to relieve us of his loathsome presence."

"But how did he get away?" asked Nhô-Galo. "There was no ship out yesterday. The *Canavieiras* doesn't sail till this evening."

"By bus, by train . . ."

Neither by bus, nor by train, nor on horseback, nor on foot: the Chief would swear to it. About four o'clock little Tuísca, greatly excited, came to the police with a clue. Of all the Sherlocks who had presented themselves that day, he was the only one to offer something concrete. A short, fat, well-dressed fellow —and it could well have been the cook, for he had a pointed mustache and swung his hips as he walked—had been seen late at night by a prostitute. She was coming from the Big Noise, and over by the warehouses on the waterfront she saw this man being forcibly escorted by three suspicious-looking characters. She told Tuísca all this, but when she was questioned by the police her story became vague: she thought she had seen them, she wasn't sure, she had been drinking, she didn't know who the men were, maybe she had just heard someone talking. As a matter of fact, she had quite clearly seen and recognized Nilo, Terêncio, and a third man, their leader, whose name she did not know but for whom she and all the other drabs at the Big Noise had a strong yen. A dangerous *capoeira* fighter from Bahia. With a mean reputation. She was troubled by a suspicion that the fat little man was in the water at the bottom of the bay. She had told none of this to the police and already regretted having discussed the subject with Tuísca.

It occurred to no one to extend the search to Dora's house, where Fernand wept at first and finally helped with the sewing; Dora's seamstresses were excused from coming to work that day. The thought of leaving Ilhéus that evening as a third-class passenger on the *Canavieiras* no longer seemed to trouble him very much, perhaps because Sete Voltas was sailing on the same ship. He planned to wear a sailor blouse. Dora promised to forward his baggage.

When João Fulgêncio entered the bar in the late afternoon, he found Nacib utterly despondent. How was he going to open the restaurant the next day? Everything was ready: provisions purchased, kitchen helpers hired and trained by Fernand, two waiters standing by, and the invitations out for the formal luncheon. People were coming from Itabuna (Aristóteles among them), from Água Preta, from Pirangi; Altino Brandão was coming from Rio do Braço. Nacib had no cook at all; even the one from Sergipe had gone, after a quarrel with Fernand, and had left the little back-yard room in filthy condition. Wouldn't the kitchen helpers do? Not unless he wanted to go out of business the day after. They couldn't cook at all: they only trimmed the meat, killed and cleaned chickens, and fed wood to the stove. How could he possibly find a cook on such short notice?

All of this he related almost tearfully to his good friend João Fulgêncio. He had dragged the bookseller to the poker room, where, with a bottle of undiluted cognac, he was trying to drown his troubles. His customers and friends at the tables in the bar remarked that they had never seen him looking so desperate before. Not even at the time of his break-up with Gabriela. Nacib's despair then may have been deeper and more terrible but it was silent, sober, somber, whereas now he cried out to high heaven, bewailing his ruin and loss of face.

"I'm ruined, João. What can I do?"

Ever since the bookseller arranged for the annulment of his marriage, Nacib had placed unlimited confidence in him.

"Take it easy, Nacib. We'll find a solution."

"But how? Where will I get a cook? The Dos Reis sisters won't take on an assignment like this, at a moment's notice. And even if they did, who would do the cooking for the customers on Monday?"

"I could lend you our Marocas for a few days. But she only cooks well when my wife stands beside her."

"What good would it be anyway, for just a few days?"

Nacib gulped down the cognac. He felt like crying.

"Nobody gives me any help. Just a lot of ideas that don't make sense. That crazy Dona Arminda, for instance, suggested that I hire Gabriela again. Imagine!"

João Fulgêncio jumped up.

"The country is saved, Nacib! Do you know who Dona Arminda is? She's Columbus. She's Galileo. Just think: the solution was right in front of us—the good, simple, perfect solution—and we didn't see it."

Nacib asked cautiously and suspiciously:

"Gabriela? Do you mean it? You're not kidding?"

"Why not Gabriela? Wasn't she your cook once? Why can't she be your cook again? What's wrong with that?"

"She was my wife."

"Your mistress, wasn't it? The marriage was false, remember? And besides, by hiring her again as a cook, you liquidate the marriage completely, even more than by the annulment. Don't you think so?"

"It would teach her a good lesson," reflected Nacib. "To return as the cook after being the lady of the house."

"Well then? The only mistake in the whole affair was the marriage. It was bad for you and worse for her. If you want me to, I'll go talk with her."

"Do you suppose she'll agree?"

"I guarantee that she will. I'm going right now."

"Tell her it's just for a while."

"Why that? She's a cook, and you'll keep her as long as she suits you. Why just for a while? I'll come back with her answer as soon as I can."

And so, on that same evening, Gabriela cleaned the little room in the back yard and moved into it. Earlier, at Dora's house, she had thanked Sete Voltas. When the *Canavieiras* crossed the bar and headed for Bahia, she stood at Nacib's window and waved her handkerchief.

The inaugural luncheon the next day was a huge success. The fifty-odd guests ate appetizers like those of the old days and wonderful Bahian dishes with seasoning somewhere between the sublime and the divine. Seated between Mundinho and the Judge, Nacib listened with emotion to speeches by the Captain and the Doctor. "Nacib Saad, distinguished son of Ilhéus," said the Captain. "The worthy citizen who has endowed Ilhéus with a restaurant comparable to those of the great capitals," said the Doctor. Josué responded on behalf of Nacib and added his own words of praise and thanks to the Arab. The affair culminated with some remarks by Mundinho, who wished, as he said, to "eat crow." He had brought a cook from Rio, though Nacib was against it. Nacib was right. There was no food in the world that could compare with the Bahian.

And then everybody wanted to see the artist who had prepared the lunch, the magic hands that created such delights. João Fulgêncio got up and went to the kitchen to get her. She appeared smiling, with sandals on her feet, a white apron over her blue skirt, a red rose behind her ear. The Judge cried out:

"Gabriela!"

Nacib announced in a loud voice:

"I have hired her again as a cook."

Josué and Nhô-Galo started to applaud and everybody joined in. Some stood up to honor her. She smiled and kept her eyes lowered. Her hair was tied with a ribbon.

Mundinho Falcão murmured to Aristóteles beside him:

"That son-of-a-gun of a Turk knows how to live."

GABRIELA AGAIN

After several delays, the work on the sandbar was finally completed. Now there was a new channel, deep and straight. The ships of the Lloyd, Ita, and Bahiana lines could cross the bar without danger of getting stuck and, still more important, big freighters could now enter the harbor of Ilhéus and carry cacao directly to foreign ports.

The delays were caused by the shifting sands that altered the contour of the bar, covering and destroying in a few hours the work of weeks. The engineers had to begin over, again and again. They changed the direction of the channel twenty times, in quest of a workable degree of stability. Once they became so discouraged that they began to doubt the feasibility of the project, while the more pessimistic people in town repeated the old argument that the sandbar was an insoluble problem.

But now the job was done. The tugs and dredges, the engineers and technicians departed, except that one dredge remained in Ilhéus permanently to keep the channel open.

A big farewell party, which began at the Commerce Restaurant and ended at the El Dorado cabaret, was held in honor of the engineers. The Doctor fully lived up to his reputation as an orator. In the main speech of the evening he compared the chief engineer to Napoleon, but "a Napoleon battling for peace and progress, a conqueror of the seemingly unconquerable sea, of the treacherous river, of the sands inimical to civilization, of the tenebrous winds," who could gaze with pride, from atop the lighthouse on Pernambuco Island, upon the port of Ilhéus which he had freed "from the thralldom of the bar, a harbor opened to all ships and to all flags by the intelligence and dedication of this engineer and his noble colleagues."

At the farewell on the docks, women down from the hills were crying and clinging to the sailors. One of the women was pregnant; the man promised to return. As souvenirs of this land of abundant and easy money, of courage and hard work, the chief engineer was taking with him a kinkajou and two cases of Ilhéus Sugar Cane rum.

They departed just as the annual rains came—punctually this time, well in advance of the Feast of St. George. On the plantations, the cacao trees were in bloom and thousands of young trees were yielding their first fruits. The forecast for the new crop was more favorable than ever, prices would continue to climb, and more money would flow in the towns and villages. There was nothing like it in the entire country.

From the sidewalk of the Vesuvius Bar, Nacib could see the tugboats, like little fighting cocks, battling the waves as they towed the dredges on their way south. How much had happened in Ilhéus between the arrival and the departure of the engineers and divers, the technicians and sailors! Old Colonel Ramiro would not see the big ships enter the harbor. Disembodiment had profoundly changed his character: he appeared at spiritualistic séances, offering counsel to the people of the region, preaching kindness, patience, forgiveness—at least so affirmed Dona Arminda, an authority in this mysterious field.

Ilhéus had changed a great deal during these few months. Something new almost every day: a new branch bank, new shops, new residences, new agencies of Rio and São Paulo firms and even of foreign companies. A few days before, the Union of Artisans and Workers had installed its headquarters in an old two-story house on Unhão Hill. In the same house it established its School of Industrial Arts and Crafts, where poor boys learned carpentry, masonry, and shoemaking, and where primary classes were held for dock workers, cacao sackers, and workers in the chocolate factory. Felipe the cobbler spoke at the opening ceremony, attended by the most important personages in Ilhéus. He shouted, in a mixture of Portuguese and Spanish, that the day of the workers had arrived and that in their hands lay the destiny of the world. The statement seemed so absurd that it was automatically applauded by all those present, even by Dr. Maurício Caires, even by the cacao colonels, who owned immense tracts of land and controlled the lives of hundreds of men.

Nacib's life, too, had been full of changes during those months: he had married and unmarried, he had enjoyed prosperity and faced ruin, his breast had been filled with anxiety and with happiness, then drained of all but ache and despair. He had been too happy, then too unhappy, and now his life was calm and sweet once more. The Vesuvius prospered. The customers tarried at the apéritif hour, calling for two or three drinks, and some went upstairs for lunch. At twelve o'clock, Gabriela would come down from the kitchen and pass through the bar with a smile on her lips and a rose behind her ear. The customers greeted her with pleasantries, looked at her with desire in their eyes, touched her hand; a more daring one would give her a pat on the fanny; the Doctor called her "my girl." They praised Nacib's cleverness, the way he had extricated himself, with honor and advantage, from the complications he had got himself involved in. The Arab circulated among the tables, paused now and then to hear or say something, and sat down for a couple of minutes with João Fulgêncio and the Captain, Nhô-Galo and Josué, or Ribeirinho and Amâncio Leal. It was as if, through a miracle of St. George, they had gone back in time, as if nothing bad or sad had taken place. The illusion would have been perfect but for the restaurant and the absence of Tonico Bastos, now definitely anchored at the Golden Nectar with his bitters and his elegant spats.

The restaurant turned out to be only a fairly good investment. Its profits were steady but modest, not nearly so big as Nacib and Mundinho had expected. Except when there were ships in port, on their way north or south, business in the restaurant was so slack that only lunch was served. The Ilhéans customarily took all their meals at home. But sometimes, tempted by Gabriela's dishes, men would come for lunch, either alone or with their families, for a change from the daily routine. The regular customers could be counted on one's fingers: Mundinho, nearly always with guests, Josué, and the widower Pessoa. On the other hand, the card games at night in the dining room were a huge success. The groups of players generally occupied five or six tables. Gabriela prepared snacks for them, and they drank freely. Nacib collected the kitties. He had an inner conflict, a problem of conscience: should he or should he not consider Mundinho a partner in this end of the business? Certainly not, for the exporter had put up capital for a restaurant, not for a gambling hall. Perhaps yes, he reflected reluctantly, when you considered that the rent was paid by the partnership, which also owned the tables and chairs, the dishes out of which the customers ate, and the glasses out of which they drank. Nacib would have liked to keep this money all for himself, but he feared the exporter's reprisals. He decided to speak to him on the subject.

Mundinho had a special fondness for the Arab. He maintained that Nacib was the most civilized man in Ilhéus. Feigning deep interest, he listened to his partner's exposition of the problem. Nacib wanted the exporter's opinion: did he or did he not consider himself a partner in the gambling profits?

"And what is your own opinion, Nacib?"

"Well, this is how I see it, Mr. Mundinho," he said, twisting the ends of his mustache. "From the viewpoint of an honest man, I think you are a partner in everything that we use your investment for, and you should receive half the profits. On the other hand, I could say that we have no signed agreement, that we never talked about gambling, that you're a rich man and don't need the money, that I'm a poor man trying to save up enough to buy a little cacao grove and this extra income would be a big help. Anyway, I brought the gambling records for you to examine."

He made a move to place some papers on top of Mundinho's desk, but the exporter pushed his hand away and patted him on the shoulder.

"Keep your records and your money, Mr. Nacib. I'm not your partner in the gambling business. If you want to feel completely easy in your conscience, you can pay me a small rental for the use of the dining room at night. A hundred milreis, say. Or, better still, you can contribute one hundred milreis a month toward the building of the asylum for the aged. Who ever heard of a federal congressman running a gambling house, anyway? Or maybe you doubt that I'll be elected."

"You know I don't doubt it. Thank you, Mr. Mundinho, thank you very much."

He rose to leave and Mundinho said:

"Tell me something." He lowered his voice and touched the Arab's chest with his finger. "Does it still hurt?"

Nacib smiled, his face shining.

"No, sir. Not the least bit."

Mundinho lowered his head and murmured:

"I envy you. In me, it still hurts."

He wanted to ask him if he had resumed sleeping with Gabriela but thought it indelicate to do so. Nacib left, swimming in joy, and went to deposit the money in the bank.

He really felt nothing for Gabriela: no trace remained of the ache and the emptiness. He had feared, when he rehired her, that her presence would bring back the past; he was afraid he would dream of Tonico Bastos in her bed. But nothing happened. As if it all had been a long, cruel nightmare. There was simply a resumption of the original relationship of employer and cook. She was very industrious and cheerful as she cleaned house, as she came to the restaurant to prepare the food for lunch, as she went to the bar at the apéritif hour, and as she moved from table to table announcing the menu and getting customers for the dining room. When the activity ended, about one-thirty, Nacib

would sit down to lunch. Gabriela stood near the table, served
him his food, and opened the bottle of beer. Then Lazy Chico
and the waiter ate their lunch (Nacib had let the second waiter
go, for he was not needed), while Valter (Eaglebeak's replacement) looked after the bar. Nacib would pick up an old newspaper from Bahia and light his St. Felix cigar. He would find a
rose in the bottom of his deck chair. The first few times, he
threw it out; then he began putting it in his pocket. The newspaper slid to the ground and the cigar went out. Nacib napped,
in the shade and the breeze, until awakened by João Fulgêncio's voice. Gabriela fixed the appetizers and snacks for the afternoon and evening, then left for home. Nacib would see her cross
the square, in sandals, and disappear behind the church.

What was lacking to complete his happiness? He ate Gabriela's
incomparable food. He was earning money and putting some in
the bank. Soon he would start looking for land to buy. He had
heard about a newly cleared tract beyond the Baforé Range; it
was the finest cacao land anyone had ever seen. Ribeirinho offered to take him there; it was near his own plantations. His
friends and customers came to the bar daily and sometimes patronized the restaurant. There were the games of checkers and
backgammon. There was the good talk with João Fulgêncio,
with the Captain and the Doctor, with Nhô-Galo, Amâncio, and
Ari, and with Josué and Ribeirinho. These last two were always
together, ever since Ribeirinho installed Gloria in a house of her
own near the station. Sometimes the three of them came to the
restaurant for lunch; they got along well together.

What was lacking to complete his happiness? There were no
jealousies gnawing in his breast or fears of losing his cook, for
where could she find better wages and a more secure job? And
besides, she was indifferent to offers of a furnished house, charge
accounts at the stores, silk dresses and shoes, and all the other
perquisites of a kept woman. Why, Nacib did not know; the motive was undoubtedly absurd and he was not interested enough
to seek it. Perhaps it was that idea about wild flowers not belonging in vases, of which João Fulgêncio had spoken. At any rate,
he was unconcerned about it, just as he was no longer irritated
by the words whispered to her in the bar, the smiles, the looks,

the pats on the fanny, the light touching of her arm or breast. It all served to hold the customers and keep them calling for another drink.

The Judge sometimes tried to steal the rose from behind her ear. Nacib looked on indifferently. What was lacking to complete his happiness? The Indian girl from Amazonas, in Maria Machadão's house, would show her savage teeth and ask him:

"Do you like your Mara? Do you think she is delicious?"

He thought she was delicious. Small and plump, her face wide and round, sitting cross-legged on the bed, she reminded him of a copper statue. He saw her at least once a week and lay with her. It was a frivolous liaison, without complications, without mysteries, without surprises, without violent raptures, without the howling of bitches, without death and revival. Mara had many admirers; the colonels liked that unripe fruit from Amazonas; few of her nights were free. Nacib picked up a variety of charmers, at random, in the cabarets and bordellos. He even slept once with Coriolano's new mistress, in Gloria's former house on the square; Coriolano no longer strove to learn if he was being deceived. Nacib's favorite, however, continued to be the Indian. He danced with her in the cabaret and they had beer and sandwiches together. When she was free she sent him a note, in her childish handwriting, and as soon as the bar closed he went to see her. Those were pleasant days.

What was lacking to complete his happiness? One day Mara sent him a note that she would expect him that night, "to play kittens." He smiled happily, and after closing the bar he hurried over to Maria Machadão's house. Dona Maria, the best-known madam in Ilhéus, put her arm around him. Motherly and completely trustworthy, she said:

"I'm sorry, Turk, you're out of luck tonight. Mara is with Colonel Altino Brandão. He came from Rio do Braço especially. What could she do?"

He left. He was annoyed, not at Mara—he had no right to interfere with her efforts to earn a living—but at his own frustration. Desire gnawed at him like a rat. He entered his house and undressed. In the back, from the kitchen or pantry, came the sound of a breaking dish. He went to see what it was. A cat ran out into the yard. The door to Gabriela's little back-yard room was open. Gabriela's leg hung over the edge of the bed and she was smiling in her sleep. One of her breasts was exposed. He approached the bed. She opened her eyes and said:

"Mr. Nacib . . ."

He looked at her. Dizzy with the scent of clove, he saw for a moment the humid earth, a land of hills and valleys, with a deep grotto where, very curiously, he saw himself. She extended her arms and drew him toward her.

When he lay down beside her and felt her warmth, waves of emotion suddenly swept over him: the humiliation, the anger, the hatred, the injured pride, and the joy of burning in her. He seized her violently, leaving blue marks on her cinnamon-colored skin.

"You little bitch!"

She smiled. He felt like kissing and biting her lips. Still she smiled, with her erect breasts palpitating, with her thighs aflame, with her belly dancing and waiting, and murmured:

"It don't matter."

She lay her head on his hairy chest.

"Beautiful man."

OF THE SWEDISH SHIP AND THE GOLDEN MERMAID

Next Sunday the elections would be held. No one doubted the results, not even Dr. Vitor Melo back at his office in Rio. Altino Brandão and Ribeirinho had already ordered a monumental victory dinner at the Commerce Restaurant, with champagne and skyrockets. A subscription was started—Mundinho's name headed the list—to buy and present to the Captain the house in which he was born and where he had lived with his father, Cazuzinha Oliveira, so fondly remembered by everybody. But the future mayor made a magnificent gesture: he donated the money to the dispensary for needy children established on Conquista Hill by Dr. Alfredo Bastos.

Nacib planned, after the elections, to buy a piece of that land beyond the Baforé Range for his cacao plantation. Meanwhile, he played an occasional game of backgammon, talked with his friends, and told tall tales about Syria: "In my father's country it's even worse. . . ." He snored peacefully during his siesta. He went to the cabaret with Nhô-Galo. He slept with Mara, Gabriela, and other women. Most often with Gabriela, perhaps, for none of the others was so ardent, so unrestrained in bed, so sweet in love, so born for the purpose. Nacib would sleep with his leg across her rounded flank. It was like the old days. With these differences, however: he no longer suffered from jealousy, or was fearful of losing her, or tried to change her. At siesta time, before dropping off to sleep, he would think to himself: his interest in her now was limited to the bed, his feelings for her were the same as for the others—Mara, Raquel, the redheaded Natacha—with nothing added, without the former tenderness. It was good this way. In the evening she usually went to Dora's house and made plans for the festivities during the month of Mary. Nacib knew about it, shrugged his shoulders, and even planned to attend. She was his cook, with whom he slept whenever he had the urge. And what a cook! Good in bed, too—better than good. An astonishing woman.

At Dora's house Gabriela laughed and played, sang and danced. When the clock struck eleven, she returned home and waited for Mr. Nacib. Perhaps he would come to her room, with his mustache tickling her neck, his heavy leg across her, his chest as soft as a pillow. Often she held the cat close against her face and it mewed softly. She listened to Dona Arminda tell about the spirits and about babies being born. On clear mornings she sat in the sun eating guavas and red pitanga cherries. She talked for hours on end with her friend Tuísca, who was now learning carpentry. She ran barefoot on the beach, her feet in the cold water. In the afternoons she sometimes played ring-around-a-rosy with the children in the square. It was good to be alive.

Four days before the elections, at about three in the afternoon, a Swedish freighter of a size never before seen in those parts, blew its whistle majestically in the waters of Ilhéus. Tuísca ran with the news through the center of town. People gathered on the beach avenue.

Not even the Bishop's arrival had been so exciting. Skyrockets rose and burst in the air. Two ships of the Bahiana Line blew their whistles, and conch blasts sounded from the smaller craft. Fishing boats and canoes crossed the bar, braving the open sea, to escort the Swedish vessel in.

She crossed the bar slowly, with flags of all countries flying from her masts in a riot of color. People hurried through the streets in the direction of the docks and swarmed over the piers. The band of the Thirteenth of May Euterpean Society came to the waterfront and played marches, with Joaquim beating the bass drum. The business houses closed their doors. The schools, both public and private, let out their pupils, who ran to the docks and cheered. Automobiles, trucks, and buses blew their horns. Gloria was there, between Ribeirinho and Josué; the three laughed loudly, to the annoyance of the respectable ladies standing about. Tonico Bastos, the personification of propriety, held Dona Olga's arm. Jerusa, in deep mourning, spoke to Mundinho. Nilo, with his whistle, drilled Terêncio, Traíra, and the young Batista. Father Basílio smiled at his godchildren. The peg-leg from the Big Noise looked enviously at Nacib and Plínio Araçá. The old maids crossed themselves, and the Dos Reis sisters smiled and fluttered; the freighter would figure in their next Nativity tableau. In unavoidable proximity stood upper-crust ladies, marriageable girls, prostitutes, and Maria Machadão. The Doctor cleared his throat and wondered how he could bring Ofenísia into a speech about a Swedish ship. Tuísca climbed the mast of a sailboat. Dora's shepherdesses were there, with Gabriela bearing the banner of The Three Kings. The cacao colonels drew their pistols and fired shots into the air. The whole town of Ilhéus was at the docks.

In a symbolic ceremony, suggested by João Fulgêncio, Mundinho Falcão and Stevenson, exporters, and Amâncio Leal and Ribeirinho, planters, carried a bag of cacao to the end of the pier where the ship had tied up: the first bag of cacao to be shipped abroad directly from Ilhéus. The stirring speech by the Doctor was responded to by the Swedish vice-consul, the tall agent of the steamship company.

At night, with the ship's crew on shore leave, the excitement in the town grew. The sailors were served free drinks in the bars, and the captain and other officers were taken to the cabarets. The captain was almost lifted off his feet and borne triumphantly on men's shoulders. He had drunk liquor in all the ports of the seven seas, but he passed out at the Bataclan and his new Ilhéan friends had to carry him to his ship.

On the following afternoon the sailors were again given shore leave, and they spread through the streets. They sold foreign cigarettes, bolts of cloth, bottles of perfume, and gilt trinkets. With the proceeds they drank rum and invaded the brothels. Many of them fell drunk in the streets.

During the lull between three and four-thirty, when Nacib was figuring his profits and Gabriela was leaving for home, a Swedish sailor staggered into the bar. He was blond and about six and a half feet tall. He pointed to the bottles of Ilhéus Sugar Cane, looked suppliantly at Nacib, and uttered some foreign words. Nacib had fulfilled his duty as a citizen the previous evening by serving free rum to the sailors. He now rubbed his thumb and index finger together to show that he would require payment. The blond Swede searched his pockets. Not a penny. But he did bring out a pretty trinket: a brooch with a golden mermaid. He placed this Nordic mother of waters, this Yemanjá from Stockholm, on the counter. The Arab caught sight of Gabriela as she turned the corner at the church. Surely no other woman in the world had her warmth, her tenderness. The more he slept with her, the more he wanted to. She seemed made of songs and dancing, of sunlight and moonlight, of clove and cinnamon. He had given her no presents since her return. He took the bottle of rum and filled the thick glass. The sailor raised his arm, offered a toast in Swedish, downed the liquor in two gulps, and spat. Nacib put the golden mermaid in his pocket; he smiled to himself. Gabriela would laugh happily and say: "You didn't have to. . . ."

And so ends the story of Nacib and Gabriela, with the flame of love born anew from its own ashes.

POSTSCRIPT

SOME TIME afterwards, Colonel Jesuíno Mendonça stood before a jury, accused of having shot to death his wife, Sinhàzinha Guedes Mendonça, and the dental surgeon, Osmundo Pimental, for reasons of jealousy. The lawyers talked, all in all, for twenty-eight hours. Dr. Maurício Caires quoted the Bible and referred to scandalous black stockings, morality, and depravity. Dr. Ezequiel Prado said that Ilhéus was no longer a land of bandits, a paradise of assassins; his theme was civilization and progress. With a sob he pointed to Osmundo's father and mother, in mourning and tears. For the first time in the history of Ilhéus, a cacao colonel found himself sentenced to prison for having murdered his adulterous wife and her lover.

"A charismatic storyteller. . . . No other Latin American writer is more genuinely admired by his peers, nor has any other exerted so great a creative influence on the course of Latin American fiction."
—The New York Times Book Review

DONA FLOR AND HER TWO HUSBANDS

A Moral and Amorous Tale

This captivating fable celebrates heated passions, conjugal harmony, the rhythms of the samba, and the delectable joys of cooking. Caught up in the pandemonium of Carnival, the roguish and irresponsible Vadinho dos Guimaraes dies, leaving behind his long-suffering wife, the irrepressible Dona Flor. As a widow, Flor devotes herself to her cooking school and well-meaning friends who urge her to remarry. The lonely woman finds herself attracted to Dr. Teodoro Madureria, a kind, considerate pharmacist, who is everything the reckless Vadinho was not. Though content after their marriage, Flor longs for her first husband's amorous, and exhausting, sensual pleasures. And Flor's desirous longing is so powerful that it brings the ghost of Vadinho back from the grave—right into her bed.

Fiction/0-307-27664-3